SWEETHOME

(MATT BANNISTER WESTERN 2)

KEN PRATT

Sweethome

Paperback Edition
Copyright © 2019 by Ken Pratt

CKN Christian Publishing
An Imprint of Wolfpack Publishing
6032 Wheat Penny Avenue
Las Vegas, NV 89122

christiankindlenews.com

Paperback ISBN 978-1-64119-493-8
eBook ISBN 978-1-64119-492-1

Library of Congress Control Number: 2019930742

This book is dedicated to my wife, Cathy Pratt. Thank you for sacrificing so much of your life during the writing of this book. Thank you for always being interested, willing to listen, and offering feedback that helped me to make this story as realistic as I could. Thank you, for all that you do to make it possible for me to write.

AUTHOR'S NOTE

SWEETHOME

I am still confident of this: I will see the goodness of the Lord in the land of the living. Wait for the Lord; be strong and take heart and wait for the Lord.

Psalm 27:13-14

PROLOGUE

April 1883

MAUDE LESKO HAD no interest in the street vendors or the saloons; the smell of freshly baked bread from the 7th Street Bakery didn't slow her determined pace towards Main Street, the main thoroughfare of Branson. She walked briskly with her lips turned downward and business on her mind. She was a woman of medium height, stoutly built, with a round face and aged blue eyes with a head of bright orange hair pinned up underneath her floral-brimmed hat. Beside her, walked her more timid husband, Robert Lesko, who wore a tan suit with a brown derby covering his balding head. His face was slim and long with a moustache that, at times like now, gave him the appearance of a nervous mouse.

They turned wordlessly onto the main street with its bustling mid-week traffic of wagons and horses, as well as foot traffic, which crisscrossed the street of this busy little city. Main Street ran horizontally from First through Twelfth Street where it ended at the staircase to the newly built courthouse, a large, granite block building with a formal stairway containing four columns leading to the entry. The city had boomed in growth and enterprise during the last ten years. Business of every kind employed the four thousand and still growing population. One of the more successful businesses was the Fasana Granite Mine. Three buildings had been built from its hand cut granite blocks in recent years: the large courthouse, the beautiful Monarch Hotel and the newest and smallest building, the United States Marshal's Office on the corner of Main and Ninth Streets. It was a single-story building, twice as long as it was wide. The front featured two big bay windows with the words "U.S. MARSHAL" in decorative gold on the glass. There was an awning over the front and a white sign with black lettering proclaiming "U.S. Marshal, Matt Bannister." Maude seemed to lose her determination as she stopped at the office door. Taking her husband's hand, she took a deep breath and opened the door which rang a cowbell tied to its top.

The Federal Government seemed to spare no expense as the outside granite blocks stepped up to fine mahogany paneling. Immediately inside the door, there was a partition three feet tall running the width of the office, with a gate at its center. The partition separated two desks from two sets of comfortable padded chairs, one to the left, the other to the right. Beyond the desks, centered on the back wall, was a metal door with a heavy lock on it. It was obviously the entrance to the jail. In the left corner was a private office with windows that were covered by curtains and the door was closed. Along the right-hand wall was a beautiful, securely locked gun cabinet that held half a dozen rifles next to a handsome wood stove that heated a pot of coffee. A set of cabinets held the coffee and what other supplies were needed and a coat rack held a lone garment. A bulletin board filled with wanted posters of scoundrel-looking faces hung next to a map of the Pacific Northwest, and portraits of mountain scenes were arranged neatly around the beautiful office.

The marshal's office was truly grand, although everyone knew the Federal Government wouldn't lavishly invest in such an expensive office, especially at the cost of this one. It was the subject of gossip, and rightly so. It was the big business owners of Branson, the wealthiest and most powerful that had designed and paid for the office. The businessmen of Branson used a touch of back door politics and their friends with the Union Pacific railroad to cut through the red tape and rush the petition to appoint deputy marshal Matt Bannister to federal marshal. The office was nearly completed when Matt was appointed to Marshal. It proved to some that everything had its price-even the U.S. Marshal's office! However, Maude didn't care about that anymore. She had come to see the famed marshal.

"Hello folks, can I help you?" A young man asked as he stood up behind his desk in front of Maude and Robert. He was in his twenties with a strong, handsome face under a full head of short blond hair. He wore a red shirt with a silver deputy marshal badge. He didn't wear his gun belt, but no doubt it was close at hand.

"Yes, we came to see the marshal," Maude said pointedly.

He put out his hand. "I'm Deputy Marshal Nate Robertson. Call me Nate. So how can I help you folks today?" he asked as he shook Robert's hand.

"I'm Robert Lesko and this is my wife, Maude," Robert

said before Maude took over. "Young man, we're here to see the marshal himself so if he's in could you tell him we need to speak with him. If he's not, will you tell me when he will be?"

Nate Robertson smiled lightly as he matched Maude's determined eyes. "Misses Lesko, the marshal is a busy man. Is there something I can help with?"

"No, deputy, there's not," Maude interrupted, "but the marshal can. He's the boss, yes?" she questioned impatiently and waited for his confirmation.

"Of course," he answered awkwardly.

"Then get him!" she demanded.

Nate laughed slightly. "All right," he said and went back to the private office, knocked lightly, opened it, and stuck his head inside. A moment later he came back with a hint of a red face and an embarrassed smile. He unlocked the gate in the mahogany partition and waved them through. "Come on in."

Feeling victorious, Maude walked past Nate, but slowed immediately when Matt Bannister stepped out of his office to greet the couple. He was a tall man with broad shoulders, a handsome face with dark eyes, high wide cheekbones and a nicely trimmed dark beard and mustache. His long, dark hair was pulled back in a tight ponytail and he was dressed in dark pants and a blue shirt with the sleeves rolled up. He greeted the couple pleasantly before motioning them into his office. His office had no decorations other than the beautiful mahogany paneling and a map of the Pacific Northwest with a few pins placed in it. The Leskos' sat in two comfortable padded leather chairs across from Matt's large desk, which he sat down behind. His attention went to Maude who spoke first.

"This is quite a beautiful place. Are all U.S. Marshal's

offices this lovely?" she asked nervously under the marshal's gaze. She had waited a long time to meet him. She had practiced her words over and over again, but now her throat felt dry. The thought occurred to her that the marshal had already felt the heat of the townsfolk about the price of the office.

Matt smiled half-heartedly. "No, the place was built and paid for by the businessmen of this town. The government didn't spend a red cent on it. I'm glad that you like it." He paused purposefully and added, "Nate says that you wanted to talk to me."

"Yes, yes," Maude said slowly as her breathing grew strenuous. She took her husband's hand tightly and held it to her chest. Tears began to cloud her eyes. She took a deep breath as Robert stared at the floor sadly. "We've got a problem, Marshal, and we don't know where to turn. We've been to the sheriff, he can't help, and I don't know what to do," she stopped as tears choked her.

"What's going on?" Matt asked quietly, his eyes never leaving the couple.

"Our daughter, Abby, married a man three years ago in Sweetome, Idaho, where we used to live and we haven't seen her since." She pressed her lips together tightly before continuing. "He won't let us see her. He won't let us go to her and we don't know if she's alive or dead. We can't get any help! Can you help us?" she asked Matt hopefully before adding quickly, "I'll pay you to go bring her home to us if she's alive, but I have to know! The sheriff here says it's out of his jurisdiction, but I understand it's not out of yours. Please help us," she begged desperately. "We have nowhere else to go!"

Matt was silent for a minute as his eyes read Maude

Lesko. "Your daughter willingly married some guy and you haven't seen her since?"

"Right," Maude nodded. "Not once! When we went to visit her, we were met by Brit's gunmen. They wouldn't let us onto the property and there's no way to get a message to her or from her." Maude paused, "Marshal Bannister, if anyone can go get her, it's you! Please bring my baby home."

Matt narrowed his eyes. "Couldn't you find a more local sheriff or someone who could help you? Surely there's someone of authority between there and here."

Maude grew offended and spoke loudly, "You don't understand! His family owns Sweethome. They own everything including the sheriff. He forced us out of Sweethome. We came here because we had everything taken away from us. Now you're here and we're here for your help. So can you help us or not?" she demanded, glaring angrily at Matt.

Matt reached for a pen and a piece of paper. He dipped his pen into a bottle of ink.

"Where is this?"

"Sweethome, Idaho. In Garden Valley."

"And what's the guy's name?" he asked as he wrote the information down. Maude only stared at Matt in response. He looked up from his writing, "His name?"

"Brit Thacker."

"Your daughter's name?"

"Abigail. Abby."

"The sheriff's name?"

Maude spoke with disgust, "Martin DePietro."

"Well, Mister and Misses Lesko, I'll tell you what I'll do," Matt said as he laid his pen down and leaned against the back of his chair. He put his hands behind his head. "I'll wire Sheriff Martin DePietro and have him check on your daughter and wire me back." He paused as he watched

Maude's look of frustration growing. "But you do know that it's possible that she doesn't want to see you."

"How dare you!" Maude yelled angrily. "That is our daughter. We love her dearly. She would never treat us like this. Never! Marshal, I know my daughter! Good heavens, I know my own daughter. Why is it that no one with a badge can help us? Are you all afraid of the Thackers? How far does their money go, Marshal? Did they pay for your beautiful office too? Well?" she yelled at Matt, glaring at him harshly.

He remained seated with his hands clasped behind his head. "Ma'am, I have no idea what you're talking about," he moved to put his hands upon the table. "I take it he's related to Bob Thacker?"

"Of course! Brit is his son. That probably complicates things, huh?" Maude asked sarcastically with a good dose of bitterness included.

Matt smiled. "No ma'am, but I'll wire the sheriff out there and find out what I can."

"The Thacker's own the sheriff; don't you understand? He's just one of their hired guns. It won't do any good."

"It's going to have to, Misses Lesko," Matt stated sharply. "I'm not going to jump on my horse and ride a hundred miles to find her sitting on a porch swing. That's not what I do here." He softened his voice before continuing, "But, I'll find out what I can, and I will promise you that if one of my deputies or I get over that way, we'll stop in and check on your daughter."

"What if she's dead, Marshal?"

"Then we'll find that out."

Maude wasn't pleased. "What makes you think Martin DePietro's going to tell you the truth? He's the Thacker's

7

legal henchman. He's going to say whatever they tell him to say," she finished with contempt.

Matt nodded. "Misses Lesko, I am the territorial marshal for these parts. I've been a deputy marshal for a long time." Long enough, I think that Sheriff DePietro will know who I am. If he lies to me and I catch him in it, he'll be called on it. I'll make that very clear to him, okay? In a week or two, I think you'll hear from your daughter."

"And if we don't?"

"Then I'll ask the sheriff why," Matt paused and then answered, "Look, I am asking you to trust me, Misses Lesko. I'll do what I can."

"Come on, Robert," she said with disgust, while standing from her chair. Her eyes burned hostilely into Matt. "We're wasting our time. Again!"

"Misses Lesko."

"Shush!" Maude demanded. "Do what you can! Write your letters, but it wasn't a pen that saved that girl in Willow Falls, was it?"

"I'll keep you informed," Matt commented casually.

"Don't bother. Have a good day!" she spat out like bile from her mouth as they departed from his office.

Matt shook his head as they closed the door behind them. He took another piece of paper and wrote to the sheriff of Sweethome. He already had a big enough list of missing people who were expected to be somewhere in or around Branson, Oregon. Sons, daughters, husbands and brothers, beloved sisters and estranged wives - the trail west was wide open now for dreamers of every kind. Those who didn't write back home often enough were missing. Some, Matt was sure, were dead, but like the Lesko's daughter, others were probably better-off and they had reasons not to write home. Maude Lesko seemed the type who would not only run her husband's life, but also her daughter's. Brit Thacker probably did have to hire gunmen to keep her away.

His office door opened and Nate Robertson poked his head inside with a curious look. "What'd you do to her, Matt? She stormed out of here like a raging bull."

Matt smiled wide as he stood up. "It's my charm with the ladies," he joked as he stepped over to the map of the Pacific Northwest. He looked it over and stuck a pin in the spot named Sweethome, Idaho.

Nate remarked, through a smile, "Maybe you should work on that charm a little. If you keep that up, you'll never find a wife."

Matt smiled slightly. "Probably not. Will you take this letter down to the post office and mail it to one Sheriff Martin DePietro in Sweethome, Idaho? Check the spelling of his name with the postmaster, but it's Sheriff Martin DePietro."

"Sure. Anything else?"

"No," Matt said slowly as he reread his letter. "I was going to wire the sheriff, but sometimes meanings become much clearer in handwritten letters. Take it and go please, ask him how long it will take for the letter to arrive in Sweethome."

Sweethome was named because of its beautiful location nestled in the heart of Garden Valley. It was an oasis of green grass and trees at the base of Idaho's northern mountain ranges. Garden Valley was fertile, beautiful, and perfect for a town named Sweethome. The town itself had grown to over three hundred people, some farmed, others were employed at the sawmill or elsewhere. Sweethome's main business was providing the mining and logging camps in the surrounding areas with the supplies they needed to survive: tools, equipment, food, and clothing. On the weekends, of course, the miners and loggers all came running into Sweethome to spend a week's wages on whiskey and women at one of the saloons. Business owners did well in Sweethome. Others, who worked for a wage got by, but nearly every business was to serve the public in some way: most didn't differentiate between the respectable and the disrespectable as long as they were customers. During the weekday, Sweethome was a fairly dignified town of friendly and decent folks as they did their day's work, but Friday night through Sunday night, Sweethome's population doubled with dozens of men letting off a week's worth of steam. For Martin DePietro and his three deputies, weekends were a busy time breaking up fights and making some arrests. It was dangerous work of course. Miners and loggers were tough breeds of men, and they didn't necessarily like each other too well, especially after a few drinks. Add to the mix a few cowboys, gamblers and street toughs and eventually fights broke out. An occasional killing wasn't so uncommon either. As a grim reminder, Sweethome built a permanent gallows for the occasional hanging.

At forty years old, Martin DePietro enjoyed the weekdays more than the weekends. He wasn't as rough and rowdy as his younger deputies were. Martin himself enjoyed a quiet afternoon, but the quietness of this afternoon would soon be overwhelmed by a long train of wagons full of rowdy loggers and determined miners coming to Sweethome to unwind. He enjoyed the present quietness of town, but it wouldn't last long. Martin stepped through the post office door and immediately began to talk to Jeannie Bartholomew, the postmaster's wife, who worked with her husband. "Hello, Jeannie. Beautiful day, isn't it?"

She nodded. Jeannie Bartholomew was in her late-forties, slightly attractive with reddish-gold hair and a slow-to-seldom smile. "It is," she agreed, as she turned from the store's counter to retrieve the sheriff's mail out of the mailroom.

The sheriff himself wasn't a big man. He stood five foot seven with a large belly on his broad frame. He had short dark hair and a clean-shaven round face with dark eyebrows over his big brown eyes. He wore his badge with pride and his holstered gun loose and close to his hand. "I was reading in the paper that Patch Williamson was hung over in Idaho City. That guy," Martin chuckled, "was so stupid. I'm always running into fools and just plain stupid men. Every weekend I do, but Patch Williamson, I swear..." He laughed again and then continued, "Last January, Patch was in my jail and it was cold out, of course. Patch got so cold he burnt his blanket!" he laughed. "He lit his blanket on fire to keep warm!" he explained with a laugh, as Jeannie returned to the counter with a letter. "I've got some, huh?"

"Yes," Jeannie said with a slight smile left over from Martin's story. "It's from Branson. The new marshal's office."

"Huh?" he took it and opened it as he continued to speak, "yeah, I'm not surprised Patch got the rope." His attention went to the letter and his face went from humor to serious to concern as he read.

"You must have figured the cold would have frozen the fool out of him," Jeannie offered as she watched Martin's face curiously.

"Yeah," Martin offered a courteous laugh. "I'll see you later, Jeannie," he said folding the letter back up and moving towards the door. "He wants me to be his deputy marshal over in Branson. What do you know about that?" he asked and stepped outside.

A truth Martin once learned was that a gossip, especially the town gossip, needed a new piece of information to gobble on once in a while, even if it wasn't true. Normally he'd look at his watch and see how long it took the new bit of gossip to get back to him, but now he only had one thing on his mind. He needed to get this letter to Brit Thacker. Brit would know what to do; it couldn't be ignored. It was written by Matt Bannister and that made it serious.

Jenny Mae Davis was a lovely lady. She had shoulder-length wavy, light-brown hair pinned up under a bonnet revealing her almond-shaped brown eyes in a pretty oval face. She was in her mid-twenties and a beauty who had moved to town a year before with her husband, Truet. She wore a plain gray dress that buttoned up to her neck as she sat on the wagon's bench seat in front of Dutch's Hardware Store. Truet was inside buying an assortment of nails, bolts and brackets for the job he'd start on Monday. As always, Truet wanted to be prepared when he began a job, so his lumber was already stacked neatly in the bed of his wagon. Truet was a carpenter by trade and was beginning a new job for Bob Thacker. He was to build a boxing ring surrounded by bleachers on all four sides.

Jenny always rode home with Truet after teaching school. This was her first year teaching in Sweethome and she loved it. Although it paid little, it helped a lot when Truet was between jobs, which happened occasionally, but especially during the winter months. Despite her love of teaching, she was excited for Friday to come; she enjoyed her weekends with her husband. It was spring, and the sun was shining gently on Sweethome as she waited for Truet. She decided to wait on the wagon rather than go into the store, but she now regretted that decision as she saw AJ Thacker and a handsome man she didn't know, walking from the Westward Whoa Saloon across the dirt street coming directly towards her.

"Ah, Jenny girl," AJ said as he stopped at the other side of the wagon. He crossed his arms on the side of the bench seat, his dark eyes roaming over her. "Are you waiting for a prince to drive you away, cause if you are, I'll take you to paradise." He smiled ever so slightly as his friend smiled a wide handsome, yet evil, grin. Although the stranger remained silent, he eyed Jenny Mae over, as well.

"No, AJ. I'm waiting for my husband," she answered matter-of-factly.

"Oh," he snickered, "why? A real man wouldn't leave such a piece of beauty like you out in the street unattended. My gosh, a lesser man than me might think of you as wanting a man like me."

Jenny refused to make eye contact with AJ and his friend, but she could feel both men's eyes on her.

"Of course," he added, "I'm not a lesser man, and so I wouldn't think ill of you. In fact, I'd say that I'm quite fond of you."

Jenny looked at him. "I'm sure that Allison would not appreciate hearing that."

AJ laughed slightly. "Allison's a whore. I would never marry a whore! I want the best and I always get what I want, even if it takes a little time. You're the best right now, but who knows what will come into town tomorrow. You might want to consider what your future looks like with Truet and what it could be with me," he continued as she glared at him with detest. "Hey," he shrugged, "I've got a thousand to every one of your dollars. Imagine that being yours."

"I'm not interested in your money or you, AJ. Now if you'll excuse me, I'm going to find my husband," she said and began to step down from the wagon.

"No need. Here he comes," AJ said nodding towards the door of the hardware store.

Truet Davis walked to the back of the wagon carrying a wooden box filled with his purchases. He looked irritated as he saw AJ leaning on his wagon bench talking to Jenny Mae. He set the box on top of the lumber and walked around the back of the wagon towards AJ and his spot on the bench seat.

AJ turned to face Truet and puffed up his chest as his right hand fell towards his holstered colt. His friend stepped beside him and his hand also fell near his revolver, though not as intentional as AJ.

"What?" AJ challenged. "You don't want me talking to Jenny?"

Truet took a deep breath as he noticed a slight crowd slowing down to watch and listen. Truet looked at AJ's friend closely and then at AJ. "No, nor does she. Now excuse me." Truet tried to step around AJ to climb up onto his wagon's bench seat, but was stopped by AJ's chest deliberately bouncing off of Truet's.

"This is my friend, Farrian Maddox. Farrian, this is Truet Davis," AJ said coldly.

Truet's eyes went to the handsome face of Farrian Maddox, a man of medium height with a strong build, short light brown hair and the hint of a growing beard on his strong-featured face. His eyes were a bright light blue that seemed to shine like the blue of the sky, but cold as a killer's – which Farrian Maddox was. He eyed Truet with the touch of a smile on his lips. Farrian's voice was surprisingly soft; "I've heard rumors that you were pretty good with a sidearm back in the day."

"I don't wear a sidearm," Truet answered awkwardly. Farrian Maddox was a name that had become synonymous with death. He was a gunfighter, gambler, murderer, hired killer, or anything else that paid him wages. He was mostly from Idaho City and Truet had never expected to meet him in Sweethome, especially with AJ Thacker introducing them. It put a bad taste in his mouth.

"Perhaps you should," Farrian continued softly, "you never know what's around the corner."

AJ added, "Especially around here. You wouldn't want some group of highwaymen to rob you and Jenny, would you? You'd be defenseless to protect a beauty like her," he said with a nod at Jenny Mae.

Truet nodded, as he stared at the ground. "I hung my gun up when I left the cavalry, gentlemen. In my experience a gun belt invites trouble," he looked up at Farrian and AJ. "Trouble I don't want anymore," he paused and then added as he stepped up on the wagon's bench, "if you'll excuse me."

"Trouble comes whether you wear a gun belt or not," AJ threatened as Truet released the brake and 'hawed' his team of horses. "See you later, Jenny," AJ called out with a strange predatory expression on his face.

Farrian spoke to AJ, "If you want him to put his gun belt back on, just keep after his woman. He's no coward; I've seen his look before. He'll come to kill you when he puts it on."

"He's a pup!" AJ exclaimed with disgust. "If he ever came at me with a gun, why I'd have him begging for his life. Don't be fooled by his size, he's a poodle in a big dog's body."

Farrian smiled coldly. He faced AJ and said with a serious tone, "I don't get intimidated, if that's what you mean."

"I didn't say that. What I meant was, don't let his looks fool you. He's a cowardly man. Would you allow someone to talk to your wife the way I did?" AJ asked with a little chuckle.

"I would've killed you."

"I know. So would I, but not him; he just turns and walks away. I hope he does put his gun on some day. Because his lovely widow would need some comforting and I'm all for that," AJ laughed. "You too, huh?"

"I'd eat her up. She's a beauty for sure," Farrian agreed. He was watching the short and heavy Sheriff Martin DePietro walking quickly toward them. "Break the law yet today?" he asked AJ as Martin neared.

AJ smirked. "None that mattered. What's up, Martin?" AJ asked as Sheriff DePietro neared them.

"Where's Brit? I got a letter from Matt Bannister himself, for him," Martin sounded nervous.

AJ frowned. "The marshal?"

"Yeah, the new U.S. Marshal, Matt Bannister, over in Branson. He wrote a letter to me about Abby. I gotta know what Brit wants me to do."

"Let me read it," AJ said, taking the letter.

Farrian spoke, sounding sarcastic. "I didn't know there was a law higher than you, Sheriff."

Martin viewed Farrian awkwardly. "Well there is." Farrian Maddox meant trouble, especially if he was staying in town over the weekend. Farrian commonly had a severe dislike for anyone that eyed the whore that he had his eye on and that usually meant trouble.

AJ laughed. "Well, finally something interesting is happening in this lousy place. Let's all ride out to the ranch and watch Brit's face when he reads this."

"Oh, let it go, Truet. AJ is a fool," Jenny Mae said. She held on to her husband's muscular arm while he drove the wagon a mile outside of town to their home.

"A fool with a gun is the worst kind, especially if he fancies himself a gunfighter. I've seen his kind before, but you know he's friends with Farrian Maddox and Farrian's the real thing. It won't be long and AJ's going to be more dangerous than Farrian. If he isn't already," Truet explained quietly. "The sheriff obviously doesn't care about the townspeople; otherwise he'd disarm AJ and his buddies. I would. If the sheriff of this town was to take the gun away from a gunfighter, or more dangerous, a man who fancies himself as a gunfighter, then he wouldn't have his tool of the trade to fight with anymore. Eventually they would quit coming to town because they'd already know they wouldn't be able to keep their guns. It's having a gun on his hip that makes AJ so dangerous. He knows how to use it and has no consequences for using it," Truet said irritably to Jenny Mae who listened intently.

Truet continued, "If you or I shot someone there'd be an investigation, if nothing else, but shoot one of the Thacker cowboys and we'd be swinging on a rope without an investigation or a trial. The longer we stay here the more disgusted I become with the town's judicial system. AJ and his friends get away with everything and everybody knows it. What we need is a sheriff that's not afraid to do his job straight across the board. One that's not afraid to stand up to old Bob Thacker and his cowboys."

"He's your boss right now, Tru," Jenny Mae offered gently. "Not to mention he owns our mortgage."

"Exactly," Truet stressed, gazing at his lovely wife. "Old Bob owns everything! He owns this entire valley and everyone in it, and those he doesn't own are heavily encouraged to do what he wants by his handpicked sheriff or AJ and his friends. It just isn't right, Jenny. There are many good, God-fearing people in Sweethome who have to feel the way I do. AJ harasses everyone, not just you and me. Why? Because he can. A new sheriff with some hardness would change that. Bob's influence would stop, where matters of the law were concerned, if I were the sheriff."

"Truet Davis," Jenny Mae's voice warned. "You're not thinking of running against Martin are you?"

Truet eyed Jenny Mae warmly, "I'm thinking about it."

"No," she said simply, "you just told AJ and his friend that guns bring trouble. Now, you want to run for sheriff and invite that kind of trouble? I'm sorry, Tru, I'm not willing to lose you for the sake of Sweethome and its corruption."

"It's our town, Jenny. We live here now. I can't stand having a man like AJ or any man saying whatever he wants to you, or to any other man's wife, just because he can get away with it. It's wrong. It's incredibly wrong! He's terrorizing people in their own town and where can the citizens of Sweethome go? The sheriff's working for AJ and his family!" Truet's voice rose steadily, "Someone's got to be the first one to stand up to them. I think a lot of folks would like to, but no one's willing to make the first stand."

"Why you, Truet? AJ's already got an eye out for you. You've said so yourself. What do you think he'd do if you won the election?" She didn't wait for an answer and continued passionately, "He'd bring his gang of cowboys out here and kill you! That's what he'd do, and the town would be no better off than it was before, except that, I'd be without my husband."

"I said, I was thinking about it," Truet stated with a hint of a smile. "Don't work yourself into a frenzy over nothing."

"Tru, I'd rather sell out and move to another town than to have you run against Martin for the sheriff's position. This isn't our town, it's theirs. It's always been theirs and it will always be theirs. You winning the sheriff's badge wouldn't make any difference, except a battle you couldn't win."

Truet smiled with disgust, "I wouldn't be looking for a war. All I'd say is, we need some law and order, especially towards the Thackers and their cowboys. If I was the sheriff, there'd be some," he finished.

Jenny Mae didn't waste a second to speak. "No, there'd be bloodshed and a lot of it. You couldn't arrest any of those cowboys or AJ, without being assassinated by another one of them. It's not your calling, Tru." She hesitated a moment before she continued, "You were called to be a husband and a carpenter and the Lord willing, a father too, not the sheriff of a wicked town."

Truet watched his two-horse team as they quickly pulled the wagon towards home. He spoke softly, "Jenny, I'm a man. I have my principles. I believe that there are rules that need to be followed, and not just by strangers and the weaker and the poor. To me, it's all black and white. A man shouldn't have to live with his wife being terrorized by a man free to do as he pleases, just because his 'daddy' is Bob Thacker!"

"Terrorized?" Jenny interrupted with a hint of surprise in her voice. "We've never been terrorized."

Truet sighed. "Then what would you call it?"

"I'd say AJ's an idiot," she stated simply. "I think you threaten him. You're bigger, stronger and much more handsome," she finished with a smile.

Truet continued seriously, "It has nothing to do with my appearance! He wants a fight, and a fight is what he'll get whether I want it or not. It would just be better for me if I was the sheriff."

"Or," Jenny Mae offered, "you could simply ignore him and walk away."

Truet smiled in spite of his disgust. "I've lived my whole

life fighting for what's mine. Now that I finally have something worth fighting for, you want me to cower down? I can't. I won't do that anymore. I was in the cavalry, Jenny Mae. I am still a soldier in here," he patted his heart. "Acting like a coward isn't natural for me and I don't think it ever will be. But how much more can one man stand?"

"It takes a stronger man to walk away," Jenny offered and then added, "The Bible says to turn the other cheek."

"I know what the Bible says. I've been turning my cheek since we moved here. It gets harder to do every time, and every time I do, he pushes harder the next time. The time is coming, Jenny, when I have to take a stand and feel like a man."

Jenny spoke firmly, "Well, wearing your gun won't make you a better man!"

"Maybe not a better man, but a man just the same. I hung up my gun when we left Kansas. I never wanted to put it back on, Jenny, but AJ's pushing harder every time I see him. Now Farrian's going to feel comfortable pushing me too and might make his intentions known with you also," he said, looking at Jenny firmly. He continued, "Understand something, Jenny; AJ is looking to start a fight. For some reason he thinks my name would look good etched under his belt." He knew the seriousness of his situation. AJ wanted to prove his status as a gunfighter of some quality. The only way to do so was to kill someone who had already proved his mettle. Truet had proved his in the U.S. Cavalry during the Indian Wars.

"We could move," Jenny offered softly, taking her husband's huge biceps in her arms as she leaned against him lovingly.

"We've invested everything into our home. We'd never find another piece of property as beautiful. I don't want to move, Jenny Mae. I want to run for sheriff. All it takes is one person to stand up to the Thackers and the rest of the town will stand up too," he said strongly.

"No," she answered with authority in her tone. "You won't be running for sheriff or putting your weapons back on. You will build a solid boxing ring for Bob and turn your cheek to AJ every time, no matter how hard it is. It takes a bigger man to be meek and to turn the other cheek."

Martin DePietro was nervous as he rode between AJ and Farrian Maddox across the Thacker Ranch to track down AJ's older brother, Brit. Brit was working with the herd of cattle on the northern end of the ranch. AJ was in good humor, as he wanted to be there to see the expression on Brit's face when he read the marshal's letter. AJ had a way of finding humor where Martin didn't think there was any. AJ may have been impulsive and known for his quick temper and his threatening gun hand, but AJ had always been friendly with Martin. He didn't threaten Martin the way Brit did. Brit Thacker simply scared Martin. Not intentionally, perhaps, but Brit wasn't like AJ, who talked too much, Brit hardly ever said anything except for what he meant to say. He never laughed, smiled, or even seemed to enjoy anything. Brit was a hard working, mean-eyed man who looked at Martin the same way he did a coyote around a calf. It wasn't personal; Brit looked at everyone with the same cold expression. When they found Brit, he was riding alone back towards the ranch buildings. He held up, curious to greet his little brother, Farrian Maddox and Sheriff Martin DePietro. It was an unlikely trio of riders coming to see him. For being a wealthy man, Brit dressed and appeared like a ragged, poor cowboy. He had dark, bushy hair that fell below his ears and a full beard that was untrimmed and ratty. He wore a dirt and sweat-stained hat and worn clothing that had seen many better days. He wore a gun belt and carried a rifle in a leather scabbard. He spit a mouthful of brown tobacco juice on the ground.

"What?" he asked impatiently as the three rode up to him.

AJ smiled expectantly. "Brit, the sheriff's got a letter for you. You might want to read it. It's from Matt Bannister himself."

"The marshal?" Brit asked curiously, as he stepped his horse closer to Martin.

"Yeah," AJ answered and added lightly, "seems half of your cowboys are wanted men," he continued as Brit took the letter from Martin. "He's coming for all of them."

Farrian laughed, as Brit eyed AJ humorously while he opened the letter. He read:

Sheriff Martin DePietro

I hereby request from you the present condition of and whereabouts of one Abby Lesko Thacker. Her parents are quite concerned for their daughter and request a letter from her, by her own hand. I request this letter to be received within three weeks. If not received within three weeks, I'll be

coming to investigate myself.

Sincerely,

Matt Bannister

U.S. Marshal

BRIT MADE no expression of concern or surprise. He simply

folded the letter in half and stuck it in his shirt pocket. "I'll take care of it," was all he said.

Martin offered, "That's Matt Bannister. So you might wanna...."

Brit cut him off curtly, "I know who he is, Martin! Thanks for bringing it out."

"Sure," Martin said meekly.

"Actually Martin, why don't you go to the old man's house and I'll bring a letter back for you to send. I'll go home and have her write it, right now," Brit said.

"You're giving into him?" AJ asked sounding disappointed. "I say we let him come, and bury him up on the north fork where he'd never be found."

"Yeah," Farrian laughed, "that's a statement I don't want any part of."

"Ah, coward," AJ replied to Farrian lightly. "I'd like a chance against the good marshal. I'd bury him."

Brit ignored the talk. "I'll be at pa's shortly," he said and kicked his horse into a smooth gallop towards his own private homestead on the ranch.

"Well, we'd better get going," Martin offered.

"Yeah, let's go see what pa's doing. That was disappointing. I was hoping to see him get upset," AJ said aloud as they headed to the main ranch house.

"Old Bob's got a whiskey selection, doesn't he?" Farrian asked. "I'm getting a little dry."

"Yeah, we'll finish off his best bottle, then let's get back to the Westward Whoa, I feel some luck following me tonight," AJ said. He was a regular at the poker table.

Abby Thacker was tired. She had spent the day hoeing in the garden. It was her responsibility and like every year, the garden would be big, plentiful and her's. She wore a plain, well-worn, dirty brown dress, no shoes, and her legs and feet were covered in soil. Her shoulder-length greasy, straight, red hair was in a bun to keep it out of her face while she worked. Her long narrow face was covered lightly with freckles and her light blue eyes had, at one time, brought more than a few courting men to her parent's door. Those were good days; she was young and filled with wonder as her whole life was before her with various paths she could choose. Life was exciting. She had a pair of young gentlemen that courted her and treated her like a real lady. Each young man hoped to win her devotion over the other. However, neither one of the young men had anything of value to offer her, except their willingness to work and strive to create a home and a future for the two of them.

Unlike the other two young gentlemen who courted her, Brit Thacker came as he was - dirty, unshaven, quiet, hard-working and usually with a mouthful of tobacco juice. He wasn't the handsomest man, but he was handsome in a rugged cow-boyish way. He was the ranch boss and in line to own the whole Thacker Ranch and all of Bob Thacker's other lucrative investments. Abby didn't marry Brit for his finances; rather she came to adore his sad smile and soft embrace. He was known as a hard man, but to Abby and her parents he was kind, giving and loving. Abby married Brit at nineteen; he was thirty-one. That had happened three years ago, which seemed like an eternity now.

Abby sat at the kitchen table resting momentarily before starting dinner. With a start, she heard Brit's horse stop outside the front door and anxiety gripped her tightly as she hadn't expected him for another few hours at least. The front door burst open and Brit's eyes hardened when he found her sitting idly at the table. He neared her quickly with a scowl.

"Brit," she gasped, and stood up defensively with panic

spreading across her face. "What'd I do?" she squeaked as her hands moved protectively to cover her face as Brit walked quickly towards her.

Brit smacked the back of her head with his left hand and then threw a hard right into her stomach, which doubled her over in painful gasps as she tried to catch a breath. With his left hand he grabbed the tight bun of hair and quickly slammed her face down against the tabletop viciously. Blood immediately spewed from her nose. He lifted her head by the hair and slammed her face down again, this time intentionally smearing her bloody face into the growing pool of blood on the table. Abby still couldn't get her breath from the blow to her stomach. All she could do was hope that he would stop soon.

"Clean this blood up, wipe your face and go get a piece of paper and something to write with," he ordered coldly and let her go. Abby didn't ask why, she just simply did what she was told, quickly and fearfully. She brought back the writing materials after cleaning up the table and her face, although her nose still bled.

"Write this: 'Dear Mother and Dad.'"

She looked up at him strangely with her reddened, watery blue eyes. "What?" she asked in almost a whisper, surprised.

"Write it!" he warned sternly. She followed his instructions. He continued, "I am fine and living my own life. If I want to see you, I'll come to you. Please don't bother me again."

"What?" Abby asked with a desperate plea in her voice, her breathing growing heavy.

Brit slapped her viciously, splattering blood droplets across the table again as it poured down across her lips.

"Write it down, Abby! I don't have time to stand here and watch you cry. Now write it!" he yelled angrily.

"Where are my parents?" she whimpered, desperately wiping the blood off her face with her dress sleeve.

Brit grabbed her hair roughly and yanked her head back, lifting it up to reveal her long, thin throat. "Write it or you'll never see them again," he warned as he revealed his knife blade, which he had pulled from its sheath with his right hand. His eyes were mean, cold and wicked. "Write it now!" he ordered coldly.

Abby broke into terrified sobs as she wrote word for word what Brit had told her. Her body convulsed as she drew in a breath. The glimmer of hope of finding her parents had once again been ripped away. Brit snatched the letter away as soon as she finished and read it. Abby's head collapsed onto the table in a torrent of weeping. Brit folded the letter and walked quickly to the door.

Abby's tortured voice stopped him as she begged, "Where are they?"

He turned and looked at her. Through a slight grin he said, "You'll never know and now they won't be searching for you anymore either."

Abby fell from the kitchen chair to her hands and knees, wailing loudly as she pleaded to Brit, "Please tell me. Please just let me write to them. Brit, please," she begged loudly, "tell me where they are. Please!"

"You just wrote to them," Brit said simply and walked out the door, closing it behind him. He swung up onto his horse and darted quickly to the main ranch house.

Abby cried. She hadn't been allowed to see or hear from her parents since the day she married Brit. The honeymoon began when he brought her to the attractive white cottage that he had built for her for their wedding day. He carried her across the threshold and she'd never left it since. It had turned into three years of being a prisoner in what seemed like an eternal hell.

The back door opened and the large figure of Saul Wolf came to her. He kneeled down beside her with a devastated expression on his face. His voice was deep, but soft and gentle. "Good lord," he said helping her up to sit on the chair. He found a rag, which he folded to cover her bleeding nose. Abby continued to cry.

"You're okay," he said, as he sat down on the chair beside her. "You're okay," he added reassuringly. She looked at him, shook her head, and began to cry again.

"You're going to be all right," he said, leaning forward to hug her comfortingly.

"He knows where my parents are," she said weakly through her tears. "He threatened to kill me, Saul." He just held her and remained silent while she continued to speak, "He's going to kill me and I don't even care anymore. Sometimes I wish he would, then I'd be free of him."

"Shh," Saul whispered softly into her ear, "Don't talk like that. It's just for now, okay? Soon enough you will be off of this ranch."

She pulled away from Saul and looked desperately into his eyes. "Take me away from here! Please, Saul, take me somewhere far away."

Saul smiled slightly. "I can't. Not now anyway. But if I win my fight in July, I won't need Bob anymore and I could take you anywhere you want to go."

"Would you though?" she asked softly.

Saul smiled gravely. "Of course."

"What about Brit? He'd come after me."

Saul's grave smile faded. "I know. We'd just have to trust

the Lord when that time comes. Until then... well..." his voice trailed off.

She nodded knowingly. "I'm glad you weren't here when he came in."

"Me, too," he agreed. "I was just crossing the creek bed when he came riding up. I ducked down so he wouldn't see me."

"So you heard everything?"

Saul nodded sadly. "It won't be long, Abby, until this is all a bad memory. I promise you that. Nothing's going to keep me from winning that fight and you know I don't even really care about the prize money. My greatest treasure will be leaving here with you."

Abby smiled a little. Saul could always bring a smile to her and she had very little to smile about.

For the third time in their marriage, the Lesko's had a new place of business doing what they did best: Lesko Shoes and Tailoring. It was a rented building, though they still made a hefty profit; business in Branson was strong. Robert Lesko sat behind his wooden workbench fabricating a piece of leather in what would be a pair of custom boots. Maude Lesko busied herself hemming up a pair of pants for a customer who would be in later to pick them up. Her eyes grew wide when she looked up to see who had just come inside the store. It was Matt Bannister, the U.S. Marshal. He carried a white envelope. "Mister Bannister, how can...?" she paused as she stood up to step out from behind the table that she had the pants lying on.

"I'm..." Matt began, sounding compassionate, "I received a letter from Martin DePietro. This one is addressed to you from Abby," he said softly and handed it to Maude.

"Oh, my lord!" Maude exclaimed, trying to contain her excitement. She took it as Robert Lesko joined her with an excited smile. Maude's excitement disappeared as tears filled her eyes with dismay as she read. "No! No! She couldn't have written this," she struggled to say, her mouth left open speechlessly.

"Is it her hand writing?" Matt asked softly.

Maude nodded affirmatively, but she couldn't speak. Robert took hold of the letter and stared at it. His face turned to a concerned and fearful expression as he shook his head. "Marshal," he spoke meekly, "there's blood on this."

"Where?" Maude asked, taking it from Robert's hand quickly. Sure enough, on the bottom right corner was a drop of smeared blood. Robert pleaded with Matt; "She didn't write this without being forced, Marshal. I'm no lawman, but I know my daughter." His breathing grew deep with the anxiety and anger that filled him.

"You have to go get her," Maude said plainly, expectantly.

"I wish I could," Matt said gently, "but I can't afford to send someone that far for nothing."

"Nothing!" Maude exploded angrily, "My daughter is someone! And I need you to get her!"

"Misses Lesko," Matt spoke softly.

Maude's bottom lip quivered as she purposefully pronounced every word, "Marshal, I have no one else to go get my baby. Please! I'm begging you. There's blood on this letter, Marshal. That's gotta tell you something!"

Matt sighed empathetically. "That's her handwriting. I can't help you."

"Oh," Maude groaned and hopelessly set herself into the nearest chair. She hid her face in her hands. Robert said strenuously, "We've tried everything and no one can help us. Do I have to go there myself and try to bring her home?

When I'm killed would that get you there? Is that what it's gonna take?" he asked heatedly.

Matt breathed in deeply. "I've already told you, if I or any one of my deputies get over that way, we'll stop by to see her." He added as he watched the Lesko's faces fall with disgust, "That's all I can do. I'm sorry," he said truthfully. "Sorry," he said quietly and left the store.

"Come Maude, let's pray that she'll come home to us," Robert said quietly. He held out his hand to help his wife get up out of the chair.

Maude eyed him squarely. "Why?" she asked irritably, "We've been praying for three years and nothing has happened yet. Every time we find a new avenue of hope, it dead-ends. What's the point Robert? No one's going to help us," she said sounding defeated and burst into tears.

Robert knelt down in front of her. "My dear, listen to me," he said, taking hold of her shoulders lovingly, "The point is, she is alive. We didn't know that an hour ago and as long as she's alive, I won't tire of praying for her safety and her return to us. I won't do it. The Lord's got her right here," he turned his right hand over to reveal his palm.

"Right here in the palm of His hand. I don't know when she'll come back, but I won't stop believing in Jesus, and I won't quit hoping for a miracle." He added softly, "And I hope you won't either. Let's go pray for our daughter."

1

June 30th 1883

Truet Davis sat with his wife, Jenny Mae, earnestly listening to the recently hired Reverend Richard Grace, give another soul-searching sermon. The Sweethome Christian Church was a good-sized church with seating for seventy people. Though it was usually nearly full, the pews seemed emptier than the usual 'empty pew' Sunday.

The Reverend Allister Schrader, who had founded the church, had left three months earlier for retirement and had brought in the young thirty-one-year-old Richard Grace and his sweet wife, Rebecca, to take over his legacy. Some town folks had trouble adjusting to the new young minister and his passionate and convicting sermons. Some people had even stopped coming to church for a while; however, being the only church in Sweethome, it wasn't long until they all decided to come back.

Most of the people missing from this Sunday had simply taken the day off from church to get ready for the Fourth of July. This particular Fourth of July was going to be special in

Sweethome. The town, for the first time, would make head-lines all across the country as the world renowned pugilist, Jacques Christy, would be coming to fight Sweethome's very own Saul Wolf, or as Bob Thacker billed him, "Goliath." Hotel rooms were booked solid as reporters, gamblers, and spectators all seemed to slowly flow into Sweethome to see the fight.

Reverend Grace didn't miss an opportunity to put his thoughts out to the congregation, including Saul Wolf himself, who sat with Truet and Jenny Mae Davis. "I wonder, folks, this week when the world comes to our town with its wildness, drunkenness, profanity, gambling and whoring, if we'll be offended by what we hear and see? I hope so. We should never become so accustomed to the sins of the world that we sit idly by in nonchalant tolerance." Reverend Grace paused, and then continued softly, "I invite every person in our congregation to join us this Thursday, as we march in protest against the debauchery of this town. We may not close the saloons or chase the prostitutes away, but we will stand up for righteousness sake and maybe, the Lord willing, we can save a lost soul or two." Now, he continued, sounding more joyful, "we have a potluck waiting outside for us, so let's go eat and enjoy the fellowship of the Lord's own family. Oh, by the way," he added quickly and looked at Saul Wolf. "Saul, I can't condone the fighting. You already know that, but I will say the only reason David was able to kill Goliath was because God was with him. I don't think this world renowned Jacques Christy has a chance, because God's with Goliath this time," he finished with a smile as some cheers erupted. "Let's go eat!"

Outside, four picnic tables were on the church's shaded grassy lawn under the large oak trees. Twenty-five or so adults and children ate plates of good food and drank lemonade or iced tea. Church socials were becoming more common under the leadership of Richard Grace. He believed a united church, without question, would attract the lost and hopeless like a lighthouse attracts the sailing vessels off the Pacific Coast. Isn't it the purpose of every church to teach the Lord's truth and keep the fire of His love alive? Richard thought so. He believed friendships built on deeper levels discourage gossip and other things that send waves of dissension through the congregation, not by correction or dictation, but by the very characteristics of friendship itself. Of course, there are always exceptions, but for the most part Reverend Grace was pleased with the friendships being made within his congregation. The friendship between Saul Wolf, a newly converted Christian and Truet and Jenny Mae Davis was one such friendship Richard appreciated.

Truet Davis was a very handsome man. Even the Reverend's own wife, Rebecca, had commented that "Truet was the finest physical specimen of a man that she had ever seen" and she wasn't alone in that regard. Many of the town's ladies found him physically appealing. His brown hair was cut fairly short, and he had friendly, deep-brown eyes, which narrowed pleasantly when he smiled. His face was clean-shaven and strong with a square chin. Truet was a carpenter by trade and had a large muscular body that impressed both men and women.

It wasn't any wonder that a man as physically attractive as Truet would marry his equal. Jenny Mae was stunning. If Reverend Grace wasn't such a prudent man he might have said to his wife, Rebecca, "that Jenny Mae was the finest specimen of a lady he'd ever seen." The Davis' were a great couple and had become good friends of Richard and Rebecca's.

Saul Wolf was in his late twenties and the biggest man Reverend Grace had ever met. Saul was nearly six feet and four inches tall and built like a wall of muscle. He was extremely broad-chested with arms the size of a normal man's legs. His legs seemed twice as thick as an average man's. Saul was a good example of what Samson might have looked like or Goliath, if he had been a few feet taller. He had a square, flat, broad face with squinty eyes, and a flattened nose. He had yellowish blonde hair cut very short and had no neck to mention. His large head set on his muscular shoulders. He wasn't handsome in the least respect; however, Saul could take the breath away from both men and women at first sight. He was majestic.

Saul was the local hero as a proven pugilist managed by Bob Thacker himself. Saul fought under the name "Goliath" and was undefeated so far in his quest to be the American heavyweight champion. John L. Sullivan was a ways off, but in a few days he'd fight one of the greatest contenders, Jacques Christy. The fight was taking place in Sweethome as the main event of this year's Independence Day festivities. If Saul won the fight, it would elevate Goliath's name to the level of the top contenders. It was a big fight for the unbeaten, and proudly labeled "The unbeatable Goliath."

Despite the violence of his profession, Saul was one of the nicest gentlemen one could ever meet. He wasn't harsh or coarse. He laughed quickly and joy pumped through his veins since giving his life to Christ. Saul was a great man and a great fighter who many believed could become known as the next champion.

At the moment though, Saul set his hulking body at a picnic table beside the young thirty-three-year-old widow, Felisha Conway across from Truet and Jenny Mae Davis.

"When the baby's born it'll be worth it, Jenny. Nine

months of discomfort is a small sacrifice to pay for a lifetime of the greatest joy you'll ever experience," Felisha Conway expressed compassionately.

Jenny was feeling the ill effects of her fourth month of pregnancy. "I know. But I sure don't feel like it's true," Jenny Mae said, while nauseously holding her belly.

"I remember those days, but it won't be long until it's all heartburn rather than vomiting," Felisha said and then laughed at the expression Jenny Mae gave her. She added quickly, "I'm sorry, Jenny Mae. Really, it's all a temporary inconvenience. The day will come when you'll want to do it all over again just to hold another baby boy or girl. I know, because I'd like to have another child or two."

Jenny Mae smirked. "You need to get married first."

Felisha sighed. "Lord willing. My Dillon needs a father to teach him how to be a man."

Truet said, "Dillon's been helping me out at my shop. He's a good little helper boy. He's already learned how to saw a board in two and is mastering hammering nails into the ground," he chuckled. Dillon was Felisha's eight-year-old son.

Saul took a deep breath and offered to Felisha, "Well, Martin's still trying to court ya."

"Shush!" Felisha playfully scolded to the pleasure of the other three. "Martin DePietro will never court me. I will never marry a lawman. If I ever get married again it will be to a businessman."

Truet laughed lightly. "You're in the wrong town if you're looking for a businessman."

Felisha shrugged. "The Lord knows where I am. I guess if He wants me to marry someone again, He'll have to bring him here, because I can't afford to go anywhere else."

"You could always marry AJ," Saul joked and faked a sore arm when Felisha elbowed him wordlessly.

"Speak of the little devil and there he is," Truet stated. He was looking behind Saul towards the street next to the church's shaded yard.

A black buggy driven by Bob Thacker stopped at the edge of the church's yard. Bob, as always, wore a dark suit and a black Stetson hat. He was a heavyset, gray-haired man with a round face. Even though he was always neatly dressed and clean-shaven, he had a tough and domineering presence. It was his icy blue eyes that could stare down the roughest men. His round cheeks and bulbous nose were always a little red-colored. He had short gray hair on the sides of his head but had little on top.

Bob stopped the buggy and stared incredulously at Saul Wolf as Saul turned his bulky shoulders to face Bob. Bob shouted, "What the hell are you wearing your suit for? I didn't buy it for you to soil it at church! It's for the press conference on Wednesday, Saul! You know that, for crying out loud!" Bob complained loudly as his youngest son, AJ, slipped out of the buggy and neared the food laid out on a table. Bob continued, "I want you to get back home and get that suit off. I didn't buy it so you could show it off to the widowed ladies of the church." He nodded to Felisha, and then immediately turned to face Revered Richard Grace who was standing between two tables staring at Bob astonished by his blatant interruption of their potluck.

"Reverend, I heard a ridiculous little rumor that you and this congregation were planning to parade through my town protesting on the Fourth of July! I suspect it's just woman's gossip. Ain't it?" he asked with an obvious threatening tone.

"Well, yes, we are," Reverend Grace got out before AJ Thacker laughed scornfully.

AJ bit into a fried chicken leg and said, "Reverend, what are you going to protest? The fight? Whisky? Gambling? Whores?" he paused to motion to the congregation with his arms, "You have whores right here, except they're free of charge."

Richard's eyes narrowed angrily. "You need to get away from here! You are not welcome on the church's property. You have absolutely no business here. Now leave!" Richard shouted and pointed towards Bob who was still on the buggy.

Saul Wolf and Truet both began to stand to go near Richard.

"Let's go, AJ," Bob said simply.

"Go now!" Richard demanded.

AJ laughed, as Saul and Truet neared Richard. "You don't like hearing that, huh? Well hell, Richard, your own wife's been eyeing me. And Jenny Mae over there, well, Truet, I don't know if she's carrying my baby or yours."

Truet stepped forward quickly to grab AJ, but was held back by Saul who stepped in between the two men. Truet suddenly furious yelled vehemently, "I'll tear your head off, you son of a bitch!"

AJ laughed wickedly. "Oh Tru, I thought you were a Christian?" he asked mockingly and then added viciously, "Step back, Saul; let's see him tear my head off." AJ suddenly pulled his revolver and pointed it at Truet's head. "I could blow yours off a lot quicker!"

"Oh, Lord!" A lady's voice screamed out and gasps of shock and fear seemed to come from everywhere.

Bob Thacker's voice boomed out loudly as he stood up angrily. "AJ! Put that gun down now!"

AJ held his deadly gaze on Truet, as he sneered coldly,

"Don't ever threaten me again, Truet. It would be my pleasure to kill you anyway."

"You need to leave my wife alone, AJ!" Truet's voice shook with fury as Jenny Mae appeared beside him, putting her arms around him. Truet continued, "I won't allow you to talk about her like that. She's my wife, not one of your prostitutes!"

AJ eyed Jenny Mae up and down intentionally, as he lowered his gun slowly and asked, "Is there a difference?"

"Yes, there is!" Truet spit out. His eyes were wide and burning with indignation. "She's married to me and I'm not afraid of you or your father! Say anything like that again and I'll bust your jaw, AJ!"

"AJ," Bob ordered, "you and Goliath get on this buggy, right now!"

Saul spoke uneasily, "Come on AJ, let's go home" and tried to nudge AJ towards the buggy.

"You sound like a mighty tough man for not wearing a gun," AJ said calmly to Truet. "You might want to consider putting one on if you're going to threaten me. I already told Jenny, I always get what I want. She knows that and so do I. You're just in the way," he finished with a cold sneer and turned towards the buggy.

Truet began to speak and follow AJ, but Saul stepped in front of him and gently pushed Truet backwards and said softly, "Let it go, Tru. He's leaving."

Bob Thacker raised his voice to address the congregation as AJ and Saul climbed aboard the buggy. "I put a lot of time and money into this Independence Day celebration. I recommend you enjoy it and not embarrass me with your religious banter. If we wanted to hear it, we'd come to your church. If you invade my party, folks, I'll invade yours," he warned coldly. With AJ beside him and Saul sitting on the back, he drove away.

Richard Grace scowled at Truet with an infuriated expression. His voice seethed with determination with every word, "We will fear no man! We will march as Christian soldiers and we will march all the louder. He just invaded our party, now let's invade his!"

2

————

Truet drove the empty wagon slowly towards their home while Jenny Mae grew more nauseated as she bounced and rocked with the wagon's movement. Her breathing was growing heavier and her pretty face had lost its color. It wouldn't be long until she vomited. She was in her early months of pregnancy and Truet hoped and prayed the nausea wouldn't last much longer. They'd been married for five years and she'd finally conceived, and now they were expecting a child. The timing really couldn't be better in hindsight; it was amazing how the Lord knows exactly when to answer prayer. His timing is always perfect.

Truet and Jenny Mae Davis came to Sweethome over a year before and fell in love with the valley and its fertile land. It seemed a miracle when they came to answer the want ad for a carpenter, and once in town the teaching position opened up in the school. The two jobs fell in place all too easily, and the biggest miracle of them all was about to take place when they went to the Thacker, DePietro Land Company and met Bob Thacker. Bob showed them a beautiful two-story home a mile out of town with solid outbuildings on twelve acres of land already cleared and planted with hay that Bob himself would harvest and buy from them on a yearly basis. The homestead was a steal for only five thousand dollars. It was a blessing from the Lord and now with a home of their own and as respected citizens of their new town; they were expecting a child. Truly, it couldn't come at a better time as he had constant work at his carpenter's shop and Jenny Mae was the schoolmaster. Their home was solid, warm in the winter and for the first time in five years of marriage, they were finally settled and it felt good. Truet rejoiced inside as he eyed his twelve acres of hay and the two-story white-painted home with black trim around the door and windows. It had a large covered front porch that faced the northwest, quite often revealing beautiful sunsets over the fields of golden hay, and the green tree line behind it.

"Stop!" Jenny Mae said suddenly and started to climb down off of the wagon. She turned away from Truet and bent over, vomiting. It was the second time since they'd left Sweethome. This time all that came up was bile. They had just stopped shy of the house, so Truet locked the brake and joined his suffering wife's side.

"Are you all right, my lady?" he asked as he put his hand gently across her shoulders.

She shook her head. "No," she moaned breathlessly, "I'm sick, Tru." She eyed him with hostility and wiped off her mouth and then her tearful eyes.

"Let me walk you inside. You go lay down and rest, I can't have my lady out here not feeling well."

"Oh, I swear I'm going to whip this baby when he's born," she said as she walked towards the house with Truet.

He laughed. "If it keeps up this nonsense, I'll whip it myself."

"It's a boy, Tru. You always refer to him as 'it,'" she looked Truet in the eyes warmly. "I don't think he likes that and I'm paying for it."

Truet smiled and took his wife lovingly into his arms. "It could be a girl, my love."

"No, no young lady would treat her mother like this. He's an awful, awful boy. Just like his father was," she said and slapped his bicep playfully.

Truet laughed and kissed her quickly on the lips.

"Tru, I just vomited," she said covering her lips with her hand, embarrassed.

He smiled his handsome smile. "Go lay down, my love. Get some rest."

"Tru, don't let me sleep too long, I have dinner to make tonight. I wouldn't want you to starve on my account. Besides, I need something else to vomit up later."

Truet laughed as he gazed upon his wife. "I love you, Jenny Mae, I really do."

She smiled slightly. "I love you too, Tru. Truly I do," she said softly while she held her husband tightly.

LATER TO JENNY MAE'S relief and appreciation, the Reverend Richard Grace, his wife, Rebecca, and their two children showed up with Saul Wolf and a basket packed with a ready-made dinner to share with the Davis'. It was a welcomed surprise.

After dinner Truet led the two men outside to sit on the porch and talk while Rebecca and Jenny Mae cleaned up. The two Grace children, Luke, who was five, and three-year-old Sarah, played outside near the porch.

Truet sat on the porch swing with Reverend Grace while Saul Wolf sat on the porch rail facing them. It was Reverend

Grace that spoke as he nodded toward his children. "Sarah's going to love playing with your baby. A few more years and you'll have a couple of little treasures running around like that."

Truet watched the children play with a warm smile on his face. "I can hardly wait. I haven't told Jenny, but I'm making a cradle for our baby. It's at the shop. You two should stop by and look at it. I don't want to sound vain, but it's the best work I've ever done. It's not put together quite yet, but it's coming together well."

Richard nodded. "That's because it's made with love, a father's love."

"I suppose," Truet smiled.

Saul added, "I hope you put some love for a friend into that boxing ring you made. I'd hate for it to collapse when Jacques goes down and they stop the fight because of it. I don't want the bleachers to fall either. I gotta win this fight fair and square."

"Nope," Truet spoke seriously, "I double-bolted every joint and set every support beam in three feet of mortar. It took a lot of work, but the ring and the bleachers are as solid as they can be. The only way someone's going to get hurt is if they get into the ring with you." He smiled and winked at his friend. He added, as if it was a matter of fact, "If I was a betting man, I'd bet on you, Saul."

Saul nodded. "I appreciate it, Truet. But Jacques Christy's a professional. He's had over a hundred fights all over the world and now he's coming here to fight me. He's not like the other men I've fought. Jacques Christy is a legend, Bob says."

"Oh, come on now," Truet interrupted with a smile, "he's just a man. Besides, like Richard said today, God's with Goliath this time."

Saul nodded without any response to Truet's words. "I am a preliminary fight to him as he travels east. Bob set it up while we were in San Francisco. Now all these rich men are coming here to bet on Jacques Christy, the legend, or me; the unbeaten Goliath." He paused sadly and added, "I have to win."

Truet shrugged. "Even if you don't, it'll only be your first loss. Certainly losing to Jacques Christy won't end your career. A loss to Richard Grace would though." Truet laughed, joined by Richard.

"No," Saul said uncomfortably, and then cleared his throat. "Can I tell you two something, something serious?"

Reverend Grace answered, "Sure, Saul."

"It can't leave this porch; you two have to promise you won't repeat it. I've never told anyone and no one else can know. Not even your wives, okay?" the expression on Saul's face showed much anxiety.

"You've got my word."

"Mine as well, Saul," Truet answered.

Even though the two men gave their word, Saul was still hesitant to speak as they patiently waited. His voice cracked slightly as he lowered his voice to a light whisper. "I'm in love with a married woman. We're going to run away when I can afford to get us away. That's why I have to win this fight. There's more depending on it than just my pride or record."

"Who is she?" Reverend Grace asked leaning forward towards Saul.

Saul took a deep breath. "You can't tell anyone."

"We gave our word."

Saul spoke through another deep breath, "Abby Thacker."

"That's?" Reverend Grace shrugged unknowingly.

"She's married to Brit," Saul answered. He knew neither

44

man knew anything of her; off of the Thacker Ranch, Abby didn't exist. Even those who may have known her once seemed to have forgotten about her, as he never heard anyone ask about or even mention her name.

"You committed adultery with her?" Truet asked with concern in his voice.

Saul shook his head. "No. Our love's built on friendship. I've held her in my arms and kissed her, but nothing that far."

Reverend Grace frowned. "Obviously, Brit doesn't know you have these feelings." He personally had never met Brit Thacker, but he had heard that Brit was a hard man.

"No!" Saul stated sharply, "and he'd better not find out or I'm dead! He's not a nice man. She's always bruised or bleeding. Every time I see her, he's beaten her again for no reason other than he wants to." Saul's face softened as he said, "I love her. I want to take her away from here."

Truet stammered, "You've never even mentioned her before, so excuse me if I'm not being overly supportive, Saul. But, she's married to another man! You can't just run off with her and expect it all to be okay, especially when it's Brit Thacker's wife!" Truet had a serious expression on his face. He eyed his friend Richard and explained, "I don't know Brit particularly, but I met him a few times and I have to say I wouldn't want to be caught leaving with his wife!"

Saul smiled despite himself as he said, "Me neither." He added seriously, "Trust me, I know, but it doesn't matter. All I care about is Abby. If I win this fight I'll have enough money to take her away, just about to anywhere."

"And do what?" Truet asked pointedly. "The Thackers won't let you just leave, especially with her! You have to think about this, Saul. You're right at the doorstep of becoming great. You're going to throw it away?"

"Tru, I don't know what else to do."

"Stop this little affair and seek the Lord, Saul. Repent and focus on fighting, that's a good start! You can't have a love affair with another man's wife and expect it all to turn out all right. It's Brit Thacker's wife!" Truet finished, glaring harshly at Saul.

"I didn't plan on falling in love with Abby. I know it's not right, but it's the only thing right in my life and certainly in hers," he paused dramatically before continuing. "Fighting isn't my dream anymore, having a wife is."

Truet sighed with frustration. "She's already someone's wife, Saul! It's not right. You're making a mistake. What are you going to do to support your family, clean pig pens? You won't be able to fight, not with the Thackers searching for you."

Saul's eyes flickered with irritation as he answered Truet. "Tru, I would rather clean pig pens for very little and have the girl I love, than to be the champion of the whole world and have to know that Brit was beating the daylights out of the woman I love. Do you realize," he added pointedly, "that he has broken her ribs, her nose, her wrist and beaten two babies out of her? Not counting the hundreds of bruises he's given her over the past three years. She hasn't been allowed to see her parents since she married him. Her parents used to live right here in Sweethome, but they were chased off by the Thackers. She doesn't even know where they live now. A few months back I got to witness Brit beating her bloody and forcing her to write a letter to her parents asking them to leave her alone forever!" He breathed in deep and continued in a softer tone, "She hasn't been allowed to even come to town in three years, not since her wedding day. What would you do if that were Jenny Mae, Tru? Would you risk everything for a chance to start a

46

life with her, or would you turn your back on her and go to work knowing the woman you love was being beaten every day?"

Truet sighed and buried his head in his hands. He wanted to reply, he wanted to say something wise and profound, he wanted to, but he couldn't; his tongue was tied. He knew what Saul wanted to hear, but he couldn't justify Saul's actions. However, he was getting ready to answer with the only thought he could muster when Richard's soft and caring voice answered for him.

"You've gotten yourself into quite a jam, huh?" he asked Saul.

"Yeah," Saul answered quickly. "I don't know what to do other than leaving with her."

"Could she divorce him?" Richard asked.

"Brit?" Saul shook his head. "She can't even leave her house. He'd kill her if she mentioned it. He told her, if she ever tried to leave him he'd kill her."

Truet spoke quickly, "And if he finds out you left with her, he'll kill you too. Saul, you're flirting with fire! You really need to think about this. Are you really willing to give up everything, including your life, for this girl? I keep emphasizing this, but Saul, you're one fight away from being a top contender for the American heavyweight championship. That's something you shouldn't just walk away from! If you do this and do get away from here, old Bob and Brit will search high and low for you. You'd always live in fear of being found. You'd always be looking over your shoulder, because you're too big of a man not to be noticed!" Truet emphasized and added simply, "I think it's better to just end it now, ask God for forgiveness and pray no one ever finds out."

"I agree with him, Saul," the Reverend Richard Grace

said softly. "I feel for this lady and I'll certainly pray for her well being, but I think you should reconsider your plans."

Saul seemed defeated as he said sadly, "I promised her. I can't let him hurt her anymore. One of these days he's going to kill her and at that point he might as well kill me, because I'm in love with her."

The front door opened as Jenny Mae and Rebecca Grace came outside with a laugh as they finished a conversation between themselves. Rebecca carried a tray of glasses filled with lemonade. "Are you men ready for some lemonade and womanish conversation?" she happily asked.

Richard eyed his wife pleasantly, though the expression on his face showed a hidden concern and sadness that she immediately recognized. It wasn't uncommon for a member of his flock to confide in the reverend. He always had the same expression when something troubled him. She knew she would never know what was confided to him unless Richard asked her opinion in the privacy of their home.

Jenny Mae didn't give Richard or the others a chance to answer as she quickly handed glasses of lemonade out to her guests and husband. "So, what kind of man talk are we interrupting, anyway?" she asked.

"Oh," Truet sighed, "wagon wheels and horse tails," he finished with a slight smile and a "thank you."

Jenny Mae quipped without a moment's thought, "Oddly enough, so were we."

Saul laughed. "Well then, you're welcome to join in. A ladies' perspective is always something to ponder on."

Jenny Mae eyed Saul seriously as she stood in the middle of the porch. "Thought exercises the mind. King Solomon had a thousand wives and concubines combined. Do you think that had anything to do with his becoming the wisest man that ever lived?" she asked with a quick jovial laugh.

The Reverend Richard Grace couldn't resist. "Ah Jenny, you should heed the proverb Solomon wrote that says, 'Beginning a quarrel is like opening a floodgate, so drop the matter before a dispute breaks out.'" He smiled and added, "Solomon answered in his own words the wisdom of having a thousand wives. 'It's better to live on the corner of the roof than to share a house with a quarrelsome wife.'"

Jenny Mae said to Truet who was laughing, "What are you laughing at?"

Truet answered, "If you notice, Solomon said 'wife,' not wives. It strikes me as funny that he thought one's bad enough!"

"Am I bad enough?" Jenny Mae asked playfully, as she leaned against the rail next to Saul.

"Heavens, no! You're perfect to me. In fact, here, let me get up so you can sit down," Truet said as he stood from the porch swing.

"Yeah, what am I thinking? Here, my dear," the Reverend said to Rebecca. He and Truet leaned on the rail so that their two lovely brides could sit comfortably in the porch swing.

3

The moon lit up the small bedroom as it came in through the window. The night was refreshingly cool and the distant sound of coyotes yipping in the night brought a slight comfort to her soul. Over the years the coyotes had become the only symbol of freedom she knew. It didn't matter how many coyotes Brit and his cowboys killed, their sweet sounding cries left a sense of triumph within her. At least he couldn't control the coyote. They were free; through their nightly cries a part of her spirit remained free as well. As desperate as it seemed, it was the only sense of freedom she knew.

It wasn't always like that though. She remembered being eighteen and nineteen and being courted by three different men. Life was filled with youthful excitement and her laughter was her strongest feature. So often the townsfolk would comment on her joyful laugh, and why not, she had her whole life ahead of her. A life that by all noticeable appearances seemed destined to bring prosperity and happiness. Who could have ever known how wrong she'd been?

Brit Thacker was a rich man. He already had a lovely little home built for her on the Thacker Ranch and promised everything imaginable to a nineteen-year-old girl if she'd marry him. Her dreams of having wealth and prosperity were ready-made promises. She wasn't bought by his promises alone; she had actually fallen in love with the older man. He was kind and lavished his attention onto her. He was considerate and interested in her thoughts. He smiled and laughed in her presence and gazed upon her with soft and adoring eyes. It was that same sensitive boy-like desire in his eyes that convinced her to marry him.

They wed in the church in a splendid Christian ceremony with a long guest list, and she in her beautiful wedding dress. A girl couldn't want a grander wedding and the adoration in his eyes melted her heart as they looked into each other's eyes. The reception party was exceptional; her parents were excited and jovial, as were the many friends who celebrated the matrimony. Many commented on how much Brit had changed since she came into his life. It was a good day. Little did she know it would be the last time she saw her family or Sweethome again.

Brit took her to their beautiful small home and as he carried her across the threshold of the door, the adoration in his eyes that she had fallen for, turned into a brutal stranger's as he ravaged her without any consideration to her modesty, fears, displeasure or cries of pain. He had set the tone for the rest of her life; he cared nothing for her desires, wishes, or courtesies. She was and would always be nothing more than someone to cook, clean, and give him a warm body to feel at night.

She laid on her side, naked and used. Brit slept soundly as he pulled her body close to his. His heavy breathing was sounding in her ear as his naked body pressed against hers and his arms held her tightly. To a visitor passing by it might seem loving; however, to Abby it was repulsive. She hated Brit, with hatred so deep that she couldn't imagine ever forgiving him. The only other emotion she had for him was terror. Brit seemed to like it that way though; the closest thing to a smile on his face was the grimace he had when he was about to strike her. He neared a smile at times, when she lay on the floor in a fetal position begging him to stop hitting her.

Why he didn't just put her out of her misery, she didn't know. He showed more emotion and compassion for his cattle than he did for his wife. She didn't understand why. She had done nothing to him other than marrying him. He only grew colder and more heartless and brutal with time. She fully expected to be beaten to death eventually and sadly enough nobody would realize she was gone; nobody would question where she was even if they did notice she was gone. She was no longer a person per se, but a piece of private property, Brit's private piece of livestock to do with as he pleased.

There was only one person in the world, as she knew it, who cared for her, and that was Saul. He was the sole reason she opened her eyes in the morning and closed her eyes at night. The very actions made it one-day sooner when he was going to take her away from Brit and his God-forsaken ranch once and for all. That day was coming. It was coming up on Independence Day when Saul fought the Frenchman, Jacques Christy. Saul had promised her he'd win this fight and take her away.

Of course, getting away would be their greatest worry. If they were seen leaving together by anyone of the Thacker ranch hands they would most certainly tell Brit and he would kill them both, she had no doubt. Leaving had to be planned, and it had to be planned well. The planning she would coordinate with Saul. He would gather all the information she needed such as the stagecoach schedules and the train heading east out of Boise City. The trouble with running was they had nowhere to go. But then again, staying where she was wasn't an option. It was better to die with the man she loved than to live as a slave to a master that hated her.

Saul was her hope. He somehow loved her enough to leave his future and risk his own life for her. How, she didn't sometimes understand, as she knew she looked a wreck. She was no longer pretty, and true to Brit's words, she felt undesirable. It still amazed her that anyone of Saul's caliber would desire her, and he must, as he still was risking everything for her. As for her, she loved Saul with everything she had. He was the only reason she could have some hope for a future. Her whole soul anguished to be with Saul. The desire that filled her was to be lying beside the man she loved. The one man that spoke softly to her and made her feel like a human being again. It was nice to just be treated like a real person. Saul was her only friend, and he loved her. He really did.

For Abby to lie as still as she could with the fear of disturbing Brit's sleep if she moved was troubling enough, but to lie there being held by the man she despised, while she dreamed of Saul was a kind of torture. She had once believed in God and grew up in a Christian home memorizing the Bible verses that taught of a loving and kind God who actually cared about His people. Abby once believed it all, but then she married Brit and she learned first-hand that not everyone's a believer in the Bible. Brit had burned her Bible and forced her to watch it burn. She'd been praying for three years for the Lord to save her from her lonesome hell and for three years Brit had continued to do as he wished. She had given up on the hope of any God coming to rescue her. Her hope was in Saul Wolf. The mightiest man she'd ever known. He would save her or at least they'd die together.

4

The town of Sweethome was in an excited buzz Tuesday afternoon with the arrival of Jacques Christy and his entourage. Jacques and his associates checked into the Dills' Sweethome Hotel, where many curious people gathered hoping to get a look at the legendary fighter. The whole town seemed to come alive and double in size as more stage coaches and wagons brought in more spectators wanting to find a bed before everything was sold out for the big fight on Thursday. Jacques Christy himself, like some others, wanted a day's rest to recoup from traveling before celebrating the Fourth of July.

The surrounding logging camps and miners were filling the saloons with the excitement of a long-awaited stretch of fun in town. The holiday celebration was already beginning and the main street of Sweethome would run wild all night, every night for nearly a week.

For Felisha Conway, it brought business into her boarding house, which was her primary income. Her rates were double that of the hotels, but it was her home and she treated her guests well. She made a decent living with her home. It was her primary tool of supporting herself and her son since her husband's death four years before.

Delbert Conway was the bank manager with an accounting business on the side. He was a strong business-oriented man with a desire to earn money any way he could. His work ethic was to succeed. Being a small-framed man he had the large Victorian home built bigger than they would ever need. His reasoning was his desire to have more children. They had Dillon, lost an infant girl they named Mandy, and Felisha had miscarried twice.

One April afternoon, Delbert climbed up onto the roof of the big home to find a leak and apparently slipped and fell off. The fall had critically injured him. He lingered for a few hours in great pain and then passed away. Felisha was left alone and had lost her family's sustainable income. She turned her large home into a boarding house and took over Delbert's accounting business, which she did from her home.

"Mister and Misses Bannister, I could draw you a bath if you'd like. Many of my guests like to bathe after a hard day of traveling," she spoke to the married couple who had arrived in the late afternoon. They were obviously weary from traveling and were resting comfortably at a table on the long front porch, drinking a glass of iced tea.

"Not right now, thank you. I think we'll just sit here in the shade and enjoy the afternoon. By the way, call me Lee and this is Regina," Lee Bannister said softly. He and his beautiful wife were quite obviously well-to-do and must've been important as Bob Thacker made the reservations for them himself.

Felisha smiled kindly. "Well, Lee and Regina, you're welcome to bathe whenever you want. Dinner will be served at six o'clock, but until then if you're hungry, I could make you a light snack."

Regina Bannister smiled appreciatively. "No, thank you, we can wait until six." She was in her late twenties, with big brown eyes in a flawless angelic face. Her dark hair was pinned up under a flower-trimmed hat, and she was stunning in a yellow flowered dress.

Lee spoke, "We might take a stroll around your town pretty soon and look around, but we'll be back before dinner."

"There's not a lot to see in Sweethome. I imagine you're here to see the fight on Thursday?" she asked and then feared it was asked too bluntly, as she waited for the answer.

Lee nodded. "Yes, Bob assured me it would be worth the trip. I'm a fan of fisticuffs and Jacques Christy is one of the best. It's worth the trip to watch him." Lee shrugged casually and then asked, "Do you know Goliath? I understand he's local."

Felisha nodded. "His name is Saul Wolf. We go to the same church. The only person who calls Saul 'Goliath' is Bob Thacker," she said with a hint of disgust. "The rest of us call him Saul."

Lee squinted his eyes momentarily and then asked, "Are you a fan of Saul's? Do you think he'll win?"

"Mister Bannister, I don't like the fighting, but Saul is a friend of mine. I guess I have to hope he wins."

"Call me Lee," Lee said simply. "But you're not betting on him?" he asked knowingly.

"No. I won't bet on anyone. I suppose, I'm not in a position to risk losing what money I do have. Not even on Saul. I don't think it's wise."

"Ah!" Lee jested, "Then you do think he'll win?"

Felisha smiled slightly. "I cannot imagine a man beating him. Have you seen Saul, Mister Bannister?"

"No. I've not."

"Well, when you do you might wish you had bet on him," she stopped as a woman's scream came from within the house, followed by a man's surprised rough voice reprimanding a child.

Dillon's voice called out, "Mama!" as his feet ran through the house.

"Out here!" she called, concerned over the other guests' voices.

Quickly her eight-year-old son, Dillon, ran out the front door carrying a two-foot long bull snake in his hands. His excited young face beamed, as Regina screamed unexpectedly and leaned towards Lee.

Dillon spoke excitedly, "I caught it, Mama, all by myself! It tried to bite me!" He held it out to Felisha. "It's not a ratler!" he finished, nearly out of breath.

Lee laughed pleasantly, as Felisha took the snake into her hands. "What have I told you about bringing things into the house, Dillon James Conway! You can't do that, young man!"

Her attention went to the older man who stepped irritably out the front door. He was another guest, who arrived for the fight with his wife. His name was Clarence W. Tibbs, a gray-haired businessman from Boise City, who was another one of Bob Thacker's personal guests. Clarence Tibbs was quite irritated as he said, "Miss Conway, I understand the boy doesn't have a father to whip some manners into him, but the child needs to be taught a lesson. He pert near scared my Misses to death. If you haven't got the heart to whip him, I'll gladly find a durable switch and teach the lesson for you!"

Felisha's eyes hardened as Dillon's excitement changed quickly to alarm. He backed in to Felisha's protective body. Her voice was controlled, but strong, "I apologize, Mister Tibbs, for my son's frightening Misses Tibbs. It was wrong of him and we were just discussing that."

"Talk is worthless, Miss Conway. Children need to be punished, the harder the better, because then they keep it in mind. Talk, my dear, goes in one ear and out the other. A switch stings the lesson learned right into them!"

Felisha's face blushed with a reddening mixture between embarrassment and anger. Her eyes grew a little wider and deepened as she fought to control her temper. In no uncertain terms would she tolerate such an impertinent man such as Clarence Tibbs. However, he was a special guest of Bob Thacker's and she feared if she spoke her mind, Bob might not use her boarding house for his guests any longer, and Bob sent her a lot of business. Felisha was thankful to hear Lee Bannister come to her rescue.

"Clarence," Lee said from his sitting position, "the boy caught a snake and it isn't a rat-ler," he used Dillon's pronunciation with a smile. "I think we should congratulate him for not getting himself bit. Felisha was doing a fine job reprimanding her son for carrying the snake through the house and scaring the Misses and you. I don't think it would be wise for anyone to overstep his or her welcome, especially when we're staying in their home," Lee finished pointedly. His voice was gentle, but the warning was clear to see in his eyes, as he silently eyed Clarence W. Tibbs.

Clarence looked from Lee to Felisha and clenched his jaw tightly. He didn't have much professional contact with Lee Bannister, but he knew it wasn't wise to get on Lee's bad side. Lee was a powerful man. "Perhaps I'm overreacting. I apologize, Miss Conway. It's been a long day." He explained, forcing his anger down.

"I understand, Mister Tibbs. Rest assured my young Dillon won't make this mistake again. Will you young man?" she asked glaring down at Dillon, who still stood pressed against her. Dillon looked up at her with his light-colored hair and deep-brown eyes like his mother's and shook his head wordlessly. "Apologize to Mister Tibbs," she warned.

Dillon looked Mister Tibbs in the eye and said softly, "I'm sorry, sir."

"Apology accepted, young man." Clarence turned to Lee, nodded and went back inside.

Felisha sighed, as she carefully handed the bull snake back to Dillon. "Keep it out of the house, Dillon. Why don't you take it out by the cellar and let it go."

"Oh Mother, Can't I play with it for a little while?"

Lee laughed. "Dillon, my name's Lee. You know, I have girls and they're afraid of snakes like their mother. So how about we go out to the cellar and play with the snake for a few minutes," he eyed Regina humorously as he stood. "I haven't played with a snake since, I don't know when," he laughed and turned to Dillon. "This bull snake will eat any rat-ler that comes near your cellar. Did you know that?" he asked as he grasped the snake from Dillon.

"Yip! My mother taught me that. I'm not supposed to catch rat-lers."

Lee laughed heartedly. "That's a good idea."

"Thank you, Mister Bannister," Felisha said somewhat quietly, "for saying what you did to Mister Tibbs. I was..." she stopped.

Lee nodded. "You're welcome. Some people just don't like children. I do," he said and followed Dillon off of the front porch.

Regina eyed Felisha with a small smile. "I can't believe you held that vile creature."

Felisha smiled. "I have to teach my son how to be a boy. He doesn't have a father anymore, so snakes, snails, slugs or whatever else he finds, I get to hold. I was raised with brothers on a farm. I was a bit of a tomboy, I'm afraid," she explained to Regina and added, "Well, I better get dinner started."

"Felisha, why not rest a bit and sit with me? I'd enjoy the company," Regina stated, and then added quickly, "If you don't sit with me, I'll just follow you."

Felisha laughed uncomfortably and hesitantly sat in a seat. "I usually don't have time to sit down when I've got a full house."

Regina shrugged. "It didn't sound like the Tibbs appreciate you anyway, so you might as well talk to me."

5

It was going to be a busy day at the ranch. Everyone, including Brit and his cowboys, were working to clean up every visible part of the ranch. Bob wanted his property at its finest for his special guests this evening. Not only did he want his property looking nice, he wanted everyone who worked for him looking their best as well. It gave plenty for Brit to complain about and he had, although he wouldn't bathe or trim up his hair and beard until later this afternoon. He had dusted off his best suit, which he hadn't worn since his wedding day three years before. He would finally wear it again.

Abby's beautifully made wedding dress, however, would remain hanging in the closet. She would not be going to the Thacker Ranch barbeque feast. She was not invited; she had never been invited, and she would never be invited. She was an intentionally forgotten part of the Thacker Ranch. She was kept out of sight and out of mind, hidden like an ugly monster imprisoned in her own pretty little home. She was Brit's personal property; he owned her, controlled her, and could do as he pleased with her. Nobody on the Thacker

Ranch would interfere or much less care if she disappeared, except for Saul Wolf.

Despite being the only one excluded from any kind of socializing, and despite the bruises that speckled her body, Abby hummed a little song of hope as she hoed the weeds out of her vegetable garden. She could hardly contain her growing excitement as it would only be a week or two until she and Saul left the Thacker Ranch behind. Of course they were risking their lives if they were caught, but it was a risk worth taking. Fear wasn't going to keep her from leaving. She had been living with fear everyday for three years. She had nothing else to fear, except death. Even death didn't seem such a terrifying transition since she was raised in a Christian home and had known Jesus as her Savior. She hadn't read the Bible in three years because Brit had burned her Bible a week or so after they married. The only reason she still believed was her heart told her to. Saul's conversion to Christianity edified her and he explained what he learned at church from week to week. He encouraged her and shared his Bible with her as she'd read it to him. She believed Jesus would help them escape the prison of the Thacker Ranch after Saul won his fight.

Abby wiped the sweat from her brow. It was only ten in the morning and it was already getting warm. It was then that she noticed Saul standing at the edge of the garden with his loving smile on his face.

"You look beautiful," he said softly.

Abby smiled shyly. "I don't." She wore a simple gray dress that was dirty and stood in her bare feet. Her bright red hair fell lazily over her shoulders unbrushed. She felt anything except beautiful.

"You do," he reinforced softly and then walked on the grass around the garden to where she met him at the garden's edge. Saul wore a pair of bib overalls without a shirt. "I can't be here long, but I had to see you while I could. They'll be looking for me soon enough. I'm the reason for the celebration, I guess," he shrugged.

Abby looked directly into his eyes. "Yes, you are, and tomorrow they'll have another reason to celebrate. Our celebration will come when we're far away from here," she said with a slight smile. Her arms slipped up around his neck carelessly. She went to kiss him, but he pulled away.

"You can't do that out here. There are too many places someone could be," he said watching the brush and tree line that surrounded the garden. "Let's go inside," he suggested hungrily.

He had fallen in love with Abby and now every time he was near her he had a tougher time controlling himself when they were together. The hunger to hold and kiss her was increasingly expanding to new territories where he'd never been before. Every new encounter proved to go a little further and more passionate. She, as well, seemed to want more of him with every moment they had together. He wished they were married so he could hold his beloved Abby. He couldn't wait until they were free to do as they willed without the threat of being seen together.

He kissed her fully and pulled her gently on top of him as he lay back across her bed, his hands roaming over her body lovingly. She unclasped the two hitches for his bib coveralls and pulled the material down to reveal his hair-covered, massive chest. She kissed his chest, stood up to pull her dress up and over her head. She then tossed it to the floor exposing her black and blue-spotted, naked body to Saul.

He stared awestruck at her pale, nude, freckled skin and moved his overalls down past his knees. His breathing was heavy as his heart pumped quickly within his chest. Saul kissed her passionately, while he held her close and felt the warmth and beauty of the woman he loved. She pulled her face away from his to watch the facial expressions of the man she loved. Her eyes widened in horror and she leapt off of Saul quickly when she saw Brit through the bedroom window. He was riding his horse up to the front door. She cried out in a panic, "Brit's here! Go now, oh, my God! He's going to kill me," she said as she pulled her dress back on quickly.

Saul glanced out the window and then ran out of the bedroom and out the back door. He ran across the garden holding his coveralls up with one hand. His heart raced like it never had before. He prayed Brit hadn't heard him run through the house or seen him cross the back yard towards the creek and the cover of the trees.

Brit stepped into his home and saw Abby standing in the center of the living room. She stood still and stared at him with a terrified expression on her reddened and perspiring face. He eyed her suspiciously. "What's wrong with you?" he asked curtly.

"Nothing," she answered quickly, "I'm just surprised that you're here." She sounded scared.

"I live here," he said and then added, "Make me a bath. The old man's beginning to panic. He wants everyone dressed up by noon now. It's not like I don't have work to do. But no, I have to walk around and act like I'm interested in his friends. It makes me sick! Draw that bath!" He walked out the back door to go to the outhouse, but stopped beside the garden where he noticed a mighty big pair of boot prints cutting across the dirt of his garden. They came from the direct line of his back door and headed towards a trail in the brush across from the garden. The man who left the tracks had run quickly from his back door. The boot prints could belong to only one man, Saul Wolf. He was the only one with feet that big and heavy enough to leave tracks that deep in the freshly hoed soil. Brit glared back towards the house with a snarl on his face and continued to the outhouse. It didn't take a cowboy long to read the signs, but it would take a little longer to decide what to do about it. He would let the rage build until it was time to be released. One thing for sure, he thought, they'd both pay heavily.

Brit left the outhouse with a deep breath and entered the house; he scowled at Abby as she heated water for his bath. She was nervous and shaking, more so than usual. It confirmed his suspicions. "So what have you done today? Are you feverish? You look hot." He stared at her coldly.

"No, I feel fine. I was working in the garden. I must've worked too hard," she said, casting a quick nervous glance at Brit. "It's getting hot outside."

"Hmm, you were inside," he said as he walked up behind her. "Come on," he said and led her towards their bedroom by her arm.

"What about your bath?" she asked anxiously.

"Later, right now I want you in the bedroom," he said roughly. He was filling with an unquenchable rage, one that he'd take out on her. But he would not say a word until after he dealt with Saul.

6

Bob Thacker wore a clean and pressed black suit and tie over a white shirt. He also wore his black Stetson to keep the sun out of his eyes. He held a glass of wine in one hand and a large cigar in the other as he stepped up onto a two-foot tall elevated platform that he had his cowhands build. It was decorated with red, white, and blue ribbons around the base.

He was in a jovial mood and smiled widely as he spoke loudly to be heard by the many guests that gathered to eat the good food and have the chance to meet the two fighters. "Ladies and gentlemen, welcome to the Thacker Ranch. It's my pleasure to have you all here and before we open up the chow line, I just want you to know that I spent a lot of money to provide a feast worthy of this occasion. We've got my best steer turned into barbequed steak; we have salmon and chicken as well. I got the best that money can buy, and I paid for the tastiest desserts and liquor. The bounty is plentiful so don't be shy. We'll open the chow line in a moment and then you can go eat your fill. Trust me, the food's worth the price I spent." He chuckled to himself, and added after a puff on his cigar, "But we're not just here to eat, get drunk and dance, are we? By the way, the band's going to play after dinner and they're going to keep playing until the last lady standing is done," he said with a smile. He added seriously, "Ladies and gentleman, let me introduce you to the one and only, Jacques Christy!"

Jacques Christy stepped onto the platform wearing a tan suit and a gray derby. He was a man of normal height and broad muscular shoulders. He had dark short hair that was thinning in the front. He had an aged face of forty years and a handle-bar mustache. He smiled and waved to the crowd that cheered. "Thank you," he said, holding a drink.

Bob called out loudly, "And his opponent, our very own, the unbeatable Goliath!" The small crowd applauded as Saul stepped onto the platform. He was in his dark suit and looked like a giant as he stood six inches over Jacques and seemed to be twice the thickness of Jacques as well. Saul waved uncomfortably.

Bob said, "Well, Jacques, you're looking at your opponent. Do you have anything to say about tomorrow's fight with Goliath?"

Jacques reached out and lightly pushed on Saul's stomach. "Yes. He's a big man. No doubt he's gonna hit me hard and I'm going to feel it the day after." He laughed with the crowd and then added seriously, "But if you talk to any lumberjack, he'll tell you the biggest tree will fall if you keep chopping at the body. The same is true of any man, even this Goliath," Jacques said with a touch of indignation in his voice.

Bob laughed lightheartedly. "Goliath, say a few words."

Saul stood awkwardly. "I don't have much to say. Jacques is a great fighter and I'm lucky to have this chance," he finished, to light applause. He shook Jacques' hand good-naturedly.

Bob smiled. He'd win more money if his guests put their money on Jacques. "There you have it, folks! Now let's eat all the food I bought and mingle with our fighters and get drunk and dance."

The food tables opened and everyone filled their plates with good food and found a seat at one of the many tables spread out across the lawn of the large Thacker home. A bar served whiskey, beer and wine, where a good portion of the spruced-up Thacker cowboys were standing, talking and laughing among themselves as they were not socializing with Bob's first-class guests. So far, the cowboys were behaving and none of them wore a gun belt. Bob had made it clear to every one of them, especially his two sons, that there would be no guns allowed in sight.

Away from the group of cowboys, the select collection of guests stood or sat in small groups and talked to each other. Mixing within the circles of men were the first-class ladies who had found their own small groups in which to mingle.

Bob moved from group to group and occasionally sent a pair of young servant girls after drinks for his guests. He was dragging both of the fighters with him to personally introduce them to his guests. Bob approached Lee Bannister, who stood with his lovely wife talking to a distinguished-appearing silver-haired man in his late fifties named Abner Sullivan, and Abner's late-twenty-something son, James.

"Gentlemen, this is Jacques Christy. Jacques, this is Abner Sullivan. Abner owns the Sullivan Gold Mine in Nevada. And this is Lee Bannister, he owns much of the city of Branson, including the Monarch Hotel," Bob announced proudly.

Jacques smiled. "It's good to meet you gentlemen,"

Jacques said and added as he shook their hands, "who is this beautiful lady?"

Lee answered, "This is my wife, Regina."

"Of course," Jacques answered and shook her hand gently with a polite bow. "It is my pleasure, Regina."

"Thank you," she said.

James Sullivan put out his hand to shake with Jacques. "I'm James Sullivan. I'm inheriting the Sullivan Gold Mine," he said disdainfully as he eyed Bob Thacker.

Jacques shook his hand. "Nice to meet you, James. I hope you gentlemen are ready to watch a fight tomorrow. It should be a good one, huh?"

James Sullivan nodded towards Saul. "He's a big man."

Jacques smiled confidently. "The size of a man doesn't matter as much as the heart and stamina of the man. He's young, inexperienced, and slow. Full of muscle, tall and thick, but his abdomen is weak. Gentleman, like I said earlier, I'm going to drop him like a tree. Now if you'll excuse me, I need another drink and find the closest privy," he said and walked toward the nearest servant girl to get his drink, while he stopped to talk to the next man in a suit.

"Goliath!" Bob ordered and waved Saul over. When Saul arrived, Bob again introduced Lee, Abner, and included James Sullivan, but again, neglected to introduce Regina.

Saul shook the three men's hands and then looked at Regina nervously. "I'm Saul," he said holding his giant hand out to shake hers.

"I'm Regina Bannister," she said. Her hand was like a child's in the gigantic grip of Saul's hand.

"Nice to meet you, Regina," he said awkwardly and pulled his attention back to the three men, who asked what he thought about his fight with Jacques.

Saul shrugged with a nervous smile. "We'll find out

tomorrow. I'm sorry, but I won't walk around bad-talking Jacques like he is me. All I'll say is this; I won't step into the ring already beaten, and I won't step out of the ring defeated."

Bob laughed loudly. It sounded much too intentional. "Well, gentleman, you heard him. It's gonna be a hell of a fight!" Bob said and walked away to talk to another small group of guests.

Lee studied Saul carefully and said seriously, "You said some mighty big words. Do you think you can stand by them tomorrow when you're in the ring with Jacques?"

Saul looked over towards Bob to make sure he couldn't over-hear him. "I have my own personal reasons to win this fight. I do not have the option to lose, Mister Bannister. I have to win it," Saul said and excused himself from the presence of the men as again Bob called out for him.

"Who's your money on?" Lee asked James.

"I'll stick with the experience of Jacques. What about you?"

Lee tilted his head with a shrug. "I think I'll place mine on the underdog. I like his fire."

"Jacques has a strategy. The big boy wants to brawl. Jacques' experience and strategy, I think, will be hard for a brawler to beat. No matter how much he wants to win," James replied thoughtfully.

Lee nodded in agreement. "True," he said and then added to Regina, "Come dear, let's go get a drink." He took her arm in his to lead her over to the bar.

"Lee!" Bob Thacker called, getting Lee's attention. "This is my business partner, Jeb DePietro, and his son, Martin. Martin's our town sheriff," Bob said bringing the father and son over to meet Lee. He continued, "This is Lee Bannister, the man I was telling you about. He owns most of Branson and if he doesn't own it, it's because he doesn't want it. Right?" Bob laughed.

"Yeah," Lee said awkwardly. He shook the men's hands, but cut the meeting short, as he wanted a drink.

"I've got servants for that," Bob stated and disappeared to find one of the girls.

"Nice to meet you," Lee spoke to Jeb and Martin and quickly walked his wife towards the bar, which was thirty yards away. The ranch's cowboys, that continued to be ignored by Bob and the other guests, surrounded it. They stared hungrily at Regina as they neared.

"Do you ever get the feeling that you're being used to heighten someone else's glory? Because I do," Lee commented quietly as he led her towards the bar.

"Everyday," she replied with a loving smile at Lee.

He laughed lightly. "Well that's true. Unfortunately, our host hasn't even acknowledged you. Not one time. I hope you don't plan on dancing all night, because I'm about done with this place."

Regina raised her eyebrows sarcastically. "Aren't you honored to be in the company of the most successful people in the west?"

Lee shook his head with a smile. "It's all a charade, my love. It's all a charade," he remarked as he neared the table that was transformed into a bar. Lee nodded to the nearest cowboy and then addressed the bartender, "Can we get a glass of wine and a glass of cold beer please?"

"Yes sir," The bartender replied and went about getting the two drinks.

"You're Lee Bannister?" A thin young cowboy with short dark hair asked. He was well-groomed and well-dressed with a black Stetson hat on his head. He held a glass of beer in his hand.

"Yes, I am," Lee answered and asked, "And you are?"

"My name's, AJ Thacker. Bob's son." He put out his hand to shake and nodded to a cowboy with a rough demeanor. "That there's my brother, Brit," AJ finished proudly. Brit was wearing a tan suit that was too tight, and a sweat-stained and dirty Stetson. He leaned casually against a large barrel of ice containing a smaller keg of beer. Brit held a glass of beer in his hand.

Lee shook AJ's hand and nodded to Brit, who didn't show an ounce of interest in Lee. He and the other cowboys mostly stayed quiet and stared lustfully at Regina. "Nice to meet you," Lee said and added, "This is my wife, Regina."

Regina reluctantly shook AJ's hand; she could feel the many eyes upon her and didn't like what she was feeling. Especially, the way AJ held her hand in his while he said, "Regina. What a beautiful name. It figures though. Me and the boys were just saying we've never seen a woman more beautiful than you," he finished, and let her hand go. His eyes never left her.

"Thank you," Regina answered awkwardly. She snuggled closer to Lee. AJ's gaze was unsettling; he seemed to be intruding into her own private essence. He was frightening.

"So," AJ said turning back to Lee, "I understand the marshal's your brother."

Lee nodded as he was handed the glasses of wine and beer. He handed the wine to Regina. "Yes, he is," he responded and took a drink of his beer.

"I'm told he's top of the food chain when it comes to gunplay," AJ touched his hip lightly. "I'm feeling a little naked without my set up, but I'm pretty good myself. The old man set strict rules about wearing our guns tonight; otherwise, you'd see what I mean. What about you? Do you have your brother's brass with a gun?" AJ paused and then added, "Because with a woman like Regina, you'd be a fool not to carry one."

Lee's eyes narrowed and hardened, but before he could respond AJ's brother Brit stepped forward. His eyes were cold, dark and dangerous as he said, "Leave him alone AJ, or Pa's gonna bust your head."

"I'm not doing anything," AJ stated and then asked Lee, "Am I? All I did was ask a question or two. Right?" he asked with a touch of foreboding in his voice. He puffed out his chest and squared off with Lee. "Certainly you're not going to go whining to my pa that I frightened you, are you? I mean my brother's acting like I'm causing trouble or something. Am I? Am I intimidating you, Lee?" AJ asked sarcastically with a smirk on his face. He stepped closer to Lee, staring into his eyes.

Lee kept his gaze on AJ and slowly gave a small smile himself as his eyes flickered irritably. "Not in the slightest little bit. I know a good ruse when I see one," he said pointedly and turned from AJ to step away.

"Yeah, and I know a coward when I see one!" AJ spoke heatedly, though he kept his voice down. "Regina, maybe you'd like to dance with me when the music starts. You don't have to die to go to heaven with me, hon."

Lee turned around quickly, his eyes engulfed with the vehement desire to beat the intolerable young man to near unconsciousness. "One more word and I'll oblige you! If you want to fight me, say another word!" Lee warned heatedly as he stepped forward towards AJ. AJ stepped back.

"Lee, don't!" Regina ordered sharply.

Brit Thacker stepped in front of Lee; his face was tense and mean. "This isn't happening today. Forget him and go back to your people, you belong over there, not over here."

Lee nodded. "True enough," he agreed. He scanned AJ

and scoffed condescendingly before turning to leave with Regina.

"Bannister," Brit's voice said getting Lee's attention, "Tell your brother if he ever comes snooping around here, I'll put a bullet between his eyes!"

Taken back by surprise, Lee eyed Brit, puzzled by the comment, shrugged his shoulders, and said, "I'll let him know." He scoffed with a shake of his head and escorted Regina back towards the first-class guests saying, "I think, my dear, that I am ready to go back to Felisha's. She's the only normal person I've met here."

"I agree. I don't want to be here after dark," she said. Her heart was still pounding from the slight altercation with AJ Thacker.

THE LAST RAYS of sunlight settled over the western horizon releasing a reddish glow across the sky. As beautiful as it was, Saul Wolf watched the older couple of Clarence W. Tibbs and his wife, Ruth, dancing together to the music that the band played. Clarence and Ruth smiled as they looked into each other's eyes, and the sight of them together represented to Saul all he wanted out of his life. He wanted to grow old and gray with the woman he loved and still be in love with her all those years down the road. The love that showed between Clarence and his wife was true, joyful, and very much alive.

Saul dreamed of the day when he could hold Abby close on the dance floor and gaze lovingly into her eyes without having to hide from everyone around them. He dreamed of a day when he could walk hand in hand with her in complete security, without a single concern of being seen together. He sat at a table abandoned by the many strangers that had come to see him fight. He felt alone and heavy-hearted, as he longed to hold Abby. It was a warm night, perfect for dancing. He had such a simple desire, one that most people took for granted, to just dance with the girl he loved. However, until he won his fight, and they eloped together it was an absolute impossibility. It was a heart-breaking realization that as the music played on such a beautiful evening as this one, the woman he loved was sitting alone in a dark, empty and silent house less than a mile away.

Saul sipped cold water that he had gotten from the melted ice from around the beer keg. He was the underdog in the fight and it showed overwhelmingly as people still surrounded Jacques Christy like a celebrity as he was drinking himself silly. Saul sat alone and would've been thankful for Brit, AJ and a cowboy named Barry McCorkle joining him, except that he couldn't stand AJ when he was drinking, and he didn't feel comfortable around Brit. Especially now that he had momentarily been inside Brit's wife.

"Mind if we join you?" Brit asked and sat down across the table from Saul. Barry and AJ sat on the two other sides. "Are you nervous about the fight tomorrow?" Brit asked curiously.

Saul nodded slowly. "Some." He was melancholy from his thoughts of Abby. He wished he could dance with her, just once. So simple a wish or a silent prayer offered up to an infinite God, yet it was so unattainable.

"I thought you might be," Brit said and added, "Hey, I'm putting some money on you, so I'm going to help you. Okay?" he asked with a slight smile.

Saul watched him curiously. "Oh, how?"

Brit smiled. "I'm taking you hunting in the morning.

Listen, the way I see it, it'll take your mind off of the fight for a while. It'll loosen you up a bit."

Saul shook his head declining. "I don't like to hunt."

"Doesn't matter," Brit replied shortly. "I'm risking a hundred dollars of my own money on you to win. My pa's risking a lot more. Everyone here believes you can whip Jacques. But we don't want you sitting around all day getting anxious and at fight time you're so frozen by fear that you lose," Brit paused with a comforting smile. "So, we're going hunting. It'll get your mind off Jacques and we'll bring home some venison. You like that don't you?"

"I do, but I don't want to go hunting," Saul said uneasily.

AJ sighed. "You're going!" he stated sharply, and then added, "I'll drag you out of bed myself if I have to, you might be a hot shot around here tonight, but you know as well as I do, that you're nothing compared to me. And I say you're coming with us," AJ stated irritably. "I'll see you in the morning!" he rose up and walked away towards the make-shift bar.

"What's wrong with him?" Saul asked.

"He wants you to go hunting. I'll see you in the morning. Be ready!" Brit warned and began to turn away.

"Did you ask your pa about that? I mean, he might already have some kind of plans," Saul tried to explain.

Brit turned back to Saul and eyed him coldly. "We'll be back by the time he's had brunch. Let's go, Barry," he said and walked away.

Saul was aggravated that he didn't apparently have a choice in going hunting. He had never been invited to go anywhere by Brit before, and it brought a certain amount of anxiety. After all, if Brit had caught him inside his house earlier in the day, he would've killed him. Brit was not a man to cross, but Saul had done more than that.

7

Felisha Conway sat on a padded sofa on her covered front porch holding her son Dillon close. He was tired and was snuggling with his mother before he went to bed.

Truet and Jenny Mae Davis sat on the porch swing and were about to leave when the elegant four-horse carriage Bob Thacker hired to taxi his guests arrived at Felisha's front door. They all watched as Lee and Regina stepped out of the coach. Felisha said, as they stepped onto the porch, "I wasn't expecting you back until late."

Lee nodded at Truet and Jenny Mae and answered sarcastically. "Well, let's see, I've never wanted to bust someone's head open as much as I wanted to bust AJ's. My brother's life was threatened, and I felt like a whore, as Bob strutted around introducing me like I'm his good friend. And to top it all off, he never, not even once, acknowledged Regina," he finished irritated. "So we decided to leave before it could possibly get worse."

Truet laughed light-heartedly as he asked, "I don't mean to laugh, but I feel like busting AJ's head open every time I see him. Let me guess, he made some insulting statement to your wife and then he tried to scare you. Probably saying something like, 'if you wore a gun I'd kill ya.' Am I right?" Truet asked.

Lee eyed Truet carefully as he answered, "That's basically what happened. He didn't have his gun belt on, but he told me about it. He was trying to test me at first, but then resorted to going after my wife to get a reaction." Lee waved off the thought of it with his hand. "I had enough of that tough-man crap in the cavalry. It takes more than some damn spoiled kid with a posse of cowboys and an older brother to scare me. I don't care who his daddy is. You could see the fear in the little coward's eyes when I didn't back down. Just because a man chooses not to wear a sidearm doesn't mean he can't use one. I was pretty good with mine, as a matter of fact. I'm sorry, but I really would've liked to give him a beating," Lee finally finished with a smile.

"Lee," Felisha motioned to a table with four chairs. "You and Regina come sit and join us, please. These are my good friends, Truet and Jenny Mae Davis. This is Lee and Regina Bannister. They're from Branson."

They shook hands and Truet offered, "I was in the cavalry, I understand what you mean, Lee. I did my time and spilt my share of blood. I was glad to leave it behind me. I'm a carpenter now. What about you?"

"Real estate mostly. I have a few investments that turned out all right," Lee shrugged casually and changed the subject back to AJ. "So that arrogant little snake acts like that in town, too? I'm at a loss for words to describe how dumbfounded I am by the actions of Bob's two sons. I'll admit, in my youth I was a bit of a hellion, but I was never utterly disrespectful to an invited guest, and certainly not to another man's lady!"

"My sentiments exactly," Truet agreed. "I warned him

not to mistake niceness for weakness, but he keeps pushing. Just the other day I nearly tore into him at our church's potluck. I can't stand him, and he apparently can't stand me because he is constantly provoking me."

Lee shrugged. "Why not just lay him out? I can read people fairly well, and I can tell you're a man that can handle himself. So why not just teach him some respect? Obviously Bob never taught him any."

Truet shook his head with a frown and explained, "I'd be shot in the back. There's no law here that isn't controlled by Bob. AJ can do no wrong here; he can shoot a man down in cold blood and walk away a free man. He's done it before. The Thackers own our Sheriff Martin Depietro. All those cowboys have a free run of this town. Most folks just stay out of their way. The only one that causes trouble really is AJ. Brit seldom even comes to town, and he keeps the others in line for the most part."

"Brit's the one that threatened to kill my brother," Lee said.

Felisha asked, "I was going to ask you, do you have a brother that came here, too? I could've made room for him," she offered.

"No," Lee answered, "He's not here."

"Then why would Brit threaten to kill him?" Truet asked.

"My brother's Matt Bannister, the U.S. Marshal. He has an office set up over in Branson now. Apparently, Brit doesn't want him coming around here and AJ would like a chance to shoot against him if he does," Lee laughed slightly and added, "Personally, I'd like to introduce them."

Truet laughed, as Felisha asked, "Matt Bannister's your brother? Isn't he a killer? I mean he's killed lots of people, hasn't he?"

Regina answered for Lee. "I thought the same thing

when I first met Matthew, but he's a very decent man. The killings come along with being a lawman."

"Your brothers got a mean reputation," Truet offered, "Very mean."

Lee smiled. "Yes, he does, but I don't see that side of him."

Jenny Mae yawned and said to Regina, "It must be a good feeling to be able to walk through town without being harassed by people like AJ with him being your brother-in law. With his reputation, I bet no one bothers you, do they?"

Regina shrugged. "No, but they never really have. Branson's a friendly little city. The bad elements stay on Rose Street, mostly. If you don't like it here, you should think about moving to Branson. There's nothing Lee can't get you set up with - a job or a home."

"What about teaching?" Jenny asked interested, "I teach and Tru's a carpenter. A very good carpenter," she emphasized rubbing Truet's leg.

Regina nodded. "A good carpenter will never be out of work, and with our recommendation you'd be set for a teaching position. Trust me, if you're interested, we can help you get settled in."

Jenny Mae asked Truet softly, "What do you think about it?"

Truet laughed good-naturedly. "I think we've never considered moving," he finished with a genuine smile.

"I know, but it would be a new life without AJ bothering us," she explained.

Truet's smile faded as he spoke, "I'm not selling out and running away from our home and friends, because of AJ. I've never been a coward, Jenny. I'm not becoming one now!" he stated firmly. He eyed Lee slightly embarrassed.

"I wasn't implying that you were," Jenny said uncomfortably. "It's just an idea, Tru."

"No," Truet said obviously offended, "you're saying we should move so AJ won't bother us anymore. We should pack up and move a hundred miles away to Branson because of why? AJ Thacker? No, Jenny. What I should've done a long time ago is knocked him on his ass and we wouldn't be in this situation."

"Tru!" Jenny Mae gasped. "You know the good Lord said to turn the other cheek. He made it very clear in the Sermon on the Mount to be meek. A real man is a gentle, God-fearing and loving man. Not a heathen given over to fighting with his fists or guns to spare his precious pride!"

Truet's face reddened a bit, as he eyed Lee with a hint of embarrassment. He smiled uncomfortably as he spoke, "I was a soldier, Jenny Mae. I know what it's like to fight with both, guns and fists; I've done plenty of both. But I have never in my life been bullied and degraded by a worthless piece of..." he stopped to choose another word, "rubbish, as AJ. Had I met him before we were married he'd be very respectful now. Oh, I know what the Bible says, but I can also tell you I don't feel much like a man when AJ's doing his thing. I don't think that's pride, I think it's natural for any man, Christian or not!"

Jenny Mae answered gently. "Pride is a natural part of the human condition. That's why it's so hard to be meek, my love."

It was apparent that Truet was trying to keep a friendly front, but was obviously growing irritated with his lovely wife. Regina said uneasily, as a momentarily pause occurred, "I didn't mean to cause an argument. I was simply offering a suggestion."

"There's no argument, Regina," Truet offered and added

softly, "Like your husband, I'd just love to break his head open and some of his ribs too."

Lee casually explained to Jenny Mae, "It's great to be nice and meek, but there comes a time when you have to stand your ground, especially, when it's your own wife he's offending. Being an ex-soldier myself, I understand exactly what Truet's saying. We fought for our country, why shouldn't we fight for the honor of our wives, our property and the threat of losing our lives? It's what we were trained for."

"Exactly," Truet said in agreement.

Jenny Mae was suddenly incensed and spoke candidly to Truet, "You know as well as I do what would happen if you struck AJ, so all of this soldier talk means nothing anymore. We either live here with it or sell our home and move away," she said sharply. She added to Felisha, who sat quietly snuggling with her tired son, "Felisha, I'd like some more of your cake. Perhaps, we could invite Regina into the parlor with us to have some, and leave the men out here to talk nonsense!"

Felisha shrugged. "Certainly. I have to put Dillon to bed, anyway. Regina, will you join us?"

"Sure," Regina said sounding unsure and cast a questioning glance at Lee, as she followed the ladies inside.

For a moment neither man said a word and then Lee offered, "She might have a point. Standing your ground now might cause some trouble."

Truet shook his head in frustration. "Jenny's adamant about me turning the other cheek and being meek. I don't argue with her because that's what the Lord said to do, but it goes against everything that I feel I should do. I'm supposed to be a man, not a coward!" he paused and then continued, "I feel like a coward every time AJ confronts me and I'm not, or maybe I should say, I never used to be until I got married."

"You're not a coward," Lee said simply. "But again, she's right about your choices. If you consider moving to Branson, I'll personally set you both up with jobs and a place to live. It can only get worse for you both here."

"How so?" Truet asked.

"Well, if you stand up and challenge him, he'll save his face anyway he can, probably shooting you in the back. And if you ignore him, like it sounds like you've been doing, he'll just become more aggressive to you and Jenny, until the day you snap and the results are the same as the first scenario," Lee said pointedly with a short hesitation before he added, "It's not a good ending either way."

Truet sounded irritated as he asked, "So you're suggesting I just sell out, pack up my wagon and move to Branson?" he finished; seemingly astonished that Lee should recommend such an action.

Lee shrugged. "What's keeping you here?"

"Friends, Lee. Many good friends. This is our home. That's what keeps us here."

"Well, perhaps you're right. But if you change your mind, just look me up, Truet. My offer will remain open."

"Thanks, but we've built a life together here in Sweethome, a good and happy life that I don't want to uproot, just because of AJ. I won't let him chase me away," Truet said with conviction.

8

Saul Wolf carried one of Brit's Winchester rifles across his lap, as he rode a large bay horse and looked for a deer to shoot. However, he doubted he'd see one as Brit and AJ talked too loudly with the other two cowboys, Barry McCracken and Jimmy 'The Colt' Lang, who came along for the hunt.

The morning was a beautiful one for a ride through the country as they slowly rode towards Hopewell Creek, not too far ahead at the northern most edge of the ranch. The soothing ride in the fresh morning air calmed Saul's nerves, and he was enjoying the hunting trip, except that none of the other men had said too much to him, and even now ignored him. He followed lazily behind content with his own thoughts. He would like to see a deer so he could at least shoot at one and maybe even take his trophy back to the cookhouse for a night or two of venison. However, his hunting partners found it more interesting to talk about the party from the night before.

Brit, of course, stayed sober all night, but Saul knew AJ, Barry and Jimmy were all probably still drunk or hung-over at best, as all three made spectacles of themselves before the night was through. It wasn't surprising that none of them were very sociable at first this morning, but now, two hours of riding in circles, they were finally talking to each other and laughing occasionally over the night's drunken events. Brit, being himself, was less talkative and led the small hunting party with a solemn expression on his face.

Saul, being ignored, found contentment in the cool of the morning and the scent of the woods as they ventured deeper into the forest surrounding Hopewell Creek. The cool morning sun filtered down through the trees casting rays of sunlight through the branches wonderfully lighting the forest floor. The air felt fresh and renewing to Saul as he rode behind his friends. It would have been a glorious moment to worship his Lord and silently sing a private song of praise, except for the foolish babbling of his hunting partners. Obviously, they didn't care if they got a deer or not. Saul didn't care either really; he was just enjoying the moment of fresh air out in God's creation. Again, he wished Abby were with him to enjoy this very simple pleasure. He silently prayed for the day when he could ride through the woods on a beautiful morning like this one or sit with Abby and watch a sunset without worrying who would see them together or of her being punished for it by another man. And that day was nearly here.

Saul felt good! He felt strong and ready to unleash every ounce of energy and strength he could give to beat the arrogant Jacques Christy. He had been worried about the fight, but now that he'd met Jacques and listened to his over-confident banter, he felt confident that he'd beat the older and smaller man. Especially, after watching Jacques get as drunk as he did the night before. It must have been part of Bob's plan all along. Jacques was very drunk by the end of the night and would be hung-over and lethargic today as well.

"Saul," he heard Brit call softly and waved Saul to come up beside him. Brit continued once Saul was close beside him. "There was a herd of game camped up here by the creek last week. We'll ride in slow and easy, but get your rifle ready, because they'll scatter quickly," Brit said with a set of cold eyes. "You boys be ready, but save one for Saul," he added to the others.

AJ pulled out his ivory handled Colt.45, smiled at Saul and said, "Let's go!"

Jimmy 'The Colt' Lang nudged Saul's arm and asked, "Are you ready, Goliath? Let's go get em."

Brit moved his horse forward and picked up the pace as they neared the edge of Hopewell Creek. Down an embankment nestled within a grove of trees was a pair of small gray tents separated by a campfire. It was the camp of some Chinese miners, who were working hard on their sluice box in the creek.

AJ aimed his pistol quickly at the nearest Chinese man and pulled the trigger. The man fell backwards into the shallow water dead with a shot to his head.

At the same time Jimmy 'The Colt,' pulled his namesake revolver and shot another Chinese miner as he stared at the mounted invader in horror. The Chinese man fell wounded and struggled to get to his feet. He cried out in a high-pitched plethora of foreign words as he began to run. Jimmy aimed carefully and fired a killing shot into the man's back.

Much too quickly, shots were fired leaving screams of pain and terror to fill the once tranquil morning air. A moment later, four Chinese men lay in the creek dead or silently dying without any warning or reason. There was momentary chaos and confusion and then silence, not a single bird dared to whistle in the deadening stillness. The sound of shallow running water over the creek bed seemed to roar against the deafening quiet. One lone Chinese man was left standing next to the sluice box; he was wearing black pantaloons and a loose fitting gray shirt with a wide-brimmed straw hat. He trembled in absolute terror with tears streaming down his face as he began to beg in Chinese for his life. He pleaded with Brit, who calmly sat on his horse in front of the Chinese man with his pistol drawn on him. In the water around the unnamed Chinese man, lay his four dead companions, whether they were friends or family, no one cared.

Saul was horror-struck as he stared at the four bodies and at the lone man left standing under Brit's deadly gaze. AJ laughed wildly, as he commented on his superior shooting over Jimmy's. Just as easily Jimmy answered back words that Saul didn't hear. Saul sat on his horse, gazing at the bodies of the freshly murdered men, and tried to wake up from the nightmare he had just witnessed.

Brit pointed toward the tents and ordered the Chinese man with a deadly tone, "Go over there!" The Chinese man held up his hands and tried to plead for mercy in quick Chinese. His native tongue was a mystery, but his meaning was universal as he begged for his life. With his horse, Brit herded the man towards the dirt bank over by the tents. Brit's eyes flamed with ferocity as he looked at Saul and ordered viciously, "Shoot him!"

"What?" Saul asked with a jolt. His friends, AJ, Jimmy and Barry, who waited for him to follow Brit's instructions, suddenly surrounded him to block any escape route in case he decided to flee.

"Shoot him. What do you think I gave you the rifle for? Now shoot him!" Brit yelled dangerously.

Thick tears of terror filled Saul's eyes, a fear like none he'd ever felt before completely surrounded him. The beating of his heart was all he could feel and hear as dread, as thick as the trees were high, filled him. "I can't," he whispered. The small Chinese man fell to his knees putting his hands together in a praying fashion, begging and crying uncontrollably, as he lamented desperately in his Chinese language.

Brit cursed bitterly and then turned his revolver onto Saul. "Aim that gun and pull the trigger!" he cursed again, and demanded with deadly venom in his voice, "Do it now!"

"Come on, Saul!" AJ urged him. "Send the Chinaman back to hell."

"I can't," Saul said with a quivering voice, his hands and body trembled. "No, I can't do this."

"Take the rifle in your hands and shoot him!" Brit warned, as he pulled the hammer back on his revolver. It clicked loudly, as it pointed at Saul's head.

"I can't!" Saul yelled out desperately through his terror-struck tears, "I'm not going to kill him!"

In a rage, Brit swung his pistol from Saul to the nameless Chinese man and pulled the trigger. The man screamed loudly, as he grabbed his leg in pain. He fell and rolled onto his side and wailed helplessly. Brit cocked his revolver and stared at Saul. "Do you like the sound of that?"

"No!" Saul stated in horror.

"Get off your horse, Saul," Brit ordered, his own voice cracked with a contained fury that sounded like it was about to erupt.

"Why?" Saul asked, suddenly realizing he could become more afraid than he already was.

"Because I said! Now get off your horse and help that rat up."

Slowly, Saul slipped off of his horse and walked over to the agonizing Chinese man. He knelt down and grabbed the smaller man by the arm and lifted him just enough to reach his other hand underneath his armpit and easily lifted the man up. The Chinese man cried out in a combination of pain and terror. Saul helped support him once he was standing. He watched Brit's incensed expression, waiting to hear Brit's next order. He waited silently, while Brit stared at him with cold and murderous eyes, his pistol resting on his leg. An awkward moment of silence came and went. Gradually Saul realized Brit, AJ and Jimmy were all staring at him like he was the prey. Barry McCracken appeared very nervous and unsure. Saul suddenly understood that he was in trouble. The expression on Brit's face revealed it all. *He knew about Abby*. Saul's eyes widened in horror as a spear of terror for himself and for Abby plunged into his heart. His breathing grew heavy and his mouth suddenly went dry. He felt the immediate urge to run, but it was too late for that, he was left the single option to beg for his life like the unknown Chinese man had done.

Before Saul could vocalize his thoughts Brit spoke in an icy voice. "I saw your boot prints in my garden, Saul, and Abby's lying face!" he turned the revolver aiming it towards Saul. "If you weren't my daddy's toy pup, I'd kill you right now. That's the only reason I don't! You stay away from my house. If I ever catch you near it or my wife, I'll kill you anyway!" Brit promised, and then quickly moved his gun and shot the Chinese man in the chest. He flew back out of Saul's arm. Saul screamed as he watched the Chinese man fall and lay dying. Petrified, Saul stared up at Brit. Brit spoke calmly, "I'll kill you just as easily as I killed these rats. Stay away from my wife, even if you hear her screaming and you might, as soon as I get home. Hell, I may just take her to

Johnny Niehus' place, give her to him, and tell him to make her a free whore. She's not worth much more than that now."

"Don't," Saul cried out, beginning to break down, "Please don't, she hasn't done anything wrong." His voice was full of emotion.

Much too quickly Brit jumped off of his horse, holstering his revolver as he did and neared Saul. Without a word he threw a hard right hand to Saul's face. It was a solid hit and Saul stumbled back and fell. He remained on the ground and with his eyes transfixed on Brit with a tear sliding down his cheek. Brit pointed at him. "You're nothing, Saul! Get back on your horse and let's go. You have a fight to win and if you don't, I expect pa will kill you anyway," Brit said and then added with disgust, "And quit crying like a baby! I thought you were tough."

9

The Independence Day celebration started at sun up with the ceremonial flag raising and a brass band Bob Thacker hired to play patriotic songs. The residents that made it a point to attend the flag raising were treated to a beautiful morning and a proud moment as the American flag caught a slight morning breeze and waved its colors proudly.

The day's festivities didn't officially begin until ten in the morning. Jeb DePietro, the mayor of Sweethome and partner in the Thacker, DePietro Land Company, opened the ceremonies with a speech as the town orator. Jeb finished with a shot at a prayer before Bob Thacker took a turn at speaking. Bob was jovial and inviting as he mentioned the day's many fine events. There were foot races scheduled for various distances for both men and women, including three-legged races and children's events as well. Other events and games were set up for all individuals to enjoy. Vendors from other towns came to Sweethome to set up on the main street and sell their goods. Bob had scheduled the brass band to play at various times throughout the day to keep the atmosphere exciting. A large potluck was scheduled from one to three, and two of Bob's beeves were being barbequed to make sure there was plenty of meat. He paid for large quantities of other dishes, but the good folks of Sweethome brought most of the food.

Later in the afternoon, the horse-racing would begin, where the men could place bets. The saloons were scheduled to open up an hour before the betting opened. To make alcohol more accessible, a portable bar was set up outside near the boxing ring and bleachers that Truet had made for this very day.

A grand parade was scheduled for five o'clock after a break for dinner; the main attraction was scheduled for seven o'clock. Sweethome's very own "Unbeatable Goliath" would step into the ring against the "World-renowned Jacques Christy."

After the fight, no matter who won, there was a community dance that would last well after midnight. The dance was scheduled to pause at ten o'clock for an extravagant fireworks show, but then the dance would continue until late. Bob Thacker had planned for over a year to make this Independence Day one that could be long remembered as the most lavish and coveted celebration in the entire West. Such patriotic celebrations made headlines. Those headlines could possibly bring new residents to Sweethome. And they would need the services of the Thacker, DePietro Land Company.

The day was a complete success. The streets were full of people having a genuinely good time. Sweethome was filled with the music of the band and the cheers of encouragement for the many various race competitors. Laughter echoed through the streets and children beamed with delight. As the day wore on, though, most everyone grew red-faced and exhausted from the heat of the day and the day's exertion.

The food was delicious and plentiful enough to feed everyone. The vendors made a killing selling candies, flavored ice drinks, and other fine treats. The day's expenditures could be considered a success, as even Bob's higher class, out-of-town friends enjoyed the continuous activities throughout the day. There had been no trouble with the lumbermen coming into town or with the miners. Martin DePietro and his deputies patrolled the town's streets casually and enjoyed themselves in the excitement of the celebration. In every direction there were only friendly discussions, introductions, competitions of some kind or another and the excitement and smiles of those who enjoyed the festivities.

It wasn't until nearly seven o'clock when Bob and his guests filled one set of bleachers and spectators filled the other three, leaving standing room only. Hundreds of men tried to wrangle for a good view of the elevated ring. The fight had brought many people to Sweethome, but only Bob and his guests were sitting comfortably with space between them, as Martin and his deputies and some of Bob's cowboys kept a barrier between the crowd and their first-class bleacher.

There was an excitement in the air so thick that it felt like it could be cut with a knife. Goliath was dressed in black stockings and was without a shirt as the referee tied the three-ounce leather gloves onto the giant of a man. Goliath appeared to be scared, more so than Bob had ever seen him look before. Jacques also wore black stockings and was without a shirt. Jacques appeared confident and ready to fight.

After a year of planning, the fight of the century was

nearly happening and the entire crowd was excited, but no one was more so than Bob. All of the money and traveling he did to get Goliath this far was about to pay off. Bob didn't think anyone could beat Goliath, hence the title, "The Unbeatable Goliath." The unlimited number of rounds under the *Marquess of Queensbury* rules would either propel Goliath to national fame or drop his name out of the ranks altogether. It was all about to begin, the wait was over, and the anticipation was killing him.

It was then, at the moment of the referee's introduction, that Bob's face hardened and flushed with immediate indignation when he first heard and then saw the members of the Christian church marching down the main street towards the boxing ring. The Reverend Grace led the loud parade followed by some fifty members of his congregation including, Truet and Jenny Mae Davis and Felisha Conway. They proudly sang hymns while carrying signs protesting drinking, gambling, and sexual immorality. Some carried signs that read, "Jesus saves." Bob bit his bottom lip as he silently raged within. The protesting church members marched loudly by the boxing spectators and lingered while they raised their voices and lifted their signs higher to be further noticed.

Bob's breathing grew heavy while the crowd of boxing fans grew quiet in the uncomfortable moments of being the center of a protest. Gradually, the protesters circled back around and marched back towards the center of town and the saloons. They made three passes back and forth through town and the boxing ring, interrupting the first, second and part of the third round before they called it a successful protest and stopped for the night.

. . .

THE BELL RANG ENDING the seventh round as Jacques Christy, beaten and exhausted stepped to his corner and sat on a wooden stool. His mouth hung open breathing heavily, his hair was soaked by sweat and blood covered his face and chest. The sight of him left no doubt to who was winning the fight. His left eye was swollen nearly closed and possibly damaged by its coloration, while a large cut above the eye bled profusely. His nose was probably broken, made evident by the amount that it bled. His right eye was also swollen and discolored and he had a large cut on his right cheek-bone. Despite the severity of his wounds, it was the exhaustion that showed itself boldly on Jacques Christy's face.

In the other corner, Goliath sat on a wooden stool catching his breath as well. A cut on his cheek, a red knot on his left eyebrow, and a lightly swollen right eye were all that marked Goliath's face. His lower body however, was red from Jacques pounding on it throughout the fight as he had promised to do.

The crowd cheered excitedly, as the moment of Goliath's greatest victory seemed inevitable. "Goliath!" Bob Thacker's voice boomed from the bleacher where he sat with his friends and Jacques' entourage. Bob was standing up and hollering through cupped hands. "You stay on him! Keep it up, he won't last long, you hit him and hit him hard!"

Saul nodded. He had a renewed strength building within him; he knew he was winning this fight, and his love for Abby fed his stamina. The only hope of having a life with the woman he loved was to win this fight, and he was resolute on winning it. He didn't need Bob to tell him to keep it up. He would win.

"Saul!" Brit Thacker's voice yelled, getting Saul's attention quickly. Brit was standing at the ring's edge near his corner with hard eyes and venom in his voice as he pointed at Saul. "You end it this round!" he snarled and stepped away just as the bell rang to start the eighth round.

Saul stood and watched Jacques Christy stand up slowly. He was tired. Saul raised his gloves and waited as Jacques neared him, Saul stepped forward quickly and threw a hard overhand right that was partially blocked by Jacques. The force of the blow staggered Jacques backwards a couple of steps and blood once again spilled over his face. The crowd cheered loudly. Saul advanced with a low roundhouse right to Jacques' ribs and then jabbed his left into Jacques' face. Saul tossed a left hook to Jacques' head, and followed it with a powerful right, which landed just above Jacques' ear while he tried to duck. The force of the blow again knocked Jacques back a couple of staggering steps. Saul followed after Jacques and offered another powerful right, which landed on top of Jacques' gloves as he covered his head. Saul threw another left hook, followed by another quick solid right to Jacques' already bloody face.

Jacques, trapped against the ropes, scrambled to break free, and lunged forward to grab hold of Saul. He held on. Saul waited for the referee to break them apart. When he did, Jacques stepped behind the referee to gain access to the middle of the ring. He tried unsuccessfully to wipe the blood out of his eyes while he waited for Saul.

Saul immediately followed and flung a left jab to Jacques' face, and then followed it with a left hook to his body; it landed solidly and brought Jacques' hands down from guarding his face. Saul propelled a hard overhand right into Jacques' face. Jacques stumbled backwards off balance and caught himself on the ropes to stop his fall. Sensing an end to the fight, and hearing the excitement of the crowd, Saul hurriedly went after him and heaved a haymaker of a right toward Jacques' head, but Jacques ducked the blow and again lunged forward to grab hold of Saul.

Again, the referee separated them and Jacques stayed near the ropes when he did. Saul threw a strong right at Jacques' face; Jacques' gloves mostly blocked it. A sudden left hook to Jacques nearly blind right side connected, which brought Jacques' gloves up automatically to cover his face. Saul blasted a hard right hook into Jacques' exposed ribs, which contorted Jacques body painfully and again brought his gloves down.

Jacques tried to grab hold of Saul, but Saul sidestepped and barely scraped Jacques' head with a short right as Jacques fell forward to the heavy canvas floor.

The crowd screamed with excitement, while Saul stood back and waited for the referee to begin to count. With great persistence and effort, Jacques stood back up by an eight count and tried to wipe the blood from his eyes with the back of his glove.

The referee motioned for the fighters to continue and stepped out of the way. Saul, feeling the crowd's exhilaration running through him, stepped forward quickly, while drawing his right arm back to put Jacques down one more time. Jacques, knowing he was in trouble gathered all of his strength and stepped towards Saul quickly with a barrage of quick lefts and rights to Saul's rib cage. When Saul's hands fell to cover his sore ribs, Jacques launched a hard right into Saul's face followed by a left to the ribs.

Saul backed up two steps and when Jacques stepped forward, Saul threw a vicious right that connected solidly to Jacques head. Jacques fell back against the ropes hurt and exhausted. In desperation, he hurled a wild right towards Saul's face just as Saul stepped in closer to finish the fight. Jacques' glove connected solidly with Saul's throat. To

Jacques' surprise, Saul stumbled backwards holding his throat and fell to the canvas unable to breathe.

The crowd quieted momentarily in shock and then erupted wildly for Saul to stand up. Bob Thacker most prominently led the screaming. Saul himself didn't care about getting up. He couldn't breathe and the gloves stopped him from holding his throat like he desperately tried to do. He had rolled to his stomach and climbed up on his hands and knees to position his body to open up his throat. He coughed and gagged painfully, but couldn't get his breath. Fear of dying crossed his mind, as he panicked and prayed for the Lord's help to help him breathe. A breath of air filled his lungs just as the bell rang a few times. He had been knocked out in the eighth round. He had lost. As he caught his breath he glanced over at Bob Thacker, who was glaring at him. Bob's face was red. He was furious! Saul's head dropped to the mat ashamed and suddenly filled with a hopelessness that couldn't be consoled. The cheers of the Jacques Christy fans rang in Saul's ears as he fought not to break into tears.

10

The fireworks show was all it promised to be and more. It would be hard to imagine a grander fireworks display anywhere in a hundred-mile radius. Even Boise City would come up short of the exhilarating display that Bob Thacker had brought to Sweethome, as the grand finale for this Independence Day.

The large audience cheered excitedly at its conclusion as a token of appreciation to Bob. It had been the finest fireworks show most of the people had ever seen. Even Lee Bannister was hard pressed to say he'd seen a better one, even in Branson. Bob had outdone himself.

"Well Lee," Richard Grace asked. "How'd you like our Independence Day festivities? How did it compare to Branson?" He was walking with his wife Rebecca and their two children down the main street towards their home. Walking with them were Lee and Regina, Truet and Jenny Mae, Felisha and Dillon Conway. They were leaving a grassy field just outside of town where they had watched the fireworks display.

"Very comparable," Lee said and continued, "I'm

impressed. I hated to miss our festivities over in Branson because I helped plan them. But I couldn't miss a chance at seeing Jacques Christy fight either." He looked at Richard with a smile, and finished, "I enjoyed myself today."

"Very good," Richard said, "So did I. I have to ask, did you bet on Jacques?"

"I did."

Truet shook his head. "I'll bet you were sweating a bit in that last round. Saul had him beaten. Jacques got lucky with that last hit."

"True, he did. I never thought Jacques would get beaten so badly. I don't know what kept him up, but one thing's for sure, he won't leave town as arrogantly as he entered. That Saul is one tough customer."

"No," Jenny Mae offered tiredly, "Saul's one of the most perfect gentleman you'd ever meet. He's a gentle giant. If you met him at church, you'd never guess he was a pugilist."

"Well," Regina replied, "I can't say I am a fan of fighting. I abhor the whole idea of two men beating each other for money. This particular fight I found very gruesome. Not that I've been to any other," she added quickly.

Felisha asked, as she held an arm around Dillon, who was tiredly leaning against her side. "So can we count on you and Lee coming back for Saul's next fight?" she asked Regina with a hopeful smile.

Regina laughed lightly as she answered, "I don't think I could stomach another fight, but I'd definitely come back with Lee. I've enjoyed getting to know you ladies."

"Next time," Rebecca Grace offered, "we'll all have to get together and have dinner. That would be fun. I've really enjoyed your company this evening, Regina."

"Yeah," Richard Grace added. "But you can't keep trying

to talk Jenny Mae into moving to Branson. We can't allow that," he joked.

"Thank you, Richard," Truet said. He looked at Lee quipping lightly as they walked, "If you moved over here you'd be closer to your friend, Bob. You could go over there for dinner a few times a week."

Lee smiled. "I would, except I already had dinner at his house. Once is enough for me. Trust me, if you ever do get over to Branson and we have you over for dinner, I won't talk about how much it costs me," Lee chuckled.

"Mama, I'm tired," young Dillon said to his mother, rubbing his eyes.

"I know, sweetheart. It's been a busy day, hasn't it?"

"Yes," he agreed nodding.

"And we stayed up way past our bedtime, haven't we?"

"Yes," he agreed again.

"Oh great. Look who's coming," Rebecca said at the same time that they all saw AJ Thacker and a group of four men walking from the Westward Whoa Saloon towards them. AJ smiled like he wanted to cause some trouble.

Jenny Mae spoke softly as she grabbed Truet's arm. "Just stay calm and be meek," she emphasized.

"Easy for you to say," Truet said. His tone had turned serious.

AJ smirked, as he drew near with a drink in his left hand, his right hand near his holstered revolver. AJ and his friend Farrian Maddox stood in front of Truet and Jenny Mae, while three of the ranch cowboys, Jimmy 'The Colt' Lang, Skip Kinnish, and Mick Rodman formed a half circle around the group of friends walking home with their children. All of the cowboys had been drinking and wore their gun belts. "Well, if it isn't the mother of my baby and the other town whores," AJ said and went to touch Jenny Mae's belly that was beginning to show.

Jenny Mae pushed his hand away angrily and yelled with rare venom in her voice. "Don't touch me!"

AJ pleasantly surprised, smiled wickedly. "Why not? You didn't complain before. Let me say 'hello' to my son," he said and reached over to touch her belly again.

Jenny Mae automatically slapped AJ across the face with a loud and stinging strike. AJ's reaction was just as quick; he tossed his drink into Jenny Mae's face with his left hand and followed it with a hard right-handed slap across Jenny Mae's wet face. She fell to the ground instantaneously.

Truet enraged, exploded with a hard right-handed fist squarely into AJ's face knocking AJ down flat on his back. AJ stared helplessly, as Truet jumped on top of him, pinning him to the ground by sitting on AJ's chest and pinning his arms down with his knees. Truet began to unleash his stored-up wrath and plowed one rage-filled, right-handed fist after another into his face.

With a struggle, Richard, Lee, and two of the cowboys pulled Truet off of AJ. Truet, filled with fury, wanted to keep hitting him. Farrian Maddox and Skip Kinnish stepped in and pulled AJ up off of the ground. He was bloody and dazed momentarily before he seemed to comprehend the loud commotion that was spinning around him. Jenny Mae was crying, as were the Grace's children. The ladies and the men argued with his cowboys, and other bystanders stood back watching in a large and growing circle. AJ watched his blood drip quickly from his face to the ground and realized he had been beaten severely by Truet Davis in front of most of the town. His eyes found Truet and his hand impulsively went to pull his revolver, but Farrian alertly grabbed his arm and forcefully took the revolver away from him. "Calm down!" Farrian yelled at AJ, "I won't let you kill an unarmed man in the middle of the street. So calm down!"

AJ glared furiously at Farrian momentarily before gaining control of himself. He looked at Truet who was holding his weeping wife in a loving embrace. Truet's eyes burned back into his. AJ wiped the blood from his face with his sleeve and said to Truet through his deep breaths. "You're a dead man! You crossed the line, Truet. I'm going to kill you soon. And you!" he spit out at Jenny Mae, "I'm going to do a lot more than touch you. You better believe that!"

Truet stepped towards AJ yelling, "You leave my wife alone, you son of a..."

"Or what?" AJ shouted, "You're both going to pay for my blood loss tonight! Believe me; you're both going to bleed!" He added to the Reverend Grace and his wife Rebecca, "You two as well! Do you really think you can march your church around town and embarrass my father the way you did and get away with it? Don't be surprised if your houses burn down - the church will for sure! You're all going to pay. My father warned you. I'm going to collect the debt!" He pointed at Felisha, "You too."

Dillon, already startled from the fighting and the yelling began to cry. He hugged his mother all the tighter while she said boldly, "You're scaring my son."

"He should be scared!" AJ yelled harshly, "I'm collecting in blood. Believe me; you're all going to pay!"

"Enough!" Truet yelled with contempt. "Leave. Just get away from here!"

Richard Grace declared, "The Lord will protect our homes and our church. Even if the buildings do burn down, you won't end our church."

Upon hearing the reverend's words, AJ focused on him and smiled a bloody smile. "Yes, Reverend, I will. Just wait and see. This town belongs to my family, there's no room for you or your church here."

"Let's go," Farrian ordered.

AJ sneered at Lee. "You better get your pretty wife out of here, or I'll do to her what I'm going to do to the others here. And there's nothing you or your brother can do about it. Isn't that right, Farrian? If the Marshal Matt Bannister comes here, we'll just bury him in the woods. Huh?"

"Matt Bannister?" Farrian asked.

"AJ," one of the cowboys named Mick Rodman said, "He's your father's guest. Let's move on."

Farrian asked again. "What does Matt Bannister have to do with anything?"

"This is his brother." AJ motioned to Lee with a careless sigh. "This is my friend, Farrian Maddox. You've heard of him, yes?"

Lee's eyes narrowed with the name recognition. He stared at Farrian and nodded.

"Matt's your brother?" Farrian asked.

"Yes, he is. Do you know him?"

"Not personally. But I know your cousin William. He's a friend of mine," Farrian said and added to AJ, "Come on AJ, let's go. You don't want any trouble with him."

"Trouble? He doesn't want trouble with me!"

"No!" Farrian spoke impatiently, "You don't want trouble with him! If his brother or his cousin William come here looking for you, you wouldn't have a chance. And there's no way I'd go up against either one of them for you. So let's go!"

"William who?"

"William Fasana. Now let's go."

"Fine!" AJ shouted and then turned to Truet and Jenny Mae. "I'll see you two soon."

11

Saul had slept very little during the night, even though Bob had ordered him to go home when the fight was over. Under the circumstances, Bob had done his best to act slightly disappointed, though still jovial to his invited guests. In private, Bob had shown his true emotions and held nothing back as he snarled and verbally tore into Saul.

"The unbeatable Goliath has been beaten, Saul! Not just beaten, but knocked out!" Bob hissed dangerously, with his eyes bulging out of his reddened face. His breathing was heavy, and he shook with anger. "You're done! We have nowhere else to go, Saul. We could backtrack to mediocre fighters, but it'll take years before anyone gives us a chance at the title. I told you we had one chance, and you lost it! I'm out thousands of dollars because of you tonight. The party I threw, all of the ceremony and food I bought was for nothing!" he paused and glared at Saul with hard eyes. "Get back to the ranch and stay out of my sight until I want to see you. Brit, take him home."

Brit had nothing good to say to Saul on the way home either, as he had lost a lot of money on the fight himself. Brit didn't say so, he said very little, but Saul could feel that Brit would've liked nothing more than to put the finishing bullet into Saul's head, or a rope around his neck. Brit's final words as he left Saul at the bunkhouse front door were, "If you come around my house or my wife again, I will kill you." With that being said, he drove the wagon towards his home. Brit's tone wasn't harsh or threatening, it was simply honest.

Fear found a home in Saul's heart. He couldn't sleep, as he wondered through the night what would happen to him in the morning. After all, Bob had lost thousands of dollars, and he wasn't a man that liked to lose anything, especially a dream or money.

Saul's future as a fighter was controlled completely by Bob in every aspect of the business. Without Bob's financial backing and his administrative skills in acquiring bouts and promoting the name of "Goliath," Saul had no hope of ever fighting big names again. All Saul did in their business partnership was fight. That was all he knew about the business he was in; Bob did everything else.

Now that he had lost the biggest fight of their career together, he didn't know where he stood with Bob. He was not a forgiving man and could hold a mighty bitter grudge. Bob was unpredictable when he was angry and Saul felt he had reason to worry.

He had watched in horror as Brit, AJ, and the others killed those innocent men in cold blood, just twenty-four hours before. The five murders were committed for the sole purpose of relaying a visual message to him, a very simple message - leave Abby alone.

Brit and the others had no remorse or hesitation when it came to killing those five unarmed men. Saul knew Brit would have no second thoughts about killing him. He'd do it as simply as stepping on a spider and have as much remorse as well. AJ was supposed to be a friend, but it had been made clear that friendships meant nothing on the Thacker Ranch. AJ would shoot him much too easily given the chance. The only reason he was still alive was because Bob wanted him alive. But now that Bob had made it clear that his career was over, it left him at the mercy of Bob's decision of keeping him around to fight again or removing his protective shield from him. If Bob chose to cut their ties, Brit would have his chance to kill him if he wanted to. The uncertainty of his fate wore heavily upon his mind all through the night.

One thing was for sure though; he had failed in his quest to take Abby away. He would never be able to leave with the woman he loved. She would continue to live in Brit's house, and be his wife, beaten and bruised, as long as she lived, and Saul would live knowing that he had failed to keep his promise to the woman he loved.

Though his bunkhouse room had a window that let the morning sunshine in, he could not lose the dark and heavy atmosphere that loomed over him like a heavy blanket of thick fog, as he lay on his bed in the isolation of his small private room. His ribs hurt, as did a few areas of his face, but his hands hurt him the most. It hurt to move his fingers and slight bruising discolored his knuckles as he stared at his only hope for the future; his hands. He had nothing in his life, except dependence upon Bob Thacker for every aspect of it. He no longer had any hope in a brighter future. His boxing career was practically finished and his love for Abby was no longer an option that he could risk. That hurt worse than his ribs or hands combined. Without Abby there was nothing to dream about anymore. Saul tried to convince himself that he should have some hope in the Lord for his future, but no matter how hard he tried, he just could not drag himself out of the lingering despair that weighed heavily upon him.

It was Brit's voice that yelled down the bunkhouse corridor that sent a chill down Saul's spine, "Saul! Pa wants to see you. Now!"

Painfully, Saul stood up. "Father, please help me," he said and stepped into the hallway of the bunkhouse. Most bunkhouses were nothing more than a large open room with bunks and a woodstove. On the Thacker Ranch, the cowboys were year-round ranch hands and had their own personal room within the bunkhouse. Even if it was just a small room, at least it was theirs and that meant something to all of them.

Three hundred yards away from the bunkhouse and the main ranch facilities was the white colonial home of Bob Thacker. It was a large two-story home with a covered front porch with four white columns supporting the high roof. It was surrounded by green grass and shade trees. The outside of the house was impressive enough, but inside, it was decorated with fine furniture and rugs spread out across the oak flooring. Paintings hung on the walls and the home was noticeably neat and clean. An older lady named Lucille, worked as the Thacker's live-in servant. She pointed Saul towards the library where Bob and Brit were expecting him. Saul tried to swallow, but his mouth was dry. He prayed earnestly while the anxiety multiplied within him as he entered into the library.

The library was a dark-paneled room with matching bookshelves on all four walls filled completely with books. In the center of the room set a large desk with Bob's chair behind it. Two stuffed leather chairs set in front of the desk. The wall behind the desk had a large window between the two bookshelves to allow the sunlight into the room.

Bob stood behind his desk smoking a cigar and leaned forward on the desk as Saul entered the library. Brit had turned his chair to watch Saul as well; he looked as unfriendly as always.

Bob spoke seriously, "I told you last night that you can't go by the name, 'The Unbeatable Goliath' anymore because you got knocked out. You got beat. So what are we going to do?" he glared coldly at Saul and waited.

Saul shrugged nervously; his voice wavered as he said, "I can still fight."

Bob puffed his cigar as he eyed Saul thoughtfully, and then he smiled easily and stated with growing enthusiasm, "And fight you shall! But we're changing your name to 'The Killer Goliath.' Jacques Christy is dead! You killed him, Saul!" Bob laughed excitedly. "We're changing our promotion. It's gonna say: 'The Killer Goliath, you might die trying to beat him,' or something like that. What do you think, huh, my boy?" Bob asked cheerfully and walked over to pat Saul's large bicep proudly.

"He died?" Saul asked in horror. "How?"

"You beat the hell out of him! Apparently he went to bed with a headache and he never woke up. We lost some money last night, but we got bigger things coming. Now you're famous, Saul! Now people will come from everywhere to see you fight," he laughed and added. "You'll be bigger than the champion. You are 'The Killer Goliath!'" he yelled out with enthusiasm.

"I," Saul stopped, as tears appeared in his eyes. "I killed him?"

"You sure as hell did! Hey, don't feel bad about it, son, it's just part of the game. He took a chance getting in the ring with you. You did great! People are going to talk about you for a long time to come!"

"I'm gonna go back to my room," Saul said softly.

"Okay, go rest up. I'll set up an interview with the newspapers for tomorrow or the next day. I want you rested and ready to fight again when they come here."

"Saul," Brit stated with a slight smile before Saul could leave, "Congratulations on your first real kill."

Saul nearly ran the three hundred yards back to the bunkhouse and into his small room. He closed the door behind him, collapsed onto his knees beside his bed, and cried bitterly into his hands as he prayed. "Father, forgive me, please! I never wanted to hurt him. Oh Lord, I don't want to do this anymore. Jesus, help me. Get me out of here!" he begged. "And if You will, let me take Abby, Lord. My life's nothing without her, I love her so much. Please help me," he sobbed heavily. "Father, I feel so lost and scared. I need you Jesus, please help me." He opened his eyes and looked at his bruised knuckles, the cost of taking another man's life. Saul whispered, "God forgive me." He wept as his discolored hands covered his face.

12

Truet and Jenny Mae heeded the suggestions of their friends and stayed the night at Felisha's. The risk of driving his wagon through town and running into AJ, as drunk and angry as he was, could've easily been a mistake. They agreed to sleep over and leave in the morning when AJ and his friends would be sleeping the night's intake off.

After breakfast, while they were saying goodbye to their new friends, Lee and Regina Bannister, the news ran through town like a wildfire fed by high winds that Jacques Christy had died in his sleep. The news shocked everyone, but it seemed to disturb Lee Bannister more than anyone else, as he won a good deal of money on the fight. Lee didn't say too much about it, but it was clear that the money felt dirty to him after hearing the news. Truet could sense it in his new friend's eyes after Jenny Mae made the comment that just like in the annuals of Roman gladiators, it was blood money that changed hands. Lee appeared heavily burdened by that statement.

The dirt streets of Sweethome were littered with trash and men were sleeping on the ground where they fell the night before. Most were prospectors and loggers that came into town to celebrate. Jenny Mae had commented, "It looks like a great time," as they drove their wagon past one man in particular, who lay in his own vomit on the street.

After the chores were done at their home, Truet and Jenny Mae took the day to relax and enjoy each other, as they lazily sat on their porch swing watching a rare Friday pass by without having work to do. After a few hours, Jenny Mae went inside to lie down for a while; she was exhausted from staying up so late watching the fireworks and then talking with their friends until early into the morning.

Truet walked into his woodshed to work on the cradle for his unborn child. He didn't care whether it would be a baby boy or girl. He was excited to be having a child with Jenny Mae; that's all he cared about. He was going to be a father and being so, he wanted his child to have a love-crafted cradle from his own hand. The design was simple, the head and foot ends were solid pieces with slightly angled rockers so it would rock some, but never be able to turn over. The bed and side rails were also solid and deep enough to be used for a year or so without worrying too much about the baby crawling out of it and falling to the floor. The wood had been sanded to the smoothness of a child's precious skin. Now that all the hard work was done, he could assemble it together, and he did so that afternoon. Once it was put together, he stared at it proudly. All that was left to do was stain it, and he would do that soon. When the time was right he'd surprise Jenny Mae with it.

The day was slow and restful. All the business that came with working for a living and keeping up a small property was put aside to enjoy the day itself. It was a needed day of rest after an enjoyable evening was ruined by AJ slapping Jenny Mae. Truet hadn't felt a rage like that since he was in the heat of battle during the Indian wars. Of course, that was a different kind of rage, one that was brought on by the fear incurred while fighting to survive. Last night's rage was simply brought on by another man insulting, touching, and slapping Jenny Mae to the ground. It had happened so fast that Truet didn't remember actually hitting AJ with the first hit. All he remembered was the desire to beat AJ to death, or as close to it as he could. There was no fear, just reactionary justification. He didn't think about it, he simply reacted. And rightly so. No man has the right to treat another man's wife in such a manner. AJ, for whatever the reason, thought he could and get away with it. While, it was true that Truet had allowed AJ to start his nonsense when they moved to Sweethome, it wasn't cowardice that stopped Truet from acting upon it earlier; it was his trying to be obedient to the Bible. "The meek shall inherit the earth," Jesus promised on the Sermon on the Mount. Again, He said, "If someone strikes your cheek, turn to him the other as well." The entire principle went against everything that was inside of Truet to do naturally. He was in the cavalry and he fought battles against the enemy and he also fought other soldiers to earn his due respect. He was not a weak-willed man or a coward; he was a Christian. Being a Christian meant losing his pride to replace it with meekness. It hurt to do so.

Many times before, he fought his reactionary desires to physically beat AJ Thacker. Each time he managed to fight the natural desire down, AJ only grew more comfortable and aggressive in his gradual progression of disrespect towards Truet and harassment of Jenny Mae. Now it was to the point where AJ felt compelled to make a mockery of them both publicly, without a moment's hesitance to consider any kind of consequence. AJ had no respect for Truet and propositioned Jenny Mae whenever and wherever he pleased. AJ had consistently grown bolder, more aggressive and threatening as time went along. It was no surprise that it would come to a head, eventually. The surprise was that Truet drew first blood and walked away unharmed.

Truet could not find any regret for his actions the night before, but hitting AJ was the best he'd felt in a long time. However, AJ's threats towards him had caused great concern among the ladies, especially Jenny Mae. Now, even more than before, Jenny Mae earnestly suggested moving to Branson to get away from AJ and his friends. She wanted to start over in a bigger city that wasn't controlled by one family. Lee and Regina Bannister seemed to be people of some weight in the city of Branson and promised to assist them with housing and employment opportunities. Jenny Mae wanted to move to Branson immediately and leave everything behind to do so. She feared for the life of her husband.

"Tru, he touched our baby, and then threatened to kill you. He's not right in his head - you know that! So what are we waiting for, him to hurt me or kill you? AJ would've shot you if Farrian hadn't taken away his gun," Jenny Mae emphasized, as they sat on their front porch swing in the evening, drinking a glass of iced tea.

Truet glanced out at the rolling hay field in front of his house which was about ready to be harvested. There was an oak tree line at the top where the woods surrounded the field. His right hand was around his wife lovingly. "AJ was drunk, sweetheart. After he sleeps it off he'll probably threaten some more, but that's all it is, just threats." His voice didn't sound convincing even to himself.

"AJ," Jenny Mae said slowly, "is going to look in the mirror everyday and see his black eye and know it was you who gave it to him. He's going to want revenge, Tru."

"Are you scared?" Truet asked.

"I am! He's not reasonable," she stressed anxiously. "Truet, this house and our friends are not worth losing our lives for. We can keep our friends for the rest of our lives, but we could do so in a new home in Branson. I want to move."

Truet scoffed lightly. "We have worked so hard for what we have, Jenny. This is our little piece of paradise. I don't want to give it up because of one man."

"And I don't want to lose my husband because of one man, but I could! We're having a baby, Tru. I don't want to raise it alone. Let's just cut our losses and leave."

Truet took a deep breath. "Do you really want to leave? We don't even know Lee and Regina. Maybe we'll get there and they'll act like they never met us. Some rich people do that around their own friends, you know."

"They won't. They're different; they're more like we are. I like them, Truet, and so did you."

"Oh, I liked them, but that doesn't mean we should put our whole future in their offering to help us get situated. We don't know them well enough to put our trust in them."

"What if I was to wire them and let them know we're coming?"

"You can. But we really need to make sure that's what we want to do. I mean neither one of us have ever even been to Branson before. We might hate the place, Jenny." Truet shook his head slowly; his emotions were torn. He knew Jenny Mae was right about AJ, but the fact was, he hated to throw away everything he'd worked so hard for. He despised putting his tail between his legs, selling out and moving out of his home because of AJ Thacker. It wasn't right.

"Sweetheart," he said after a minute. "I understand that you're afraid, but Jenny, I don't scare easily. You can wire Lee and Regina, but before we run away like cowards let's just wait and see what happens. We have the Lord on our side; AJ doesn't. Like the Bible says, '*If the Lord's with us, who can stand against us*?'" He paused, "I suggest we wait, and see what the Lord does, Jenny Mae."

Jenny Mae answered slowly. "I'm wiring them tomorrow, okay? We'll wait if we must, but if he makes another threat or touches me again, we're leaving. Agreed?"

Truet sighed with another deep breath. "Agreed."

"I love you, Truet. It's not worth losing you," she said.

"I love you," Truet said, and kissed his beautiful wife.

13

By Sunday the news about Jacques Christy was old news. The newest news that burned through Sweethome was of the massacre of five Chinese miners out on Hopewell Creek. There were no witnesses or suspects. Whoever had committed the crime had long since vanished with whatever gold the Chinese men had. The news was startling, but many strangers came to Sweethome for the Independence Day celebration. The unknown gunmen were probably passing through and came upon the Chinese men's claim. Sheriff Martin DePietro washed his hands of the whole unsolvable tragedy.

The other bit of gossip that traveled quickly was of Truet Davis beating AJ Thacker bloody in the middle of the street. It was the town's general consensus that AJ had it coming.

The church rejoiced in a bold and successful turnout for the Independence Day protest. They may not have saved any souls that particular day, but maybe they planted a few seeds that would eventually grow and lead someone to the Lord. If nothing else, they stood up for what they believed in, the Lord Jesus Christ, and His word, the Bible.

After church, Truet and many others worried about where Saul had been since his loss on Thursday night. No one had seen hide or hair of him since then. They had a special prayer for him; they all knew Saul would be very upset about Jacques dying the way he did. Reverend Grace and Truet both expected Saul to come by their homes before Sunday, but he had not. When he didn't show up for church, their concern grew stronger. He was their friend, after all.

Truet helped Jenny Mae up onto the wagon and waved to the last of the congregation that stood around talking in front of the church. He climbed up onto the bench seat beside Jenny Mae, released the brake and started his wagon team down Fourth Street one block and made a left turn onto Independence Street, Sweethome's main street. It was surrounded on both sides by the town's main businesses. Most were closed on Sundays. The only ones open were the restaurants and Chinese laundry. Soon the saloons would open up as well. The streets were fairly empty on Sundays until the early afternoon when the saloons opened up. It gave the migrant workers one more day to spend their earnings before they slowly made their way back to the logging and mining camps, broke and weak from their weekend exertions.

Truet passed the sheriff's office at the corner of Third and Independence Streets, across from the Sweethome Bank. He continued towards Second Street as he passed the Dills' Hotel where Jacques Christy expired in his sleep. He passed the Westward Whoa Saloon across the street from the Schultz Hardware and Lumber Store, where Truet often went. A clothing store and others filled the double-long block between Third and Second streets. As he neared First Street, he passed a photography shop, the

Snyder Meat Market, and Truet's own carpenter's shop. Next door to his shop was the blacksmith's shop of old-timer, George Ogle. Across the street was the Burkhalter Livery Stable. It was a large livery stable with corrals behind the main building. Wes Burkhalter's house was beside the stable and was the border of Sweethome's city limits.

It was there that Truet felt a cold flash of fear run down his spine as he saw AJ Thacker and his group of friends waiting for him on Wes' front porch. When they saw Truet's wagon, AJ stepped off the porch and walked out into the street with his friends beside him, although his friends, Farrian Maddox, Jimmy Lang, Skip Kinnish and Mick Rodman stood back on the edge of the street leaving AJ to continue alone.

"Oh, Jesus, please," Jenny Mae said worriedly.

"It'll be all right. Just stay calm," Truet reassured his wife. He reached down to pat her leg comfortingly. His words were confident, though he was more scared than he let on. "We'll be okay," he repeated. AJ held up his hand to stop them as they neared him and walked to Truet's side of the wagon. His left eye was blackened and still swollen. Truet felt his heart pounding as AJ neared him. AJ's hand was close to his gun belt. Worried, Jenny Mae slid close to Truet and held his arm tightly with both of her arms.

AJ looked up at Truet and nodded. "I owe you an apology, Truet. You too, Jenny Mae. I was out of line on Thursday night. I drank too much. You know how it is. I apologize though; I had no right to slap Jenny, Truet. I hope there's no hard feelings," he said and held out his hand to shake Truet's.

Taken off guard, Truet stared at AJ with a perplexed expression. He never imagined AJ would apologize to him.

He shook AJ's hand, still bewildered by the apology. "Apology accepted," is all he could say.

AJ sighed with relief. "I would ask you to apologize for the black eye, but I deserved it. I am sorry for hitting you, Jenny Mae," he paused to receive any feedback, but Jenny said nothing. "Well, I just wanted to apologize; you two have a nice day," he stated and stepped back to get out of the wagon's way.

"Thank you," Truet said and started the wagon towards his home. When he passed the bleachers he had built around the boxing ring for Saul's Independence Day fight, he said to Jenny Mae. "Can you believe that? Wow, the Lord is good!"

Jenny Mae smiled with relief. "I never would've believed it if I hadn't been there myself to see it. You know what Rebecca and Felisha are going to say, don't you? They're going to call us liars," she quipped. "I love you, Truet," she said while she stared at him, "I love you very much. That's the only reason I wanted to leave here."

"I know, sweetheart," Truet responded, "But we'll be fine. You can't run from trouble. Sometimes you have to fight back. Then you earn the respect of others. Turning the other cheek only invites more trouble with guys like AJ. If I remember right, I said that when we moved here," he finished with a smile.

Jenny smiled. "Okay, so you were right about that, this time. But I, at least, had the courage to hit him first," she joked.

He laughed. "You just wait until we get home. Then we'll see how tough you are."

"Uh, huh, it's your fault I'm in this condition," Jenny Mae patted her stomach, which was barely showing now at four months pregnant. "For some reason, I get the feeling that I'll be pregnant for the rest of my life because of you," she said with a smile.

Truet laughed. "I hope so. You're very beautiful when you're vomiting in the yard."

"Tru!" she slapped his large bicep with an astonished smile. "I can't believe you'd say that to me, your one and only wife!"

"I wouldn't want it any other way, Jenny Mae. I love you, my beautiful bride."

"And I love you, my chosen husband," she said and drew close to him for the ride home.

14

Saul had not left the confines of the ranch since Independence Day. He had nowhere to go, really; he no longer desired to leave his room. His body and especially his hands felt better after a couple of days of rest. However, he had no desire to face anyone in town and hear how shocked they were to hear about Jacques Christy dying. He had no desire to feel like everyone on the street thought him guilty of killing Jacques. He didn't want to be stared at, whispered about or as they did at the ranch, call him "a killer." There would also be those who had bet on him winning and lost their hard-earned money. He feared they might comment about his being knocked out by one punch. He didn't want to hear it; he'd heard it enough from the ranch hands, and, of course, Bob and his sons.

He'd seen Brit Thacker more in the past few days then he had in all of his time at the ranch put together. Brit had made it a point to check up on Saul on a daily basis. The times were sporadic, but often. It seemed Brit's hard days of working from dawn till dusk had been replaced with the obsession of knowing where Saul was from the moment Brit left his home until he came back to it. Sometimes, Brit would just open Saul's bunkhouse room door, peak in with a scowl on his face and leave. Sometimes, he'd make a comment about the fight or losing his money, but the most painful comments he'd make about Abby. Brit found a cruel humor in obscene comments and gestures about Abby and what he was going to do to her when he got home. Sometimes it was a threat of hurting her, sometimes it was bragging in front of the other cowboys about what he was going to do sexually.

The worst was the ongoing threat of taking her to Johnny Niehus' Hideaway Brothel and putting her in a cheap room with a "free" sign on the door for all the loggers and miners to enjoy. The hideaway was already the worst of the town's establishments. It was cheap, dirty, and the women were long past their prime. They were mostly older, unattractive and had nothing left to offer, except a warm body for a very short time. The prices were so low that the quantity of men that came and went made up the difference. The beds all had oil cloths laid across the foot of the bed to protect the linens from getting dirty from the men's boots as they spent their fifteen minutes' worth of change, while the next man waited in line outside of the door. It was the bottom rung of a downward spiral and the only way out to many was death. Suicide wasn't that uncommon among the destitute women at the Hideaway. It may have been an ugly, dark truth hidden from view of the public eye, but it also made Johnny Niehus a fairly wealthy man.

He owned an entire city block that contained his whole livelihood. He had a large building that was filled with multiple rows of bunk beds called the "bunkhouse hotel," which was for the weekend army of loggers and miners that came to town to drink, eat and be with a woman. Johnny

Niehus supplied it all to his guests; he had a large saloon that was filled with younger, prettier, and costlier women and he also had a cookhouse-style restaurant to feed his army of guests. Behind his other buildings, hidden from view, were the tiny rooms of the penny-for-profit ladies that hosted the busy traffic of the Hideaway Brothel.

The idea of Brit taking Abby there terrified Saul. He could not imagine a worse fate for any woman, let alone the one he loved. It would literally kill him to find out Brit had done so. His promise to take her away from the Thacker Ranch and give her a normal life where she could live free of fear had been shattered by a single punch. He would never take her away from the Thacker Ranch and the cute little cottage that had become her prison. She was at the mercy of her murderous husband to do as he willed. Saul was helpless to help her. He was in a very similar situation himself as he couldn't leave the ranch either and was at the mercy of Bob Thacker. After witnessing the murders of the Chinese men, Saul had no doubt his life was literally in Bob's hands. AJ was the closest he had to a friend on the ranch and trusted him to a certain extent. It was sad how hard it was to find real friendship. The friendship he thought he had with AJ wasn't friendship at all, but he never would've known that if he hadn't met Truet Davis.

Saul met Truet when Bob Thacker sent him to Truet's carpenter shop with a damaged dresser. Saul found Truet to be quite different from his cowboy pals or the men at the places he'd worked at before. Truet was physically bigger and stronger than most men Saul had seen, but Truet didn't seem to care about proving how tough he was. On the contrary, he was friendly, easy-spoken and in a strange way, he was like a breath of fresh air to be around. Saul went back to Truet's shop everyday that he could and then he was invited to church one Sunday morning. That Sunday changed Saul's life forever. Saul was introduced to the Lord Jesus Christ, and he accepted Him as his Savior. Little did Saul know how much his lonely existence was going to change in the next year. He met Jenny Mae, and the others that day that were now his friends and brothers and sisters in the Lord.

For the first time in his life he had friends that cared about him without wanting something in return. He could be himself and was accepted just as he was; he wasn't made fun of or picked on like he was at the ranch. Among his new friends he was appreciated and felt complete with the Lord's own people. Once he lived with an emptiness in his soul that always left his life feeling incomplete, and no matter what he did to fill it, whether the drinking, womanizing, or fighting, he always remained unsatisfied and searching for something that he couldn't quite identify. Thanks to Truet for inviting him to church that first Sunday, Saul found Jesus. The Spirit of the Lord was what Saul had been missing in his life. Now he was complete. He had the same peace in his soul that Truet had when he first met him. He was set apart from the cowboys that he lived with. They noticed the changes in Saul immediately, and they hadn't let up yet with their mocking and at times downright mean-spirited persecution of his new faith. It was his friends Truet and Richard that read to him the verses of the Bible that said to expect to be treated the way he was by unbelievers.

It was the words of Reverend Richard Grace that stuck with him and kept repeating themselves in his head. "Saul, God does not promise you wealth, health, or a trouble-free life. On the contrary, He does promise you will be hated for His name's sake. He does promise that troubles will come. But Jesus also promises to help you through those troubles, one day at a time. He promises to hear you and never leave you. He promises to love you and give you eternal life if you accept Him as your Savior."

Being illiterate, owning a Bible did little good, except for the comfort it brought to simply hold it tightly, and knowing it was the Word of God. Being so, Saul found willing people to tutor him with reading. Jenny Mae, being the town's schoolteacher naturally spent time teaching him the alphabet and the basics of how to read and write. Felisha Conway offered to teach him his figures and the fundamentals of monetary balancing. There was no shortage of teachers willing to give Saul an education; late though it may be in his life, no one asked anything in return for their time. Saul had made friends, real friends who cared about him, who loved him for who he was.

And that love for his friends is what pushed him to keep running through the moon-lit night. He ran through a grove of trees and then across a field of grass hay onto the road again, where it circled around the field. He ran as the sweat poured out of his body and his chest felt like it was going to explode. He didn't have much time; he was supposed to stay with the wagon in Sweethome, while AJ and a couple of other cowboys went into the Westward Whoa to have a few drinks and to be with the women. It gave Saul some time, but he didn't know how much, so he ran.

He ran as fast as he could for as far as he could. His side cramped and his breath was hard to catch, but he kept running through the dark countryside until he saw the homestead with a light in the windows. He ran faster knowing his destination was in sight.

His big hand pounded on the door as he bent over to catch his breath.

"Who's there?" Truet's voice asked from the other side of the door.

"Me. Saul," he huffed heavily.

"Saul?" Truet asked and opened the door quickly. Concern was on his face. "Saul, what's wrong? Are you all right? Come inside."

Saul, still bent over, held up a hand to decline, as he tried to catch his breath. "No, listen I heard what happened Thursday night," Saul got out as he struggled to breathe and sweat poured off his face. "AJ's out to hurt you, Jenny Mae too. He's been talking about it, Tru. You need to take Jenny Mae and get out of town. I'd hate to see you two get hurt by him."

Truet shook his head to argue. "Saul, AJ apologized to us today for what happened that night. He agreed he went too far and deserved what happened."

Saul raised his voice slightly. "Don't believe him, Tru. I..." Saul stopped, as his bottom lip began to quiver and tears filled his eyes. It plainly wasn't sadness that brought them, but panic and fear.

"You what?" Truet asked concerned. Jenny Mae moved beside Truet with a distressed expression on her attractive face. She held Truet's arm with both hands.

"I watched AJ and Brit kill those men. Truet please, take Jenny and go."

Jenny Mae asked with great anxiety in her voice. "What men? Saul, what are you talking about?"

"Those Chinese men?" Truet asked.

Saul nodded as his face contorted in anguish. "They murdered them because of me," he said as his lip trembled.

Truet reached out to Saul. "Come inside and tell us about it."

"No!" Saul stated sharply, "I can't, I gotta get back. I came to warn you AJ's a murderer. He'll do it again, Tru, except this time he's planning on killing you," he said through his heavy breathing.

"What do you mean they killed them because of you?"

Saul sighed impatiently. "Brit found my footprints at his house, because of Abby! They killed those men to warn me!" Saul stated loudly and fought his sobs again as guilt filled him. He added emotionally, "I had to bury them."

"Oh, my Lord!" Jenny Mae stated sharply. "Who's Abby?"

Truet ignored her question and said, "You could tell the sheriff."

Saul shouted sharply, "He knows! Martin knows who did it! But he won't do anything about it. You know that, Tru! There's nothing we can do! But I don't want it to happen to you and Jenny Mae," Saul's eyes filled again with tears. He added as he backed up and stepped off the porch, "Please, Tru, take Jenny Mae and go. He's not playing around. You made him bleed; he's planning on killing you."

"Saul," Truet asked softly, "Are you all right?"

Saul shook his head painfully. "No. I have to go. Get out of town my friend, please!" Saul pleaded and then ran back towards town.

"Tru, I'm frightened," Jenny Mae said as they watched Saul run into the darkness.

Truet held his wife. "We'll be all right," he said as he closed the door. He had nothing else to say, but fear crept into his heart. He held Jenny Mae in his arms in silence. "Let's go pray, Jenny Mae," he said.

"Tru, I want to move to Branson. I'm wiring Lee and Regina tomorrow; I think we should leave right away. I can't live like this. Let's just go. Please, Tru," Jenny Mae pleaded with urgency in her voice and tears in her large, beautiful eyes.

Truet nodded. "Okay, you start packing up and I'll take care of everything in town tomorrow. We'll have to sell everything, everything we've made of our life here."

"Maybe it's just better to leave alive from here!" Jenny Mae snapped quickly and then apologized quietly, "I'm sorry Tru. We can start over again."

"I don't want to start over! That's the problem Jenny; I don't want to start over! We've worked too hard to get what we've got. We have a family here. You can say we'll make new friends over there, but these friends are our family, Jenny Mae. I don't want to throw it all away because of one man!"

Jenny Mae stepped away from Truet and shouted, "And what if that one man's a murderer? What if that one man has plans of murdering you? Is staying here worth that?"

"It's gossip! AJ apologized. He was sincere. Maybe he did say a bunch of garbage, but then he apologized. Maybe Saul was just panicking over nothing."

Astonished, Jenny Mae stared at Truet. "Truet, I just saw the biggest and toughest man I've ever seen shaking in terror for our safety! And he just buried those dead Chinese men that AJ murdered just to teach a lesson of some kind?" she paused to glare at Truet. "It sounds credible to me! Maybe he has a reason to panic! And perhaps we should too."

15

A decision was made after hours of discussion to sell out and move to Branson as soon as they could. It was a heart-wrenching decision for Truet to make, but for the sake of Jenny Mae, he agreed to follow her wishes.

They had gone into town on Monday and wired Lee and Regina Bannister in Branson informing them of their plans to move over to Branson and to expect them within two weeks. They planned on selling their home back to the Thacker DePietro Land Company and all of their personal belongings to whoever would buy them, except for what they could load on their wagon. They figured it would take five to six days to drive their team and wagon to Branson. They hoped to leave Sweethome within a week. But it took money to start over again, and they had to sell everything to get that.

After wiring the Bannisters, they had walked over to the Thacker DePietro Land Company and had spoken with Jeb DePietro about selling their home and acreage back to them. Jeb declined to discuss it without his partner, Bob Thacker, in the office because Bob was the one who sold them the property. It would be Bob's due responsibility to buy it back from them. However, Bob seldom worked in the land company's office on a set schedule. Jeb assured them that he would set up a meeting with Bob on Tuesday at one o'clock for them. By the time they left the Thacker DePietro Land Company, the news of their moving to Branson had already made its way through the streets of Sweethome. Jeannie Bartholomew, the general store and postal clerk, had already told as many of her neighbors as she could.

The rest of the day was spent with their friends, Richard and Rebecca Grace and Felisha Conway, as they owed it to them to tell them the news of their decision themselves before the gossip on the street did. The news wasn't received well as none of them wanted Truet and Jenny Mae to move. Richard was most adamant about them staying in Sweethome to confront their fears, but in the end there was no changing the mind of Jenny Mae, and they had left their dear friends deeply saddened. Whether they understood or not didn't really matter, Truet and Jenny Mae were leaving.

TRUET STOPPED the wagon outside of the Thacker DePietro Land Company for their Tuesday afternoon meeting with Bob Thacker and gently helped his wife down off of the wagon. She was looking particularly pretty in her long, light blue dress with a white floral pattern. Her brown hair was pinned up under a blue tinted bonnet exposing the soft white skin on the back of her neck.

"Are you sure you want to do this? It's not too late to change our minds," Truet questioned as they stood by the front door of the office.

Jenny Mae smiled through the soft tears that filled her

eyes. "Yes, I'm sure," she stated and hugged Truet tightly while her tears fell from her closed eyes.

"You don't seem so sure," Truet said softly. He held her in his arms lovingly.

"No, I'm sure," she said wiping the tears from her eyes. "No matter what Branson holds for us, at least I'll have you with me. That's all I care about, Truet, having the father of my baby with me. I love you too much to risk staying here." She hugged him again and kissed him in public. "I love you, Truet Davis."

He smiled his handsome smile. "I love you more, Jenny Mae Davis."

"Let's go sell our home," she said and led the way through the door.

Inside, Bob Thacker stood up from behind his desk and walked out to greet them with a sincere expression of sadness on his face. "Truet and Jenny Mae, I was hoping you'd change your minds and wouldn't show up today. I understand you wanted to put your place up for sale. Please, come sit down and let's talk about it," he motioned towards two chairs in front of his large oak desk while he sat behind it.

Truet and Jenny Mae's attention wasn't on Bob or the expensively decorated office they were standing in. It was on AJ Thacker, who was standing by the window where he had been watching them outside. He stared at them without a smile or any other sign of emotion.

"Please," Bob motioned toward two chairs. The office was small and designed with walnut-paneled walls and plaster ceilings with four large metal chandeliers that provided a lot of light as each chandelier held four lanterns. The design was simple: two large desks in the middle of the room with two chairs in front of them. There was a private room in the back, but they sat in the main room at Bob's desk. Truet and Jenny Mae reluctantly took their seat in the chairs, uncomfortably putting their backs to AJ.

"So, I hear you're wanting to move to Branson," Bob remarked once they were seated. He held a file in his hand, but spoke frankly without opening it. "I was told you wired Lee Bannister. Lee's a fair man, I think, but he won't give you the deal I did. You won't find a beautiful home on acreage for what you paid for it here," Bob paused to sigh. "Lee's a self-made man just like I am. I won't kid you; he didn't get where he is by giving anything to anyone for free. You're taking a chance by throwing yourself upon the graces of a greedy and immoral man like Lee. You're giving everything away, just like that. May I ask why?"

"Um, well," Truet started to speak, but paused when he heard AJ's boots walk up behind them, AJ stepped around his father's desk to the empty seat at Jeb's desk four feet from Bob's. AJ leaned back in the high-back chair putting his hands behind his head and stared at Truet while he continued.

"We're looking to start over, and Branson has the opportunities," Truet replied casting his eyes quickly from Bob to AJ.

"Hmm... The opportunities in Branson were ten years ago. Carpenters there are a dime a dozen, and teachers, well, you'd better get used to something else. The teaching positions are taken ten times over. The only opportunities you may find are labor jobs requiring very little skill and a lot of physical labor and muscle. The two major opportunities in Branson are the silver mine and timber industries. I wish you both luck, but I have to warn you, Branson's no paradise. You know," Bob asked sincerely, "I don't understand what kind of opportunities you're looking for. You have a beautiful home, a thriving business and Jenny's the teacher of our school." Bob shrugged and continued, "What more could you possibly want?"

"We have our reasons," Truet stated and glanced over at AJ, who looked at them with his blackened eye.

"Well, certainly there's something I can do to keep you here," Bob suggested and leaned over his desk, as he grabbed the opened file. "We can refinance the farm. Renegotiate the carpenter shop agreement or redo the teacher's contract. I'm willing to negotiate within reason to keep you both here. Here, let me be frank with you," Bob said and then continued. "Years ago Jeb and I sponsored this town and grew it to be what it's become, the hub of a circle, if you will, of centralized trade. We've accomplished that and reached our goal. Sweethome's not going anywhere; we're here to stay. However, it's still known as a roughneck town. We're trying to cure that. We're trying to make Sweethome a family-friendly town, if you will. We need people like you to stay here. So, what can I do to keep you and Jenny Mae here? You give me your thoughts and we'll negotiate a fair deal."

"Well, Bob, I don't really know that...," Truet was saying when Jenny Mae cut in sharply.

"There isn't going to be a deal! We came to sell," she spat out, sounding definite. She glared furiously at AJ. He had licked his lips at her while Truet was speaking. She added in the same incensed manner to Bob, "And you can chain your son up like the dog he is! That might help as well."

AJ laughed quietly, as Bob expressed his concern. "Keep my son chained? Why I understand that he's had some slight disagreements with you two, but it looks to me like that was settled once and for all last Thursday night. Am I right AJ? Didn't you apologize to them?" he asked irritably.

"Yes I did, Pa. Just like you told me to, and I meant it," AJ said quickly, sounding insincere.

"You better mean it!" Bob warned and then asked, "Have you been bothering them?"

"No sir," AJ said as his face slightly reddened.

Bob turned back to Truet. "Please tell me you're not running away because of him!"

Truet shook his head. "No, we have our reasons."

"Mister Thacker," Jenny Mae said boldly, "We are not negotiating a deal. We are moving to Branson as soon as we can. Truet's finishing the work at his shop tomorrow and liquidating his supplies to the hardware store. The ladies are coming over tomorrow to help me clear out our home. We are not changing our minds, but since you asked I will tell you. Your son has been the thorn of our existence since we've arrived in Sweethome. He has insulted Truet and me beyond every reasonable boundary; he has touched me, cornered, and harassed us to no end. Now, Truet's very life has been threatened and we will not stay here and risk our family because of your crazy son! Just a moment ago he was licking his lips at me, right here in your office! So now, you tell me what would make us want to stay here? No amount of money is worth putting up with your son!" she finished heatedly.

"When was your life threatened?" Bob asked Truet with increasing irritation and interest.

"Almost every time I see AJ," Truet said honestly. He was quickly getting irritated at Jenny Mae for bringing it up to Bob. He suddenly felt like a coward and his face was turning red. He had been caught in an embarrassing situation thanks to Jenny Mae's mouth getting the best of her.

"Is that true, AJ?" Bob roared at AJ.

"No Pa, of course it ain't. They just don't understand

Thacker humor, I guess. I don't know, but I've never threatened them," AJ said with a wave of his hand. "And if I have, it was all in jest. I have no reason to kill Truet or a reason to want to." He laughed with a shrug of his shoulders. His smile faded when he saw Jenny Mae glaring at him with detestation showing on her face.

"Maybe we're having a misunderstanding. Maybe this is all a mistake. Perhaps AJ's so-called threats weren't meant as such, and you're over-reacting a bit," Bob suggested diplomatically.

"We're not over-reacting," Jenny Mae spoke in a no-nonsense fashion. "We want to sell; so will you buy back our place? Yes, or no? I'm not staying here any longer than I have to. Don't even try to talk us into staying. I can no longer stomach this town and particularly your son!" she stood up from her chair and said to AJ, "You are the most repulsive man I have ever met!" she glared at him and then added to Truet, "Let's go. Mister Thacker, we will sell for a fair amount. We'll come back by tomorrow at one o'clock to finish this. Have a reasonable offer on the table," she finished and walked out the door.

Bob's face reddened, as he burst out heatedly, "I will not stand to be talked to like that, especially when you want me to do you a favor! Truet, you need to control your woman. A man's wife should never talk out of line, much less come to a business meeting! Come by tomorrow about noon, Truet, and we'll finish this up, but leave her at home. It sounds to me like the only one who's being attacked is AJ!" Bob stated gruffly.

Truet nodded as he stood. "I'm coming into town early so I'll be around. I apologize for Jenny," he said softly. He walked towards the door.

"Truet," Bob called. "You need to teach your damn

woman a lesson about keeping her mouth shut! I'm beginning to understand why AJ smacked her. A woman that speaks like that needs to be beaten. Take her home and make a lady out of her."

Truet stood in the middle of the doorway looking at Bob with a growing resentment. It showed on his face, but wordlessly, he opened the door and stepped outside as AJ's voice was heard saying, "Only a coward let's his wife do the talking, Pa."

16

"I know we won't get back what we've paid, but don't let him cheat us either. All we need is enough to get settled. Between our home and all the furnishings we should make three thousand to thirty-five hundred, at the least. Don't you think?" Jenny Mae asked questionably. She sat at the dining room table writing down figures on a piece of paper. They had received a wire from Lee Bannister acknowledging their wire and noting that he'd have a home for them to move into when they arrived. It was temporary of course, until they chose a home of their own. It was all the affirmation they both needed to grow excited enough to sell off what they owned and pack up what they cherished the most. Truet's wagon couldn't carry all that much after all.

"I think Bob is going to low-ball us. We didn't leave yesterday on the best of terms, my dear," he said from across the room with an accusing expression that made her laugh.

"Yes, of course! God forbid a woman has a mind and the courage to express it."

"Yes dear, I should knock you around for that," Truet teased with a smile and walked over to where Jenny sat at their dining table. He put his hands on her shoulders and kissed the top of her head.

"I love you, my dear. I better get going; I have a lot to do today."

She stood and faced him. "I know, me too. I can't believe how much we've acquired in such a short amount of time. It's going to be tough deciding what to load onto the wagon. We have so much."

Truet smiled.

"What?" she asked.

"Wait here. I probably need to show you something before you start packing up everything," he said and walked out the back door leaving the house.

"Where are you going?" she asked.

A few minutes later, Truet entered through the back door and said, "Close your eyes."

"What are you doing, Tru?" she asked with a smile.

"Open them."

Jenny Mae's eyes opened wide as she stared at the cradle he had made. He held it in his hands proudly. "Oh, my goodness! Truet, it's beautiful! You made it for our baby?" she asked, tears filling her eyes.

Truet's smile grew while he watched Jenny Mae's reaction. "I've never put more care into anything more than I did this. I want to take it to Branson with us."

Jenny smiled approvingly through her quiet, teary eyes. "Of course. It's the most beautiful thing we own, Truet. Thank you." She hugged Truet tightly while he set the cradle down on the table. "Thank you, Truet. I love it. I love you."

He chuckled lightly while he wrapped his arms around her. "Well, I'm glad you like it."

"I love it. You are so wonderful to me," she said gazing

deep into his eyes. "I think our son is going to be a lucky young man to have such a wonderful father."

"It could be a girl."

"Nope. He's too ornery to be a girl. I keep telling you a girl wouldn't treat her mother like this."

Truet kissed her with a pleasant smile. "I have to go or I'll never get done today. I love you, my lady. I'll see you later today."

"Have a good day, Tru, and be firm with Bob today. Don't let him steal our home."

"I won't," he said blowing a kiss to Jenny Mae from the front door and walked out closing the door behind him.

Jenny Mae watched him step up into the wagon and drive towards town. An enduring warmth filled her soul while she watched Truet leave. When he was out of sightshe sat at the dining table and looked fondly at Truet's workmanship on the cradle. They had no other furniture or supplies for the baby and the cradle was perfect. She never expected one so beautiful. It was comforting to know that he was thrilled about having the baby too. He always said he was excited, but the love he put into the cradle actually showed it. She ran her finger along the cradle feeling for any rough edges, but the wood was smooth. The day would come before they knew it when she'd be a mother and Truet would be a father. They were beginning a family together. There are times in a lady's life when she needs to sit quietly and relish the small moments of the day. Moments of joy, laughter, or as now, deep and quiet appreciation of all Truet had given her. People seemed to struggle all of their lives to find happiness, but failing to recognize that happiness was conditional, so it could never be found for long. Happiness, like all other emotions, depended upon circumstance. Jenny Mae was happy, but more importantly, her life was built around the Lord Jesus and His Word. She knew no matter where Truet and she moved they'd be in the Lord's good graces and she would be content with the life the Lord gave her. Other people might struggle to find lasting fulfillment and happiness in their lives, but Jenny Mae had already found it and she was thankful for it.

She studied the craftsmanship of the cradle with great fondness, but a quiet melancholy filled her because she knew the home they had come to love would've been a dream home in which to raise a family. The home was large for just the two of them, but for the price they paid, it was a steal, especially considering the outbuildings and acreage of hay leased back to Bob to plant and harvest. The home was beautiful, and it had plenty of space for their family to expand and grow. It had three bedrooms upstairs and a large bedroom downstairs, which was theirs. It was hidden in the back corner of the house behind the kitchen and the short hallway to the backdoor. The dining room was the open area beside the kitchen where the dining table was placed. The large living room had a cozy wood stove surrounded by two stuffed chairs, a davenport, and tables. It was an inviting room that had been used to host get-together dinners and many discussions over the past year. The walls were wallpapered, and a stairway led upstairs along one wall. The design of the home was wonderful, so was the condition of it. They would not be able to buy another homestead like this one ever again, not with their incomes. Not even Lee Bannister, as nice as he seemed, would be willing to sell a property equal to theirs for the same price.

Bob Thacker had made them a great deal to keep them in Sweethome. Perhaps it was the need for a schoolmistress or the need for a gifted carpenter, or maybe a little of both combined with the need to sell the property that enticed Bob to sell it for so little. The Lord had led them to Sweethome at just the right time to fall into such a blessing as their homestead. In truth, she hated to sell the lovely home and move away from her dear friends and students, but Truet's safety and being free from the likes of AJ Thacker was worth the move. It was doubtful that their new home would have nearly the same quality, but no one knew what the future had in store. One thing was for sure though; AJ wouldn't harm Truet in Branson. He could get away with murder in Sweethome, but not in Branson.

Jenny Mae couldn't explain why she trusted Lee and Regina Bannister to deliver on their promise to help relocate them and find suitable work, but she did. She had liked them immediately and somehow knew that they were good people and had the potential to be good friends. Jenny Mae was counting on them to help her and Truet, like she would a long-time friend; she was heavily relying on them to help. According to the wire they received from Lee, she was right about them. They were going to help and promised to have everything set up when they arrived. The comfort it brought to have them to rely on under the circumstances of moving to a large new town was substantial. She was at ease with moving to Branson.

The greatest trouble with moving a hundred and some miles away was that very few furnishings and equipment could be taken. There was a well-used road to Branson; stagecoaches, freighters, and anyone else making the journey west used it. If the railroad had been completed they'd take the train, but the railroad wouldn't arrive in Branson for another six months to a year. The only option was loading the wagon with absolute necessities and leaving the rest behind, just as they had once before. It would be tough and she was in charge of the difficult job of deciding what went and what stayed. The cradle was the first item she wrote on her list of necessities going, followed by her family china set her mother had given her. Truet's guns and tools would have to go, as she knew he would never leave them behind. There were photos and other personal items that she could not part with as well. Of course, she couldn't allow herself to get too sentimental, as they would need room to live in the wagon, most uncomfortably, until they arrived in Branson. They could set up a tent at night to sleep in, but they still had to pack water and food, bedding, and their clothing just to survive the five to six-day trip to Branson. And so the work began, first the list of the non-negotiable, then the expected negotiating with Truet about items he'd insist on taking and then the selling off of almost everything they owned. What wasn't absolutely necessary was to be sold for as reasonable a price as could be asked.

The silence of the morning was suddenly broken by the back door being kicked open. It slammed against the wall forcefully shattering the glass window.

Jenny Mae jumped up startled and stared toward the hallway that concealed the back door from view. Jimmy 'The Colt' Lang stepped into view, followed by another man, a Thacker cowboy she recognized, but whose name she did not know. He had necked-length straight black hair and a scruffy beard. They both eyed her ferociously with wolf-like smiles on their unshaved faces. Terrified, she backed up quickly towards the front door and turned towards it to run. She froze in place when the door opened and AJ Thacker stepped inside of her home, followed by Skip Kinnish who closed the door behind him.

AJ's eyes were bloodshot and hostile. "Surprise!" he stated with devilish glee and continued toward her. Jenny

Mae backed herself into the large living room with sheer panic on her face. "I told you, I always get what I want. Even you!"

"Felisha and Rebecca are on their way here. You better leave now," Jenny Mae heard herself utter through her panic-stricken voice and a quivering lip. Her heart pounded against her chest rapidly and she couldn't believe these men had come into her home.

AJ smiled lightly. "Not until ten I heard. That gives us a bit more than an hour."

Jenny shook her head desperately as the men stepped closer. "They're coming now!" she said. She was suddenly backed into the corner of the family room with the four cowboys moving closer still, a combination of animalistic savagery and lust in their eyes. They meant to hurt her.

"Good," Jimmy Lang replied, "I'd like to have that preacher's wife, too."

"Get out of my house!" Jenny Mae screamed with all her available energy. Tears of desperation and terror flooded her eyes as she began to break down and pleaded with them, "I'm with child, please get out!"

AJ flung his right hand and slapped Jenny Mae's face hard with the back of his knuckles. "That's for the other night!" he spit out viciously.

She fell to the floor and stared horrified at the blood on her hand that fell from her split lip. She looked up at AJ and begged, "Please don't. I'm having a baby."

"Pick her up boys. Let's put her on the table," she heard AJ say as she watched him heartlessly turn around and walk over to her dining table and throw the cradle carelessly off of it, as well as her center-candle piece. She felt the hands of Jimmy Lang and the others pulling her up to her feet roughly.

"No!" she screamed and tried to fight off her attackers while they manhandled her to the table, "Let go of me! You have no right to..."

A hard blow to her stomach by AJ took her breath and will to fight away. The pain consumed her abdomen. AJ grabbed her hair, which was tied up in a bun and jerked her head back to glare into her pain-filled face. "You're gonna give us all a present to remember you by after you leave, Jenny Mae. Like it or not! Take her to the table and strip her!" he hissed.

"No, please, my baby," she barely got out, as she tried to catch her breath. The men picked her up easily and carried her the short distance to the dining table. She couldn't breathe, but she frantically cried out in desperation, "Lord, help me." She was laid across the table and held down by her arms by Skip Kinnish and the other cowboy whose name she didn't know. Jimmy Lang tore at her dress and underclothes with a rapacious thirst. Once she was laying exposed for all to see, Jimmy ripped off his gun belt and impatiently undid his jeans, but AJ's voice stopped him.

"She's mine and she'll be mine until I'm done with her! You boys just hold her down," he said as he undid his jeans and leaned over Jenny Mae. He positioned himself and forced her to face him while he sneered, "And I'm going to hurt you!"

17

"Well, a mistake or not, she needs our help, and a friend is always a friend, even if we can't quite agree with her choices," Rebecca Grace said. She rode beside Felisha, who drove the wagon to the Davis home. It was the Grace's wagon and horse, but Felisha was more experienced with driving a wagon and livestock than Rebecca was. Young Dillon sat on a blanket on the wood plank bed of the wagon.

Felisha shook her head irritably. "Jenny never considered moving until Regina suggested it. It's absolutely ridiculous to sell everything and move like they are. Not that I'm judging her necessarily, but I have to say it's a terrible idea. I can't believe they're actually leaving. It just makes me angry," she spoke quietly so not to be heard by Dillon, who often repeated what he heard.

"I agree," Rebecca said simply. Her black hair was in a bun under a white sunbonnet and she wore a simple peach-colored dress. Soft freckles speckled her nose and cheeks. She eyed the Davis home sadly when they pulled up to the house. "But Felisha, if we can't reason with her, then we have to support her. She's our friend. Maybe if we were in her shoes we'd do the same thing."

Felisha stopped the wagon and set the brake next to the front porch. Felisha looked at Rebecca squarely. "I lost my husband and have battled the Thackers as well. I stayed and fought to keep the life we'd made. I never considered selling out and leaving. Never once."

"Yes, Felisha, but your husband's death was accidental. His life wasn't threatened," Rebecca emphasized before she climbed off the bench seat of the wagon. "Let's go inside and help our friend."

"Of course. Come along, Dillon," Felisha called for her son, while she opened the front door and stepped inside. "Jenny Mae? Oh, my lord!"

Jenny Mae was naked and curled up in the fetal position holding onto her abdomen. She was crying and writhing in pain. Blood smeared her face and her inner thighs; where blood pooled on the floor beneath her. Her breasts and upper shoulders and back had bite marks exposing some blood where the teeth marks penetrated the skin. Her face had been severely beaten and her dress and undergarments had been ripped off carelessly and cast beside the table. It left no doubts as to what happened as blood was smeared across the tabletop as well.

Felisha went to Jenny Mae immediately. "Dillon, go outside please!" she ordered curtly.

"Mama?" Dillon asked, disturbed by the sight of Jenny Mae.

"Get outside!" Felisha shouted and then addressed Jenny Mae. "Jenny, I have to get you to the doctor. I think you might be losing the baby," Felisha said, her voice cracking with emotion.

"No," Jenny Mae sobbed softly. "Not my baby. Please,"

she cried through her split lips. She held her lower abdomen. "It hurts."

Rebecca came over and quickly offered a prayer over Jenny Mae's body that the child might be saved. As soon as she finished, Felisha told her to go grab a blanket to cover Jenny Mae. "We have to get her to the doctor right away."

"Don't touch me! It hurts," Jenny Mae cried.

"Who did this?" Felisha asked, but she already had a good idea.

"AJ and his friends," Jenny Mae said and sobbed. "They..." she tried to say, but sobbed uncontrollably while her friends lifted her up to wrap her in a blanket for the trip to town. Her sobs were loud and uncontrollable. She could barely stand, let alone walk.

18

"Ve're goin' to miss ya," Dutch Schultz said to Truet from across the counter of Dutch's Hardware Store. "Ya one of my best customers," Dutch finished with a heavy accent of German decent. He was an older man of fifty-some with graying dark hair and thick sideburns.

Truet smiled sadly. He had made a good friendship with the older man. "Ah Dutch, you could sell out here and start over again in Branson. I'm sure there's hardware stores there already, but they don't have you."

"No. I moved cross the ocean, and then cross dis country. I no more move ever. Dis is my home now."

"Are you glad you moved? I mean, was it worth it to just start over again? It must be, yeah?"

Dutch nodded. "Very gute fir me. It be gute fir ya, too. Jest work hard and honest. Same as here."

Truet smiled his handsome smile. "Have you ever been to Branson, Dutch?"

"No. I stop here," Dutch replied and then asked, "Ya?"

Truet shook his head slowly. "No. Like you, I stopped here. It's rather exciting not knowing what's going to happen, but leaving it all up to the Lord. It's how we wound up here in Sweethome. I imagine it'll be similar in Branson."

"Ya, I tink so," Dutch agreed. "I still hate to see ya go."

"I know. It won't be easy leaving all of our friends behind." His attention went to a young boy named Mark, who burst through the door in a hurry.

"Is Truet in here? Truet," he stated urgently when he saw Truet. "You need to get to Doc Bladine's office. It's your wife, she's been hurt!"

"What happened?" Truet's voice filled with panic.

"I don't know. But everyone's crying!" Mark announced urgently. Truet ran out of Dutch Schultz's hardware store without another word.

Truet ran the three blocks to Doctor Clint Bladine's office. He burst through the door and was greeted by the sight of a small group of his church family standing in a small office area with concern and sorrow mingling on their faces. Reverend Richard Grace stepped forward to console Truet.

"What's going on? Where's Jenny?" Truet questioned with panic in his eyes. "Richard, where's Jenny Mae? What happened?"

Before Richard could answer, Jenny Mae's anguish-filled voice cried out in pain from behind a closed door. Truet glanced at the door and in exasperation looked back at Richard. It was then that Truet noticed Rebecca crying and appeared to be very upset while holding her two children and Dillon. "Richard, what is wrong?" Truet demanded, raising his voice.

Richard swallowed and said as carefully as he could, "Jenny Mae is losing the baby."

The words stunned Truet visibly as the color left his face and his body appeared to slump. His eyes grew misty as he replied softly, "I have to be with her." He stepped towards the door.

"Tru," Richard said, quickly stopping him. Richard's eyes grew thick with pain-filled tears. "That's not all."

Truet watched Richard's expression and felt the sudden strike of the dread that lingered gravely on Richard's face. Bracing for the unknown, Truet asked, "What do you mean?"

Inside of the small procedure room, Doctor Bladine had Jenny Mae lying on a sheet-covered table with her knees bent up and her legs spread apart. Felisha held her hand comforting her, while Dr. Bladine assisted with the miscarriage of the nearly five-month-old fetus. Jenny Mae had to push, as her body was forcing the fetus out. She was bleeding and in great pain, but Dr. Bladine chose not to give her any type of painkiller until the unborn baby was delivered. He needed her to keep pushing.

Truet was shattered by what Richard had told him. Even after being warned of her condition, Truet was wholly unprepared to see his beautiful wife lying on the doctor's table beaten and bleeding while giving birth to their dead child. Nothing on this earth could've prepared him for what he saw or the horrific expression she had on her face when she looked at him. She raised her arms up reaching for him to come to her. She pressed her lips together and began to cry.

No words could easily describe the emotions Truet felt as he held Jenny Mae. Devastated, he held her close while she wept. Felisha stepped away to allow some space for Truet to hold and comfort his wife.

"I couldn't stop them," she cried into Truet's shoulder. "I couldn't stop them! I'm sorry Tru," she wept heavily.

"Shh! It's not your fault," Truet said. A tear slipped down his cheek. "It's okay, Jenny. I'm here."

"The baby's dead. They killed our baby!" she wailed grievously from within Truet's loving arms.

"Shh," Truet whispered into her ear. He held her close as he felt tears burn down his cheek. There was nothing that came to mind to say. All he longed to do was hold her.

"Tru," Dr. Bladine said, "I need her to push. She's bleeding heavily; the sooner she gets it out, the better we'll be," he finished with a sense of urgency to his voice.

"Okay. Jenny, sweetheart, push. Let's get this done and go home. Okay?" he asked softly while he looked into her beaten face.

She nodded agreeably, let go of Truet, and lay back flat on the table. Her face transformed into a determined scowl as she pushed with renewed purpose. She moaned loudly with pain while giving a strong effort, and then quit pushing to rest. Her breathing was heavy and her face was covered with sweat. She was forced to push again before she was ready to, as her body contracted to push the fetus out. She squeezed Truet's hand tightly with her right hand and reached over with her left hand to take Felisha's as well. She yelled out in agony as she strenuously squeezed her abdomen.

"Push, Jenny," Felisha encouraged her.

"I see it coming," Dr. Bladine said. "One more big push and I'll take it out, Misses Davis."

With that being said, Jenny Mae drew in a deep breath and pushed as hard as she could. The terrible pain she had endured was suddenly released when she felt the fetus being pulled out. Upon feeling the alleviation from the pain, she looked at the heartbroken face of her husband. She didn't say anything. She just stared at him. She was exhausted and wanted to sleep. But not there, she wanted to go home and sleep in her own bed, next to her husband.

"It's over. I'll step outside for a bit," Felisha said with an empathetic smile. She began to walk away towards the door.

"Wait!" Dr. Bladine called to Felisha. His attention went back to Jenny Mae. "Grab me a towel! She's..." he looked up at Truet with a grim expression on his face. "She's hemorrhaging, Truet. I... I can't stop it. I'm sorry."

"What do you mean you can't stop it?" Truet hammered out in alarm. "Do something! You're the doctor, damn it!"

"The damage is too deep inside. The uterus walls have been torn, there's nothing I can do. She's bleeding to death, Truet. I am sorry. You have very little time," he said as sincerely as he could to make Truet realize the facts. Jenny Mae was dying.

Felisha gasped. She struggled to breathe while she watched Jenny Mae holding Truet's hands lovingly. Felisha didn't want to leave the room, but the doctor's soft-spoken words to leave them alone moved her out the door to where their other friends waited with concern. Felisha took one last look at her friend before entering the waiting room. Her body quivered as she fought to control her emotions. She stepped out of the procedure room and her will collapsed at the sight of her friends, who were expecting her to inform them of Jenny Mae's condition. As the door closed behind her, her grievous sobbing could be heard.

Jenny Mae found comfort in staring at her husband, who knelt down to be face to face with her. Tears fell one after another down his cheeks. He didn't know what to say. It had become clear that she was leaving him, but he couldn't say anything. He stared at her helplessly and kissed her hand. "I love you, Jenny Mae," he said. He stared into her eyes, refusing to break eye-contact with her.

Her face was growing paler and her eyes struggled to stay open. "I love you, Truet Davis. I'm sorry about losing our baby," she said and closed her eyes painfully.

"No, no, don't be sorry, my love. It isn't your fault. It's not!" he said trying to comfort her. His breathing quickened as he knew she didn't have long.

She opened her eyes and gazed at him with great affection. "I'm sorry, Tru."

"You have no reason to be sorry, my lady," Truet reassured her again.

A tear fell from Jenny Mae's eye. "For leaving you," she whispered through an agonizing expression. Her voice cracked with emotion.

Truet squeezed his eyes and lips together tightly to try to keep his composure. His whole being wanted to burst open and fall apart. He wanted to wail loudly and perhaps even kick and scream, but he fought to keep from doing so. He focused on Jenny Mae. "You are still beautiful," he said fondly. "The most beautiful lady in the world," he whispered.

"I love you, Tru. Truly I do, Tru," she whispered and smiled weakly. It was once a play on words that she'd use when they first got together.

He smiled slightly through his anguish and watched her eyes close slowly. Her smile faded and her hand went limp. She was gone.

Truet squeezed her hand and held it to his face while he convulsed with hard sobs and wailed loudly. "No! Jenny please don't leave me! Jenny! Don't you do it, my love! Oh Lord, please. Don't take her!" he cried. He stood up and leaned over Jenny Mae trying to hold her, as he sobbed. "Jenny!" he screamed loudly trying to wake her up, but she did not wake. She was gone.

Richard Grace stepped into the room closing the door behind him and gently approached Truet while he still held the lifeless body of Jenny Mae. "I'm sorry," is all Richard said. He stood by and waited for his friend.

After a few minutes, Truet seemed to take notice of Richard and released Jenny Mae's body. As he did, he seemed to take notice of the bruising and bite marks on her body for the first time. He wiped his nose as he asked, "Who did this?"

"Come to my house for the night."

"Who did it?" Truet demanded loudly.

Richard said bluntly, "Come to my house and I'll tell you there."

"Who did this to my wife?" Truet asked with a growing wrath no one could've imagined coming from him.

Felisha stood in the doorway with a tear-covered face. Her peach-colored dress was spotted heavily with Jenny Mae's blood. She spoke in a doleful tone as she stared at Jenny Mae's lifeless body covered partly by a sheet. "AJ and his friends; Jimmy, Skip and Mick Rodman by the description she gave me." She eyed Truet evenly. "They showed up after you left this morning and left before we got there. But they did it. She told me."

"I'll go get Martin," Dr. Bladine said softly and slipped out of the office to seek out the sheriff, Martin DePietro.

"He won't arrest them," Felisha stated with disgust and left it at that.

"Let's pray," Richard said and began to pray for the Lord's comfort in the midst of this great tragedy. He thanked the Lord for Jenny Mae's life and her faith. He prayed for Truet and that justice might be done. He prayed for comfort as they all had lost a good friend.

Truet himself didn't hear the prayer. He was focused on

a bite mark that penetrated the skin on top of Jenny Mae's shoulder. 'It must've hurt,' he thought. Someone intentionally hurt her. The pounding of his wrath-filled heart grew stronger as his eyes studied his beautiful wife's face, blackened eyes, split lip, bruised cheek, and a bleeding ear. Before he left, he would look under the sheet that covered her and see what else he could see.

"Amen," he said on cue with the rest, but remained fixed on his thoughts at hand. Gradually he lifted the sheet to see what else had been done. He grit his teeth and covered his beloved Jenny Mae. She was now in God's hands and would rest in peace. But Truet's torment was just beginning.

19

Saul Wolf sat in the shade of the cookhouse peeling a basket of potatoes with a sharp, but small paring knife. The work was monotonous of course, but it didn't take long. It was part of his new described duties to keep him busy and earning his keep, now that he had lost his fight.

Things had changed. He was expected to work around the ranch doing whatever the cowboys no longer wanted to do, such as cookhouse help, clean the horse stalls and pig pens, cut firewood, clean up after the others and basically do it all, except cowboying. It wasn't too long ago when he enjoyed doing very little, except what he had to do to be ready to fight. After losing this fight to Jacques, the rules had changed. Brit especially, found great pleasure in finding the worst jobs possible for Saul to do, including burying the five murdered Chinese men. The most humiliating was when Brit ordered Saul and the boys to lift the privy off of the six-foot deep hole underneath it, tossed his pocketknife into the excrement, and ordered Saul down into the pit to dig out his knife. Brit and the cowboys laughed at him with mixed gagging, while Saul stood waist deep in the retched filth feeling for the knife. Once he found it, Brit tossed it back into the foul smelling muck before returning the privy to its usual place over the hole. Saul had become a despised object to push around and poke fun at. Even his faith in God and his desire to go to church became a personal attack against his intelligence, character, as well as his physical appearance.

It didn't matter that Jacques Christy had died and "The Killer Goliath" was now more famous throughout the world than anyone, especially Bob, could've dreamed. There was even a reporter coming out from New York City to interview "The Killer Goliath," so that the East Coast could meet the new boxing legend. Bob was excited to have reporters come to Sweethome. He answered the questions while Saul stood solid and quiet, as his picture was taken. That was the way it had always been and it would always be the same way. The only difference was now he was big news with newspapers all around the boxing world. It didn't matter though, he still had to live in the bunkhouse, wash dishes, do laundry, clean stalls, and wallow in feces to fulfill Brit's disdain for him. When the newspapermen came out to interview him, Saul would be in his gentleman's suit for the interview and then put on his leggings to show his intimidating power for photographs. Bob would lie to make himself appear to be a great manager by selling himself to the reporters as Saul's trainer. Bob would somehow always get the glory for Saul's work. He always had and he always would. Saul was the strength and the power while Bob basked in the glory, and kept most of Saul's winnings, too.

'It didn't matter though,' Saul thought, as he peeled another potato. He had no dreams left to fulfill or any needs to be met. He had no deep desire or for that matter, any real desire to achieve anything. If he had a home back in Iowa, he'd pack up and leave, but he didn't. He didn't have a whole lot of anything, just a duffel bag of clothes and that's about it. His new name was spreading across the world and all he was, was contained in one small room in a smelly bunkhouse, in a canvas duffel bag.

Who was he to ever think he could run away and finance a life with Abby? It was a fool's dream. Brit and his boys would've tracked them down all too quickly and sent Abby to Johnny Niehus' brothel with a "free" placard on her room's door. Saul would've been hung on a tree somewhere by "strangers traveling through town" of all things, just like the story that Martin DePietro had settled upon for the Chinese miner massacre, that seemed to be quite a mystery in Sweethome.

Saul peeled potatoes. What else was there for him to do? Saul glanced up when he heard horses riding up to Bob Thacker's house, about three hundred yards away. Bob and his business partner, Jeb DePietro, stepped out of Bob's black buggy, while Martin DePietro and two of his deputies stepped down off of their horses. All five men walked into Bob's house. Most of the time Jeb came alone, sometimes he'd bring Martin along, but he'd never seen Martin bring two deputes with him. "Hmm," Saul shrugged, noticing the oddity of it and kept peeling potatoes.

BOB THACKER CARRIED a pitcher of ice water from his dining room up the stairs to the room where AJ continued to sleep covered only by a sheet. Bob opened the door, stepped inside and emptied the contents of the pitcher onto AJ's body.

AJ jumped quickly out of bed with fierce blasphemous cursing and hard, angry eyes glaring at his father. His hand had naturally gone toward his gun belt, which hung on the bedpost. He glared at his father and yelled, "What the hell did you do that for? You have no business doing that! What the hell's your problem, old man?"

"What the hell have you done, AJ?" Bob kept his angry voice low, but his body vibrated. Any doubts were immediately eliminated; AJ's face had four long and deep scratches running down the left side of his cheek. The first two knuckles of his right hand were bruised and swollen. "What have you done, son?" Bob's voice turned sad.

"I haven't done anything. What are you talking about?" AJ said with animosity, while he grabbed a clean white shirt out of his dresser.

"She's dead, AJ."

"Who is?" he turned to face his father.

"Jenny Mae. She miscarried the baby and bled to death."

"So? What's that have to do with me?" AJ asked. He pulled on his shirt and then rubbed his scratched cheek. "It's not my baby."

Bob's breathing grew heavier, as his face turned red. He sneered under his breath. "She was our school teacher, AJ. She's Truet's wife and one of the most loved citizens of our community. She was raped and beaten this morning by you and those other fools. That's what it has to do with you, AJ. She named you all, and now, she's dead!" He paused to take a deep breath and added calmly, "Jeb and Martin are downstairs. Get dressed and let's go."

AJ stared at Bob and smiled slightly. "Named me? Well, Pa, just so you know, I had nothing to do with it."

"And your face?" Bob accused.

"I have a scratch on my back too. I was drunk last night and got into a wrestling match with Skip. He scratched me. You can ask him yourself."

"Damn it, AJ! This whole town's going to be crying out for your blood, and the blood of the others, Skip's included. This cannot be wiped under the rug. Jenny Mae was someone special here, not some Johnny Niehus whore!" Bob shouted loudly trying to get his son to understand the seriousness of the situation.

AJ eyed his father while he sat on a dry spot on the edge of the bed, to pull on his boots. "Pa, I'm sure amongst us all, that we can agree that I'm innocent of all charges. Anyone could've beaten her. Raped? I have trouble believing that. She'd lay down with anyone for a dollar after Truet went to work. Ask Jimmy, he did her," he said with a smug smile. "Nah," he continued, "she just named me because she was dreaming. I'm sure we can prove I was elsewhere, you know, because I was," AJ said simply as he stood. "She was a whore, Pa, whores die."

Bob said thoughtfully, "If it wasn't you and the boys, then who did it?"

"Strangers, Pa. They had to be."

SAUL STEPPED WEARILY into Bob's large home. A middle-aged deputy named Henry Kyle had walked down to the cookhouse and asked Saul to come to Bob's house, where Bob was expecting him.

Henry Kyle hadn't said anything to Saul about why they wanted him or what was the purpose of their being there. So he was naturally cautious when he walked inside and the two deputies, Henry Kyle and Jessie Hoff, remained on the front porch.

Inside Jeb and Martin DePietro both sat comfortably in the large Thacker family room, as did AJ, who had four scratches down his face. Bob stood waiting by a stone fireplace with a large cigar in his mouth. Jeb and Martin both smoked one as well.

"Saul," Bob stated. "Come on in here, son. There's been a horrible tragedy that you need to know about. Jenny Mae Davis had a miscarriage and died today. She had..."

"What?" Saul interrupted Bob. The words sent a jolt through him like a spear through the heart.

"Well, I'm telling you!" Bob said curtly. "She hemorrhaged after miscarrying and died, nobody's fault. But it happened."

Saul's facial features twitched. The impact of the news left a medley of emotions. A wave of shock had enveloped him followed by disbelief and a shortness of breath as he tried to grasp the news of his friend. He shook his head. "I just seen her," he said in shock. His eyes slowly teared. "I have to go see Truet. Thanks for telling me," he said and nodded to the others and turned to leave.

"That's not all I have to say," Bob said and waited for Saul to turn and face him. Bob leaned against the fireplace mantel and held his cigar in his right hand. "Jenny Mae was brutalized by a couple of strangers, we figure, after Truet went to work today. She was in pretty bad shape when they found her. She apparently told one of the women in town that it was AJ and a couple of our boys here that attacked her."

Martin DePietro began to speak as Bob ended. "She probably never even saw her attackers, because she had bite marks on her back, here and here," he suggested as he reached over his own shoulders. "We figure she was attacked from behind and she probably never even seen who attacked her," he repeated to reinforce his point.

A burning animosity continued to grow in Saul's face as he glared at AJ. He turned to Martin with a surprisingly mean expression on his face. Saul's voice quivered with loathing. "And what about her scratching one of those attackers?" he nodded at AJ.

"What are you saying, Saul?" AJ challenged him dangerously, standing up from his seat quickly.

Saul refused to back down, he squared his shoulders to AJ. "I know you did it! Those scratches prove it. Martin, if Jenny Mae said he did it, then he did it. You know darn well that Jenny Mae never lied. Look at the scratches on his face, for crying out loud! AJ wanted to hurt them. I even warned Truet and Jenny Mae about him," he stated and turned back to AJ. "I know you did it," Saul accused boldly. He clenched his fists with rage as he eyed him.

"I didn't do anything!" AJ shouted heatedly. "But I might put a bullet in your head just for saying that kind of crap!"

Bob's voice boomed. "AJ! Tell him where you got the scratches!"

"A dog scratched me last night when I reached down to pet it. Then, I broke its leg and then I killed it. Don't mess with me, Saul! I have absolutely no pity for your broken little heart. 'Ooh, Jenny Mae,'" he mocked him by rubbing his eyes in mock tears.

"Enough!" Bob yelled, followed by a flurry of cursing. "Saul, I need you to tell Truet and your other church friends that AJ and the boys were with you here on the ranch all day, and especially this morning."

"I won't do that. They weren't here," Saul stated sharply and with great disdain.

"The hell you won't!" Bob yelled and walked up into Saul's personal space and glared wildly at Saul. Bob's face was red with anger and his breathing hard. "You'll tell everyone in town exactly that and nothing else! Or I swear to that god of yours that my daughter-in-law will pay for it!

That's right, Saul, Abby." Saul's face lost its thunder. "I'll have AJ take her to Johnny Niehus' and give her away. Don't think I won't either! Do you understand me?"

"Yes!" Saul uttered through inflamed, tear-filled eyes.

"Then what are you going to say?" Bob asked in a sinister manner.

"AJ and the boys were with me all morning out at the ranch! There's no way they could've done it," Saul spat out, repulsed with each word that came from his lips.

"Very good," Bob said in a gentler tone, "very good indeed. Okay, Martin, did you hear that? Jeb?"

Martin shrugged. "I've heard enough. Unless the judge overrides me, I won't arrest them."

Jeb puffed his cigar. "There's no evidence to back up her false claims. I believe they are innocent and have a solid alibi," he affirmed as the Sweethome Judicial Judge.

Saul shook his head at the inconceivable conversation he had just witnessed. He turned and walked out the door exasperated and slammed the door behind him.

"Thank you, gentlemen. Once again justice has prevailed," Bob said with a slight smile and then scowled at his son. "Get out of my sight."

20

The Grace home was filled with Truet's close friends as they stayed with him to express their love for him and their own grief over Jenny Mae. The hugs and kind words would mean so much on any other occasion, but on this particular day and at this particular moment they meant absolutely nothing. Truet didn't want sympathy, hugs, or compassion. He wanted his wife back! He wanted to be left alone!

Still though, people came by the Grace residence to offer their condolences and to ask if they could do anything to help him through this time of loss. "Loss," it was beginning to sound like Jenny Mae was misplaced and could be found someday, perhaps even accidentally found, like so often happened with his small tools. If one more person was sorry for "his loss" he thought he might scream in aggravation and run away to somewhere, anywhere, to just be alone.

The shock had worn off over the hours after Jenny Mae passed away in his arms. Now he knew she was gone, but he couldn't believe it. It didn't seem possible. He expected her to step out of the Grace's kitchen or in through their front door with her bright smile and large brown eyes shining, ever so full of life. But for the first time since they were married, she wasn't there. Although he anticipated her to walk through the door at any moment, he knew she wasn't coming. He could not come to terms with that and he doubted that he ever would. Personally, it felt like a strange nightmare that he could not escape. He was numb and emotionally unstable as tears often flooded his eyes. It was already past suppertime, and he still had no desire to eat. The Grace home was full of food as many fine people brought food to offer assistance in any way they could. Everyone in town knew Truet was at the Grace home. Where else did he really have to go? Without Jenny Mae, his home would never be home again.

"Truet," Richard Grace said softly, "Martin is here. So is Saul."

Truet glanced up from the backdoor steps where he'd been sitting to be alone and followed Richard through the crowded house to where Martin was standing inside the front door next to Saul and the two deputies, Henry Kyle and Jessie Hoff.

"Hello, Truet," Martin said, with a compassionate smile. "Again, I'm sorry about your loss. Jenny Mae was an incredible lady."

Truet nodded. "She was. So what's happening with AJ?" he asked with a taste of poison in his voice. He watched Saul who appeared uncommonly uncomfortable, more likely scared. He listened for Martin's voice, but his eyes focused on reading Saul's nervous expression. "How are you, Saul?" Truet asked. He shook Saul's giant hand. Truet's own breathing grew quicker with a clenched jaw, as he noticed Saul would not look into his eyes. It was getting plain to see why when he listened to Martin's words.

"Well," Martin began, not giving Saul a chance to

answer, "I know what Jenny Mae said, but AJ and the others were on the ranch all day, including in the time frame that Jenny Mae was attacked."

"Bullshit!" George Ogle, the blacksmith shouted, incensed. He was an older man of sixty-some with a rough exterior and no hair on his head. He was thin and wiry and wearing his stained work clothes. He was visibly upset. "I seen them riding through town around nine-thirty or so. Don't sell your soul to save those bastards, Martin!"

"They've got an alibi," Martin argued loudly, over the voices of those who agreed with George. Truet kept his eyes on Saul, as Martin continued, "Saul, please tell them."

Saul closed his eyes and said loudly through tight lips. "They were with me all throughout the day. AJ and the others were at the ranch. There's no way they did this to Jenny Mae." He allowed the tears to fall from his eyes as he made eye contact with Truet.

"Bull!" George yelled again. "They are not your friends, Saul! How can you lie like this? Saul, she loved you," George pleaded angrily. George's words were mixed with the other people's, who were outraged as well and said so.

"Please!" Martin yelled holding up an arm. "There are no charges being filed against AJ, Jimmy, Skip or Mick. It must've been strangers that attacked her! Her back was bitten. She probably never even seen who attacked her."

In the heated verbal arguing that followed between Martin, George, and the others in the house, Saul quickly reached over and hugged Truet tightly. While he held Truet close he whispered into Truet's ear, "They did it to her, Tru. God forgive me, but they did. I'm sorry. I have no choice. God, I'm sorry, Tru." Although he tried to fight his tears, he couldn't, his body began to tremble, and he broke down crying in Truet's arms. He quickly let go of Truet, turned, and walked quickly out the door with his head turned down. His sudden departure drew the attention of the others and quieted the room.

Truet watched Saul leave and then his eyes hardened and shifted to Martin. He yelled forcefully, "She had bites on her breast, too! Bites on her shoulders and was beaten in the face. Are you telling me she didn't see who did it?" he demanded.

"Truet," Martin replied nervously while trying to calm the angry husband. "Maybe she saw them, maybe not. All I know is, it wasn't AJ and the Thacker cowboys. We think it was strangers passing by."

"Just like the Chinese men, huh? Well, Martin, let me ask you, are you going to track them down or not? Because I am going to and maybe you better stay out of my way when I do, because, Martin, I am going to kill those strangers when I find them!" he paused and then added, "No matter who they are."

"Tru, I know you're upset, but trust me, we're doing what we can. Unfortunately, Jenny Mae made a mistake, and we wasted a day investigating AJ and the boys," Martin said turning red-faced and getting frustrated.

Rebecca Grace had heard enough and shouted through her own tears as she pointed at the door. "Get out of my home, Sheriff! You are as crooked as your father and have no business with a badge! Get out!"

Martin raised a hand in retreat and walked outside with haste. George Ogle and some of the others made unkind comments as they followed him out. He and his deputies stepped up into their saddles and turned their horses to leave when Truet walked outside and neared Martin's horse.

"Martin, I just want you to know that I'm going to find those men responsible and I'm going to kill them," he said and then added pointedly, "When I do, you better leave me well enough alone, just like you're doing right now. Because I'll gladly put a hole in your heart like they've done to mine. But yours will come from a .45 caliber slug. Do you understand me?"

"Are you threatening me, Truet?" Martin asked, taken back by surprise.

Truet shook his head. "I'm warning you. When the time comes, leave it well enough alone."

"What's that mean?"

Truet shrugged. "Just talking."

"Listen Truet, I really am sorry about Jenny Mae, but my hands are tied. They have a solid alibi and it appears it's someone other than who Jenny Mae said."

Truet nodded as he curled his lips together in anger. "So be it," he said and walked away towards the house.

"Saul's lying!" Richard snarled. "Speak of Judas among us."

Truet answered simply. "They've got something over him. He told me he was lying. He was forced to say that, Richard." Truet laughed painfully in disbelief. He said aloud, "Oh God, where's the justice? I can't let them get away with this, Richard."

"Vengeance is the Lord's, Truet," Richard answered quickly. "The Lord said so, let Him have them. He can't work His plans if we interfere with it."

21

Truet couldn't sleep. Lying alone without Jenny Mae beside him for the first time in five years seemed unnatural. He lay on an uncomfortable bed staring at the dark ceiling of the small bedroom in the Grace's home. Despite his friend's good intentions, Truet had no desire to sleep or to lie there throughout the night. He rose, put on his boots and quietly left the home of his caring friends. He stepped out into the summer night's cool light breeze and breathed in the fresh air. He walked down the street without a particular destination in mind. It was a beautiful night as the nearly full moon cast its light down upon Sweethome's empty streets. He needed to get out of the Grace's home and spend some time alone without anyone asking if he was okay. He was not okay. He was, in fact, devastated. Even though Jenny Mae had died in his arms, a part of him denied that she was really gone.

Truet stopped outside the doctor's office and stared at its dark windows wondering if Jenny Mae still lay inside, undisturbed, or had they moved her to the ice cellar, like they usually did. Truet would normally be the one to build the simple plank casket for the burial. He wondered who had made her casket or did she have one yet? Of all the things Sweethome didn't have, it was a local undertaker. The servicing of the body and funeral service was a community-sponsored event; it was all volunteer labor. Given the frequency of the death and dying around Sweethome, it was quite surprising that there wasn't an undertaker to provide such services. The funeral for Jenny Mae was set for the following day at noon in the cemetery. Truet had no desire to go, of course. Twenty-four hours from now she'd be buried in the ground. He would never snuggle close beside her again, he realized, as he stood there staring at the dark windows numbly.

Truet wiped his eyes and walked away towards the only audible sound that was heard, the piano music of the Westward Whoa Saloon. As Truet got closer to the saloon through the windows he could see AJ, Jimmy, Skip and a young cowboy named Mike Moye. They were sitting at a table playing poker with three ladies of the establishment clinging onto them. They were in good humor and laughed together while they played and talked lightly. Truet's breathing nearly stopped, and his eyes burned with bitter tears, when he saw with his own two eyes the evidence left behind by Jenny Mae, as she obviously fought to save herself and their baby from AJ and the others. A rage like none he'd ever experienced filled him when he saw the four deep scratches that ran down AJ's left cheek. Truet fought to control the rage that built inside of him. He closed his eyes and taking deep breaths, he leaned heavily against the side of the building to compose himself. A physical weakness suddenly overtook him.

Gathering his courage and forcing himself to gain some self-control, he took a deep breath, stepped through the two swinging bat-wing doors and walked up to the bar. His entrance became the main attraction of the moment. The player piano continued to play, but every man's attention went to Truet as he found a place at the bar.

Mitch Hampton, the barkeep approached Truet with a look of urgency on his face. "What are you doing here, Tru? I advise you to leave before you can't do it on your own," Mitch was saying quietly. He was a tall and lean man in his late forties with black short hair and long sideburns that also made a mustache.

"I need a drink, Mitch. How about your best whisky," Truet said and buried his face into his hands on the bar, and then glanced up into the bar mirror and saw AJ and his group staring at him.

Mitch handed him a shot glass of golden brown liquor and left the bottle on the bar. "I'm sorry about Jenny Mae, Truet. I really am. Tonight's on the house."

"Thanks," Truet said dryly. He carried the bottle with him to walk over to AJ's table. "May I join you?" he asked and sat down at a table parallel to theirs without waiting to be invited.

"Sure," AJ answered cautiously. He maneuvered his girlfriend, the Westward Whoa's Madam, Allison Nurmi, away from the angle of his gun hand and Truet. Jimmy 'The Colt' and Skip Kinnish also did the same.

Truet began to speak while he sadly refilled his shot glass of liquor. "Saul told me it wasn't you guys that killed my wife. Martin doesn't seem to have much to go on, but I intend on hunting those men down tomorrow." He looked at AJ questionably. "Where'd the scratches come from?" he asked simply. It would be suspicious, he thought, if he didn't ask the obvious.

"A dog scratched me. The bitch ended up dying from the

beating she got. So I guess, I showed her, huh?" AJ asked, with a hint of arrogant pride and sarcasm.

Jimmy 'The Colt' Lang smiled and tried not to laugh. He was a short and thin rail of a man in his mid-twenties. He had short blonde hair and a thin frail face. However, Jimmy 'The Colt' was a cold-hearted and trigger-happy man of low repute.

Skip Kinnish scoffed in disbelief and gave a short laugh while he shook his head. Skip was bigger than both AJ and Jimmy. He was a good-sized man with neck-length brown greasy hair and an unshaved face. Skip was known as a good cowboy; however, he had a reputation for excessive drinking and an occasional fight. He wasn't a gunfighter, or a known killer, but Skip Kinnish could often be a town bully.

Mike Moye reacted to AJ's comment with a horrified expression on his face. Mike Moye was nineteen years old, of medium build, and size. He had a youthful face and medium-length brown hair. His reputation had not yet been laid. He mostly worked cattle, but tonight he was with AJ and the others having a drink in town.

Truet squeezed his jaw tightly at AJ's words and forced himself to continue acting blind to AJ's obvious admission. "Sounds like," Truet agreed and continued, "Your dog?"

AJ smirked. "No, she was someone else's bitch," he said, eyeing Truet tauntingly; his finger tapped his revolver's ivory handle. Jimmy laughed lightly.

"Hmm," Truet drank his shot of whisky quickly and refilled his glass. "Like I was saying, I want to track those men down and..."

"Arrest them!" AJ interjected sarcastically, drawing laughter from his friends.

"No," Truet said slowly. He eyed AJ evenly, "I have plans to kill them. That's why I'm here; I'd like for you and your guys to come with me and help track them down. I learned how to track in the cavalry, but I'll need men with me who aren't afraid to kill. You're the only one I can count on. Will you help me?"

AJ stared at Truet and then smiled peculiarly. "I thought your wife claimed I was the one that did it to her."

"At first I thought so, but then Saul told me you and the others were with him all morning. Saul's a good friend of Jenny Mae's and mine. I don't believe he'd lie to me about that. Besides, there's evidence that she was attacked from behind. She may not have seen who it was. At least that's what Doctor Bladine says, anyway."

"What kind of evidence?" Jimmy asked.

Truet shrugged. "I'm not sure. He wouldn't tell me. So, will you join me? I don't believe Martin's got any tracking experience and I can't let them get away with this. I'm asking you to help me bring them to justice, AJ," Truet said with tears flooding his eyes despite his efforts to hide them.

"Well, yeah, we'll help," AJ agreed with a shrug. "Hell, when shall we meet up to trail these murderous scum?" he asked and laughed, as did the others. AJ added, "Forgive me, we've had a bit to drink. But hell yeah, I'd be honored to ride after them with you. Wouldn't you, Jimmy?"

"Truly I would," Jimmy said, hiding a smile.

"Good," Truet agreed. "Be at my house at seven or so, perhaps eight, whenever you get there. I'll be waiting," Truet said and stood up to leave.

"Why don't you meet us in town, Tru," AJ spoke seriously. "Yeah, if you want our help, you meet us here in town. We'll be waiting." He didn't like the feeling he got from Truet's last statement.

Truet shrugged. "Their trail's at my place."

AJ nodded his head. "If you want my help, you come meet us in town."

"Fine. I'll be here early," Truet agreed and meant to leave.

"Truet," Allison Nurmi said softly. She was thirty-five years old and still quite pretty. She had blonde hair and caring blue eyes that gazed upon Truet sympathetically. She was the madam of the saloon's bedding stock. Even though she could've stolen the heart of any man that came to town, she had a solitary and lasting devotion to AJ. She was convinced that the younger man was going to marry her and everyone knew AJ had no mind to, no matter what he told her. She spoke with great sincerity, "I'm sorry about what happened to your wife. She seemed to be a very sweet lady. I know everyone in town loved her," she finished softly.

"Yeah, they did!" Jimmy 'The Colt' quipped quietly, bringing some laughter.

"Thank you," Truet said softly and added to Jimmy specifically, "I'll see you in the morning."

Truet stepped outside of the saloon where he could still hear AJ's and Jimmy's laughter over the others. Truet could barely breathe when he went to the livery stable to get his horse and wagon. He was going home.

Nearly obliviousness to what was around him, Truet instinctively put his horse away and fed her. He looked at his cow that called to be fed and milked. He tossed some hay down to her as well and then left the barn to enter his house. There was no reason to milk ole bossy; he no longer had a family to feed.

He entered through the broken back door and fumbled over furnishings that were tipped over and on the floor. The house was silent and dark until he found and lit a lantern. The dining table had been stripped of all its usual decorations and Jenny Mae's torn clothing lay on the floor around the table leg. A pool of dried blood stained the wood flooring where Jenny had lain when she was found. Looking around, Truet saw the cradle lying on its side about six feet away where it had been thrown. He walked over, picked it up, and carried it back to the table. He stood up one of the tipped over chairs and sat down at the head of the table where he'd normally sit to eat. He set the cradle on the table and began to sob as he picked up Jenny's dress; he closed his eyes while he held her dress to his face to breathe in his beautiful wife's scent that still lingered within its fibers. Exhaling deeply, he opened his eyes and noticed the dried blood on the table. Truet in one quick movement stood and flung the cradle across the room while he screamed in agony. He grabbed the lantern and went into his bedroom. On the wall were his rifles and hanging from the gun rack was his cartridge belt with its cavalry buckle and holstered Colt Single Action Army.45 revolver. He reached over and grabbed his gun belt.

22

_____

"Eldon, will you run over to the Westward Whoa and tell AJ and his friends that I'm saddling up their horses, while I'm waiting," Truet asked the twelve-year-old stable boy, named Eldon Richards. He was a red-haired and severely freckled boy of sweet disposition.

"The Westward Whoa's closed, Mister Davis," he answered softly.

"Run up the back stairs to the ladies' floor. Knock loud and one of them will open it. You've done it before, Eldon, I'm sure," Truet snapped impatiently. Eldon often ran errands to and from various places for people everyday. It wouldn't be the first time he'd awaken the bevy of ladies.

Eldon seemed troubled. "Miss Nurmi done warned me not to wake her up before nine again. She says no one should see her before she's at her finest. Not even me."

Truet was in no mood to smile, but a quick hint of one passed through his face. "Please go relay my message, Eldon. They're expecting me, so she won't be angry."

"Mister Davis," Eldon said before leaving to run his errand, "I hope you find those men."

"Eldon," Truet said as he dug in his pocket for some change, "when you finish with that, I want you to run down to Erma's Restaurant and order two big breakfasts, one for you and one for me. You stay there and wait for me. Do you understand?"

"Sure, but I thought you wanted to leave right away."

"We are, were. You and I are having breakfast while they shake off their drinks from last night. I don't want to pay for them to eat, so don't mention it to them, okay?"

"All right, how do you want your eggs?"

"Over easy. Eldon, don't mention it to the others, I mean it. I'll see you there," Truet said and watched the boy walk off towards the Westward Whoa.

He took a step back inside of the dark and musky smelling, large livery stable. His own bay mare, named Fanny, was saddled and tethered to a rail, ready to leave in a moment's instance. She was loaded with two large saddle-bags filled with an extra horseshoe, nails, currycomb and brush, and some grain and a feedbag. Saddlebag space was limited and valuable, but it was necessary to care for Fanny before his own needs were met, as his life depended upon her and her conditioning. He packed his ammunition, flint and steel, small tin pot and finally, food he bought for himself that morning; jerky, dried fruit and hard tack. A tarpaulin was rolled up tightly containing his slicker and bedroll. He had his rifles in their scabbards and his canteen filled with water. Truet considered his supplies and felt comfortable with what he had. The years in the cavalry had taught him how to travel comfortably and quickly with limited supplies.

He had just closed his bank account when the bank opened and with his money and the supplies he bought, he was ready. He hadn't slept at all, and he was moving ahead on a quickly decided plan that could end up badly. However, he didn't care. He wanted justice, and he was going to get it.

The Bible said, "*The meek shall inherit the earth.*" Wasn't it that very verse that Jenny Mae preached to him every time he wanted to strike AJ? He tried to be meek; all that meekness got him was his wife brutally raped and beaten and ultimately her death and that of his unborn son. No, there would be no more meekness.

Truet closed the left side of the large double swinging door half way to force the men to walk around the door into the open when they finally did come. He leaned against a support post in the shadows to watch the street in the direction of the Westward Whoa. He pulled a photo out of his shirt pocket of Jenny Mae and him, taken a year before. In the picture they sat closely together and stared straight ahead with their heads tilted slightly towards each other's. Truet had a slight smile while Jenny Mae's eyes beamed with joy. Their hands held each other's tightly.

Truet's eyes burned with tears as he stared at Jenny Mae's beautiful face and remembered the moment much too clearly. He wiped his eyes and looked up to see Allison Nurmi open the front door of the Westward Whoa and AJ, Skip, Jimmy, and young Mike Moye step out into the morning sun. AJ carried a bottle of whiskey in his hand, which explained why they came out the front door rather than coming down the back stairs. Allison stood outside in her Victorian dress. She was as pretty as ever while she watched them walking toward the livery stable. They seemed much too jovial at the prospect of going to hunt down the men that harmed Jenny Mae, Truet thought to himself. He replaced the photo in his pocket and said quietly, "I swear to you, Jenny Mae. I'm going to send them to hell for what they did to you."

Truet walked over to Fanny and pulled his double-barreled, dual hammer, twelve-gauge shotgun out of its scabbard and walked to the half-closed door to listen, as their voices drew closer. He reached down and unsnapped the union flap holding his Colt.45 in the holster. He pulled both side hammers back on his shotgun.

"Ssssh!" AJ said with a laugh, "Let's not say anything too loud. My god, Jimmy, you're getting too anxious," AJ laughed. "Trust me, there will be plenty of..." he stopped suddenly.

Truet spun around the door with his shotgun and pointed it at AJ, who was within six feet of him. Truet pulled the trigger hitting AJ squarely in the center of his chest; he flew backwards to the ground with a horrified expression on his face.

Truet immediately moved the shotgun past Skip Kinnish to Jimmy 'The Colt' Lang, who was quickly trying to draw his colt, but was also hit squarely in the chest with the second round of twelve-gauge buckshot. He also flew backward to the ground, dead.

Truet dropped the shotgun and pulled his colt quickly, Skip Kinnish had turned to run away. Truet aimed quickly and placed a .45 slug into the back of Skip's head. He fell face first to the ground, dead.

Truet spun his colt over to young Mike Moye and held it. His eyes held a ferocity that most men on the receiving end seldom live through; his voice was firm and dangerous. "This doesn't involve you! Don't be a fool, boy. Tell Mick Rodman this isn't over until he's dead too. Now run!" Truet ordered dangerously to the shaking boy. Mike back-peddled quickly, turned, and ran.

Truet heard Allison screaming, but now noticed the commotion on the street. Allison Nurmi was running towards the dead bodies, still screaming, while the town's people stood stunned. Truet holstered his colt, picked up the empty shotgun and went inside of the livery stable to Fanny. He grabbed two new shotgun shells out of his saddle-bag, reloaded, mounted Fanny, and galloped out of the livery stable with the shotgun in his left hand and his colt in his right. He controlled Fanny with his legs as she came out of the livery stable; he pressed his left knee into her ribs causing her to turn left and kicked her to pick up her speed.

Allison Nurmi, kneeling over AJ's body picked up AJ's revolver, screamed through her bitter tears "murderer" and fired a round at Truet as he rode out of the stable door. It missed. On instinct, Truet kicked Fanny, leveled his shotgun and fired, killing Allison with a shot to her chest, shredding her Victorian dress as he rode by.

Mike Moye had run to the corner and pulled his pistol as Truet rode towards him. He fired at Truet and missed. Truet swung the shotgun over the saddle and fired. The shotgun blast hit Mike on the right side of his upper arm. He spun around and fell down in a great amount of burning pain. Young Mike's scream was filled with anguish.

Truet rode through Sweethome as fast as he could. He passed the sheriff's office just as deputy Henry Kyle stepped outside, followed by Martin DePietro. Truet wished the deputy wasn't standing in the way of his killing Martin DePietro. He didn't have time to lose. He had to get out of town quickly and put as much space between the law and himself as he could. As he passed Erma's restaurant, he made eye contact with young Eldon Richardson, as he rode by. Justice was served. Now he was on the run.

23

The Reverend Richard Grace held his Bible in his hands while he stood at the head of the grave and the pine box coffin that held the remains of Jenny Mae Davis. His eyes were affected by the loss of Jenny Mae like the rest of the large crowd that came to the funeral. It wasn't just the loss of their friend and beloved schoolteacher that left the strange and bewildering foggy haze over the town of Sweethome on this beautiful Thursday afternoon. The tragic loss of Jenny Mae and her unborn child was heartbreaking enough, but the four murders by Truet that morning had left the town stunned, even now as they buried the beloved Jenny Mae Davis.

"What more could be said about Jenny Mae?" Richard asked, as he peered at the crowd of mourners, mostly dressed in black and wiping their eyes. He looked at his own wife, Rebecca, who was dressed in a long black dress and a dark bonnet. She held her children near her like a frightened mother bird protecting its young. Felisha Conway stood beside Rebecca similarly with her son, Dillon. Richard continued, "Jenny Mae was a good friend. She was a good wife to her husband and a good teacher to our children. Jenny Mae was also a faithful servant of our Lord Jesus Christ. So as we stand here and mourn for our loss, let's keep in mind that she's receiving her reward in the presence of Jesus himself, as He says to her, 'Well done, my good and faithful servant.'" He paused momentarily, as he noticed a group of riders coming towards them, led by Bob Thacker. He continued, "Jenny Mae Davis, our friend, our sister in the Lord, went home. What, my dear friends, can be better than that?" he paused and then continued.

"The twenty-third psalm is often read at funerals. I've read it myself many times during funerals. However, I'll let you know something; it has nothing to do with dying. It has everything to do with living. It's for us; so as I read this, apply it to your life today, not when you're Heaven-bound," he said and glanced at Bob Thacker as he drew closer. Reverend Grace looked down at the Bible in his hands.

"The Lord is my shepherd; I shall not want. He maketh me lie down in green pastures; he leadeth me beside the still waters. He restoreth my soul; he leadeth me in the paths of righteousness for his name's sake."

Richard glanced up again as Bob Thacker and his group of armed riders stopped. Bob stared at him disdainfully. Richard continued, "Yeah, though I walk through the valley of the shadow of death, I will fear no evil: for thou art with me. Thy rod and thy staff they comfort me. Thou preparest a table before me in the presence of mine enemies: Thou anointest my head with oil: my cup runneth over. Surely goodness and mercy shall follow me all the days of my life: and I will dwell in the house of the Lord forever," he paused as he eyed Bob curiously. "Forever and forever will we dwell in the house of the Lord with Jenny Mae. May I say we'll see her again, my friends." He added softly, "Let us pray."

Bob Thacker's voice interrupted uncaringly, "I ain't got time to listen to you pray now, Reverend. We're after Truet, so if any of you know where he is, you'd be wise to speak up. I'll have no quarter upon anyone who helps that murdering son of a..."

"You are invading the funeral for our friend!" Richard stated abruptly. "You have no right to interrupt our service. No one knows where Truet went, Bob. Now please leave, so we can finish our service," he demanded.

Bob Thacker's face turned red, as he leaned forward and yelled at Richard with a merciless glare, "I don't give a damn about your service or your prayer. I want the man that killed my son! And if any of you help Truet in any way, you'll be just as guilty as he is and I'll hang you, too!"

Felisha Conway couldn't control herself. "I didn't know you were the law, Bob."

"Martin's the law! And he'll do as I tell him. So if you're hiding Truet, you better come clean right now, otherwise you'll pay for it!"

Rebecca Grace, despite her usual quiet demeanor, heard herself speak out with great hostility, "Just like AJ and his friends paid for what they did!"

Bob exploded into a fiery, verbal torrent from his mount; he glared murderously at Rebecca and her children, whom she guided behind her with her arms. "AJ didn't do a damn thing to her!" He pointed at the simple pine box. "If she miscarried, she miscarried, but don't blame my son for her bad luck. Every woman wanted my son. She lied about AJ and you all know it. And I don't want to hear anymore about it. If the whore laid down for AJ and the boys, it was on her own account. She didn't have to lie about it!"

"How dare you!" Richard demanded loudly. "Get away from here before I pull you from that horse and lash into you for your lack of respect!" Richard stepped around the grave towards Bob. "Your son got what he deserved! He's still getting what he deserves for what he did to Jenny Mae. And just so you know all of us at Sweethome Christian Church, will help Truet in any way we can. But most of all, we'll pray to our Lord for his protection from you and your men!"

"Then you'll pay the consequences, Reverend," Bob said simply and turned to leave.

Rebecca's voice stopped him instantly, "Just like you're paying the consequences for not holding your son accountable for his actions during his rotten life! I hope your son accepted Jesus as his Savior at some point in his life; otherwise he's in hell. And you know, it's kind of comforting to know that!"

"Rebecca!" Richard rebuked her. His eyes burned into her with surprise and disgust.

Bob Thacker glared at Rebecca. His eyes raged with the venom of hate and thirst for violence, but hidden under the venom was the anguish of losing his son. He spoke in a casual voice with intense overtones, "I want all of you to get out of my town. I'm burning your church down and building another whorehouse. Pack your things, people, because after the church burns, I'm burning your houses down. You don't believe me, but you believe an ancient book? Let me tell you something, people don't rise from the dead! And I'll prove it to you when I hang Truet!" he hissed ferociously. He angrily turned his horse and galloped the way he came from, with his small posse following behind him.

The funeral was silenced by Bob's interruption. Richard looked at Rebecca, he was astounded by the day's events that just kept spiraling out of control. He didn't have any more words to say and none were needed, as Rebecca came to him and they embraced tightly. Her body convulsed into heavy sobbing as she held him. Looking up from holding his wife, Richard noticed Felisha Conway standing alone with her hands on her son's shoulders. She was staring at Richard with her lips pressed tightly together trying to suppress the tears that fell anyway. Richard scanned over the distant horizon and prayed silently for Truet; wherever he was, he would be alone.

24

Truet wore a coat and wrapped himself in a wool blanket to keep warm. On the crest of the mountain where he camped, the temperature dropped significantly. The stars were bright while the moon cast its light down over the mountains and the neighboring valleys full of timber. The clear July night brought a downright coldness to the mountains.

Huddled in his coat and blanket Truet chose not to make a fire because a fire at night could be seen for miles, especially up on a mountain. He knew there would be men coming after him, but he saw no distant glow of a fire in the valleys below him, especially on his back trail that he had taken up to his position. It was doubtful, but possible, that like him a posse wasn't willing to compromise their position with a fire. He doubted that anyone from Sweethome was behind him reading his trail because he left a hard one to follow. He rode out of Sweethome on the northern road to Blue Hill. He could've gone east to McCall, but instead, he chose to continue north toward the mining camp of Butterstown. Halfway to Butterstown, Truet turned off of the dirt muleskinner's road and onto a miner's trail down a gentle, long slope to a running creek along the base of the mountain. He rode on the bedrock of the creek for two miles or so until he found a ravine lined with rock that came down a steep slope. He rode up it to hide his tracks. From there, he rode on the layers of needles that fell from the trees and stayed hidden in the woods, ever losing himself deeper in the forest. He rode on rock and water sources as much as possible as he climbed up to where he made his camp. Truet guessed he had ridden close to fifteen miles, mostly through uncut forest. One thing the cavalry had taught him was how to ride long distances, and the Indian guides taught him a little about how not to leave an obvious trail for others to follow. However, his regiment horse was used to long and intense days of riding. Fanny wasn't. He had pushed her far; probably much further than he should have and now she had to rest before they moved on again. He looked Fanny over for any injuries or swelling, checked her shoes and brushed her, fed her some grain and tethered her to a tree near his bedroll. He was fairly confident that he could stay put for a day or two before venturing deeper into the woods. He couldn't live off of the land forever though; he'd have to go to a town eventually. He just wanted it to be a distant town.

He sat on the cool ground looking out over the tree-covered mountain range and valleys under the brightly lit sky. The tranquil beauty of the night's scenery did nothing to move him, except to anger him more. He looked up into the heavens from his seated position and snarled out bitterly, "You could create all of this, but You couldn't save my wife! You couldn't protect her from AJ? You created the world, Lord! How can You not be able to save her? Why didn't You spare her? She was carrying my baby." His eyes filled with water and slid down his cheek.

"I thought You were my God. I thought You loved me, Lord. The Bible promises You're our protection from men like them. Where were You, Jesus? Where were You when they raped Jenny Mae? Where were You when she miscarried our child? Where were You, Father?" he screamed, and then stood up and glared into the heavens.

"We served You everyday of our lives together. We worked hard, and we wrapped our lives around Your Word. For five years we prayed for a baby and finally You gave us a child. But now You've taken them both away from me! Why? Why, Lord?" he paused seemingly wanting a response. His tears continued to fall."I thought living for You brought goodness. Isn't that what the Bible says, that our Heavenly Father gives good gifts? Blessings, Lord, not stealing my dreams away when they're right here!" he yelled, while holding out his hands. His voice echoed through the valleys. He pointed towards the heavens with his tears blurring his eyes. "You could've stopped them! You could've stopped the bleeding! You could've saved my child if You wanted to. You could've spared Jenny Mae, Lord! You could've at least done that!" His voice crumbled into pain-filled sobs as he dropped to his knees weakly. "I love her. Oh Jesus, what am I going to do? You should've taken me too. I don't want to live without her. But..." he spoke in a stronger tone, as he stood, "I have one more man to kill. I know Your word says vengeance is Yours, but it also says You love and care for me. I don't see it. You could've saved her, but You didn't. How is that a good gift for me? We were Your followers. How could You let this happen? We counted on you, Lord, and You did nothing to help her. Why?" he finished quietly and waited momentarily before going over to his bedroll. His bedroll was placed between a fold in his canvas tarpaulin to keep the bedroll dry on all sides. He glared up at the stars bitterly. "You have destroyed everything that I care about. What more is there to say?"

25

By Sunday morning Sweethome had become anything but sweet to every member of the Sweethome Christian Church. The three-day-old hunt for Truet Davis had become a personal obsession to Bob Thacker and his promise to run the church out of town was already in practice. Nearly every home belonging to the congregation had been forcefully burst into under the false pretense of finding Truet hiding inside. Bob's hired men had no accountability for the injuries or property damage they afflicted while invading a home. Some of the congregation had been severely beaten and the lives of their wives and children had been threatened if they didn't tell them where Truet could be found. The search for Truet wasn't exclusive to the church membership, but the reign of terror was. Any intimidation, threat, beating or property damage was intentionally directed at them. Some people got it worse than others, such as Reverend Grace and his family, while others like Felisha Conway, unexplainably, weren't terribly troubled at all. Still others quit coming to church to spare themselves the trouble. Bob promised the harassment would end to anyone who quit the church. His determination to run the church out of town literally showed on the faces of the congregation who still came on Sunday morning. Many of the men and even some of the women had visual reminders of the cowboys' visit on their faces. None had more bruises than the church's reverend, Richard Grace.

Reverend Grace stood at the podium, in a dark suit, white shirt and black tie. His face was discolored with two blackened eyes, swollen nose and split lip. Richard had received a severe beating by three cowboys in front of his wife and children, all in the name of justice in the search for Truet. It was a ruse, though, to end the people's commitment to the Sweethome Christian Church, because every church is only as strong as its committed followers. Bob was determined to break those who were committed and burn the building down.

Richard Grace wasn't the kind of man who ran easily or was easily intimidated by the pressures of his enemies. He was the kind of man who dug his feet into the trenches and fought for what he thought was right. But when he knew it was right, he'd die for it. He was willing to die for the Gospel of Jesus Christ.

"I will not turn my cheek to these men, nor will I turn my back to them and run away like they want us to. They can hit me; they can burn my house down. They can burn this church down and maybe they will, as we learned this week just what these men are capable of." Richard paused and looked out over his frightened congregation with a serious expression on his face. "I don't know what's happened to Truet and quite frankly, I'm frightened for Saul. We are all in a very strange time where there is no justice to be found. There is no accountability to what's right or wrong and we are being persecuted because of our faith!

Make no mistake about it, my friends, I promise you; if you denounced Jesus Christ to Bob Thacker and his men, they'll leave you alone. Just ask some of our congregation who no longer come here. You won't have any more trouble with them. Your bruises, broken noses and ribs can heal and you will have no more reason to fear. You will be left alone and all you have to do is denounce your Lord and Savior, Jesus Christ. Not deny him like Peter did, but denounce him like Judas Iscariot did! That's all you have to do to live without fear during these strange and unbelievable days." He paused silently for a moment to let his words sink into his frightened congregation. Reverend Grace continued with a serious emphasis in his voice, "Let me ask you a question that could happen today or on any given Sunday. What if Bob and his men circled our church and said they were going to nail the door closed and burn us alive, but anyone who denounced Jesus could leave freely. What would you do?" Richard paused momentarily again before continuing, "I

PROPOSE to each and every one of you that I would choose to stay here and die for my Lord, than to fall under the weight of persecution. I propose to each one of you that God is in control of everything that's happening. I will remind you, children of

the Almighty, that He loves his children. I will also remind you that Jesus never promised wealth, health or even happiness. He did promise trials and persecution for His name's sake! Brothers and sisters, Jesus is just keeping His promise." He smiled slowly and then added joyfully, "But also let me remind you that the Lord promises never to leave us. In fact, the twenty-third Psalm says; *"You prepare a table before me in the presence of my enemies."* Richard paused to let it sink in. To clarify he added, "It's a promise from God. When it's all said and done, we will win this battle. We have nothing to fear. So we take a licking; so did Jesus. We are bruised; so was Jesus. So we have broken bones; Jesus hung on a cross. If we are killed for believing in Him; so, He died willingly for you and me. We shall overcome this, because we are the loved children of the Lord Almighty! Do not doubt it and do not forget it when the wolf comes knocking on your door. Just remember we have a firm foundation. We can withstand it because our Father in heaven is the rock on which we stand." Richard added strongly as he peered out over the congregation, "So stand! Let the Sweethome Christian Church be known as a church that will stand to the death for the Lord Jesus Christ! Let our faith say more than our words or songs ever can to them. '*Though they slay me, yet I shall believe!*' Is it true for you?" Richard asked pointedly, with a dramatic pause. "Let's end our service with the hymn "Be Still My Soul." Pay close attention to the words, as we sing them because these words say so much about the Lord we serve. My friends, let's repose in our Lord and wait for His goodness, as this hymn so clearly speaks."

'BE STILL, *my soul, the Lord is on thy side; bear patiently the cross of grief or pain. Leave to thy God to order and provide. In every change He faithful will remain. Be still my soul, Thy best, Thy heavenly Friend thro' thorny ways leads to a joyful end.*

Be still my soul, thy God doth undertake to guide the future as He has the past. Thy hope, Thy confidence let nothing shake. All now mysterious shall be bright at last. Be still my soul; the waves and winds still know His voice who ruled them while He dwelt below.

Be still my soul: The hour is hasting on when we shall be forever with the Lord, when disappointment, grief, and fear are gone. Sorrow forgot, love's purest joys restored. Be still my soul: when change and tears are past, all safe and blessed we shall meet at last.'

26

"Saul!" Barry McCracken called as he pulled his horse to a stop. He had ridden out to the north end of the ranch, where Saul was splitting wood to haul back to the ranch for the winter. "The news just came in. Farrian Maddox is dead! Truet killed him in a saloon in the town of Gold Springs. Bob wants everyone to come to the house immediately. He's arranging another posse to go after him," Barry explained quickly.

Saul was shirtless and covered in sweat under his bib overalls. He held a twenty-pound maul next to a pile of split wood. "So Tru's still alive?" he asked with a hint of a satisfied smile. He had feared for his friend's life when Bob Thacker hired Farrian Maddox to track down Truet.

"Yeah, he's alive. He's at Gold Springs, at least he was yesterday. Come on, Bob's waiting."

"I've got the wagon, so I'll be a bit getting there. But let him know I'm coming," Saul said and with one hand planted the maul into his stout cutting block.

The trip back to the ranch was a little over a half hour, but Saul was in no hurry and could make it last an extra fifteen minutes while he lazily rode the wagon behind the casually walking mules. He quite simply no longer cared. A man can fear something for only so long before he becomes accustomed to the circumstances and hardens his point of view. In Saul's case, he couldn't run and he couldn't hide, so he had to endure the daily humiliation of being made into the ranch's imbecile and the possibility of receiving a full dose of Brit's wrath with his constant verbal attacks. Now three weeks after AJ's death, Saul no longer feared for his life. He had no reason to live, anyway; Abby was locked away in her small cottage and Brit still held the key. He would never be able to rob Brit of that key and free the lady that he loved more than the very life he lived. He had put her life in jeopardy once; if he was ever caught around her again, he knew Brit would take her to Johnny Niehus'. She'd become the star attraction to every penniless man at the hideaway hotel. The thought was horrifying to Saul. Any temptation to go see Abby was halted by the consequences of being spotted by one of the cowboys or caught by Brit himself. Saul wasn't so concerned for himself. His life meant nothing without Abby, but Abby's life meant everything to him. Even when Brit went after Truet, Saul dared not leave his bunkhouse room to stop any risk to her. He loved her; perhaps someday she'd understand why he didn't make any effort to see her. It was better to be heartbroken and alone in Brit's home, than to be like the concubine in Judges 19 of the Bible, that was raped by multiple men throughout the night and died in the morning.

Every time Saul saw Mick Rodman, he was reminded of such an event. Mick was one of the men that contributed to Jenny Mae's miscarriage and eventual death. For Saul, it was especially hard to be cordial, let alone share the ranch with Mick. He could not stand the man and he could not forgive

Mick for what he'd done. Saul would've liked nothing more than to beat Mick until he was finished with the beating. Whether Mick lived or died, he wouldn't care.

Brit would care though. He'd already lost two good cowboys and a third, young Mike Moye, had his right arm amputated. Brit couldn't afford to lose another cowboy to Saul's wrath. Bob ordered Brit to keep Mick on the ranch and always in the company of another to protect him against a free and raging Truet Davis. Neither Bob nor Brit found any loyalty to Mick; especially after considering what happened to AJ. It was Bob's hope that keeping Mick on the ranch might just bring Truet to him. Mick was quite content with being the bait while the other cowboys were sent to disturb and torment the Christians that still attended the Sweethome Christian Church. It was interesting to Saul how Mick claimed he wanted to go raise hell and draw blood with the others, but Bob wouldn't let him. Mick swore to all the cowboys that he could pull the truth from the reverend if he only got the opportunity. However, Saul knew Mick had no desire to go to town. In fact, it was disgusting to hear his worthless banter and watch him nonchalantly smile and go about his day after the others left for town.

Saul, as well, was not allowed to go into town. The reasons were different, of course; he just wasn't allowed to speak to his Christian friends anymore. Bob forbade it. Saul was to be kept on the ranch. His life and Abby's were now very similar, as he had little more freedom than she did. The Thacker Ranch had become a prison camp, but to keep Abby safe, he'd do what he was told for as long as he was told. There were no exceptions.

As Saul drove his wagon to Bob Thacker's large home, he felt a wave of hopelessness flow through him when he saw Brit Thacker and a couple of other cowboys waiting on the front porch. As usual, there were no smiles on their faces.

Saul stepped down from his wagon as Bob Thacker stepped out onto the large colonial front porch patting the sweat on his forehead with a folded handkerchief. "You're late again. We're finished with our meeting. You might as well get back out there and keep cutting wood. It's becoming the only good purpose for keeping you here!" Bob stated coldly. He looked with animosity at a cowboy named Dave Redle, who was leaning against one of the porch columns. "Am I paying you to stand here? Get busy with something. Is this what you call managing the ranch, Brit? Hell, your worthless wife could do a better job than you! At least she'd keep her boys busy, huh?" Bob finished with a glare. He scowled at Brit and his cowboys silently while they left the porch and walked away.

Bob turned his attention to Saul who was still standing beside his wagon. "What?" he snapped.

"Barry said you wanted me."

"And I told you, we were done!"

"Barry said Farrian was killed by Truet."

Bob nodded. "Yes, he was. But now we know the whereabouts of Truet." He cupped his hands and yelled out after Brit, "But no one on this damn ranch can track him. Nobody on my ranch has got the guts to track him down. Maybe I should send your wife after him. She always seems to get her man! You're nothing, but a worthless coward! AJ would've had him shot, hung and gutted by now, if you'd been shot!" Bob finished and watched Brit continue to walk away, seething in anger.

Bob said to Saul with disgust, "I wired Branson for Matt Bannister to come handle hunting down Truet for us. I expect him in a week or so, maybe less. He'll find Truet and kill him for us. If not, then Truet will kill the marshal and then everyone under the western sun will want Truet dead." He eyed Saul carefully, and then added with a slight smile, "Truet's days are numbered."

"Matt Bannister, the U.S. Marshal?" Saul asked with a touch of alarm in his voice.

"The same. Truet better be enjoying today, because when Matt gets here, death's going to be knocking on Truet's door."

Matt Bannister had killed more men than any other U.S. Marshal in the nation. He had a brutal reputation and even to law-abiding citizens like Saul, the name of Matt Bannister was frightening. The idea of the famous marshal going after Truet sent a chill down Saul's spine. Nobody had outrun Matt Bannister yet, or so the stories read in both newspapers and dime novels. Saul was speechless. He just shrugged and climbed back up onto his wagon. "I'd better get back," he said quietly. He needed time to pray.

"Oh," Bob said suddenly, "remember AJ, and the boys were with you that morning. So if you lie to the marshal about it, then you know what'll happen to you and to Brit's whore of a wife."

27

Felisha Conway rubbed flour on her hands to continue kneading the ball of dough for the two loaves of bread she'd need for the night's dinner and the breakfast she was planning in the morning. She could, and occasionally did, buy bread and desserts from the local bakery, but usually she made her own to feed the guests that stayed in her boarding rooms. It only seemed right to feed her guests as well as she could. Besides, it was much cheaper to make her own bread than to buy it and, in her opinion; it was simply better-tasting bread.

Her attention went to the back door as Dillon came running excitedly into the kitchen from the back yard calling for her. He carried a milk bucket full of sloshing water that spilt over the top of it and onto the floor. His face was elated even though his pants were covered in mud and very wet. A sign that he listened at least, was that he had taken his muddy shoes off at the door, but he still tracked wet and dirty barefooted tracks into the kitchen.

"Mama, look what I caught," he called excitedly. Inside of the milk bucket sat a large bullfrog floating prostrate in the swishing water. "Can I keep him, Mama? His name's 'Bo,' it's short for bullfrog. I'll take care of him and he can live in this bucket beside my bed. It would be okay. Huh?" he asked quickly with a proud smile.

"No!" Felisha answered sternly. A slight smile parted her lips as she looked at her son's mud-speckled face. She asked in a more reasonable tone, "How would you keep him quiet at night when our guests are trying to sleep?"

"He's just singing, Mama. I'll teach him to sing quieter," Dillon said with innocent enthusiasm.

Felisha laughed lightly as she kneaded the dough. "No, Dillon. You may not keep Bo. Now take him outside and you know you're not supposed to get so muddy. Take the frog outside, come back in and clean up your mess, please," she finished patiently.

"Okay, Mother, but..." he paused as the bullfrog kicked unexpectedly and the force of it doing so startled Dillon. He dropped the bucket, spilling the contents out onto the kitchen floor.

"Dillon!" Felisha yelled, "Get that frog out of here. For heaven's sake!" she continued while watching Dillon reaching for Bo. The frog jumped across the kitchen floor away from him. Dillon ran through the water to catch the frog. He slipped and fell on the floor spreading the mud from his jeans. He scrambled to his hands and knees after the frog that jumped again and again towards the parlor.

"Don't worry, Mama, I'll catch him again," Dillon offered while he crawled quickly across the floor spreading the mud as he went. He dove after the frog that once again jumped out of his reach.

"I've told you before not to bring animals into this home, young man! This is exactly why, Dillon. I can't have frogs and snakes running loose in my house!" she yelled angrily while she followed Dillon into the front room. She stopped in horror when she saw a dark-haired and bearded stranger standing in her opened front door wearing a dark suit and holding a parker shotgun in his right hand, a Winchester rifle in his left, two saddle bags over his shoulders and a gun belt around his waist, the holster was tied to his leg. He was smiling with great humor on his handsome face from watching the muddy and wet boy chasing the frog through the parlor leaving a trail of mud behind him while being chased by his angry and flour-covered mother.

"Hi," Felisha said awkwardly. She was embarrassed by the situation and filthiness of her home. "Can I help you?" she asked mortified. She wiped her brow leaving a trace of flour.

The man laughed lightly. "My name's Matt Bannister. I'm looking for a Miss Felisha Conway."

"I'm Felisha."

"I got him!" Dillon shouted excitedly. "I told you I'd catch him. I'm getting good at this, huh, Ma?" he finished. He held the frog in his hands and neared his mother with a proud smile on his face.

"Get him outside, Dillon. Right now! And then get that mess cleaned up in there. I want it done now!" her voice was restrained due to her present company, but was still quite firm.

Dillon stood in front of Felisha, stared straight up at her, and asked sincerely, "Can I keep him though?"

"No. Now get moving. I want the kitchen floor clean, young man." Felisha's large brown eyes burned warningly at Dillon. "Now!"

"Fine, Mother. But I could've put him in a box so he couldn't jump out," Dillon offered as he exited out through the kitchen in a hurried and angry pace.

Felisha, greatly embarrassed, was already turning red. She turned to face the dark-haired stranger, who stood in the doorway obviously amused. "I apologize, Mister Bannister. My son has a fascination with bugs, lizards, snakes, and frogs. Really it's anything that he can catch."

"He sounds like a regular healthy boy. I used to do the same things," he finished awkwardly. He stared at Felisha a little longer than necessary before he added,

"I hope you're expecting me."

"Oh, yes, come inside. I'm sorry, Mister Bannister. I'm completely off-kilter at the moment. I'm terribly embarrassed. Please come in, I'll show you to your room. You must be tired after such a long way," she offered. She led Matt up a set of stairs and into a small cozy room with a comfortable single bed on a wrought iron frame covered with an attractive quilt. A small kerosene lamp set on a bedside table with a vase of freshly picked flowers. The room was furnished with a small desk, chair, and a large set of dresser drawers with a wash basin set on top of it. A clean folded towel lay neatly beside the wash basin. Paintings of various types of flowers decorated the walls.

Felisha stood nervously beside the bed with her arms at her side. "I hope it's suitable enough for you, Mister Bannister."

Matt leaned his rifles carefully against the wall beside the dresser and set his saddlebags down on the floor. "It's great. I would sure like it if you called me Matt, though. Lee and Regina send their regards and were deeply disturbed by the news about your friends. They must have been quite a couple to make such a friendship with Lee and Regina so quickly. Not just them, but you and the reverend's family as well. I've heard nothing except high praise about all of you. By the way, Regina wanted me to give you this letter when I arrived," he said and pulled a sealed envelope out of his inner coat pocket and gave it to her.

"Thank you," she said, taking the letter. "Jenny Mae was my best friend, Mister Bannister, Matt," she corrected herself. "It has not been easy since she died, not for any of us. She was a very dear friend. But the reason I asked you to come here is because the Thacker cowboys have been terrorizing many of our congregation about the whereabouts of Truet. Reverend Grace has been beat-up twice now. Rebecca, his wife, has been threatened, harassed and I'm quite afraid she'll be the next one to be raped, like Jenny Mae was. The Thacker cowboys have had free reign to do as they wanted to anyone who continues to come to our church. I'm afraid they'll eventually kill someone if nothing's done about it soon. Richard and Rebecca have gotten the worst of it, but he's the reverend, so of course, he would. We are Christians, that may not mean anything to you, but we should have the Constitutional right to be so without being harassed or beaten up for our faith." She paused and continued, "Truet's up north and they know that, but they are still busting into people's homes under the suspicion that Truet's there! Mister Bannister, we need your help. Maybe you can get the sheriff to protect us like he's supposed to, rather than sitting on his duff watching and even helping them out sometimes," she finished with concern in her voice. She waited to hear what he had to say now that she reiterated why she asked him to come to Sweethome.

"Miss Conway, I'm a Christian myself. So I understand what you're saying perfectly. I do need to tell you something though. I got a letter from Bob Thacker about Truet Davis killing his son AJ and a few others, including an unarmed lady. He asked me to track Truet down and bring him back here for justice to be served. In his words, 'either dead or alive.'"

Felisha's eyes opened and grew tense with anger. "Well, you can't do that! Truet is not the bad guy here. I'm the one that wrote to you as the U.S. Marshal to stop the Thackers from hurting my friends. Not for you to come here and hunt down my friend! Don't you dare go after him. Those men deserved to die for what they did to Jenny Mae!" she finished heatedly.

"Miss Conway..."

"Felisha," she said curtly.

Matt smiled and gently explained, "Felisha, I'm stepping into the middle of a hornet's nest I think, and quite simply when you want to kill the nest safely, you don't kick it. I'll listen to both sides of the story and do what's right. I've been doing this for a long time, Felisha. I only ask you to trust me, okay?"

28

The Reverend Richard Grace sat beside his lovely wife, Rebecca, on Felisha's front porch staring at the famous U.S. Marshal, Matt Bannister, with a combination of surprise and a touch of trepidation. The well-known marshal had killed close to thirty men in his long and bloody career. The stories Richard had read about this man and the rumors he'd heard about him over the years had fed a pre-existent expectation of what the marshal might be like. He was expecting a mean-spirited, rough and dangerous older man with little education and a foul mouth whose only good quality was wearing a badge.

Richard was surprised by the well-dressed, well-groomed and soft-spoken man of thirty-four or five, who seemed to be quite perceptive and inquisitive about the town of Sweethome and the people who lived in it. Occasionally, he wrote down a name or side note on a piece of paper that he'd pull out of his shirt pocket. Matt Bannister was nothing like Richard's pre-conceived notions. He was, in fact, everything that he wasn't expecting.

Matt was a clean-cut man, with long dark hair that he kept in a ponytail and a well-groomed beard. He had a friendly face, but with a certain toughness that was undeniable and commanded authority. He spoke with a gentle voice and was respectful of the others in his company. His brown eyes weren't cold and deadly like Richard had expected, but rather, they were bright, inviting and warm. Most of all, Richard was surprised to learn that the famous U.S. Marshal was a Christian. It just didn't seem possible that this man in front of him was the same Matt Bannister that he'd heard so much about.

Rebecca Grace explained to Matt, "In a moment of bad judgment, I told Bob that AJ was in Hell where he belonged. That was when they began to attack us. It started that day; his cowboys began ransacking the homes of our congregation searching for Truet; but the truth is, they were there to hurt us. They burst in to our home and three of them beat up my

husband in front of my children," Rebecca said and choked on her emotions as large tears built up in her eyes. "Marshal, my children should never have to see that kind of thing."

Richard reached over and put an arm around his wife, comforting her. "They broke out the church's windows and our windows. They broke Jim Walker's arm and beat his teenage boy senseless for trying to help his daddy. They've frightened every lady in our congregation so much that none of them will go out alone anymore. We have families that have quit coming to church because of Bob's men. Everyone's afraid of what might happen next." Richard emphasized, "They even went so far as to put a gun to Neil and Doris Carter's little five-year-old son's head and threatened to kill him, if they didn't tell them where Truet was. Nobody knows where Truet is, but they don't care; they're trying to run us all out of town. That's what they're trying to do!"

"And the sheriff?" Matt asked.

Richard scoffed. "Well, he's either standing back watching or in his office telling jokes. He won't do anything, except for what Bob tells him to do."

Felisha spoke, "Two of his deputies have quit over this, Henry Kyle, who's also a member of our church and Paul Reed. You should talk to them two, if you want to hear the truth within our sheriff's office. Things have gotten bad. That's why I wrote to you before anyone got killed."

Matt nodded slowly and asked, "What about you? Your house seems to be in pretty good shape."

Felisha sighed guiltily. "My late husband and Bob were business partners. Bob must've told his men to leave me alone. I can walk right by them and they don't say a word, but I have no other explanation, except that. I've never stopped going to church," she finished with a shrug.

"Maybe he's sweet on you," Matt offered. "Is he?"

Felisha's expression changed to annoyance. "If he is, I have given him no reason to be. I have never liked Bob or his two sons."

"I wasn't implying that you did, it just might explain why you weren't included," Matt explained simply.

Richard changed the subject. "Now that you're here, things might settle down a bit. Maybe even go back to normal," he said, sounding hopeful.

Matt shook his head. "I wouldn't count on it. I can bring some peace and put the responsibility of all of this onto your sheriff for allowing it to happen. But, in my experience when I leave, it will start back up, unless there's some changes in key positions. It sounds like your sheriff needs to be removed from office, to me."

"Undoubtedly," Richard agreed. He paused momentarily, as young Dillon came running around the house, up onto the porch and into the house in a hurry. Richard continued, "But I don't see how. Bob and Jeb, Martin's father, think they own this town. They appointed Martin to that position and there's no such thing as a fair and impartial election for that position. Not here, this is Sweethome - Bob and Jeb's town," he finished sarcastically.

Matt smiled slightly and was about to speak when Dillon came out of the house carrying a coffee cup of water in his hands.

"Where are you going with that, young man?" Felisha asked, in her motherly tone.

Dillon stopped and looked at his mother. "I have to teach my caterpillar how to swim," he answered sincerely.

Matt laughed, as did Richard and Rebecca.

Dillon smiled, pleased to be the source of the laughter. He asked, "What?"

Felisha said with a smile, "Just bring the cup back, please." She watched as Dillon left the porch and ran back to the side of the house. "I swear that boy finds the oddest things to do," she said and then explained to Richard and Rebecca what had happened earlier in the day with "Bo," the bullfrog. Through the laugher that followed and Matt's added commentary of the events he witnessed upon arriving, the mood had lightened. Felisha had just refilled their glasses of iced tea and returned to her seat when her face grew somber and asked, "Have you met Bob Thacker yet, Matt?"

"No, not yet," he replied, before taking a drink of the tea.

"You're about to. Here he comes," Felisha said.

A one-horse buggy came towards the house. Bob Thacker drove his buggy, dressed in a clean brown suit and tie. His black Stetson shadowed his aged round face from the late afternoon sun. Beside him, Brit Thacker sat looking as unpleasant as ever. He was dressed in dingy jeans and dirt-stained gray shirt. His well-worn, sweat-stained brown Stetson covered his unkempt hair. His arms were on his lap and he glared at the group on the porch as they neared.

"Evening," Bob stated, sounding friendly with a big smile, while stopping the buggy. "Felisha, you look as fresh as ever this evening. I don't know what would be better, a glass of your tea on a summer's evening or the Pacific breeze on a hot day," he paused, to wait for a reply.

"Why, thank you, Bob," she said uncomfortably. His compliment was unexpected and unusual.

"Why Reverend, it looks like your Misses caught you at the saloon again," Bob laughed. He referred to the two fading blackened eyes on Richards's face. Without waiting for any kind of reply he continued, "So who's that with you? Are you the marshal?"

"I am," Matt said, as he stood. He removed the leather thong hooked over the hammer of his revolver so smoothly that it was nearly unnoticeable to anyone, except Felisha. Matt stepped down the steps and walked over to the buggy reading the cold eyes of both men easily. "I'm Matt Bannister," he announced.

"Well, Matt, I'm the one that wired for you to come. I'm Bob Thacker," Bob said, reaching his hand across Brit to shake Matt's. "This is my son, Brit," Bob introduced Brit with a nod.

Brit's hands remained on his lap. "My hands are clean," Brit said disdainfully.

Matt smiled slightly while looking into Brit's eyes and then looked back at Bob. "Nice to meet you, Bob. I had plans of finding your place tomorrow."

"Tomorrow?" Bob questioned. "Hell, grab your gear and hop aboard. I have a room all made up for you out at the ranch. Fact is, I heard you were in town and came all the way here to save you from the vultures in town that'll rob you blind for a night's rent. Go ahead, grab your belongings and we'll take you to the ranch. We got a lot to talk about, you know."

Matt nodded. "I understand. But I already paid for a room for the night."

"No, I insist," Bob stressed. "I wired for you to come to Sweethome, and I'll host you while you're here. Hell, your brother Lee is a friend of mine. I'll treat you right. Go get your gear and let's go. We'll talk tonight and you can leave in the morning. That murderer, Truet, is getting further away by the day."

"Mister Thacker, I appreciate the offer, but I already paid."

"Get your money back!" He leaned closer and said, "If it's liquor and a whore you want, you're at the wrong place. Felisha will kick you out to the street if you come in smelling of liquor or a whore's perfume," he laughed. "Come on home with me and I'll fix you up with the finest of both."

"Mister Thacker, I've already told you I've purchased a room for the night. I won't change my mind," Matt said with finality in his voice. "It's nice to meet you, and I'll talk with you tomorrow."

"You don't understand, Marshal," Bob stressed, his face

turning red and his breathing growing heavier while his eyes grew angry. "I wired for you to come here and hunt down the man that killed my son and you're sitting on the porch drinking tea with Truet's best friends! They're filling your head with lies about my son and lies about me too, probably. Have they told you how great Truet is and his whore of a wife, Jenny Mae? I could give you a list an arms-length long of men that I know of that had been with her. You could ask any one of them and they'll tell you the same. My boy didn't touch that girl. He was with Saul that whole morning. Now my son's dead and Truet's out there getting away with murder, while you sit here drinking tea with his friends! Now I'm demanding you come home with me, Marshal!" He clenched his jaw together tightly and his eyes burned into Matt.

Matt was about to answer when young Dillon came to his side carrying his cup of water in his hand. "Mister Bannister? Do you want to see my caterpillar drowned?" he asked with a smile, his big brown eyes looking up at Matt with boyish excitement.

It was Brit's curdling snarl that answered for Matt. "Get away from here, you little bastard, before I pinch your head off!"

Instantaneously, Dillon's eyes raced to Brit and then back to Matt's before he quickly ran back to the porch in tears to his mother. Matt had seen the surprise, fear, and the hurt that flashed through in the young boy's eyes. It was a repugnant action by a callous man and it immediately angered Matt. He looked at Brit with a hard, indignant glare.

Brit asked mockingly, "Is there a federal law against teaching a little bastard some manners?"

"No, but I wish there was," Matt answered sharply. His tone made it obvious that he had an immediate dislike for

Brit. "It doesn't take much of a man to scare a child, or much character to do so!"

"Hey, boys," Bob interrupted. "Brit, apologize to the boy and shake the marshal's hand. There's no reason to start out on bad terms. Shake his hand!" Bob ordered, as he nudged Brit's shoulder with his own. "We're all on the same side here."

Brit glared at Matt, gritting his teeth into a sneer and extended his hand out to shake.

Matt shook his head, refusing to shake hands, and stepped back. "I'll find you tomorrow when it's time to talk. Don't come knocking on the door for me, Bob. I'll see you tomorrow." He stepped back another step, not taking his eyes off of Brit. When Bob started his buggy down the road, Matt turned and walked up the steps to the porch. He watched the buggy roll out of sight.

Richard Grace said, "See? They're not pleasant people. He's got a temper and now you might understand."

Matt looked down at Dillon, who was hiding his tears in his mother's side while she held him close. "I told Felisha earlier and I'll say it again," he said to Richard and Rebecca, "When you want to get rid of a hornet's nest you want to use some tact, some planning to avoid getting stung. But sometimes, you just need to grab your shotgun and blow it to hell," Matt said irritably. "Forgive me; I shouldn't have said it that way. But I have absolutely no patience for any man treating a child like that. Now, do any of you know anything about Brit's wife?"

"Of course. Abby's her name. Why? How do you know about her?" Felisha questioned and explained what she knew of her parents being run out of town after she married Brit. It was a scandal at the time, but now it had died down after three years of no sight or sound of her.

Richard Grace added, "She's been having a love affair with Saul."

"What?" Both of the ladies exclaimed.

"Yeah, one night he told Truet and me. He made us swear not to tell anyone. So I haven't."

"Tell me everything he said," Matt stated with interest. He shifted in his seat and took a drink of his tea.

29

"Why?" Bob sounded outraged. He stood in his long gaming room filled with elk, deer and bear trophies mounted on the walls and a billiard table in the center of the room. He leaned against the table with a drink in his hand. "I've already told you everything! Why in the hell would you want to talk to Saul? He can't tell you anything that I already haven't."

"That's probably very true," Matt said in an agreeing tone. "But he's AJ's alibi, which means I need to talk to him. In private," he added pointedly.

"Why Saul? What have those liars in town told you? Marshal, what's going on here? I asked you to come to find the man that killed my son, not to listen to the gossip in town."

Matt frowned impatiently. "Bob, if Saul tells me AJ was with him, then I'll leave first thing in the morning to track down Truet. I've been doing this for a long time, Bob. One thing I know is there's always another side to the story. The fact is that AJ, two other men, and one woman are dead, and one teenage boy is missing an arm because of Truet.

Nobody can deny that. From what Lee has told me about you, everything they said last night sounds a bit out of your character. Now, if I can talk to Saul and get on my way."

"Fine," Bob conceded. He spoke to Brit, who was sitting in a chair, "Go bring Saul here. Tell him the marshal wants to talk to him." He finished in a threatening tone to make his point clear to Brit. It wasn't unnoticed by Matt.

MATT WALKED CASUALLY beside Saul as they walked away from the prying ears and eyes of the ranch house. They walked towards town on the dusty road surrounded by tall, dry grass. Matt adjusted his brown Stetson hat against the sun with a skeptical smirk on his face. He remained silent to allow Saul to keep talking.

Even when Saul paused, Matt remained silent, which under the circumstances proved too much for Saul to bear, so he'd reinforce his story, each time adding a new layer of mixed lies.

Lee had told Matt about the fight in Sweethome between an unknown giant named Goliath, and the renowned Jacques Christy. Lee had bet on Jacques, but ended up stunned and greatly impressed by Goliath. Lee had stated that he felt Goliath would be the world champion someday. This giant of a man with arms the size of Matt's legs, the very giant of a man that killed a legend in a boxing ring with his own hands, was now scared to death and stuttering his words while he tried to find some to keep himself speaking. The thought of it, and watching Saul nervously sweat through his lies, caused Matt to smile.

"Yep," Saul continued, as he walked along with Matt. As usual, Saul was in his bib overalls and had on a dirty sweat-drenched cotton, long-sleeved shirt. He wore a well-worn straw hat. "Jenny Mae had lost a lot of blood by the time she mentioned AJ and the boys. I think she was, what do you call it, imagining it or seeing things? I told Tru, AJ and the boys couldn't have done it since they were here on the ranch with me. But he killed them anyway; that's all I know." Saul glanced quickly at Matt and then quickly away. He slowed his pace hoping to turn around and get back to the house. Matt kept walking forward at the same casual pace forcing Saul to speed up to catch up with him.

Saul continued to speak nervously, "Tru should've thought about what he was doing, I guess. I wish he'd listened to me. AJ was a good man. He never would've hurt Jenny Mae or anyone else."

"Saul," Matt finally spoke once they were out of sight of the house. He broke off a tall dry piece of grass along-side the road and put its broken end between his teeth to suck on. "You refer to Truet as Tru. Were you friends?"

"Yeah, good friends," Saul answered honestly.

"Then why are you lying? Let me tell you something, you are a terrible liar. That's a good thing though; it means you're not accustomed to it. Which by the way," Matt turned to watch Saul, "I like. Do you know who I am, Saul?" he asked seriously with no friendliness showing in his eyes.

"Yeah," he answered with a trembling voice.

"Then you know why Bob wants me here. He wants me to go track down Truet and bring him back here as a prisoner to be hung or to kill him myself. If you know anything about me, you know I've done plenty of both. Rest assured, I will find him, Saul. Now, I'll ask you one more time, and one time only. Was AJ with you that morning? Yes, or no!" Matt demanded forcefully. His eyes had grown intensely dangerous.

Saul swallowed and his eyes grew thick with water. "No,"

he whispered and appeared as though he was ready to crumble down into an emotional breakdown. His bottom lip quivered uncontrollably.

"Let's walk," Matt said and turned to keep walking away from the house. "Felisha Conway wrote me a letter; Bob wired me too, but it was Felisha's letter that brought me here. You see, you met my brother Lee and his wife Regina before your fight. They took an immediate liking to Felisha, and especially to Truet and Jenny Mae. They also mentioned in other terms Bob Thacker and his two sons AJ and Brit. The news of what happened didn't surprise either one of them when they heard it. Jenny Mae had wired Regina the day before her death to say they were selling out and moving to Branson." Matt paused and then continued, "It's a pretty clear picture of what happened, isn't it? I just wonder why you'd be so willing to encourage me to believe that Truet was a murderer and allow me to go after him and possibly even kill him. He was a friend of yours, I understand. I was told all of you were a close group of friends. What happened? What are you so afraid of, Saul?"

"Tru is my best friend. So was Jenny Mae," Saul said suddenly. His voice was full of emotion as he continued, "I told them to leave! AJ had every intention of doing what he did to Jenny Mae and to kill Truet. I didn't want anything to happen to them, Marshal. They were my friends." Saul's voice broke, and the tears slipped heavily down his face. "I loved them both, but I didn't have a choice. I had to lie! You don't understand, Marshal. I can't leave this place. I can't go to town or anywhere else unless Bob says so. I had no choice! I had to lie, and you can't tell them that I told you the truth, or..." he paused. Fear gripped him tightly; panic became the only clear expression on his face. "You can't tell Bob that I told you AJ wasn't with me," he begged.

Matt frowned. "Why not?"

"Because you can't! My life's on the line after you leave."

"Come with me then. They can't hurt you if you leave with me."

"I'm not leaving! There's no way, but you can't tell Bob either, Marshal, please!" Saul was becoming desperate. He appeared to be traumatically afraid for his life. Matt had just given Saul an opportunity to escape the ranch, and he still refused to leave even under the protection of a U.S. Marshal.

"Does this have to do with Abby?" Matt asked and watched Saul's face closely. It revealed his surprise.

"You know about Abby?" he asked astonished.

"The good reverend told me. So is Abby alive?"

"Of course! But if you tell Bob about me telling the truth, she won't be."

"Do you love her, Saul?" Matt stopped in the middle of the road to receive Saul's answer.

Saul looked Matt in the eyes and said with certainty in his voice, "With every ounce of who I am."

Matt nodded. He looked Saul in the eyes and spoke in a serious manner, "Then use that love you have for her to inspire you to become a better liar. This might get a little worse before it gets better, and if you want to live through it, you better learn to lie well. Let's get you back and get our story straight on the way. But first, why don't you tell me everything you know about her and Brit."

As expected, Bob, Brit and a couple of the other cowboys had been standing on the front porch watching the two men walking. They remained curious, anxious, and quiet, as Matt and Saul approached.

Matt removed his hat with his left hand and wiped his forehead with his forearm.

"Well, Bob, you'll be pleased to know that I'll be leaving first thing in the morning to track Truet Davis."

A great relief came across Bob's face. He smiled. "I figured you would be. If you need any men, I'll send some with you. I want that man dead!"

Matt replaced his hat. "You're going to get that one way or the other. Now I have the unfortunate task of telling Felisha and the good reverend that I'm going after Truet. I don't think they'll take that well," he said looking at Bob.

Bob scoffed light-heartedly. "Well, if she kicks you out, I have an extra room. You should've just came home with me yesterday when I told you to. You have no business talking to them anyway. This isn't any of their affair. I'm the one that wired you to come." Bob paused, as he changed the subject. "So are you interested in taking some of my boys? I've got some good hands that can follow orders and shoot straight."

Matt shook his head. "No. I ride alone, Bob. I always have and prefer to keep it that way."

"Are you sure?"

"I'm sure," Matt said simply. He glanced at Saul, who was standing near him uneasily. "You can however, let my brother Lee and me know when his next fight is." He nodded to Saul. "Lee told me you had a future champion on your hands. Lee said he was big, but I never imagined how big. You've got a good man there, Bob. It's not easy to be honest when a quick lie could have saved your best friend's life. Men of integrity like that are rare. Take care of him and I have no doubt he'll win that title for you," Matt finished and stepped up onto his horse.

Bob grinned. "I have no doubt that the Killer Goliath will be the next champion. He's unbeatable, and if you do beat him, just like Jacques Christy found out, you'll be killed doing it," Bob proudly announced.

"Well, I enjoy a good fight. Let me know," Matt said half-heartedly.

Brit scoffed. "He ain't nothing. I've knocked him around like a child before and probably will again. Don't be fooled by his size, he ain't nothing. My wife puts up a better fight!"

Matt eyed Brit momentarily with no emotion on his face and then smiled slightly. "You know, Bob, that may not be a bad idea. I'd pay to see it."

"I'm afraid my son feels bigger than his britches sometimes," Bob said irritably.

Matt smiled, as Brit grit his teeth with humiliation. "One more thing," Matt added, "Now that we know the whereabouts of Truet, how about you have your boys lay off the church membership. I'd like to go back to Felisha's with some good news to tell them to soften the blow about going after Truet. I'd appreciate it."

Bob smiled a big joyful smile. "I'll spread the word. And my word's law here, Marshal. Hell, maybe I'll even go to church this Sunday," he laughed. "Thank you, Marshal."

"I'm just doing my job," Matt said and rode away.

30

"Gosh," Jeannie Bartholomew said, disappointed by the news that the Marshal Matt Bannister wasn't presently at Felisha's home. She stood on the front porch holding a cherry pie and a wired telegram that came from Branson. "I was hoping to give my condolences myself. I'm glad you're here though, Reverend Grace. He'll need some spiritual guidance, I'm sure. Do you know when he'll be back, Felisha? I feel it's my duty as the postmistress to deliver the wire myself."

"I have no idea," Felisha answered her, growing irritable by Jeannie's persistence. Jeannie Bartholomew could be a caring and sweet lady when she wanted to, but it always came with a price, namely, the community knowing the issue at hand before sundown.

"Heavens," Jeannie uttered, overly exaggerating her predicament. It was obvious that she wanted to be invited to sit down with the others on the porch and wait, but the invitation wasn't offered. "What to do? I went and baked this cherry pie and expected to deliver my condolences and return home before long. I know Tom is tending the store for another hour before he comes home for dinner, but I sure hate to go home, and then after dinner, come back here," she debated thoughtfully.

"You could just leave them and when he comes back, I'll tell him you baked the pie for him and wish him your condolences," Felisha offered. She stood by the front door willing to take the pie into the home, while Richard and Rebecca Grace waited patiently for her to rejoin them on the porch.

"No, that just won't do. It's my duty to hand-deliver this to him," Jeannie laughed lightly to herself. "What kind of a postmistress would I be if I let you do my duty for me? No, I must hand-deliver it myself."

Rebecca Grace said simply, "I thought Tom was the postmaster."

A flash of anger flickered across Jeannie's face momentarily and then it was covered over with a forced smile and a quick laugh. "Oh, Tom is my husband, Rebecca. It's his name on the paper, but it's my responsibility. Even you should know that the government gives such professions to men over ladies."

Felisha said, "Well, I don't know when to expect him. So I really couldn't tell you what to do."

Jeannie sighed dramatically. "Well, I suppose I could go back to the store and keep watching out for him. Do you think you could send Dillon to fetch me when he arrives?"

"Of course," Felisha agreed.

"Actually," Richard Grace said. "There he is."

"Oh, really!" Jeannie stated and turned toward the street to see Matt drive up to Felisha's house in a black buggy being pulled by one horse. Matt set the brake, stepped down and walked up to the porch steps where he paused. Felisha was standing by the door talking to an older reddish-golden-haired lady in her mid-to-late forties who held a pie. Richard and Rebecca stood up from their chairs and stepped nearer to the other two ladies. They all watched him somberly from the front porch.

Richard said, "Matt, this is Jeannie, she's the postmistress."

"Hello, Marshal," Jeannie said before Richard could finish his introduction. "I wish we could meet under different circumstances. I have an emergency wire for you from your brother," she said and handed the paper to Matt.

Matt frowned, opened the folded paper and read it. His expression changed quickly from concern to shock, and then a look of sadness revealed itself in his face as he stared at the paper.

Jeannie held out the cherry pie with both hands and said, "I brought this cherry pie as a token of my condolences to you. Like I said, I wish we could've met under better circumstances, Marshal."

Matt made eye contact with Felisha and said, "My brother-in-law is dead. He apparently got drunk with some of his friends in Branson and went for a midnight swim in the river and drowned." His eyes momentarily filled with water as they stared into Felisha's helplessly.

"I'm sorry," she said sensitively.

Matt took his eyes off of her and nodded to Jeannie. "Well, thank you, Ma'am, for the pie. That's very kind of you," he said to Jeannie as he took the pie.

"Why, you're welcome, it's the least I could do. If you'd like, you could come over to my house for dinner and conversation. I just live a couple of blocks away and I'm a great listener if you need someone to talk to. I know how hard it is to lose a family member," Jeannie said as she put a comforting hand onto his shoulder. "I am so sorry for your loss, Marshal. If there's anything I can do?"

"Thank you. Actually, what you could do is return a wire back to my brother and tell him to send my love to my sister. And let him know I'll be awhile before coming home."

"Of course," she put a hand on his shoulder again. "Were you close to him?"

Matt shook his head. "Not really. I just met him this past Christmas," he said quickly and looked at Felisha again. "Felisha, I was hoping you and Dillon might take a buggy ride with me out to Truet's place. I know it's a sudden decision to make without asking first. But I rented the buggy just in case."

"Well, I don't..." she stammered and stopped, as Richard quickly interrupted, "Of course she'll go, Matt. And we'll even watch Dillon for you."

Rebecca shot a strange expression towards Richard, but said nothing.

"I have to begin dinner," Felisha sounded reluctant.

"I'll make dinner for you," Rebecca said volunteering after being nudged by her husband and then added with a shrug. "I'll just feed Dillon with my family tonight."

"No, I couldn't," Felisha meekly argued, her face turning red.

"Trust me," Richard was insistent. "It's no trouble at all."

Felisha looked from Richard to Matt, who stood at the bottom of the steps holding the pie, waiting for her with a silent pleading in his eyes.

"Okay," she agreed. "Let me grab a shawl and we'll go."

A subtle awkward silence fell over the porch once Felisha walked inside. Rebecca appeared to be slightly agitated at her husband and Jeannie seemed to be pleasantly surprised to notice it. She stood on the porch with her mouth slightly agape watching the Reverend and his wife. Matt, noticing, asked Jeannie, "Are you part of the church congregation here, Jeannie?"

"Of course! I am one of the founding members as a matter of fact. My husband and I were on the committee to bring a church to Sweethome and were vital contributors to the building fund as well. So yes, I would say I was a large part of our church, Marshal. Of course, it has changed substantially since its wonderful beginning. But it's still the only church in town; if it weren't for me campaigning so hard to bring a church to Sweethome then we probably wouldn't even have one. It's just too bad Reverend Schrader retired. Oh, not to say Reverend Grace doesn't do a fantastic job though," she finished with a large smile, though her sincerity sounded questionable.

"We've missed you the past few weeks, Jeannie," Rebecca casually mentioned.

"Ah! I know it," she said dramatically. Her face reddened a touch as she cast a quick glance of irritation at Rebecca. "Between Tom and me not feeling well and the store's business, well, we've just not made it to church recently," she said uneasily and then changed the subject back to Matt. "So, Marshal, I understand Bob wanted you to stay at his place yesterday?"

WHEN MATT and Felisha rode away on the buggy, Rebecca turned to her husband and asked, "What's this all about? How can you explain yourself this time?"

Richard laughed lightly. "Sweetheart, when a man takes a liking to a lady and includes her son in his relationship with her, well, dear, that's the man you don't let slip away.

Many men would say there's no room for Dillon on that buggy. Matt included him," he finished pointedly.

Jeannie asked frankly, "What are you saying, Reverend?"

Rebecca asked him, "You think Matt's attracted to Felisha?"

"I don't think it, ladies, I know he is. I know that look in his eyes a mile away."

"Well!" Jeannie said, "I haven't noticed her being interested in him, which is only proper, given his reputation. A Christian woman has no business being courted by a godless man."

"That's true enough, Jeannie, I couldn't agree more with you on that. But Matt's a Christian," Richard said with a smile.

31

"The blood stain on the floor is where we found her. She was beaten and bleeding." Felisha covered her mouth with her hands as her eyes filled up with tears that slid down her cheek. "I'm sorry," she said and stepped outside to be alone.

Matt watched her step out onto the porch and sit heavily onto a porch swing. She buried her face in her hands and wept.

The home of Truet and Jenny Mae Davis was a well-kept home that was filled with furnishings and had the obvious touch of a God-filled woman. Framed embroidery stitched Bible verses proclaiming their faith in God hung on the walls. One embroidered plaque in particular showed a finely stitched house with the words that read, *"Choose this day whom you shall serve, as for me and my house we will serve the Lord."* Under that plaque were two stuffed chairs separated by a table with two Bibles on it. It was obvious that one Bible belonged to Jenny Mae and the other to Truet. Matt picked up the Bible closest to what would've been Jenny Mae's chair. He could tell by the pink and yellow square-patterned crocheted blanket set neatly across the back of the chair. Her loving parents inscribed her Bible on Christmas 1870. Flipping through the pages, he saw many underlined versus throughout the old and new testaments. He laid it down and picked up Truet's. Inside the front cover were the words.

To my husband,

'I am still confident of this: I will see the goodness of the Lord in the land of the living. Wait for the Lord; be strong and take heart and wait for the Lord!' Psalm 27:13-14

Never lose heart, my love, and never lose your faith in our Lord. No matter how hard or for how long. Be strong, take heart, and wait for the Lord.

I love you Tru, Truly I do.

Your loving wife,

Jenny Mae Davis

Matt closed the Bible and held onto it as he walked around the clean and orderly home. He nearly expected to run into Jenny Mae and Truet, as it was left exactly the way it was when they last left it, including Jenny Mae's torn dress that laid on the table wadded up as if someone had been holding it tightly and laid it down.

In the bedroom, the bed was neatly made and the gun rack was empty. All of the small personal items that were left out on the big dresser were untouched and visible to his eye. A picture of Truet in his cavalry uniform was set on the dresser. He pulled a wanted poster for Truet out of his pants pocket that Bob had given him and looked at it closely, studying it and comparing the picture to the hand-drawn likeness on the wanted poster. He looked for scars or any other obvious features that couldn't be hidden or altered. The man he was searching for appeared to be a powerful man with a strong-featured face that was very handsome by all accounts that he'd heard. He looked for a picture of Jenny Mae, but there wasn't one to be found. Truet must have taken them with him.

After a few minutes of investigating the bedroom, he replaced his folded wanted poster and stepped out into the small hallway which went to the kicked-in back door; he then walked into the kitchen once again.

"What are you looking for?" Felisha asked. She sniffled and wiped her eyes as she came back inside.

"You can tell a lot about the character of a person, man or woman, by their home. If I know Truet's character, I'll be able to track him easier."

"Track him?" Felisha asked stunned. Indignation entered her face, especially around her large brown eyes. "You're not going after him, are you? You said you just wanted to see the house for evidence; there's Jenny Mae's blood on the floor! What more do you need? Saul's lying and you know it. If you kill Truet, you'll be killing an innocent man and I will never forgive you! And if you bring him back here, Bob will kill him and you'll still be to blame!" Felisha's eye's glared fiercely at Matt.

"I'm not going after him to arrest him, Felisha," Matt explained gently. "I'm going to find him and bring him back to Boise City where he can be tried by a fair and impartial jury to be freed from these charges. So that he can walk out of there a free man. If I don't, he will be killed sooner or later. He'll either be shot or hung. It's just the way it goes. No one can run and hide for very long. They all get caught eventually. Trust me, Bob's money and wanted posters are drawing a lot of attention, and I'm not the only good tracker out there. The sooner I leave, the safer he'll be." Matt added softly, "I don't want to hurt your friend; I want to help him."

"How do I know you're not wanting Bob's money? Five hundred dollars is a lot of money. He's bought everyone else, why not you?"

Matt frowned and then handed Truet's Bible to her. "Read the front cover." As she read the front cover, her eyes filled with tears. Matt spoke softly, "He did nothing I wouldn't have done myself if Jenny Mae was my wife and the law was paid to look the other way. I've made my fair share of mistakes, Felisha, but I would not and could not hunt an innocent man down for money. The money goes away eventually, the guilt does not." She looked up at him filled with emotion from the words Jenny Mae had penned to her husband. Her eyes were pools of deep water that somehow remained suspended in place. He continued, "That man's life was shattered when he lost his wife. I'm going to find him and give his life back to him. If there's air in his lungs and Jesus on his side, there's still hope of a life worth living. I discovered that; Lord willing so will he."

"And Bob and Saul? Saul's story will hold up, even in Boise City."

"Saul told me the truth. For now, he's sticking to his story to keep Bob happy. Bob thinks I'm going after Truet to bring him back here. I'm not. It's better if you keep it quiet, because the fewer people who know about Saul, the safer he'll be. While I'm gone he's my concern here."

"Saul betrayed Jenny Mae and Truet. He's betrayed all of us!" Felisha spit out angrily.

"He had no choice. When this is all done and over with, you'll understand. Until then just remember he's a good man, Felisha. He has his reasons."

She flailed her hands and asked, "Why all the secrecy?

Why not just go out there and say AJ was guilty and stop his man hunt for Truet and bring him home?"

"Because quite simply, Bob's a powerful man with paid men, and many acres. He could shoot me in the back and bury me just about anywhere and no one would be able to prove he did anything wrong. He could do the same to Saul and Truet, or you. So be careful who you talk to, Felisha. I mean it."

Felisha seemed to understand and momentarily let his words sink in. Her demeanor quieted, and she said sincerely, "You too, Matt. That Jeannie you met is the biggest gossip in town. The entire town probably already knows about your brother-in-law and about our buggy ride."

"I suppose the town can know about either one of those," he said with a shrug.

"So you don't know your brother-in-law too well? Because you appeared very sad to me," Felisha asked sincerely.

"Oh, I am. He was a..." he paused and continued slowly, "he was a nice man. He had his faults, but he loved my sister and my nephew and nieces. My heart is broken for them. He was a good man," Matt said and then walked towards the front door.

Felisha followed. "I can relate to your sister. My husband fell off of our roof and died. It was a very difficult time. I won't say you ever get over it, but it was made easier by already having a book-accounting business and a big enough house to start the boarding. What did your brother-in-law do? Can your sister start a boarding house or something to keep finances coming in?"

Matt stepped out onto the front porch and leaned against the rail. "She's the co-owner of my aunt and uncle's ranch in Willow Falls. Financially, she'll be fine. In fact, her husband worked on the ranch for her. I don't think he really liked it though. He'd come to Branson once or twice a month for a couple of days and hang around one of the saloons to drink and gamble. I never heard of him frequenting a prostitute. I can say that for him. Apparently, on one of those days he and his pals decided to go swimming." He shook his head and added, "Tragic."

"I'm sorry, Matt," she said, taking a seat on the porch swing. "How many children do they have?"

Matt took a deep breath. "Three; a boy and two young girls." After a short pause he continued, "My mother died giving birth to my sister when I was seven. My father couldn't handle six kids, so he dropped us all off at my aunt and uncle's ranch and they raised us. I never saw my father much after that. He gave up the responsibility of being a husband and father for the drink of a bottle. It's not a fair trade, in my opinion. Anyway, my aunt and uncle loved us and raised us like their own. We're blessed with that." He paused and then continued, "Felisha, I don't have any children to raise of my own, but I love children and despise any man that doesn't. I've seen all kinds of unimaginable things in my years as a marshal. I've hunted down and arrested or killed some terribly wicked men over the years, but some of those men I've killed were much kinder to their children than some of the law-abiding citizens that I've seen, are to theirs. It just breaks my heart that my nephew and nieces are going through this. Kyle may have been a little lazy here and there, but he treated his wife and children the way a man should. He loved them." His said with a sad expression.

"I understand that," Felisha said and explained, "Dillon's growing up without his father. It is difficult to be a single woman raising a boy alone. It's not easy being a single parent and the only source of income. I was blessed to already have what I do have. Otherwise, I don't know what I would've done. But I can't afford to get sick or take a day off. This," she motioned to the front porch of her old friend's home, "is a luxury to be here while someone else makes dinner for my son." She laughed lightly.

Matt smiled and gazed at her affectionately. "You have a nice laugh, Felisha. Dillon's a good boy; you're doing a good job raising him. He's definitely a boy," he stated with a small smile.

"Thank you. I try, and pray," she laughed lightly. "He's always intrigued with catching bugs, frogs and, you know, anything else that moves. I'm afraid he'll reach down and catch a rattlesnake one of these days and get bit."

Matt laughed. "My aunt would tell you to enjoy it while you can, because little boys grow up and all of that boyish adventure becomes practical responsibility. She raised five boys."

"Poor woman," Felisha joked.

"Ha, my uncle Charlie helped. So what about you, any brothers or sisters?"

"I have a brother in Boise City and another one in Portland."

"Are you a bit of a tomboy?" Matt asked.

"Let's just say I'm not afraid of snakes," she answered with a smile as she stared at Matt.

He laughed.

32

The sun was still low on the eastern horizon as Matt stood beside his horse, Betty, at the hitching post in front of Felisha's home. Matt had Betty packed with his rifles, saddlebags of supplies and bedroll. He looked tired and somewhat awkward standing by the street holding Betty by the reins and staring at Felisha with an unspoken longing to stay. She stood on the steps holding a cloth bag of food in her hands. She was physically exhausted herself and felt an unexpected sadness to see him leaving. "Here's some food I made up for you. And a little note too," she added with a genuine sad smile.

"Thank you," he said accepting the bag from her. "Well, thank you again for your hospitality. I enjoyed your company," he said uncomfortably.

"You're welcome, Matt. You're welcome to come back anytime," she said softly.

Matt nodded. "I'll do so. Hey," he spoke seriously as he swung up into the saddle. "Is it all right if I write to you from time to time? Just to let you know where I am."

"Of course," she answered quickly and added, "you could add a little about how you are, too."

Matt smiled lightly. "I will. Take care of yourself, Felisha, and tell Dillon I'll see him later. Until we meet again, my friend."

"Matt, be careful and I'll pray for you to find Truet quickly."

Matt nodded. He lingered in place, silently debating with his second thoughts as he nervously said, "Maybe, if I come back we can take another buggy ride to someplace else. Somewhere a bit more fun though, perhaps. Sound all right?"

She smiled warmly. "That sounds wonderful."

"I'll come back then. I'll see you soon, Felisha," he said before turning Betty and riding out of her sight.

Felisha reached into her dress pocket and pulled out the note from Regina that Matt had given her the day he arrived. She opened the envelope and re-read the letter she'd already read four or five times just since leaving the Davis home the day before.

MY DEAR FELISHA,

My utmost empathy and heartache to you and the Graces' for the loss of our friend, Jenny Mae. Much more your friend than mine, I still know she was a wonderful person and must've been a beautiful friend. I regret to not have had the opportunity to experience her friendship in the capacity that you did.

Lee and I convinced Matthew to come to your rescue a day before Bob's wire came. Do not be dismayed by his reputation; Matthew is as decent and kind a man that you'll ever meet. He will not harm you or Dillon.

With our deepest sympathy and warmest regards,

Your friend,

Regina Bannister

P.S. Matthew is single and would make you a fine husband and father to Dillon.

Helpful hint- he loves cinnamon rolls.

FELISHA SMILED TO HERSELF, Matt would be pleasantly surprised to find three cinnamon rolls in his knapsack when he opened it. She sighed and stepped back onto her porch. Normally, she'd be making breakfast for her boarders and Dillon, but for once her home was empty of boarders. She sat down on her bench swing and watched the morning pass while the town came to life with people preparing to fix breakfast and begin the day.

It was nice to take a moment to relax and enjoy the crisp morning air. She and Matt had stayed up late talking about their lives, their families, friends, and views. It was nice to be able to talk to a man the way she was able to with Matt. He listened and showed interest in her and her thoughts. He allowed her to speak honestly and share more in their conversation than she had shared with any man since her husband passed away. Actually, it was even longer as her husband had found his business more important and more pressing than listening to her long before he passed away. She missed being listened to; she missed having long conversations with a man.

"Father," she prayed, "watch over Matt as he goes to find Truet. I ask that You'll guide his path to find Truet quickly. Watch over Truet as well, Lord. I pray You'll bring both men home safely, Father. In Jesus' name, Amen."

33

Oddly enough, Wylooska wasn't on the map of Idaho that Matt had gotten recently. Wylooska was nothing more than a clearing in the woods near a decent-sized stream, where someone decided to open up a saloon. Probably within weeks, other saloons, hotels and brothel were built up. Where people congregated, a store was bound to follow. The tiny town wasn't at all attractive or inviting. It was, in fact, a group of closely built buildings offering alcohol, gambling, prostitution, food, and beds for the local logging camps to come to. Wylooska had no other purpose than to be an outlet for the loggers to spend their hard-earned wages.

The only reason Matt found his way to Wylooska was that it was one of the farthest northern towns, of such, that hosted loggers. He'd been to other towns and isolated logging camps over the past ten days without finding Truet, but Matt gradually worked north and was running out of logging camps, except for the few farther up near Wylooska.

Matt tied Betty to the hitching rail outside of a single story, hand-hewn building with the word "saloon" painted on the bare wood. He stepped into the dark and dirty saloon. The bar was roughly nailed together out of boards; the bar was about twelve feet long and four feet high. Behind the bar was a tall cabinet half full of clear bottles with various levels of liquid in them, a medium-sized mirror and a good painting of a seascape. The walls were bare except for a few paintings of nude women. Lanterns for light were mounted on the walls and hung from the ceiling. The floor was made of wide planks covered with dirt and tattered by the many calked boots that visited the facility. There were square tables for card games and a small beaten-up piano in one corner. There were no attempts to impress anyone by the owner; it was all very simple with homemade furnishings that served a very practical purpose.

There were four men inside drinking whiskey and refilling their shot glasses from an unlabeled bottle they'd bought, as they sat talking with the bartender behind the bar. All of their eyes turned to Matt with interest as they noticed his tin star pinned to the left side of his shirt.

"Can I get ya a drink?" A balding man asked from behind the bar. He turned to the other men at the bar sarcastically. "Sheriff?"

A burly, heavyset man sitting at the bar spit a mouthful of brown tobacco juice to the floor and said with a laugh, "Did Wylooska hire a sheriff, Jim? There's no room for law 'round here. You might choose to go back down the trail, fella. The folks 'round here might not take kindly to your staking claim here," he finished in a fairly friendly manner. He had long, curly black hair under his dingy felt hat, and a thick beard covered in tobacco juice.

Matt leaned against the bar, keeping his right hand near his holster. He held out a piece of paper with a drawing of a man on it. It had been a wanted poster with Truet's likeness drawn on it. However, Matt cut the paper so all it showed was the likeness. He had also drawn in a beard to fit what he thought Truet might now look like. He spoke clearly and purposely as he eyed the four men cautiously back and forth. "My name's Matt Bannister. I'm a U.S. Marshal and I'm looking for this man. Does he look familiar to you?"

The burly man nearly choked on his spit. "You're Matt Bannister? The Matt Bannister from Cheyenne?"

"I am. I'm now over in Branson, though," he said with a nod.

The men all looked at each other. "Matt Bannister. What are you doing here?" one man asked.

"Imagine meeting you here," another stated. "Did you run all the murderers out of Wyoming? Why'd you go to Branson? You should be down there in the New Mexico area cleaning it up a bit now."

"Is he a killer?" the big man asked nodding at the likeness Matt had handed him.

"No. I was just asked to find him. He's in no real trouble at all. Does he look familiar to any of you?" Matt asked again hoping to get their attention on the likeness rather than on him.

"Hard to say," the bartender named Jim said. "It kinda looks like every one of the men that come in here. What's his name?"

"Truet. Truet Davis."

"Never heard the name. What about you, Isaac? You get up to the camps."

The burly man named Isaac took the likeness and studied it closely. He shook his head. "I don't know." He took his finger and placed it over the hair in the hand-drawn likeness. "It kinda looks like that new guy up at the Old Crows

Camp." He looked up at Matt as he spoke, "he doesn't say much and looks like he'd just as well kill you as to say hello. His name's Daniel though, and he has no hair."

"Does he come to town?"

"No sir. He keeps to himself. Not an overly friendly one at all. Think he's the one you're looking for?"

"Is he tall and lanky?" Matt asked.

Isaac shook his head with a scoff. "No sir! This man looks like he could beat the bark off the trees, and I think he's mean enough to do it too."

"Well, the man I'm searching for is about six feet and a hundred and fifty pounds. He's missing two fingers on his left hand. Sound familiar?"

Isaac turned his head. "I haven't seen him."

"Well, thanks, gentlemen. Is there a hotel in town?" Matt asked.

"Not a good one, Marshal," Jim answered from behind the bar. "There's just a room full of beds and the whore's rooms if you want one. But I have to tell you; they're having a hell of a time with bed bugs and lice. If you'd like, I could rent you the extra room at my house. It's not much, but it's got a clean bed," Jim offered with a shrug.

"Lice, huh?" Matt asked in thought.

"Not at my house, but if you stay anywhere else I'll guarantee you, you'll get them."

LATER THAT NIGHT, Matt sat cross-legged on a narrow bed in Jim's tiny spare room with barely enough room to stand up in. He sat under a kerosene lantern hung from the low ceiling using his Bible as a solid backing as he wrote a letter to Felisha.

. . .

To my friend, Felisha,

How many days has it been since I left the kindness of your hospitality? Though it's only been ten, I fear it seems much longer. I find myself in a camp of pleasure for the loggers to waste their earnings on, named Wylooska. A terrible, but necessary evil I suppose, as these logging camps are farther out then any others. Why a man would want to live and work so far from society is beyond me, unless of course, they are running from the law. I do expect to find Truet in one of these last few camps. I will be taking my star off to enter the camps, as many of those men could be wanted and react to my encroachment with hostility. I will be careful.

I sit here in Wylooska and think of you, my friend. You are a ray of sunlight that breaks through the dark clouds of a stormy day. Warm, kind, thoughtful and comforting. I enjoyed your company greatly and look forward, with great anticipation, to our buggy ride when I return. I hope all is well. Tell Dillon hello. I hope to return shortly.

Sincerely,

Matt

Matt reread his letter and folded it up. Jim, the bartender and owner of his guest room said the mail went out once a week. It just so happened it was leaving the next day.

He had already mailed off two long letters and now this one. He couldn't explain why he wrote so often to Felisha. He hadn't written two letters in ten days in years, if ever. He couldn't help it; he was compelled to write to her for some reason that he could not explain. He had just written his third letter and if he could, he'd happily write another. There was a comfort in writing her name and revealing himself to her little by little, word by word, letter after letter. He was not a man that was easily swayed by an attractive woman, but for the first time in many years he was smitten by a woman that he couldn't get out of his mind. He could not explain it nor could he understand what was happening inside of him. All he truly knew was he wanted her to see him for who he really was, and letters opened a door through the walls he'd made over the years.

The thought of her made him smile and filled him with a childlike anticipation to see her again. He wanted to talk to her and watch her dark brown eyes light up with her hypnotic smile. For the first time in his long career he wanted to quit searching for a wanted man and go back empty-handed, just to be near Felisha. However, that was not an option. Felisha would kick him off of her porch if he failed to find her friend, Truet. In the morning he would continue his search thanks to Isaac, the local freight driver, who delivered food and supplies to all three logging camps in the surrounding area. Matt had a good idea of where Truet was, what he looked like now and what he was calling himself. Matt was looking for a hard and bitter muscular man, with a shaved head and ungroomed beard named Daniel, who kept to himself up at the old crows camp.

Matt lay on his bunk for the night and opened up his Bible to read. Tomorrow he would track Daniel; tonight he would seek his Lord. It always puzzled Matt how so many people claimed to know Jesus as their Lord, but they never read their Bibles. It only seems reasonable that a man should be interested in getting to know Jesus up close and personally. After all, He is the only salvation man has and can ever hope for. A Christian should desire to know what the Bible has to say on a daily basis as they draw closer to their Lord. Of all the "works" a Christian is called, led or chooses to do, none are as important or as vital, as seeking the Lord daily in prayer and Bible reading. To Matt it came down to one question really: how important is the Lord to you?

34

Brit Thacker glared at Abby with the purest hatred she'd ever seen in his eyes yet. He gritted his teeth in an almost animalistic snarl while he leaned over her, breathing heavily with rage. "I should just kill you and be done with it. I married the ugliest girl in the world. You're disgusting, look at yourself!"

Abby lay on the floor with her hands held upwards to protect herself from any more of his wrath. Her nose bled as did her bottom lip from his earlier punches. She wore a thin paisley dress over her bare skin. Her legs were blotched with dirt and bruises. She made no comment; all she could do was cry.

Quickly, Brit grabbed her red hair and pulled her up to her feet forcefully. She cried out in pain, but knew better than to fight back. He dragged her through the house into their bedroom and forced her to look into the mirror that hung over the dresser. He pushed her face next to the glass and yelled loudly, "You're ugly! What happened to the beautiful girl I married? I'll tell you what," he answered, his voice growing meaner. "She got married, fat and lazy. That's what!

Do you think just because you married me you can let yourself go to hell? Do you?" he shouted, demanding an answer.

"No," she cried weakly and tried to keep her eyes turned down. Her body convulsed lightly with the struggle to not sob.

"Like hell!" he let go of her hair and stepped back. "Brush your hair, make yourself pretty. Do it!" he ordered.

She fearfully reached down and took hold of her brush. "Please don't," she pleaded softly while viewing him in the mirror, her blue eyes pleading for mercy.

"Brush your hair," he demanded in a low and threatening voice, "I'm gonna stand right here until you make yourself pretty. Or don't I deserve a pretty wife? I do, don't I?"

"Yes," she nodded. She dared not take her eyes off of him in the mirror. She slowly brushed her long straight red hair.

"There now," he said in a softer voice. He had gone into the other room to grab the bottle of whiskey that he'd been drinking. He took a long drink and stepped behind her. He looked at her in the mirror. The blood was still drying on her face, but her hair was brushed. "Here," he spoke softly and spit into a rag, he wiped the blood gently from her face. Her eyes filled with tears while he gently cleaned up her face. "There now, see? You can clean up nicely. Now, put on the makeup, heavy like the whores wear it."

"What?" she gasped. Alarm ran through her suddenly. He had threatened numerous times to take her to Johnny Niehus' bordello. She began to shake visibly.

"Put on the makeup!" he ordered sternly. He sat on the edge of the bed and added kindly, "I want to see you beautiful, like you used to be."

The only makeup she had was a small tin of rouge for her cheeks; she put it on wondering if there was a purpose.

She cried out to God silently, terror gripped her like a vice. Brit had never before wanted her to get "pretty" as he had put it. It was frightening to wonder if she was moving out to Johnny's or to the cowboy's bunkhouse. She could barely apply her rouge as her hands shook so much. When she had finished, she looked at Brit in the mirror. He watched her with a scowl on his rugged face. She put her hands down at her side and waited for whatever came next.

Brit smiled slightly while he stood up from the bed and walked up behind her. She turned to face him nervously. His smile was almost kind, as he placed his hands on her shoulders and then quickly spun her around and forced her face close to the mirror roughly. He snarled viciously, "You're still the ugliest damn girl I've ever seen! Look at yourself, Abby! Look!" He yanked her hair forcing her to look at her own reflection. "Even with makeup you're ugly! No man is going to want you. You're too damn ugly! I couldn't charge a dime for you because no man's going to touch you. You're disgusting, Abby! Absolutely disgusting! Look..." he pulled up her dress to show her dirty and bruised spotted legs. "You're a damn pig, dirt everywhere! I married a sow, not a lady. If you wanna look like a pig, then you might as well live with the pigs!" He quickly grabbed her by the hair again and led her through the house, out the back door and towards the barn.

She cried out loudly, begging him to stop, but he stepped quickly pulling her by the hair past the garden to the small barn. He stopped at the pigpen. With one hand he held her head down and with the other he opened the gate to the pen. The pigs grunted from being disturbed from their sleep. Brit quickly led her over to the soupy filth of the corner the pigs used to relieve themselves, and with great force he threw Abby face-first down into the deep, foul smelling pool of pig feces and urine. "That's where you belong, because that's all you are!"

"Why are you doing this to me?" she screamed out, still lying in the soup of filth. "Why? Why don't you just kill me?" She began to climb to her feet, sobbing bitterly. Her face and entire front side were caked thickly with the dark and wet muck.

"I hate you!" she screamed. Her sobs had taken over.

"You hate me?" he threatened. "You hate me after all I've done for you, you hate me?" he asked and stepped towards her.

"I'm sorry, I didn't mean it," she spoke quickly as he came to her, "I'm sorry, Brit. I didn't mean it."

He slugged her in the stomach with a hard right that doubled her over unable to breathe. While she was bent over in pain, he grabbed her dress and ripped it up over her head and off of her arms exposing her in the nude. He then shoved her backwards into the soupy muck. He stood over her pointing down and yelled, "I'm the one that put this dress on your back! I put food on the table and provide everything you need. And you hate me? I gave it all to you and what do I get? A piece of pig crap for a wife! You're disgusting! Come on." He grabbed her by the hair again and pulled her up out of the pool of pig waste. "You need a bath. Maybe then you'll start caring about what you look like once we get you cleaned up!" He led her out of the pigpen, pausing to close the gate and then continued over to the horse corral. He led her to the water trough and carelessly tossed her head-first into it.

She screamed and filled with panic as Brit put his boot on her back and forced her to the bottom of the two-foot-deep water trough. She flung her arms and legs wildly, but he kept her at the bottom until air started to leave her lungs, he then removed his foot to allow her up to get some air. She sucked in the air wildly and tried to catch her breath.

He laughed coldly. "Wash up. I don't want you smelling like a pig for once tonight," he said and walked towards the house where he went inside.

Abby sat in the water trough and began to weep bitterly. She looked up at the nearly full moon and bright multitude of stars that speckled the night sky and with burning tears in her eyes. She said to God above, "I thought I was Your child, God. I thought You loved Your children. You can die on the cross for me, but You can't help me? Lord, I made a mistake marrying Brit, but forgive me, Jesus, don't forget me! What am I supposed to do? Lord, look at me," she said through her tears and raised her hands slightly. "I need You! I was a Christian before I married and I read the Bible. It says You'll never leave me. It says You'll protect me and save me. I know You saved me eternally, but what about for now?" she asked, "Jesus, I have nowhere else to go, please help me!" she pleaded.

ACROSS FROM THE GARDEN, hidden within the trees and underbrush of the creek bed, Saul Wolf watched his beloved Abby being thrown around, humiliated, and nearly drowned by Brit. He was severely tempted to run out there and beat Brit to death, but somehow he remained still and suffered through the unimaginable abuse of Abby by Brit's hand.

Tears fell freely down his face and his breathing was heavy from the emotions he couldn't identify easily, half of it was his fierce anger and the other half was the pure heartbreak he had endured by what he saw.

"Father," Saul prayed earnestly through his gritted teeth.

"I pray that You'll keep Abby safe. I pray that You'll get rid of Brit and that You'll allow me to marry her. I love her, Father. You know I do. I would never treat her like that. Lord, I would love to get my hands on Brit, even for five minutes, I really would. Lord, I'm asking You, please let me marry her and allow me to give her a life where she's treated like a lady at the very least."

Saul wanted to go to her to comfort her, but he resisted. It wasn't worth the consequences if he was caught. He quietly slipped away unnoticed and broken by what he'd seen. A man who stands by and watches the woman he loves being beaten and humiliated by another man normally doesn't feel too much like a man anymore. Men were created to be a man, and it wore deeply in Saul's soul. He climbed into his bunk and wept hopelessly.

35

Billy Sexton sat on his top bunk listening with the others, as old man Enoch played his fiddle to pass the time before they blew out the lamps and called it a night. Five-thirty came mighty early to the hard-labored men of the forest. The bunkhouse was too small for the eight bunk beds and sixteen men; a woodstove and an old Shepherd mix named "Shep," which belonged to Enoch. Enoch was the oldest at fifty-two and the muleskinner for the Old Crow Logging Camp.

Billy was the youngest man on the crew at seventeen. His father, Jack Sexton, one of the most experienced tree fallers in the outfit, slept beneath him on the bottom bunk. They worked in the logging camp during the spring, summer and into fall before returning home for the long winter. This was Billy's second year and he and his father sent their money home for safekeeping instead of wasting it in the den of sin, Wylooska, where most every one of their crewmates spent theirs. Even old Enoch occasionally went to town for a laugh and a good "letting loose," as he called it.

At Old Crow, the only day off was Sunday and usually every Sunday Billy and his father were alone in the bunkhouse, except for Daniel Yoder, who never went to Wylooska. Daniel seemed to be content simply being alone. He didn't say much and when he did, it was short and direct. He made it known to everyone he worked with that he didn't want to make friends, nor did he want to talk. He merely wanted to be left alone. He was frightening in that he looked like he'd rather beat you silly, than repeat a word twice. For some reason Billy liked Daniel. He thought Daniel was interesting, mysterious perhaps.

Interestingly, Daniel wore a wedding band on his finger. However, he never mentioned a word about his wife or wrote to her. Sometimes, Billy would catch Daniel staring at his wedding ring and watch his eyes grow glossy and then his face would harden into a stone cold sneer, which everyone agreed was reminiscent of the calm before the storm. Generally speaking, everyone stayed out of Daniel's way. He wasn't a normal man, he was vastly superior in physical strength and the coldness in his eyes said it all; he just didn't care about anyone or anything.

If anyone had a friendship with him it was Billy's father, Jack. He and Daniel stood on the springboards, while they worked together with axe and saw to fall trees, day after day. Jack respected the endurance and work ethic of Daniel and was finally beginning to build a trust between the two. The only time Billy had seen Daniel smile was in his father's company. He was a hard man to get to know because Daniel didn't want company. Nightly after dinner he would leave the camp to go sit in the forest to be alone.

Billy followed him once, maybe twice, and all Daniel did, was sit on the ground overlooking the valleys below and whittle with his pocketknife. After a few hours of whittling when daylight came to an end, he'd come back to the bunkhouse and go to bed. It was common and tonight was no different.

As Enoch played his fiddle, the bunkhouse door opened and Daniel Yoder stepped in casting a look of annoyance towards Enoch. He stepped to his bunk wordlessly. Daniel was a big man with large powerful muscles, much larger than anyone else's in the camp. He purposely shaved his head bald to fight the lice that invaded the camp mercilessly. However, Daniel had a semi-long full-faced beard and his eyes were as hard as granite itself.

Enoch stopped playing his fiddle and looked at Daniel as he was taking off his pants and shirt to climb into his bunk. "You missed the excitement after dinner, Danny. Ole Isaac came by and said he ran into the Marshal Matt Bannister."

Daniel froze and breathed in deep. Enoch continued, "The marshal's in Wylooska hunting for a man named, Honest Davis?" he glanced at one of his crewmates, questionably.

"No, Truly, or Trowed or something," the man answered.

"Truet," Jack said plainly. "Truet Davis."

"Yeah! That's it," Enoch agreed. "So maybe we'll get to meet the marshal. I've heard of him! I guess the good marshal thinks that Truet fella is around here somewhere."

Daniel lifted himself easily into his bunk and spoke to no one in particular, "Never heard of him."

"Well, I have," Billy offered. "He single-handedly saved a woman from two kidnappers this past winter in Branson. He killed them both. They say he's killed thirty to forty men. I wouldn't want to be that Truet fella," Billy laughed, "his time has come."

"William," Jack said with a soft warning, but his

meaning was clear. "Any one of the men up here in these woods could be Truet Davis. I promise more than one or two are hiding from the law. In my opinion, any man who'd pick this life rather than breaking the law again couldn't be that bad. They either made a mistake or didn't do it all."

LONG AFTER THE lamps had been blown out and the snoring of at least ten men filled the bunkhouse, Truet laid on his top bunk with his hands folded under his bald head. Panic had seized him and he was tempted to grab his belongings, take his horse out of the stable, and leave the area as fast as he could while the darkness still hid his escape. It would put him a day or two ahead of Matt Bannister possibly, but if Matt Bannister could find him here, then Matt would find him anywhere he went. He could run to Canada and begin again, but he was too physically exhausted to begin another long run. He had been running and hiding for over a month now. He had been found by Farrian Maddox in a saloon in Gold Hill, a small town where Truet never thought anyone would look for him.

He was wrong. Farrian found him and before Truet could draw his revolver, Farrian had drawn and fired a shot into the wall behind him. A second later, both revolvers fired simultaneously and Farrian fell to the floor with a .45 shell in his chest. He was still alive, but terrified of dying when Truet stepped over him carelessly with nothing more than a passing glance. He left Gold Hill quickly before someone else could shoot at him.

The news of Farrian's death left a direct route exposing Truet's back trail. He fled as quickly as Fanny could carry him. Distance was his first concern as he knew the Gold Hill sheriff would gather a posse and come after him. Once out of town a couple of miles he took the time to look for a way to escape the danger at hand. He resorted to the same tactics he'd used before by staying off of soft soil and roads as much as possible and remaining as invisible as he could. From that point on, he avoided towns and spent most nights sleeping under his makeshift tent deep in the woods.

Searching for a plan that might provide some cover and an income, he changed his appearance as much as he knew how and changed his name. He found employment at a logging camp and when he heard that the Old Crow logging site needed men, he came here to get as lost as he could from civilization and especially Bob Thacker.

Now he lay in his bunk thinking. Bob had not only sent out his ignorant cowboys, he sent gunmen like Farrian. Bob Thacker put up a reward that would bring bounty hunters by the dozens and apparently, the U.S. Marshal, Matt Bannister. The marshal, famed for his many killings and uncompromising tenacity was now on Truet's boot heels. He could not outrun the marshal. Even if he fled to Canada, which would stop the marshal legally, it wouldn't stop the bounty hunters; they would chase him until he was dead, and they claimed the bounty on his head.

There was nowhere to run; he had to make ready his stand and fight. He was already a wanted man, so killing the marshal would only raise his bounty. If he killed the marshal, he could then flee and put distance between himself and those that would follow him. Given enough time to gather distance, he could lose himself in the great wild country of Canada. One thing was sure though, he'd never get away from Matt Bannister being less than a day's ride away and on his trail.

Truet quietly pulled his firearms down from hanging on the wall above his bunk, climbed down silently and carried his weapons outside. He would do what he was forced to do. Tomorrow, if Matt Bannister came to the Old Crow Logging Camp he would be a dead man and Truet Davis would disappear.

36

Daniel Yoder seemed to be heavily preoccupied. He swung his axe with greater force and more hurriedly than Jack had yet seen him over the past two weeks of working with him. Daniel stood on a springboard on the other side of the large Douglas fir with a determined, but focused, expression on his face. A snarl appeared on his face with each deep penetration into the wood with this double-faced axe.

They were chopping out the undercut to create the direction they wanted the large tree to fall when they made the final back-cut with their ten foot, double-handed falling saw. Jack was pushing himself a little too hard to keep up the rhythm with Daniel.

A cold front had dropped down overnight leaving a heavy gray haze through the forest. It hadn't yet rained, but a fine mist gently fell through the air. Though the normal sounds of working timber men echoed through the mountains as usual, it seemed all too unnaturally eerie and quiet. There was a tension in the air that Jack couldn't explain, nor was accustomed to feeling. It made him uneasy.

Jack swung his axe, sinking it into the wood deeply and

stopped, which threw Daniel out of rhythm. He held his axe and eyed Jack irritably.

Jack asked, as he wiped his sweaty brow, "Do you feel the need to work me to death today, Daniel?"

"No, why?" he replied without any expression, except irritation.

"You seem in a bigger hurry than usual today. Any reason why? Because I'm getting too old to work twice as hard as I already do."

"I'm just doing my job."

"Me too, but keep in mind we work together. You don't have to fall this tree alone. I know some of these boys already think you're Paul Bunyon, but you're not. You might be as strong as him, but until you show me a blue ox, I'm your partner. Let's work at our usual pace," Jack said with his usual friendly smile. Jack was a heavyset man with broad shoulders and short dark hair with a long dark beard.

Daniel's expression softened momentarily, a slight smile crossed his face. "Okay, now let's bring this big old girl down."

"Okay," Jack agreed and pulled his axe out of the nearly done undercut. Daniel's axe hit the tree and was pulled back just as Jack swung his axe and again let it stop in the wood.

"What?" Daniel asked impatiently, with a hint of humor in his eyes.

"That must be him," Jack said staring down the hill behind Daniel. A bearded man with a dark ponytail under a brown hat was riding up the mountainside on a red-roan horse. He had two rifles sheathed, one on each side of his saddle and a six-shooter tied on his hip. He was about a hundred yards down hill and riding towards them. "That must be the marshal. My word, that's really him."

"Must be," Daniel agreed, watching him. "I'll be back,

time to drain the morning coffee." He jumped three feet down from the springboard and disappeared behind a near by tree.

MATT HAD SEEN one of the two tree fallers jump down from his springboard and quickly walk away after they had noticed him riding towards them. Matt took a deep breath and continued to ride up the clear-cut mountainside that was littered heavily with limbs and splintered fragments of fallen timber.

He watched the path carefully steering Betty to avoid any debris that might hurt her. While at the same time, he tried to spot the man he'd just seen walk away from the tree he was falling. He no longer could see him through the lazy, low clouds and the cover of the thick tree line. It filled Matt with an unsettling anxiety to remain steady and in the open, while the man he believed to be Truet disappeared all too quickly into the brush. Experience told him Truet was either running fast as he could hope to get away from him, or more likely, Truet was taking a position to ambush him. Matt had already talked to a young man at the bottom of the mountain and realized rumors of his coming had already beaten him to the camp. The man, known as Daniel Yoder, hadn't run and his going into the brush wasn't a coincidence either.

It was a bad plan to put himself blindly at the mercy of a stranger, a wanted man at that. Despite his better judgment, he rode Betty up the mountain in a slow and weaving pattern around piles of discarded limbs and debris. His eyes focused on the ground in front of Betty and then quickly scanned the dark woods for any sight of the man he believed to be Truet. As he crested the top and neared the tree line, he took a deep breath to calm his anxiety. He refused to touch his weapons or even un-thong his revolver from its holster. Matt whispered quietly, "Lord, I'm in Your hands," as he neared the remaining tree faller.

"Good day," Jack said, as the man on the horse rode near. He wasn't sure if it was the U.S. Marshal Matt Bannister or not because the rider did not wear a badge. Jack stepped down off of his springboard. It was a wooden board with a steel strapped toe, which was wedged into a narrow slit cut into in the tree. "My name's Jack Sexton. Can I help you?" he asked. He leaned on his axe handle.

"Perhaps," Matt answered as his eyes darted through the surrounding trees and undergrowth. His heartbeat quickened. He didn't like being exposed and the urge to pull his revolver beckoned to him strongly. He refused to touch it; he kept his hands on his saddle-horn purposefully. "My name's Matt Bannister. I'm the..." he stopped, as a bald man with a beard, stepped out from behind a thick Douglas fir with a double-barrel shotgun on his shoulder. He had it aimed at Matt carefully; both side-by-side hammers were pulled back and cocked. On his waist was a gun belt with his revolver. Matt raised his hands slowly.

"I know who you are!" he spoke bitterly and stepped forward with a determined expression on his face.

"Daniel! What are you doing?" Jack demanded in horror.

"My name's Truet," he said to Jack, his eyes never leaving Matt. "I hate to kill you, Marshal. Your brother's a friend of mine, of sorts. But you never should've come here. You should've just left me be." He added in a piercing voice, "They raped my wife, Marshal. And then they stood there and laughed about it. They beat her and I watched her die!" A painful scowl burned on his face. "I did what I had to do. They got Saul to lie to save his own life, and they were going free. So I shot them, yes I did! And if I ever see Mick Rodman again, I'll kill him too." He looked at Matt and said simply, "I won't let you take me back and I can't let you ride away. I'm sorry, but your only chance is to go for your gun!"

"I came to help you," Matt explained hurriedly. He suddenly regretted not pulling out his revolver earlier. He should've ridden up the mountain behind Truet, with his own shotgun to his shoulder rather than trusting the character of a stranger, one wanted for murder at that.

Truet smiled thinly. "Now that you're about to die you're here to help me. Imagine that?" he said sarcastically and added seriously, "Say your prayers, Marshal."

"Daniel, don't," Jack said pleading with Truet, "He's a Federal Marshal!"

With his hands still held up in a surrendering position, Matt spoke quickly, "I don't believe you're a murderer, Truet. I've talked to Reverend Grace, Felisha, and Saul. I know what happened. Saul told me the truth, Truet. I know what really happened and I'm not here to arrest you. I am here to help you get your life back." Matt continued when he saw that Truet was listening.

"I understand you don't trust me. Bob's put a price on your head and you've got your bead on me, so I might say anything to get you to believe me, but I am telling you the truth. I am here because Felisha wrote to Regina, my sister-in-law. Lee and Regina asked me to come after you. They are sorry about your wife and so am I," Matt finished sincerely. Truet lowered the shotgun a little, as his eyes stared into Matt's.

Matt continued, "I can take you back to Boise City and promise you a fair trial. With my testimony, Saul's, and the rest of the town's, you will be released a free man and free to do as you wish. You won't have to run and watch your back anymore." Matt paused for a moment and then continued, "I'm offering you a chance to start your life over again. A free man."

"Start over doing what, Marshal? I've lost everything that means anything to me. What do I have to go back to?" Truet asked bitterly.

Matt eyed him compassionately. "Your future. You're still alive, Truet. You still have a life to live if you give it a chance." He stopped suddenly and then said a touch harder, "Look, you can either come with me and we'll get you out of this mess and you can show your face in public again as a free man or you can kill me and keep running. But soon enough, one of Bob's bounty hunters will track you down like I did. They won't come peacefully. You may not even see them coming. They'll just shoot you in the back and haul you back for the money," Matt said pointedly and then added calmly, "They won't touch you if you come back with me. If you don't want to, then I suggest you run to Seattle or Portland and join a schooner bound for China or somewhere. You were found here. If you want to run, go to sea. No one will find you there."

Truet replied seriously, "How do I know I can trust you? If I lower my gun, how will I know you won't shoot me in the back when you get the chance?"

"Have your friend reach into my left side-saddle bag and find your Bible."

"My what?"

"Your Bible. If I came to kill you I wouldn't have brought the Bible your wife inscribed for you. Trust me, I came to help."

Jack went to the left saddlebag, found the black leather-bound Bible and carried it over to Truet. Truet lowered the shotgun and slowly took his Bible. He opened the front cover and his body began to tremble at the sight of Jenny Mae's handwriting. He sat heavily on the ground where he had stood, laying the shotgun aside. Truet held the Bible with both hands and buried his face into its front cover. He wept painfully.

Matt lowered his hands to the top of his saddle horn and said compassionately, "Come back with me, Truet. You still have a long life to live. Don't let Bob get his way this time. Let's go back and tear his kingdom down."

Truet looked up at Matt with a tear-stricken face that was filled with anguish. "What about Mick Rodman?"

"I'll arrest him and you can watch him hang," Matt said simply.

"I want to do it myself," Truet said coldly, beginning to stand.

Matt nodded. "I know you do. Let's get your stuff and collect your pay. Then we can start heading back; we've got a long ride ahead."

37

"Dillon, stop asking, I already told you no. You chose not to do what I asked you to do, so you will not be rewarded for disobeying," Felisha Conway said simply. She and Dillon were entering the general store and post office run by Jeannie Bartholomew and her husband, Tom.

"Yeah, but it's only a penny candy, Mother. I have a lot in my penny jar. I could pay you back," Dillon offered in all sincerity. He held his mother's hand, staring up at her with big pleading eyes.

"No," she answered again and turned her eyes to Jeannie, who stood behind the counter with a fixed smile. Felisha handed a letter to Jeannie to be mailed out. "Good afternoon, Jeannie. I have a letter to post and I'll need a dozen eggs if you have that many left. I intended to get here earlier, but I didn't," she said with a shrug. She knew all too well that people like her that didn't have their own chickens quickly bought up the eggs the Bartholomews' collected daily from other locals.

Jeannie received the letter and looked at whom it was addressed. "Mmm, you must becoming good friends with the Bannister family. I met Regina at Bob's party the night before the fight. Yes, I met Regina and her husband. What's his name?"

"Lee," Felisha responded with a small forced smile.

"Yes, that's it, Lee. How could I forget? They are a nice couple, though I have to say she seemed a bit too arrogant to me," she paused momentarily and walked away to post the letter to Regina. She continued to speak, "However, you must have gotten to know her better than I, since she and Lee stayed at your house. Some folks around here noticed how Lee and Regina preferred to stay in your company rather than that of their own social upper class. You must have made quite an impact on them. And also on the marshal, by the way," Jeannie added, as she reappeared from around the corner with a letter in her hand. She held it out to Felisha, as she continued, "The second letter in less than two weeks. He must be taken by you."

Felisha's face lit up quickly as she held the letter and then downplayed her excitement. "Oh, I don't think so. He's just letting me know how the search for Truet is going," she explained. Her face flushed slightly.

Jeannie frowned and then questioned, "Shouldn't he be notifying Bob? After all, Bob's the one he's employed by." She laughed lightly.

"Is he on Bob's payroll?" Felisha asked quickly and irritably. "I sure hope he doesn't hear that rumor when he brings Truet back. I don't believe there could be a deeper insult."

"I didn't mean it literally," Jeannie spoke quickly. "I only meant it was Bob's doing that he's even here. He should be letting Bob know how his manhunt is going, not you. But it's none of my concern. I only insinuated that I think he's smitten with you, oddly enough. And, I am out of eggs until tomorrow, unfortunately," she finished with her fake smile.

"Well, you're right. It's none of your concern. I'll come back tomorrow morning for the eggs. Have a good day, Jeannie," she expressed irritably and turned to leave. Dillon, fixed in place pulled her hand and asked, "What about my penny candy? Can't I have one, Mother? I'll do what you asked."

"No! Dillon, I've already told you that. Don't ask again. You chose not to do what I asked, didn't you?" she glared down at him, waiting.

"Yes," he admitted solemnly and lowered his head.

"Okay then, I will not reward you for a bad choice. Now let's go," Felisha said and began to lead him away.

From the counter Jeannie said, "Wait. Here you go, Dillon. I'll give you one free of charge." She held out a penny candy for Dillon. She looked at Felisha with a smirk.

Felisha's brown eyes glared fiercely at Jeannie. Her voice was strong, "No, you won't either, Jeannie. You just heard me tell him, 'No'. I won't allow you to reward him when he's being disciplined by me, his mother!" She spoke to Dillon curtly, "Now, let's go!"

Jeannie watched Felisha walk quickly through the store leading Dillon by the hand. At the door, Sheriff Martin DePietro stepped inside and held the door open for Felisha. He smiled wide and greeted her with a pleasant, "Good afternoon, Felisha. You look nice today. You always..."

"Hello, Martin," she said irritably cutting him off and walked out the door he held open without so much as a thank you.

Martin watched her walk out, closed the door behind him, and walked to the counter to talk to Jeannie. "She doesn't say much to me anymore. She doesn't even look at me," he said, leaning on the counter. "I can't seem to get her interested in me no matter what I do."

Jeannie frowned. "That's probably because she has a new man in her life. A suitor, if you will."

"Oh? Who?" Martin asked with interest. Jeannie's words caused an alarm within him. He'd been trying to court Felisha for a long time.

"One Matt Bannister," she said slowly.

"No! How do you know?"

"I've seen them together while he was in town. And he's written to her numerous times within two weeks. You tell me, Martin, would you write so frequently to a woman you weren't smitten with?"

"No, I suppose not," Martin agreed quietly, almost sadly. He added with a touch of hope in his voice, "But that doesn't mean she's interested in him."

Jeannie stared at Martin with an obvious smile. "I'm afraid, my dear, that she's already been had by the good marshal."

"What do you mean by 'had'? You're talking about Felisha, Jeannie. She won't even look at a man twice, let alone be touched by one. So what are you getting at?" Martin asked seriously. His breathing picked up a little.

Jeannie sighed heavily. "I saw the way he looked at her, Martin, and the way she looked at him. They went for a buggy ride and were gone for nearly three hours before coming back to town," she paused purposefully. "I noticed she was sitting very close to him on the way back into town, very intimately. Being a lady myself, I know what that means," she finished, nodding her head knowingly.

"What?" Martin asked with an impatient shrug.

"Martin, truly," she scoffed. "Felisha blushes like a little schoolgirl whenever someone mentions his name. And there's a glow about her recently, or haven't you noticed? It wouldn't surprise me if she were with child. We'll know in a few months."

"Oh, get out of here! We're not talking about Molly over at the Westward Whoa; we're talking about Felisha Conway, Jeannie." Martin laughed uneasily. "I think you're just talking hogwash!"

"Really? Well, then explain to me why she just handed me a letter addressed to Regina Bannister. And this is not the first letter she's written. Then explain to me why Matt Bannister keeps writing to her and why she blushes like a little girl every time I hand her a letter from him. I'm telling you, as a lady that knows about women, that Felisha has already been taken and is falling in love with Matt."

Martin scoffed. "How can she be falling in love with someone she just met? He wasn't here, but what, two days?"

Jeannie shrugged. "A better question is why is she falling in love with the marshal that's going to either kill her good friend Truet himself, or bring him back here to hang?" she paused to watch Martin's facial expression. "That's my question. It smells a little fishy to me."

Martin smiled sarcastically. "I think you have too much time on your hands, Jeannie."

Jeannie, slightly offended, looked at Martin seriously and said, "Ask Reverend Grace; he noticed it too. In fact, he and Rebecca offered to watch Dillon for the night just so Felisha and Matt could be alone. You don't have to believe me; you'll find out for yourself soon enough." She leaned over the counter and added quietly, "But don't you find it strange that she'd be falling for the man that's come to see to it that her friend is killed? I do."

Martin frowned. "I highly doubt the Reverend took Dillon so they could be alone. I'm sure Dillon was just spending the night with little Luke. Jeannie, I don't think she's falling for him. I know Felisha and she's too good for him. He's a killer; she wouldn't be interested in him. He might be smitten with her, but she'll send him away broken-hearted." He looked at Jeannie with a confident smile. "I wouldn't put much concern into it. I'm sure he is trying to win her affections, but we know how hard that is, don't we?"

38

It was late afternoon as Matt and Truet rode down a long and steep grassy hill. It ended at a shallow river at the bottom of the canyon before they were to ride up the other steep mountain, which was capped by a thick tree line. They had been riding for hours, leaving Wylooska miles behind them. They now rode towards Idalia, a town equal to Sweethome in size and stature, but it was still hours away. They wouldn't arrive until well after dark.

"You're not what I was expecting," Truet said, looking at Matt while they rode. He continued, "Your name conjures up a mean image, quite frankly, one that doesn't fit you. Are you really Matt Bannister? Because you don't seem like a man that's seen so much killing or has killed as many men as they say you have," Truet finished slowly.

"Truet," Matt replied, as he turned his head to look at him. "You're here on your own free will. I came to you as a friend. If I had come as a lawman, you never would've gotten the draw on me. I don't make myself so vulnerable."

"Why did you? I could've killed you."

"I spent a lot of time talking to your friends in Sweethome," he paused, to eye Truet. "I knew you weren't a murderer. I took a chance that I could talk to you without being shot. I was a little bit surprised to see a shotgun pointed at me."

"You didn't act surprised."

"I weighed your options. Truth be known, I prayed that the Lord would keep me safe and open your ears to what I had to say. Very few of the men I've gone after were innocent, so to answer your question," his eyes hardened momentarily. "I can be as forceful as I need to be."

"You just don't act like what I expected. I was expecting a callous and bloodthirsty man. You don't strike me as that at all," Truet paused, while they continued their steep descent down to the shallow riverbed. "I've met a lot of men who seem to thrive on their reputations. Men, who walk around thinking they're so tough that hell itself won't phase them. Men like Bob Thacker, who think they're so powerful that they can do anything and get away with it. His son, Brit, walks

through town like he's so tough that God Himself couldn't scare him. And men like AJ Thacker." His lips tightened as he proceeded to talk, "Well, they're the worst ones. AJ knew he could get away with anything because his daddy would get him out of it. He had nothing to fear. He could harass my wife, disrespect her, and even touch her and there was nothing I could do about it. AJ could've shot me in the back of my head in the middle of a busy street and gotten away with it. How do I know that? Because AJ and his friends raped my wife, and they got away with it!" Truet's eyes burned with hostility.

He continued, "Bob somehow forced Saul to become the scapegoat and Martin DePietro went along with it. My wife was raped, beaten and had bite marks on her. She said quite clearly who'd done it. People had even seen AJ and his friends ride towards my house early that morning and they were seen riding back. One person even told Martin that they saw the fresh scratches on AJ's cheek. The same scratches I saw on his cheek, the same ones he said a dog gave him after Jenny Mae had died. And they still were getting away with it!" Truet's rage was clearly evident in his voice. "AJ and his friends sat in front of me and had absolutely no fear of being prosecuted for what they did. My wife was dead because of them and they couldn't care less. But I did, and I killed every one of them except for one. I plan on killing him too, whether you let me or not," he added firmly.

"Can I ask you something, Truet? You are a very powerful man; you were in the cavalry and obviously can hold your own. So why didn't you stop AJ at the beginning?"

Truet sighed. "At first, AJ was just joking around here and there. He'd give me a little push and a little nudge, and gradually it became more disrespectful and more serious. With time he got more aggressive. Finally, it got to the point where he was threatening to shoot me and crossing every line imaginable with Jenny Mae." He looked at Matt with remorse and continued, "I wanted to beat him, I wanted to tear his head off. But Jenny Mae was adamant. She'd say over and over again, 'Be meek. If someone strikes the right side of your cheek, turn to him your left side also. The meek shall inherit the earth. You're a Christian, Truet, be meek,' she'd say."

Tears filled his eyes as he thought back to his wife. He fought against his tears and said in a quivering voice filled with emotion, "I put up with it every time. I should've busted him in the mouth the very first time he said something to Jenny Mae. But no, I tried to be meek, gentle and calm like a Christian's supposed to be." He shook his head slowly and then added quickly, "You're probably thinking if I would've been more of a man, then those sons of bitches never would have touched her in the first place and she'd still be alive. And you're right. I've been haunted by that very thought since it happened. Trust me, Matt; I wasn't raised to be a coward. I was just trying to be godly. Jenny Mae insisted that we be meek and turn the other cheek," he explained again and wiped the tears from his eyes.

"Your wife," Matt offered softly, "she took those Bible passages and forced them on you without considering the damage it could cause in your particular circumstances. Meaning it was AJ Thacker and his unfortunate ability to go untouched by the law that caused your wife's death. But even as a Christian, we have the right and the obligation to stand up for ourselves. Nowhere in the Bible does God's Word say 'be weak, be cowards!' However, it does say over and over again, '*Be strong, be courageous.*' Somewhere, I think, we have been manipulated into thinking we are required to be meek in every circumstance, even when we should be strong and courageous." Matt paused momentarily and added thoughtfully, "In the Bible there is a list of attributes in Second Peter that go hand in hand with being a believer. Among them are love and kindness, in which we ought to be loving and kind, of course. But we should never allow others to mistake our kindness for weakness, and unfortunately, I think a good portion of the time we Christians do. God never created us to be cowards, and God often commanded His people to fight."

They rode the rest of the way down to the shallow river in silence. Once there, they allowed their horses to drink. Matt stepped out of the saddle to refill his canteen and to stretch his legs.

Truet remained on his horse. "Jenny Mae really took a liking to your brother-and sister-in-law. We were making plans to move to Branson when they attacked her."

Matt nodded. "I know. Lee and Regina liked you both very much. They were troubled when they heard what happened. I know it's bad timing, but after we get you cleared of any charges, you can still come back to Branson with me. Make a new start if you want."

Truet shook his head slowly. "I don't know what I want. I've never thought about it."

"What to do now?" Matt asked, while he stood up tightening the cap to his canteen.

"Yeah."

"As difficult as it may be, you only have one choice and that's to live your life again."

"My wife was killed not even two months ago and you're telling me to start living again?" Truet asked suddenly irritable. "I don't even know where she was buried, Matt! How am I supposed to just move on and begin a new life without Jenny Mae? I have no desire to start a new life." He glared sternly down at Matt. "To be honest, there's only one thing I care about and that's killing Mick Rodman! After he's dead and I find Jenny Mae's resting place, maybe then I'll feel like living again, but until then I have nowhere to go. The past isn't done!" Truet finished with his eyes burning into Matt.

Matt nodded. "I understand," he said and swung himself up into his saddle.

Truet stared at Matt as he asked, "Have you ever been married, Matt?"

Matt shook his head. "No, I've not."

"Then there's no way you can understand!" Truet said vehemently as he kicked his horse and rode ahead of Matt.

39

Upon reaching Idalia, Matt secured a hotel room and using his notoriety, convinced the clothing store owner to open his store so that Truet could purchase some new clothes before he bathed. Back at the hotel Truet took a warm bath. It was the first time in almost two months that he was able to relax in a tub without the threat of someone finding him. After the needed bath, Truet shaved off his beard and left his hair stubble on his head to grow out.

Both had bathed and eaten a late meal at the hotel when Idalia's sheriff and two deputies came to the hotel to meet the famous marshal and his infamous prisoner, Truet Davis. Sheriff Joseph Pendergraft and his deputies came to escort Truet to their jail for the night.

"No, thanks," Matt had replied in the downstairs lobby while Truet remained upstairs in his room. "I can watch him better here."

"Yeah, but Marshal Bannister, he's a murderer, and it's fitting that he's held securely. He shouldn't be left to wander, not to mention left alone!" Sheriff Pendergraft emphasized by waving a hand towards the hotel's staircase. He was an older, distinguished-looking man in his mid-fifties, who seemed to be tough enough in his own right. However, he did appear to be a bit nervous in front of Matt.

"I understand your concern, Sheriff. But trust me, I will not allow him out of my sight. Your town's safe," Matt reassured the sheriff and quickly excused himself from their company.

In truth, they had separate rooms, and Truet was not a prisoner by any means. He was still armed and was free to leave on his own if he so desired.

As soon as Truet had laid on the comfortable bed and closed his eyes, he fell asleep. He slept like a rock until he suddenly woke up with a fright and sat up in bed. His heart pounded and his breathing was heavy as he realized it was just a dream. He lay back down and his lower lip began to tremble as his eyes burned with hot tears. He breathed in deeply as his face contorted and he broke into heavy sobs.

He dreamed he was in his home with Jenny Mae standing across the room from him. She looked beautiful with her big, brown almond eyes staring into his with more love showing in her's than they ever had before. She smiled affectionately and gracefully walked towards him, her eyes never leaving him. He reached out and held her in his arms lovingly. He could feel her body against his and smell her sweet scent as he held her close. He heard her whisper the words, "I love you." Then suddenly she was being pulled out of his arms by an invisible force that he couldn't stop or follow after no matter how hard he tried to keep hold of her. He cried out desperately for her to come back to him, but she only smiled with a peaceful grace about her as she flowed away from him and simply seemed to disappear. Then the front door of the house opened and AJ Thacker stood at the threshold of the door unable to come through it. He glared at Truet with a bitter hatred in his eyes so intense that it was unimaginable. His lip curled viciously while he gnashed his teeth in rage. Truet woke up startled.

He had seen his wife just as she used to be. He had held her in his arms, smelled the scent of her hair and heard her voice. He was with her just momentarily. It seemed so real. The love he felt for her came out in his desperate cry for her to stay with him. He felt her, he loved her and she was gone. He would never see her again during his lifetime.

The hole that her death created in his life had been filled in part by the weeks of running, hiding, and the constant worry of being found. He spent his nights fearing someone might recognize him the following day. The wanted posters that Bob had printed with a five-hundred-dollar reward were quickly spread out across the territory. It was only a matter of time until he was found and he knew that. Luckily, it was Matt who found him.

All too quickly he was learning now that without anything to fear or worry about, he had time to think about Jenny Mae and what he had lost. He had lost his only true friend; the one person he shared his hopes, dreams and frustrations with on a daily basis. She was the anchor of his life, his stability. Her constant and honest feedback was so often his guide and perhaps most of all, he lost the sincere caring of his best friend and wife, Jenny Mae. He would never feel complete without her in his life. There were married couples all over the nation, but Jenny Mae and he shared something special in their marriage, something that too often is left out of many other marriages. After five years of marriage, they were still falling in love with one another. Truet enjoyed Jenny Mae, where other husbands no longer truly enjoyed the company of their wives. Jenny Mae was his best friend.

Truet sat back up in the darkness and turned up the oil lamp by his bed to light the room. He reached into his saddlebag and pulled out the Bible that Matt had brought to him. He opened the front cover and read the words Jenny Mae had inscribed to him. Seeing her handwriting sent a deep wave of sorrow into his heart, so deep that it literally hurt his chest as he read the words, "I love you Tru, truly I do." He pulled the Bible to his chest and slid off the bed to the floor.

"Oh God," he cried out quietly. "God, I love her. Why didn't You protect her, Lord? She loved You more than she loved me and You let her down!" His voice grew angry. "You could've saved her, you could've protected her from them," his voice grew higher in pitch. "Why'd You take her away from me? I need You to answer me. How am I supposed to live without her, Lord? It's not fair! I loved her with everything I am. How could You let this happen? Why, God?" He stared bitterly up at the window where faint moonlight could be seen through the closed curtains. "Why didn't You protect her? She was my wife! I thought You loved us." He adjusted his body to sit with his back against the side of the bed. He sat in silence for a few minutes staring in thought at the floor. He sighed heavily and then looked up at the window again. "Take me too, Lord. I'm no use without Jenny Mae. You've taken the only thing that matters to me, so You might as well take me too. I trusted You. I thought You were going to help us, not destroy us. Lord, I can't believe she's gone," he said and began to weep. "Why didn't You save her? She was pregnant with my child. How could You take them from me? What did I do, Jesus, to deserve this?" he asked tearfully. "What did I do? Lord, I miss her." He lay prostrate on the floor and wept painfully.

40

_____

"Why are you sending Felisha a letter? We'll be in Sweet-home before that letter arrives there," Truet said. They were leaving the Idalia Postal Office, which was inside the local bank. Their horses were saddled and hitched outside of the restaurant where they had eaten breakfast. They had walked the short distance to mail the letter Matt had spent the evening writing in his room.

"We're not going to Sweethome. We're going to Boise City. Besides, maybe I'd like for her to get a letter before I see her again," Matt explained. His expression quickly changed, as he noticed the town's sheriff, Joseph Pender-graft, and one of his deputies on horseback near a group of men, some with rifles, standing by Matt and Truet's horses.

"Keep quiet," Matt ordered bluntly, while he unthonged the leather loop from his revolver. He noticed Truet unsnapped his holsters leather cover, as they walked towards the men. "Morning," Matt said as he neared them. He watched the sheriff and the others carefully.

"Morning, Marshal. We noticed that your prisoner's armed, and we decided to ride along with you two till

Gerhard, where one of them there can assist you further," Sheriff Pendergraft said. He appeared to be a man of his word and of uncompromising principle. He had short gray hair, and a weathered, clean-shaven face. He was of medium height and stocky build and was set in his decision to assist the marshal with the lawless prisoner.

"I don't need..."

"Maybe you don't understand how dangerous that man is, Marshal!" Sheriff Pendergraft cut Matt off. "He's done kilt three men, a woman, and a child. A man like that should just be hung where he stands! I insist that we go. I already wired south to say we're coming. A man like that will shoot you in the back the first chance he gets. He can't be trusted!" he stated to Matt and then added to the men standing on the ground, "Take his gun belt, Travis. We're gonna shackle him."

Matt spoke firmly to the men standing, "Take one step towards my prisoner and I'll lay you out on the ground!" He eyed the sheriff coldly as his hand touched the butt of his revolver. "And you take your men and get away from me. I told you politely last night that your services weren't needed. I won't tell you again!" Matt warned sternly. The sheriff taking it upon himself to wire south without Matt's knowledge angered him. It could potentially ruin his plan to take Truet to Boise City without Bob Thacker knowing his whereabouts. "Now step away from me and mind your own business. You had no business wiring anything about me to anyone, Sheriff! Now excuse us," Matt barked angrily and swung up onto Betty. He watched closely as Truet did the same.

"Marshal, there's a twenty-five-mile distance to Gerhard from here, and it's rugged country. This killer could shoot you and disappear again," the sheriff argued. "It'll be safer if you let us help you. We don't want his likes running free around our town. At least disarm him, for crying out loud, Marshal!" Joseph pleaded, angered by Matt's lack of reason.

Matt noticed Truet's hand was resting near his revolver, just as Matt's own hand lightly rested. He said dangerously to the sheriff and his men, "If you want to disarm Mister Davis, I invited you to kill me if you can, and disarm him. Otherwise, go about your day and forget all about Mister Davis and me. I will not repeat myself again." He added coldly, "If I catch you following us, I will not hesitate to join with Truet in shooting you! That is your only warning, Sheriff. There are some things you just don't need to know right now. But, I will tell you that I am leaving Mister Davis armed for his own protection. Good day," he stated harshly and turned Betty to leave town.

"Now you understand why I'm here," Matt explained as they were leaving town. He sounded irritable. "Every bounty hunter, two-bit gunman, gambler and store clerk in the West is hunting for you. It isn't just the reward money Bob's offering; it's the lies Bob's created. Any man that shoots a woman and child is inexcusable."

"I didn't intend to shoot Allison or young Mike. I returned fire at both of them because they were shooting at me," Truet said with a hint of remorse in his voice.

"I know, but that's not what Bob printed. The boy didn't die anyway. He lost his arm, but not his life," Matt eyed Truet seriously. "Bob wants you dead. He's saying whatever he has to say to get it done." Again, he sounded angry as he said, "I just hope Bob doesn't receive that wire the sheriff sent and send his cowboys to come escort us back to Sweethome. I'm going to have to wire him myself and remind him that I work alone."

"If they come," Truet said with the taste of blood in his

voice, "I just want Mick Rodman to come, and then they can hang me for all I care."

"No, I can't allow them to do that," Matt said. "I already had a friend hung once; it'll never happen again if I'm still alive."

"Want to talk about it?" Truet asked. He noticed the pain that entered Matt's eyes when he mentioned it.

"Not particularly," Matt declined, putting the matter to rest. "How'd you sleep?" he asked, to change the subject.

"Fine for awhile," Truet said rubbing his clean-shaven chin. "I dreamed that I was holding Jenny Mae. It woke me up." His eyes lightly misted up with tears as he spoke, "It seemed so real, like I was really holding her. I didn't sleep much after that. Last night it really hit me that she's gone," he said softly. His eyes were red and moist. Matt left him to his thoughts.

After a little while Truet asked Matt, "So what did you write to Felisha?"

"Nothing really," Matt answered, a touch uncomfortably.

"Must've been something," Truet began, "You certainly were adamant about sending it. It looked like a long one."

"No. It's just a letter," Matt shrugged.

Truet smiled. "Are you sweet on Felisha?"

"No. She's just," Matt paused and glanced at Truet with a slight grin. "I like Felisha. I haven't felt like this about a woman since, well, a long time."

"Really? Well, she is a good woman. Is she interested in you?" Truet asked.

Matt shrugged. "I don't know. I hope so, but I can't tell. I'm good at tracking men down, but when it comes to women, I'm a bit of a fool. I can't read them," Matt admitted.

"I wouldn't worry about reading women as a whole. When you find one you like, like Felisha perhaps, become her friend. Get to know her and then you'll be able to read her. At least I could with Jenny Mae. I knew when she was worried, sad or not feeling well, just by the expression on her face. She didn't have to say a word. I knew her, and I loved her for who she was." His emotions welled up again. "I'm sorry," he said as he wiped his eyes.

"Felisha and I have become friends," Matt said ignoring Truet's statement. "I got a message from Branson stating that my brother-in-law drowned while I was staying at Felisha's place. It gave us some common ground, I guess. She and I talked until the very early morning hours, around three or so." Matt paused, noticing Truet casting a perplexed expression at him. He continued, "I'll have to tell you about my love life sometime, but I haven't talked to a girl like that in years. Don't get me wrong; I was attracted to her at first sight. But I have never in my life felt this kind of, well, being drawn to her like I am. I can't explain it."

"Wait a second," Truet questioned, "your brother-in-law died. And you still came after me?"

Matt nodded. "I did."

"Why?" Truet asked quickly. "Wouldn't your sister need you? You told me your family all lived around the Branson area. So why didn't you go back home to be with your family instead of coming after me?" Truet seemed disturbed.

Matt took a deep breath. "Because you're still alive. I got the wire from Lee and Regina saying Kyle had drowned. They asked me to stay and find you." Matt paused and added sadly, "Kyle was dead, you weren't. I sent my sister a wire giving my condolences."

"But he was family," Truet pointed out.

"If I had gone home and bloody Jim Hexum or some other blood hunter found you cutting down trees and killed you with a shot in the back, what good would I have done?"

Matt asked with a shrug. He continued, "I came here for a reason and I'm glad I did. An honest man should never have to go through what you have gone through. The greatest thing I could've done is tried to make something right. My sister understands that."

"Thank you, Matt," Truet said sincerely. "I'm sorry to hear about your brother-in-law."

Matt nodded. "Me too."

"So do you think you and Felisha have a future?" Truet asked changing the subject back to Felisha.

Matt shrugged. "I have no way of knowing. She hasn't written back," he joked with a laugh. Truet smiled.

"I don't know. I feel compelled to write her letters and every one of them gets longer and longer. All I write about is me. So I don't know. She probably thinks I'm a fool or something, but I can't wait to write to her again. I'm nervous to see her, but I guess that's the day I'll find out," Matt said looking anxiously at Truet.

Truet smiled lightly. "I think you'll be all right," he sounded confident. "Do you like children? Because she has Dillon, and he's a part of her. What I'm getting at is, don't get too attached to her if you're not willing to accept her son as your own."

Matt spoke sincerely, "I have no business writing to her if I wasn't willing to accept Dillon as my son. I don't know if there's a future for us or not, but I know that I have never experienced what I am feeling before and Dillon's a part of the reason for that."

41

Jeannie Bartholomew walked purposefully down the street casting a friendly smile at the familiar faces she passed on the way.

The Thacker-DePietro Land Company office was just down the street and Jeannie wanted to hand-deliver this particular wire to Bob Thacker herself. She knew it would put a long-awaited smile on his face. She liked being the bearer of good news, especially when it came to Bob Thacker or Jeb DePietro, the two most powerful men in Sweethome.

Jeannie opened the office door. She was pleased to see Bob leaning over a community plat map that was sprawled out over a table. Jeb was beside him; they were discussing a future building site of some kind. Bob held a cup of coffee in his right hand as he glanced up to see Jeannie and stepped forward curiously.

"Do you have some news, Jeannie?" he asked hopefully. He had become increasingly impatient over the nearly two months of searching for Truet without any success. He had read her expression correctly.

Jeannie smiled excitedly as she handed Bob a piece of paper. "The marshal's found him. He's bringing Truet back as we speak. They left Idalia for Gerhard today," she said proudly.

Bob's smile grew wide as slight tears of satisfaction built into his eyes. He stared at Jeannie, speechless.

Jeannie added with a smile. "They should be here in three days or so."

"I knew Matt Bannister would find him! That boy could find the lost needle in the proverbial haystack, I swear!" Bob laughed. He added to Jeannie, "See? I told you not to worry about the marshal. He may have taken a liking to Miss Felisha, but the boy's got no loyalties, except to the law. Trust me; he's got hundreds of Felisha's spread out across his travels. He'll bring Truet here, take what he wants from Miss Proper and disappear forever." Bob added with a hint of disgust, "And she'll be left used and not so high and mighty anymore."

Jeannie said as if it was a fact, "Like I've said, I think she already has given herself away, and it wouldn't surprise me if she's with child."

Jeb DePietro scoffed. "You have no proof. Being the judge here, I'll tell you it's all speculation, Jeannie. In other words, gossip."

"Say what you will, Mister DePietro, but I saw them together with my own eyes, so it is not gossip. I do not gossip nor do I listen to the ladies in the church that do. My first person testimony to what I witnessed should stand as fact in your court of law, Judge DePietro."

Jeb smiled and shook his head. "Well, the content of their relationship does not matter to me."

"Me either," Bob agreed. He turned to his business partner and friend, Jeb. "If Truet gets here in three days, how about we give him a trial two days later and hang him ten days from now? That would be on a Saturday and a good crowd could come celebrate Truet's hanging. We could set it up like we did the Fourth of July and make a little profit too."

Jeb shrugged his shoulders uncommitted. "Set it up."

Bob nodded with a thoughtful grin. "Yeah, we could open the ring up to anyone who wanted to challenge Goliath, five hundred dollars to anyone that can beat him. We could have a dance and maybe some fireworks. Yeah, I believe this could be a good thing. An end-of-summer necktie party!" Bob laughed loudly.

Jeannie said through a smile. "The church fellowship isn't going to like this. After all, Truet was a very respected member of the church."

"So are you!" Bob stated quickly. His fiery temper suddenly showed itself. His face reddened and his voice rose hard and mean. "I don't care about the church or what they think. I'm hanging the man that killed my son! His death sentence is already signed and will be handed out officially in the court of law. There's nothing anyone can do about that, try though they may." Bob paused and added purposely to Jeannie, "This time if your church causes me any embarrassment or trouble, I will order my cowboys to beat every one of them into the ground. That includes women and children! I will not allow anything or anyone to interfere with my justice!"

"Oh, I understand," Jeannie agreed quickly. "I wouldn't dare interfere; Truet is a guilty man. It's not me you need to worry about, Bob. It's Reverend Grace and the people like Felisha who will cause a problem. They were Truet's good friends, you know. And..." Jeannie stopped intentionally.

"And what?" Bob asked.

"Well, they're all friends with Matt Bannister now. What if they ask him to stick around?"

"So what if they do?" Bob asked bitterly. "It's a fair trial. He's guilty and will be found guilty. There's no crime in carrying out a death penalty, Jeannie."

"Perhaps," Jeannie agreed. "But, I still think they can cause a lot of trouble. I still say Felisha and the marshal have an inappropriate relationship and that could sway him to take up their cause somehow."

"How?" Bob asked growing short tempered.

Jeannie shrugged. "I don't know, but it sure seems to me that if you were to somehow convince Felisha that Matt was taking advantage of her, she might not invite him to stay a night longer than necessary," she mentioned pointedly. She added quickly after seeing an expression of doubt cross Jeb's face, "You don't have to believe me. I just know how women are, that's all. The marshal's sweet on Felisha. Don't think a woman like her won't use that to her advantage to free Truet."

Bob scoffed. "She can't free him, he's guilty!"

"Then at least she'll try to save Truet's life. The point is, she's going to cause trouble for you and you can't stop it if the marshal is here, and you know that." Jeannie stated sharply and excused herself, leaving the office as suddenly as she had entered it.

"Jeb," Bob said after a few minutes of thinking about Jeannie's words. "I'm going to see Felisha," he finished sharply and headed for the door.

FELISHA WAS on her small back porch scrubbing a pair of Dillon's jeans on the washboard in a tub of soap and water. It was a weekly chore to wash their clothes and hang them out to dry on the clothesline in her backyard. She was nearly done with her washing when a deep voice called her name from inside of her home.

"Out here," she answered loudly, thinking it might be Mister Foley, her only new boarder.

Bob Thacker stepped out of the backdoor and eyed her pathetically. "I let the Chinese wash mine." He nodded at the washboard where she scrubbed. "It's one of the few things they do well," he added with a hint of a smile.

"Hi, Bob," she said surprised to see him. It was such a surprise that she immediately feared bad news. She stood up slowly, drying her reddened hands on her old apron. "What can I do for you?" she asked with a touch of concern evident in her voice.

Bob frowned. "I came to tell you that Matt Bannister has arrested Truet and is bringing him back. They should be here in a few days. I thought you'd like to know that."

Felisha sighed with relief; she had feared the worst. "That's nice of you. Thank you," she said sounding foolish, she thought to herself. She didn't know what else to say.

Bob nodded. "Truet's trial will begin two days after he arrives and he'll hang on the following Saturday. I do not expect any trouble from you or any other of your Christian friends. If there is, my cowboys have my permission to do, as they will, to any and all of you, including you! I won't restrain any of them this time around. Am I making myself clear?"

"Hmm," Felisha said thoughtfully. Though growing angry, she kept her peaceful appearance. Her tongue however, got the better of her. "Does he get a lawyer, Bob? Or is this strictly a prosecution trial! Because it sounds to me like you've already gotten him sentenced."

Bob compressed his lips tightly together, struggling to

remain calm. His voice was strained. "How dare you? He killed my son, Felisha. There is no doubt about his guilt! He will hang and I will have my justice. That is a fact!" He glared warningly at her.

Felisha put her hands on her hips. "So why are you telling me this? I'm not on the jury, am I?" she asked sarcastically.

Bob continued to eye her oppressively. "I've heard about your relationship with Matt Bannister. I don't know the extent of the relationship, but I'd question his intentions. It seems strange to me that you're so quickly taken with the marshal and he's bringing your good friend back here to hang." He smiled slightly when he saw Felisha's expression change to anger. He added intentionally, "It seems to me that maybe he's taken advantage of you. Being a single man and all, I'm sure he's mastered the art of seducing women like you all over the west. I mean, what would the townsfolk say if you had another fatherless bastard running around at your feet."

"Unfortunately for you and the others who need to concern yourselves with my business, there is no relationship other than friendship," she said defensively. Her brown eyes grew wide and fierce.

Bob laughed lightly at Felisha. "Well, it seems he's more my friend than yours. But, say what you will. Have a good day, Felisha. And again, if you and your friends get in my way when Truet gets here, my boys will run their horses right through you. Women and children won't be spared this time. Nobody's getting in my way. No one!" He pointed a finger at her and turned to go back through the house, but a young man in his mid-twenties stood behind him listening. Bob eyed him strangely and said, "Who are you?"

"Oh, my name's Nate Foley," he said and offered his

hand to Bob. Nate was a good-sized young man with a youthful face and well-groomed blonde hair.

"Do you always listen to other people's conversations, Mister Foley? It's a good way to get yourself slapped, boy!" he spat out. He stepped past Nate with a hard nudge with his shoulder to remove the young man out of the way.

Nate looked at Felisha questionably. "Did I interrupt something?"

Felisha frowned. "No. What can I do for you, Mister Foley?"

Nate shrugged. "Nothing, I just saw a man walk through the house and heard what he was saying. I don't mean to pry Miss Conway, but is everything all right?"

Felisha eyed the young man, slightly annoyed, and answered shortly, "Everything is fine, Mister Foley. Thanks for checking up on me."

When Nate had gone back inside, and she was sure she wouldn't be overheard, she smiled. Looking up into the blue sky of the afternoon sun, she said, "Thank You, Lord. I thank You for letting Matt find him safely."

42

Saul had spent the day driving one of the six wagons making the back-and-forth journey between the hayfields and the feed barn. He and a few of the other cowboys had to work with the Chinese men Brit hired to bring in the harvest of hay. They started early in the morning and worked until sundown. It would take many long hours, day after day, but eventually, it would end after many hundreds of acres of hayfields were harvested.

To Saul, it was another long, dust-filled day of sitting on the wagon's bench seat being rocked, shifted and bounced with every bump, hole or rut the wheels ran over in the fields. His job duties were simple enough. He was to drive the wagon into the field, wait for it to be loaded with hay and then drive it back to the feed barn. His particular job was easy enough, but it wore on his body like no other job did in the harvesting of hay. His body ached from the continuous jolting of the wagon and dust filled his eyes and nose. The hot sun blazed down upon him continuously without the luxury of an umbrella for shade. Brit supplied five umbrellas for the six wagon drivers. Saul, of course, didn't get one. For Saul, the worst part about driving the wagon was quite simply the hours of driving the wagon over and over again, all day long, day after day. A highlight of his day was waving to the other drivers as they'd pass by one another on their rotating cycle of hauling in the harvest.

Upon returning to the feed barn to unload, Saul was a little unnerved to see Bob Thacker sitting in his black buggy waiting for him. Bob had a cowboy named Joe Warren sitting beside him. Saul stopped the wagon underneath the large double doors at the top of the large barn. The men in the hayloft used a pulley and a large hayfork to pull the hay up into the loft where it was stacked and stored for winter.

"Saul," Bob said, pulling his buggy beside the wagon. "You come with me. Joe's gonna fill in for you."

Saul said, "hello" to Joe, who was visibly irritated about being forced to drive a wagon on the harvesting rotation. He would rather be watching over the free-ranging cattle up north like a cowboy was supposed to be doing at this time of year.

"Get on," Bob said as Saul neared. "We're going for a ride."

"Okay," Saul said nervously. His heart began to beat quicker as Bob released the brake and urged his horse to move on. "Where are we going?" he asked.

"Just for a ride," Bob replied simply as he puffed on his cigar. He was dressed in dark suit pants with black suspenders over a clean white shirt that was unbuttoned at top and his sleeves were rolled up. His black Stetson shadowed his face against the late afternoon heat. "How's the hay coming along? Are those Chinamen earning their pay? I don't want those yellow-eyed thieves to cut me out short. You gotta watch them," he stated as a warning.

"They're doing fine," Saul reassured him.

"Are you ready to fight again? I've got something in the works for ten days from now. How would you feel about having an open ring invitational? A five-hundred-dollar purse for the man that can beat the 'Killer Goliath.' Are you ready for that?" Bob asked, all business on his face.

"I guess."

"No guessing, Saul! For that kind of money those men will be giving their all to hurt you. You better be ready and willing to hurt anyone that accepts that challenge. You're 'Killer Goliath' now. You need to live up to the name."

Saul remained silent while Bob drove them away from the feedlot towards the main ranch house and other buildings. Saul grew uneasy when Bob turned towards Brit's home.

"Where are we going?" he asked.

"Just down the road," Bob said and left it at that. They rode in an uncomfortable silence until they drove right up to the front of Brit's house. Bob stopped the buggy, reached behind the seat, and pulled out a brown paper-wrapped package. "Take this to Abby for me will ya?" Bob asked. It was more of a command than a question.

"What?" Saul asked nervously. "What about Brit? I'm not supposed to..."

"Forget Brit. Go!" Bob ordered curtly with a wave of his hand.

The front door opened and Abby stood at the threshold with a perplexed expression mixed with fear on her face. "Brit's not here," she stated in a quivering voice. Her lip was swollen and had been split. Her left eye was heavily discolored.

"Good lord, Abby," Saul gasped softly, stepping down from the wagon and stepping closer. She turned her face away from him, trying to hide her face with her left hand over her eyes. Her slim body visibly shook. "I'm sorry," he added softly. He hadn't spoken to her since Independence Day, nearly two months before.

"Give her your present," Bob said sounding nearly kind.

Saul glanced back at Bob and awkwardly held the brown-papered package out to Abby. "I'm supposed to hand this to you."

Reluctantly, Abby took it and eyed Bob carefully. "What is this, Mister Thacker?" she asked weakly.

"A new dress. You'll like it; it's from Saul. Go put it on. Let's see what it looks like on you," Bob sounded kind while he smiled pleasantly.

Abby shuttered. "Please, just go away," she nearly begged in her voice.

Bob's smile faded and a nasty scowl replaced it. His voice was gruff and demanding, "Go put it on! I want to see it on you and only that, nothing else!"

Abby closed her eyes as a tear slid down her face. Without looking at Saul, she stepped inside and closed the door behind her.

Saul put his hands on his hips and stared at the ground. His breathing was heavy and his emotions swelled within him. The combination of fear, guilt, and fury swirled within him like a pot of boiling water over a fire.

"I think you'll like the dress," Bob sounded optimistic, "I'm sure it'll suit her fine, Saul. It'll be kind of nice to see her in a new pretty dress, huh?"

Saul looked at him with an unsettled expression. "Yeah," he answered.

"I thought you'd like that. It's from you," Bob mentioned again, as he puffed his cigar with a smile.

After a short moment Bob lost patience and yelled, "Hurry up and show yourself!"

The door opened a little and they could hear her fighting to keep from sobbing as she hid behind the door.

"Get out here!" Bob ordered. Abby stepped out from the door. She wore a plain white bed sheet wrapped around her tightly. Her pale skin was exposed around her shoulders and arms, her calves and feet were also exposed. She hid her face with one hand and held the sheet with the other. She gritted her teeth tightly as her will and body began to crumble. She wept.

Saul turned to Bob filled with anger. "What the hell is that?" he shouted.

Bob took a deep puff on his cigar and exhaled through a cold and sober face. He spoke deliberately, "That's all she'll be wearing day in and day out at Johnny Niehus' place if you don't do as you're told, Saul. I've already made the arrangements; it's a done deal, we're just waiting to see what you'll do."

"Me? What haven't I done?" Saul yelled out emotionally, his voice quivered. "What more do you want me to do? I've done everything you've asked me to do! You don't have to hurt her, for crying out loud. You don't have to do this to her to get to me. I'll do anything you want, just leave her be. Please!" Saul cried out. Tears of frustration filled his eyes.

Bob glared evenly at Saul. "The marshal arrested Truet and they're coming back here. You're going to sit in the courtroom in front of your friends, the town, and maybe even the marshal himself, and tell them that AJ and the boys were with you. You're going to say they were innocent; you're going to swear it on that Bible you care about. Am I right?"

"Of course," Saul choked. He forced down the temptation to pull Bob down off of his buggy and beat him to death.

Bob nodded and continued pointedly, "Truet will be

sitting there. His life will depend on your testimony. You might be temped to try to save Truet's life. Just know that if you do, our sweet lady here will be bought and sold every half hour to any man with a penny. She'll be the cheapest damn whore in town. And it'll be your fault."

Abby, distressed, suddenly cried out towards Bob, "Why are you doing this to me? What have I ever done to you? Any of you? Why don't you let me go home? I just want to go home." She wept bitterly and slowly crumbled to her knees, still holding the sheet around her breasts in the doorway. "I just want to go home to my mother."

Saul glared at Bob with hate burning in his eyes. "I'll do what you want. But you are a wicked man and you can't keep me here forever."

"No?" Bob asked as if it was a challenge. "Saul, you'll do what I want until I tell you differently," he said confidently. He looked at Abby who was still lying at the threshold blocking the door. "Woman, stop your crying! I can barely stomach you, anyway. Brit would be better off if he did sell you to Johnny." He paused and then said to Saul, "Are we understanding each other, Saul?"

"Yes!" Saul spit the word out like it was poison to his lips.

"Good. Get up here and let's go, Saul. You've had a long enough break, it's time to get you back to work." He looked at Abby with disgust. "Get inside and cry!"

Abby glared up at Bob through her tears and asked, "What have I ever done to you?"

"You married my son," he answered simply and added to Saul. "Let's go!"

Saul nodded, acknowledging Bob and turned toward Abby. He reached his hand down to her and gently helped her to her feet. Holding the door open he motioned for her to go inside. He followed her inside and let the door close on its own. Once out of Bob's sight he turned her around to face him. She looked away ashamed, but he placed his hands on her cheeks and turned her face toward his. "Now you know why I haven't come back here to see you," he spoke quickly and quietly. "I love you more than anything in this world, Abby. Don't give up on me, please. I promise I'll take you out of here soon. Just don't give up on me. Okay? Just pray, Abby."

"Why? God doesn't answer me," she said hopelessly.

Bob's voice boomed from outside, "Saul! Get out here right now!"

Saul kissed her quickly on the forehead. "God does answer prayer, especially yours. Just keep praying and keep hoping in the Lord. Our God's a God of hope, Abby. Don't lose yours." He kissed her quickly and then kissed her again. He had longed for so long to hold her again; now that he did, he didn't want to let her go. "I love you," he said and reluctantly let her go and went to the door just as Bob yelled again. Saul paused and looked back at her. "Trust in the Lord, Abby."

43

"Can I ask you a question?" Truet asked Matt as they rode through the rugged mountain terrain towards Butchart, some thirty miles south of Gerhard. They had stayed the night in Gerhard and left immediately after breakfast. It seemed the marshal's fame brought a lot of unwanted attention to them as they ventured into new towns. While in Gerhard they ate a secluded dinner and stayed the rest of their time in the confines of their shared hotel room. In the morning, they ate breakfast and left as soon as they could. It was going to be a long day of riding to reach Butchart.

"Sure," Matt agreed.

"I watched you reading your Bible last night before I rolled over and went to sleep. So I'll ask, and maybe you'll understand, but have you ever felt like God has left you?"

"Yes," Matt answered slowly and looked at Truet sincerely. "A year ago I lived in Cheyenne, Wyoming; I'd been there for numerous years. I hadn't seen my family in fifteen years and I... well, I didn't really have too much to live for anymore until this one certain day and..." he hesitated and then finished quietly. "I figured I had nothing to live for, so I put my gun to my own head to end it."

"You?" Truet asked surprised. "Really? I'm surprised to hear that because you seem so, I don't know, happy."

Matt smiled sadly. "Well, I wasn't. I knew the Lord, of course, but I didn't want to continue living with the sorrow I was living in. So I thought I'd end it and I would've, if it wasn't for my reverend stopping by just in time." Matt paused and then he continued pointedly, "I thought the Lord had left me. I couldn't feel His presence in my life anymore, but Jesus saved my life that night. He had not left me, Truet. I left Him. He promises in the Bible to never leave His people and He was there even though I felt lost and alone. God's not left you, Truet."

Truet looked out through the forest with tears clouding his eyes. "I don't know about that. Do you believe God is good? I mean really good, even in the things that happen which are absolutely not good?"

"Like what's happened to you?" Matt asked empathetically.

Truet shook his head slowly. "No, like what happened to my wife. We were expecting our first child, Matt." He raised his empty hands. "How could a good and loving God take that away from me, or anyone else for that matter," he asked with anger building in his voice and burning quietly in his eyes. He added, "It doesn't sound good or loving to me. Does it to you?"

Matt frowned. "No. Nothing like that is good or seems loving. But the fact is we live in a wicked world that's full of injustice and all kinds of terrible things that seem unfair and just simply wrong. As a marshal, I've heard countless tragic stories. Some make me wonder how anyone could be so cold-blooded and heartless to another human being, but it happens everyday," Matt paused to look at Truet. "But that's the choices and doings of humanity. God is good, loving and merciful, make no mistake about that. He is here, and He sees everything that's happening. He allows it to happen, but it isn't forgotten." Matt paused and then continued, "We live in a fallen world, Truet. Crime, misfortune, tragedy, and heartbreak are just a part of it. I think the Bible makes that pretty clear. But the Lord promised to never leave His people. He promised to never leave you."

"What about Jenny Mae?" he asked bitterly. "The Lord also promises to protect his people!"

"The Lord does protect His people. Terrible things can happen to Christians just like they can to non-believers. You know it just happens and we wonder why God didn't stop it. We can blame God for it even, but in the Bible terrible things happened to God's people and He didn't send an angel down to stop it from happening.

"The best example of that is Joseph in the book of Genesis. His brothers wanted to kill him, God protected Joseph from being killed, but God *allowed* him to be sold into slavery to the Egyptians. Over time, he became the head slave to Potifer's household and Potifer was the captain of Pharaoh's guard. In essence, Potifer was the General over the Army in today's terms. When Potifer's wife tried to seduce Joseph, Joseph rejected her for the sake of righteousness. Enraged by being rejected by a slave, she accused him of trying to rape her." Matt paused and then continued dramatically, "Now, here's the thing about this. Potifer, by all rights and power, should have had Joseph beheaded, but he didn't. God protected Joseph from being killed, but God did *not* protect Joseph from being sent to prison for a crime he did not commit. I have to wonder how unfair Joseph must've thought God was to him because he was being punished for a crime that never happened. In fact, it was his belief in God and what's right and wrong, that made him literally run from Potifer's wife.

"Joseph said it himself when he deciphered the dreams of the cupbearer and the cook. Joseph tells the cupbearer to remember him when he's restored to his position as Pharaoh's cupbearer. Joseph said something like, 'Remember me, because I'm in prison and I have done nothing wrong. I was unfairly imprisoned. I am an innocent man.' I have no doubt that Joseph felt like God had left him," Matt said with a nod toward Truet.

"The cupbearer didn't mention Joseph to Pharaoh, though. Joseph stayed in prison for years. He did, however, prove himself to be a great manager and he got to the point where he managed the supplies and work force of the prison. I wonder how many times he wondered why God had left him in that prison unfairly. I would guess many.

"But unknown to Joseph, God was working on the outside. Pharaoh was troubled by dreams, dreams that his advisors couldn't explain. The dreams must've really haunted him because that's when the cupbearer remembered Joseph and told Pharaoh about him. Joseph deciphered his dreams for him. There would be seven years of plenty, and following would be seven years of absolute famine. That's a scary thought when you live off of the land," Matt emphasized with a nod. "So Pharaoh put Joseph in charge over the entire land, everyone was under Joseph's power, except Pharaoh himself. That included Potifer and his wife. Can you possibly imagine how scared she was when that happened? It doesn't say, but I wonder if he made her confess her wrong in front of Potifer to clear his own name?" he asked. "Anyway, when the famine came, Egypt was well prepared for it and people came from all over to

Egypt for food, including Joseph's brothers, who had sold him into slavery all those years before. They didn't recognize him when they wanted his permission to buy food to feed their family. Of course, he recognized them and eventually moved his entire family to Egypt. After his father died, his brothers feared for their lives, you know, because they are the ones that sold him into slavery at the beginning. But Joseph doesn't execute them. In fact, when they fear for their lives, Joseph makes an outstanding statement, he says: *'you meant it for harm, but God meant it for good. The saving of many lives.'*"

Matt drank from his canteen. "My point is, God allows some bad to happen, but He protects too. Joseph couldn't be who he had become if he hadn't been sold into slavery and he couldn't have planned for the famine if he hadn't been in prison. He came to understand that when he looked back over his life in Egypt. God was in control and beside him the whole entire time preparing Joseph for something much larger and greater. The saving of many lives."

Truet stated sharply, "What does that have to do with God protecting Jenny Mae? She was a very committed Christian and God didn't protect her! She was raped and beaten by four men. She miscarried our baby and bled to death because of them! Where's the protection in that?" he asked bitterly.

"I don't know, Truet. All I know is God can use all circumstances for His good purposes."

Truet grew angry. "Like what, Matt? What good could God possibly bring out of my wife dying with our unborn child, huh? You tell me that!" he asked heatedly. His eyes burned into Matt's painfully.

Matt sighed. "I don't know. All I know is that He can."

"There is no good in it!" Truet yelled. "None!"

"I didn't say there was any good in it. You're right, there is none. It's a horrible crime and God knows you have the right to be angry," Matt said firmly. He added softly, "Maybe someday when you look back on this, you'll see something that you can't see now. Like Joseph did on his life. I'm not saying that it'll ever be good, but maybe you can offer someone else something good because of this. God says He can 'bring some good out of it.' Not that it's good."

"There is nothing good that can come out of this!" he snapped bitterly at Matt and then sped his horse up in front of Matt's to ride alone.

Matt nodded. He would say no more about it. God can and does bring good out of dark and painful experiences. Matt had said Truet's exact words in his lifetime, many times. Though not always explained or ever really understood, it was clear to Matt that all situations are pre-approved by God. When the sovereign Lord allows troubles to come into the lives of His children, it should never be forgotten that the Lord carries His children through them. None of His children are left to face the darkness alone.

Truet turned around in his saddle and added vehemently, "If God is the Creator of everything; He should've been big enough to save Jenny Mae!"

Matt said softly, "Yes, but He didn't. Remember Truet, we are created for His purposes, not Him for ours."

44

The sound of the crickets, frogs and an occasional coyote filled the Thacker house with the sounds of a warm August night. Bob still wore his dark suit-pants and suspenders over his unbuttoned white shirt. He stood alone in the silence of the parlor of his large home with a glass of brandy in his hand. As usual, the windows were opened to allow the night's breeze to cool his house down after the day's heat.

The parlor was the largest room in the house and decorated with expensive and lavish furnishings from around the world. There were two fine velvet-covered davenports and two sets of matching high-back padded chairs. There was enough seating for a dozen individuals comfortably. There were ornate tables and cabinets of the finest workmanship that seemed to blend perfectly with the light pastel-papered walls with a mahogany wainscot. The parlor was specifically designed to entertain guests, so a wainscot bar held a wide assortment of drinks.

Certain items were placed in the room as conversation pieces, such as the throne made of steer horns which Bob had shipped up from Texas. A Japanese samurai sword sat proudly on the mahogany mantel of a large river rock fireplace. A wolverine with a vicious snarl was mounted in a glass case, and other unique items Bob had collected were displayed in the room.

However, the object that seemed to interest his guests more than any other was the large oil portrait of a beautiful young woman in her mid-twenties. She had her long black hair in a bun and her oval-shaped face was turned slightly to her left with an amorous, yet adoring countenance expressed in her dark eyes; as if she was eyeing someone fondly nearby. Her ebony eyes gazed with such a spellbinding tranquility that it forced one to wish they were the recipients of her affection. Her long and slender neck was covered tastefully by a green dress decorated with black lace. Around her neck, a gold chain held an opened, heart-shaped locket. Each side of the locket had a little dark-haired boy's face representing their two sons, Brit and AJ. The portrait was in an ornate, oval-shaped gold frame and at the bottom was a nameplate that read "Olga." It was a painting of Bob's late wife.

The portrait wasn't painted while she was alive. It was painted long after her death from a small daguerreotype that sat below the portrait on a cherry wood table. Olga's expression on the daguerreotype was stiff, despondent and bitter. Dressed in a simple dark dress with a shawl around her shoulders, she appeared to be a young woman who had aged long before her time. Truth be known, Bob paid the artist to create a beautiful seductress from Olga's embittered expression on the daguerreotype. The daguerreotype was of little value, except that it was the only likeness he had of the boys' mother. The portrait he had painted looked nothing like her, except for the hair and the shape of her face.

The portrait of Olga brought many questions asked by

the friends he hosted. People were curious about the alluring young wife he once had. With great affection in his voice, Bob would tell the story of how he met Olga in Denver, Colorado. She was a judge's respectable daughter. They fell in love, but the judge would not allow her to marry Bob until he could raise a stable future for her and her offspring. So he headed out to California with the gold rush and did well for himself by finding a "well of gold" as he often told it. He returned to Denver, bought a home and invested in a store business. By becoming an established businessman and showing himself as a man of integrity, he earned Olga's father's blessing, and he then married Olga. After some time, they eventually sold out and moved west to Boise City to venture into the cattle business while the land was still young. He staked a claim on what is now a small portion of the Thacker Ranch. Just when life appeared like it couldn't get any better, his beautiful Olga, was kicked in the abdomen by a horse and died of internal bleeding hours later. Devastated by the loss, he buried Olga under a willow tree and committed the remainder of his life to raising their two boys alone. With a hint of tears in his eyes, he would finish by saying, "My love for Olga is the only love I will ever know." It was a good story, and it brought him a lot of empathy, but it was, after all, just a story.

Bob swirled his fine brandy and sipped it as a cool breeze blew in through the window. He looked at his hand that held the glass - his right hand. It was the very hand that built his fortune, even early on.

Bob had not met Olga before he went to California to seek the gold, nor did he find a "well of gold," as he claimed. What he did find was a distaste for the backbreaking labor it required to find the gold. Broke and discouraged, Bob left his claim and took a job as a barkeep in Jackson. It paid little, but he discovered that he could pocket gold dust easily, and over time it added up. On occasions, he'd steal from the prostitute's savings in the rooms upstairs and as often as he could from the drunken customers.

Greed was a funny thing. Given the opportunity, greed can make a man do the unthinkable, including the stalking and killing of a lone miner, for the load of dust in his purse. It was the first of a few that Bob victimized. Bob collected a good weight of dust, but he came up with an idea of how he might double or even triple his earnings. By melting lead and dropping beads of it into water, he created nuggets of lead, which he would then coat with melted-down gold. He created gold nuggets of various sizes and weights that were mostly lead. He left Jackson a much wealthier man, and he continued to sell his nuggets from town to town. He left California and moved on to Virginia City, Nevada where he once again went to work as a barkeep to start his scam all over again in a new town.

Florence Marcel was the successful madam of the "Blue Diamond Inn," which was a bordello of some reputation of quality. Florence was in her late forties and an ex-prostitute herself, who had the onset of tuberculosis. She had a daughter who was still young and pretty, who stood to inherit the bordello when Florence passed away. Though Olga Marcel was a prostitute herself, Bob courted her mercilessly until she had no choice but to be swayed by his charm. She had fallen in love with him and they married. With his own money and some borrowed from Florence, he bought a home in Virginia City. He continued to work as a barkeep and pocketed what he could, while Olga stayed at home to do the domestic chores. Tired of struggling to barely get by and desiring to have so much more, Bob grew impatient and planned his next move toward attaining the riches he deserved. He waited until Florence was having a bad day as she was often sickly. On one of those days when she struggled to breathe, he entered her room late at night and he held a pillow over Florence's face. The following day, her death was considered being by consumption.

Olga inherited Florence's considerable savings, including the bordello. Bob sold the bordello and his home, took his now pregnant wife, and moved west to Boise City.He bought a home in town and met a young lawyer named Jeb DePietro, who was struggling to make ends meet. They went into business together as partners on a saloon and with time it prospered enough to open another. Bob managed the saloons with his vast experience, while Jeb applied his legal knowledge in his law office.

Business was good. Bob had finally succeeded in having a thriving business that was beginning to pay for a big house and all that he had worked so hard for. Despite his growing financial success his home life was in trouble. Olga, tired of being beat on and watching her two young sons being manhandled by their father, decided to leave her husband. Olga demanded the worth of her mother's estate to begin a life somewhere else with her boys, who were now nine and two. Bob enraged by her request, hit her. However, this time instead of hiding in fear, Olga fought back with a knife, cutting Bob's arm. Bob beat her to the ground and while she lay on the floor he kicked her again and again as hard as he could. The two boys cried in terror as they watched helplessly, but he continued to kick her and yell out obscenities until he exhausted himself. Later that night, Bob tried to hold her close to him to make things right, but she was in terrible abdominal pain. Her refusal only angered Bob who took her anyway despite her cries of agony. By morning when he awoke, she was lying beside him, dead.

A grand jury tried to indict Bob for the murder of his wife, but with the cut on his arm, Jeb's courtroom expertise, and the testimony of nine-year-old Brit Thacker that his mother was trying to kill his father, Bob was released a free man. The rest was history. He invested in cattle and started what would become the Thacker Ranch. Eventually Bob and Jeb founded the Thacker DePietro Land Company and founded the town of Sweethome.

Bob looked at his hands; they were the hands that built his fortune. He had everything he had ever wanted and more. He had money and certainly had power. He even had a top contender for the American boxing championship. He was successful; he had it all except for his beloved son, AJ.

Bob picked up a photograph of AJ from the Cherry wood table. He was such a good-looking boy. He was a good son. A little feisty at times, but what boy wasn't when he sowed his oats? Truet Davis had murdered him and rocked Bob's whole kingdom. The shock waves of AJ's murder had left a wide range of unhealed emotions that Bob had yet to reconcile. One of the most painful was the constant reminder that AJ no longer lived at home. He did not sleep in his bed or have a sarcastic word for his father. Bob missed his son and nothing that Bob owned could fill that emptiness. It was like a widening void constantly growing deeper. There was one thing Bob was sure would fill it and that was the blood of Truet Davis. He longed to see the day when Truet would hang. He was going to make sure that Truet's face was uncovered when the trap door opened, just so Bob could stare into Truet's eyes while he strangled to death. It was already planned; there would be no quick snap of the neck. There would be no mercy for Truet, and Bob looked forward to it. In fact, he thirsted for it!

45

Jeannie Bartholomew had received another wire that morning concerning the whereabouts of Matt and Truet. They were leaving Butchart and that put them two days ride away. If they kept up their present speed they would arrive in Sweethome on Saturday. She had yet to notify Bob Thacker of that, but she figured she'd walk to his office on her lunch break at noon. Strangely enough, the marshal had never wired Bob yet with the news of finding Truet. Perhaps though, the marshal was one of those kinds of men that liked to surprise people. It was the sheriff of Butchart that had wired.

However, the marshal did write another letter to Felisha. It was a touch thicker than the others, so it must have had a lot more to say about something; she could only imagine what. She thought it interesting how he could spend so much time writing to her, but couldn't take a moment to wire Bob. She had said as much to her husband and a couple of other ladies that morning.

The door opened with the sound of the bell and Felisha

walked in with Rebecca Grace, who held the hand of her three-year-old daughter, Sarah.

"Well, good morning, ladies," Jeannie said. It was nearly eleven.

"Good morning," they both replied. It was Rebecca that added, "Jeannie, I would like to get a square of butter and a tin of cinnamon. And," she hesitated in thought. "And that's all for now, I suppose. I have enough flour," she looked questionably at Felisha to remind her.

"Eggs?" Felisha asked with a shrug.

"No, I've got eggs. Oh, tea. I need a tin of tea. Richard would just about tan my hide if I forgot his tea," she said with a smile, glad she remembered it.

Jeannie seemed to hesitate as she stared at Rebecca. "A man of God should never hit his wife! My word, if he treats his wife like that what's he going to teach the town?"

"It was a figure of speech," Rebecca replied sharply. "Richard would never, nor has he ever laid his hands on me. He is a very godly man and I am sorry that you misunderstood my meaning."

"Oh! I am glad to hear that," Jeannie stated with an intentional laugh. She turned to gather the goods that were spread out through the store. "My mother always used to say the church is only as good as the reverend that runs it. And you can always tell how good he is by how godly his family is, hum hmm," she cleared her throat as she walked back to the counter carrying a one-pound brick of butter wrapped in linen and a can of cinnamon. "Oh, the tea!" She laid the two items down and walked back around the cashier to a grocery row. "We must not forget the reverend's tea or you might get whipped," she laughed lightly.

"My husband..." Rebecca began to reply without any humor in her voice.

"I was kidding," Jeannie said quickly over Rebecca. She returned to the counter with the tea. "I think you have a lovely family. And we love the reverend. That's why it sounded so shocking when you said that," Jeannie explained with a shrug. "I will just add these to your bill, Rebecca."

"Thank you," Rebecca said with a taste of irritation to her voice.

"Anything for you today, Felisha?" Jeannie asked pleasantly.

"Not today."

"How about a piece of candy for the baby?" Jeannie asked Rebecca, reaching into a large jar of penny candies.

"No. She's not feeling well today," Rebecca replied looking at her daughter. She appeared flushed and grumpy as she stayed near her mother's side. "Have a good day," Rebecca said and turned to leave.

"Oh, Felisha, I have a letter for you," Jeannie announced as if she just remembered it and walked into the mailroom to retrieve it. Jeannie returned holding it out to Felisha with a snide smile. "It's from your secret admirer, the marshal. I can tell by the handwriting. He must fancy you because this one's thicker than all the others."

Rebecca smiled, as Felisha glanced at her quickly. Felisha's face lit up though she tried to hide her excitement. "Thank you," she said taking the letter and turning to leave.

"You're welcome," Jeannie said sweetly and then added in an insinuating tone, "I must admit, I find it rather strange that he can write endless letters to you, but he can't find the time to notify Bob of his progress either by wire or mail."

Felisha answered calmly, "I suppose you should ask him about that when he gets here, Jeannie. If it bothers you that much, that is."

"Oh," Jeannie smiled, "The sheriff in Butchart wired this morning. It seems the marshal and Truet are on their way to Louden. So, they should be here on Saturday afternoon sometime." She watched Felisha's reaction carefully. A quick flash of excitement spread momentarily across her face. Jeannie smiled knowingly.

"Good," is all Felisha said.

"Yes," Jeannie agreed. "I suppose, you'll be excited to see the marshal again," she waited expectedly.

"In fact, yes, I will be," she answered honestly and waited for Jeannie to say something more.

"I imagine so; undoubtedly he'll be expecting to see you again. I just feel bad for Truet though," she changed the subject as fast as she changed her tone, which now turned sympathetic. "Monday he'll be tried for murder and next Saturday he'll be hung. Bob has already begun to plan to make a community spectacle of it. I feel so bad for Truet. But," she paused to take a dramatic breath. "At least Matt will be here for one night before he goes back to Branson. I mean, after all, his job here will be done. He certainly has nothing important to stick around here for."

Felisha forced a small smile. "Truet will have a fair trial. After all, it's up to a jury to decide what happens to him. Not Bob."

"There's nothing to decide. The whole town witnessed Truet shooting those men and killing poor Allison the way that he did."

"Poor Allison!" Rebecca spouted; she glared at Jeannie in disbelief. "The whole town saw her shoot at him first. There's nothing poor about her. What is poor is your insistent need to criticize and gossip about everybody in this town! You can't stand the fact that Felisha might just really have a good start to a relationship with a good man, and yes, maybe he is interested in Felisha, too! Most of us would say 'great,' but not you. No..." Rebecca stepped forward; her anger was clearly expressed on her face. "You turn it into some kind of terrible gossip insinuating that it is unreasonable for Matt Bannister to be interested in Felisha. So it has to be sexual! Oh, yes, I heard what you're saying about them." Rebecca glared severely at Jeannie, who stood with her mouth open. She was surprised by the unexpected verbal attack by the normally quiet Rebecca Grace.

"You," Rebecca continued, "are supposed to be a Christian, but you are not! You thrive on other people's misery and throw out insults covered with chocolate to just hurt them a little bit more. The comment about my husband, my family! You darn well knew what I meant, and you intentionally twisted it around so you could go tell it to everybody else!" she pointed at Jeannie with an extended finger. "You are the filthy, rotten maggot in a bundle of apples. You ruin everyone around you. My husband won't say it because he just keeps hoping and praying, but I will say it because I've been waiting a long time to say it!" Rebecca took a deep breath to regain her composure. She spoke boldly, "We'd appreciate it if you didn't come to church anymore, Jeannie. It's supposed to be a place of worship, finding hope, gaining peace, and building each other up during our troubles. Not collecting gossip to tear them down and spread around. You are the wolf that causes dissension and separates the flock of the church. You are not welcomed back!"

"My, how dare you!" Jeannie protested. "I have been a member of that church long before you came here, young lady! I pay my tithe every month, much more than anyone else does. Here," she said opening her receipt ledger, "I'll just pay your bill right now because this is my week to tithe!" she finished loudly. She leaned forward over the counter and hissed angrily, "How dare you talk to me like that? I'm the one that pays your bills! I am also the church treasurer and used to play the piano before you came to town. But, I suppose that isn't enough, is it? No, it's not, because I apparently gossip. I do not gossip and I never have! Maybe you're listening to gossip about me, but I do not gossip! I love and care for every member of our church, every one of them. I would not hurt any of them, especially either of you," Jeannie said while glaring at them both.

"I can pay my own bill," Rebecca said in a controlled fashion. "You can keep your tithe. Do you really think God cares how much you tithe? It seems to me that repeatedly throughout the Bible that '*obeying*' is emphasized, not tithing. You don't need to tithe until you can *obey* what the word of God says." Rebecca turned to Felisha, "Come on, we're done in here."

"I obey! I am a Christian, unlike you two judgmental hypocrites! Don't judge me. I know what I see with my own two eyes. You both think you're so high and mighty, but I know the truth about both of you. Yeah," she spoke to Rebecca, "You and your husband act like you're so godly, but your children are little brats and you can't even pay your own bills!" She flicked the pages of her ledger pointedly. She then turned to Felisha and said, "And she can act like a lady all she wants, but I know what happened between her and Matt Bannister! I saw them together with my own eyes. Don't try to pretend to be perfect to me. You're both hypocrites! You can say what you will to the congregation about me, Rebecca. But I'm not the one sleeping with the devil! It isn't my lover that's bringing Truet back here to hang, and he is going to hang! And there's nothing you can do about it. Fair trial? It's already been decided!" She directed her fury at Felisha again, "And your lover is in on it.

He's been paid to bring Truet back here. You're just a side dish, Felisha. Don't kid yourself; Matt wouldn't be interested in an older woman with a son!" Jeannie scoffed and then turned her attention back to Rebecca, "Pack your things, because you and your husband are leaving Sweethome. You don't belong here!"

Rebecca shook her head in awe as she said simply, "You have no sense of truth whatsoever at all, do you? I'm afraid you bundle closer to the devil than you think. And just so you know, Matt's not even bringing Truet here. He's taking him to Boise City for a fair trial."

"You shouldn't have said that," Felisha stated quickly with annoyance in her voice.

"Why not?" Rebecca asked heatedly. "They're going to find out anyway. And we'll know soon enough whose side Jeannie's on." Her attention went back to Jeannie. "AJ and those men killed Jenny Mae. They were getting away with murder. Truet did what any man would do in his shoes and he deserves a fair trial. Not to be strung up like a criminal," she finished.

Jeannie's eyes were filled with deep resentment as they stared at Rebecca. She tried to control her voice as she said, "AJ was with Saul that morning, Saul already admitted that. So I don't understand how you can think Truet's innocent. He killed them, there's no doubt about that. Besides, I've seen AJ and Jenny Mae talking together many times before, and I know Allison was very jealous of Jenny Mae. So don't tell me they didn't have something going on."

Felisha laughed with disgust. "Let's go."

"And," Jeannie added, "about the marshal taking Truet to Boise City for a trial. It doesn't really matter, does it? He'll be found guilty there, too. But it does show what kind of Christians you two really are, doesn't it? Lying and deceiving, you two aren't so perfect after all. I will recommend that we replace our reverend soon. I want you out of this town."

Rebecca found a sarcastic smile. "You do that. You're right about one thing. We are not perfect, far from it, in fact, we're Christians. If you're looking for perfection, then look to Jesus because He's the only one who's perfect. Are we hypocrites? You should let the Lord decide that. He's the one we will all stand before someday to be judged on that very question, even you, Jeannie! Have a good day." She turned and left without another word.

"Maybe you should let the Lord decide, too!" Jeannie yelled out after them.

46

Nate Foley sat on Felisha's front porch reading a book in the noonday sun. It was getting hot out and he had a glass of iced tea on the table in front of him. He had been in town for a few days and, so far, it seemed like a quiet town mostly, except for Bob Thacker's visit the day before. He had stood back and listened to Bob warn Felisha. It seemed an oddity, but Nate wasn't one to pry into other people's business for the most part. However, as he happened to peer over his wire-rimmed spectacles and saw Bob Thacker walking at a brisk pace towards Felisha's porch with fury expressed on his face. Nate lowered his book and took off his spectacles just as Bob stepped up on the porch. Bob ignored Nate completely and stepped into Felisha's house, as if he owned it himself.

Bob yelled, "Felisha, get out here!"

Felisha stepped out of the kitchen drying her hands on her apron after washing the lunch dishes. "Bob," she sounded more afraid than surprised.

"Is Matt taking Truet to Boise City? Is that right?" Bob

yelled. He stepped closer to Felisha aggressively. She stepped backward towards her wall.

"I don't know," she tried to sound sincere, but it was weak.

Bob quickly grabbed her by the shoulders and shook her violently. "Damn it! Tell me the truth; are you behind all of this? I told you no one was going to get in my way. Not even you. Now tell me!" he screamed and threw her across the room. She fell to the floor in disbelief, and panic showed on her face as she watched Bob walk towards her. Dread began to fill her, but it turned to terror as she watched Dillon step in front of her and begin to swing at Bob's legs and groin to protect his mother. He screamed, "Leave my mother alone!"

Bob threw a merciless backhand that sent Dillon to the floor in tears.

Felisha stood up quickly with a ferocity of her own that burned hot in her eyes. She stepped towards Bob fearlessly as she yelled loudly, "Don't you ever touch my son again, you son of a bitch!" She slapped his face with the same viciousness that he had shown Dillon. The force of her blow turned his head. He was just about to send a hard right-handed fist into Felisha's face when he heard a deep and authoritative voice behind him say loud and clearly, "Don't you touch her!"

Bob turned to see Felisha's boarder, Nate Foley, standing near where Dillon fell. Not only was Nate a good-sized young man, but he also held a small, but lethal, two shot derringer on Bob.

"You best mind your own business, son!" Bob warned dangerously. His left cheek was reddened from the stinging slap that Felisha had given him. "You have no idea what you're getting yourself into," Bob finished.

Felisha went to Dillon, who was crying bitterly. Dillon had a red mark on his face about the size of Bob's hand. Felisha sat on the floor and scooped him up onto her lap. She held him consolingly while she eyed Bob furiously. "It's okay, baby," she whispered to her son. Tears of outrage ran down her cheek.

"Actually," Nate said to Bob as he reached into his left pocket and pulled out his silver-starred badge. He showed it to Bob. "My name's Nate Robertson. I'm a deputy U.S. Marshal, Mister Thacker." His voice grew threatening, "And I know exactly what I'm getting into here since it was Matt that sent me. Now, I recommend you leave and the next time you see me I won't be carrying this peashooter. I'll be wearing my peacemaker."

Bob glared at Nate with hostility in his eyes. He was breathing hard and grit his teeth. Tears of outrage filled his eyes. "Your badge means nothing in my town. You don't scare me, you little whelp. This isn't over by a long shot!" Bob glared down at Felisha and pointed his shaking finger. "And you! We'll finish this later; I am not through with you. I'll burn you out of this town!" he yelled and walked towards the door.

"I'm not here to scare you," Nate said as a simple fact, "but you better leave things well enough alone. Because Matt is a man you'd better fear."

Bob spun around; his face was contorted by a rage that seemed to take possession of him. His desire to murder was evident on his face. He leaned forward and spit out vehemently, "Matt can go to hell!"

"That's impossible," Nate said simply and explained, "Matt's a Christian." Bob appeared puzzled for a moment, turned, and left.

Nate looked down at the floor, where Felisha held Dillon

close. She stared up at Nate with an exasperated expression. "You lied to me?" she asked sounding more astonished than angry.

Nate nodded as he replaced the derringer into his pants pocket. "Not intentionally, Miss Conway. Matt asked me to stay here just in case something like this happened."

"I suppose I should say thank you," she said as she held her son.

"My pleasure," Nate said simply. "You must be a very important witness, because his instructions were pretty clear. No one, absolutely no one was to touch you or your son."

"I'm not a witness," she answered.

"Well, you're important enough to him that he didn't want anything to happen to you or your son. He didn't explain why."

Felisha smiled despite herself. "We're friends," she said in a way of explanation.

Nate looked at her and smiled, "That explains it all."

47

The repetition of driving the wagon from the hay fields to the hay barn was growing tedious for Saul. The late August heat burned down leaving him thirsty, and the dust kicked up by the mule team always seemed to find its way into his eyes, nose and mouth. Physically it was an easy job, but it was wearing him out day by day. The hours were exhausting and he couldn't wait until harvest was over and the cool days of fall came.

The sight of Bob Thacker driving his buggy towards him with Mike Moye sitting beside Bob, holding a shotgun in his left hand, sent a cold chill down Saul's spine. Brit Thacker rode his horse beside them. Saul closed his eyes and said a silent prayer, as he had no idea what they wanted him to do now. He pulled his mule team to a stop beside Bob. Brit halted his horse between the carriage and the wagon.

"Saul, did you know that the marshal was taking Truet to Boise City?" Bob snarled.

"What? No!" Saul acted surprised. His heart beat quicker as panic set deeply within him.

"Don't lie to me! Did you know the marshal's a Christian? He's fallen in with your Christian friends in town. Saul, did you know that he's taking Truet to Boise City to be tried? You were a Christian for awhile, so what did you tell him?"

"I told him AJ was with me," Saul said defensively. "I told him exactly what you told me to tell him."

Brit jumped into the conversation, "Did you tell him Pa told you to say that?"

"No!" Saul declared loudly, "I stuck to my story. I didn't tell him anything!"

Bob grabbed the shotgun from Mike's good arm and aimed it at Saul quickly. He pulled back the hammer and demanded loudly, "What did you tell him, Saul? I swear, I'll blow you off of that wagon if you lie to me. What did you tell him!"

"Nothing!" Saul exclaimed, suddenly shaking in fear. "I swear, I didn't tell him anything, Bob. I told him AJ, and the others were with me that morning. He tried to trick me, but I stuck to my story. I swear to you that I did!" Saul stared at the muzzle of the shotgun as he spoke. He was obviously scared.

"He's lying!" Brit shouted out angrily. "Kill him, Pa! He's lying to you. He told the marshal everything!"

"I didn't!" Saul pleaded to Bob quickly, "I swear I didn't." His lip began to tremble uncontrollably.

"Did you know about their plan to take him to Boise City? Felisha knew it. The reverend knew it. What about you? The marshal and you took a long walk!" Bob accused with his shotgun still leveled at Saul.

"I haven't talked to anyone since AJ was shot. I haven't even been to town; so how could I know?" Saul spoke desperately in a soft, quick voice as he raised his arms unknowingly. "The marshal tried to trick me, but I didn't say a word! I swear it to you."

Bob lowered the shotgun slowly as he said, "You better be telling me the truth, Saul, or I'll kill you."

"Let me kill him if you can't!" Brit spit out violently. "He's lying!"

"Shut up, Brit!" Bob said bitterly and handed the shotgun back to Mike. "Let's go talk to the men. Saul, keep working. The hay won't move by itself." Bob grunted to his horses and drove forward to turn his buggy around to go back toward the house.

Brit rode up beside Saul and glared at him with great disdain. "I know you're lying and I'll force you to say so. Then you'll be a dead man. I'll see to that myself. Enjoy your day, Saul; you've got very few left!" With that, he turned his horse and left.

Saul watched them leaving together and was filled with the same wrath he had felt the day before when Bob brought the sheet to Abby. Bob was using her as leverage to force Saul to do his will. Bob always looked for the upper hand of any angle

to enforce his will somehow. Bob had been doing it to people for a long time, but now it involved Abby, and Saul was tired of it. More and more his wrath built up and he desired nothing more than to crush the faces of those two men with his fists.

As long as Abby was kept relatively safe, he was harnessed to their will, but if they ever sent her away, he would no longer care and beat them both to death or die trying. It would be his intention, anyway. He took Matt's words to heart and used his love for Abby and his hatred for Bob and Brit to hone up his

lying skills. He feared Bob would see through him, but he hadn't. Saul might not have fooled Brit, but he would go to the grave to save his friend, Truet, from Bob's hanging party. He didn't know how it would end, but he had picked his side and planted his feet. He would not betray his friends again; his only friends were his Christian brothers and sisters. In the loving memory of Jenny Mae, he would do what was right, no matter what it cost him. Even if Abby was threatened again, he would no longer lower his head like a beaten coward. It was time to stand up for what was right and be a man.

BOB THACKER STOOD on his wide front porch surrounded by a group of six of his cowboys. They had their horses packed with bedrolls, saddlebags, ammunition, rifles and other needed supplies as they waited for Bob's last words.

Bob spoke loudly and purposely, "I know for a fact that they'll spend tonight in Louden. They've been staying in hotels the whole map down until now at Louden. They'll be there; I want you men there tonight. I want you to kill the marshal in the morning. I don't care how, but I want him dead! I want Truet alive. Do you understand me?" Bob asked forcefully.

Barry McCracken said nervously, "Bob, I signed on to work the ranch. Not to murder a United States Marshal. I won't take part in this, sir. I won't be killed for you," Barry finished and began to lead his horse away towards the barn.

"Hold it right there! Where do you think you're going, McCracken?" Bob yelled. "You signed on to do what you're told. If not, then I'll kill you right here!"

Barry glanced over at Brit, who pulled the hammer back on the shotgun that he was holding in front him. He was on the front porch near Bob.

Bob continued, "I will not allow anyone to disobey me! You're going to Louden to kill the marshal and bring Truet back alive to me. All of you are going and you will do it! If not, I'll track every one of you bastards down and kill you myself! You're hired men; this is just a part of your job."

Barry said argumentatively, "I signed on to work cattle or whatever else was needed, but you don't pay me enough to kill an innocent man. Or to get killed trying."

"All of you signed on knowing you might have to kill someone. It's the nature of ranching and you're all cowboys, damn it! If rustlers are stealing our cattle you'd shoot them, Barry. You know you would! I know you would. That's why you work for me. Am I right?"

Barry sighed. "Stealing cattle is a crime. You want us to murder a U.S. Marshal. It's our lives on the line, not yours."

Bob was silent for a moment and then nodded with a sigh. "Okay, here's my deal. I'll give the man that kills the marshal and brings Truet back alive five thousand dollars. If you all do it together, I'll give you each a thousand dollars. Leave the law to me. You just do your part, and I'll take care of each of you. If not," he paused and grew mean as he snarled, "I'll spend my fortune hunting you down! Now get going. The daylight's burning."

Mick Rodman stepped over to the porch and walked up the few steps to talk to Bob privately. "Bob, you know I'm not really much of a gunman and those five can accomplish this without me. So I was thinking, maybe I could stay here and help with the herd. You know you're leaving the ranch pretty bare by sending all six of us."

Bob's face slowly grew into a snarl and he pushed Mick off of the porch with a hard shove. Mick fell backward and landed hard on his back where he stayed, as Bob followed quickly down the steps with his finger pointed at Mick's chest. Bob was red-faced and angry. "You," he yelled loudly, "are the cause of all of this! If you'd left that woman alone, we wouldn't be doing this! I'm telling you right now, if Matt Bannister is still alive and you are too, I'm going to kill you myself. You kill him or you'll be a dead man, Mick!" Bob spun around to face Barry. "Anything else, Barry?"

Barry incensed, shook his head. "No," he replied to Bob and swung up on his horse. "Let's go, Mick," he said glaring at Bob coldly, "We've got a job to do."

"Get up!" Bob ordered, giving Mick a kick as he slowly got up off the ground.

"Joe," Bob said to Joe Warren, "I am putting you in charge and will hold you personally responsible for every man in your posse. If Barry and Mick want to ride away from our endeavor, then you better kill them or any other man that wants to leave. Do you understand me?" Bob questioned severely.

Joe Warren glanced quickly from Barry to Bob. "Barry's the foreman when Brit's not around."

"Not anymore!" Bob snapped. "He's no longer the foreman, you are. Now, you lead this posse to Louden and you kill the marshal and bring Truet back. If you do that, I'll set you up for life. I've said all I'm going to say; you've all heard my words, and my warning," he directed to Barry. "I won't tolerate cowards, insubordination, or failure."

Barry eyed Bob squarely. "You're putting Joe in charge of me? You're giving him my position on the ranch?"

"Why, yes, I am, McCracken. If you don't like it, kill the marshal," Bob finished pointedly with a smirk of pleasure on his face.

48

Matt opened his eyes to the darkness of his small hotel room. He heard Truet's breathing, as he slept on the mattress they had brought in and set on the floor near the bed where Matt slept. The sound of two men climbing the stairs, one of them wearing spurs, and walking towards his room grew closer. He heard the voice of the hotel owner begrudgingly leading the other man towards Matt's room.

Matt sat up quickly and turned the oil lamp up just enough to lighten the darkness to see across the room, but still dark enough to not cast a shadow against the windows. He stirred Truet lightly and pressed his finger to his lips when Truet opened his eyes. Matt motioned towards the door. The hotel owner's voice was heard whispering to another man in the hallway. He sounded hesitant to knock on Matt's door. Under the door, the light of the hotel's corridor cast shadows of their feet standing there.

Truet sat up and reached for his colt, while Matt grabbed hold of his Parker double-barrel shotgun. "Stay quiet, when I tell you to open the door, do it quickly and stay behind it.

It'll offer you some protection from the buckshot," Matt said, while he pulled back both hammers on the shotgun and took his position in the back of the room toward the corner.

Truet stepped beside the door with his colt in his hand. A light knock sounded at the door. The hotel owner's voice said lightly as to not waken his other guests in the neighboring rooms, "Mister Bannister, I'm sorry to bother you, but there's a man who says he needs to talk to you. Mister Bannister, are you awake?"

"Who is he?" Matt's voice asked through the door.

"I don't..." he began to answer, and by the shadows under the door it was noticeable that the other man, who wore the spurs, stepped in front of the hotel owner. "Marshal," a different voice said, "my name's Barry McCracken. I worked for Bob Thacker. Marshal, I've got to talk to you," he sounded urgent.

"Do you know him?" Matt asked Truet, who appeared surprised to hear Barry's voice.

"Yeah," Truet whispered with a concerned expression on his face as he stared at Matt.

Matt noticed Truet's troubled expression. "And?"

Truet shrugged his shoulders. "I've known him a long time. I'm surprised he's here."

Matt sounded irritated, "Is he a gunman?"

"No, he's a decent man."

"Mister McCracken," Matt stated loudly through the door, "We're going to open the door, I want your hands held up high and empty. If not, I won't hesitate to pull the trigger. Any tricks and you're the first man I'll kill. Do you understand me?" Matt asked forcefully.

"Yes, sir."

Matt knelt down on one knee and aimed the shotgun at

the door. He said quietly to Truet, "Stay behind the door; open it."

Truet stood to the side, with his left hand unlocked the lock, and swung the door open towards him, to put a barrier between himself and Matt's shotgun. No shot was fired.

Barry McCracken stood in the center of the doorway with his hands held up. "I just came to talk," he said nervously, as he saw the marshal's shotgun pointed at him.

"Come in," Matt said as he stood, still holding the shotgun on him. "Close the door," he said once Barry stepped inside.

Truet held his revolver on Barry's head as he closed the door.

"Hi, Truet," Barry sounded nervous.

"Barry," Truet greeted him suspiciously, "What are you doing here?"

Matt didn't give Barry time to answer. "I want you to slowly remove your gun belt and toss it down by my feet. You better step away, Truet, just in case."

After Barry had unarmed himself and Truet searched him for any hidden weapons, they asked him to sit in the only chair in the room. Matt sat at the head of the bed with the shotgun near at hand. Truet stood near by with his colt still in his hand.

"Now then," Matt said carefully, "What do you want?" He turned up the oil lamp slightly to see Barry's face clearly. Barry was a heavyset man of good height with greasy, dark brown hair cropped short under his weathered hat. He had a round face with dark stubble. His face appeared neither overly kind nor friendly, but certainly as a sincere man who might even be honest. His clothes were sweat-stained and dirty; he wore a six-gun and seemed uncomfortable with it being removed from his hip. He wore spurs on his well-worn heels. Matt watched Barry closely while intentionally staying out of view of the covered windows.

"I came to warn you," Barry explained, "Bob sent us up here to kill you. He's giving five thousand dollars to the man who does. I won't be a part of it, but my life was threatened if I didn't come with them. It's the least I could do to warn you; the boys plan on ambushing you in the morning."

"Five thousand dollars?" Matt asked and looked at Truet. "It was five hundred when I left Sweethome. With that kind of bounty out for you, we'd better get you to Boise City soon. He'll have every man in the territory searching for you. He must want you pretty darn bad."

Truet shrugged speechlessly.

Barry clarified. "The five thousand is for killing you," he said to Matt.

"Me?" Matt asked surprised.

"Yes, sir. He'll give the money to the man that kills you and brings Truet back alive. Bob's planning a community celebration next Saturday and your hanging is the center-piece of it," he said to Truet.

"Why's he want me dead?" Matt asked. His facial expression hardened as he listened to Barry.

"The news got out that you were taking Truet to Boise City. Bob went over to Miss Conway's to confront her about it and that's when he found out about your deputy being there. Well, let's just say that's when he realized he was being deceived and now he wants you killed. Marshal, Bob doesn't care if it's a U.S. Marshal or a child on the street, he'll kill to get what he wants. Right now he wants your blood and Truet to hang. He's sent six of us up here to do it. I won't be involved. I'm changing sides. I'd like to fight beside you tomorrow."

Matt shook his head. "Is Felisha okay?"

"She's fine. Your deputy was there."

"Good."

Truet asked Barry, "Who else came with you? Did Mick come?"

"Yeah, he's here," Barry said and added sincerely, "I'm sorry about your wife, Truet."

Truet grimaced as he asked, "Where is he?"

"The saloon. He and a couple of the others were there getting drunk."

"Who else is here?"

"Mick, Dave Redle, Ezra Loften, Alias Avery and Joe Warren," Barry answered.

Matt spoke from his position on the bed, "I suggest we grab our things and leave. We can outride them easily enough, if we ride out now."

"No way!" Truet said raising his voice, "I have some unfinished business with Mick Rodman to settle tonight, Matt. I've been waiting all of this time to kill him and now he's just down the street." He looked at Matt with determination in his eyes. "I'm going down there to kill him!"

"Not tonight you're not," Matt stated plainly.

"He killed my wife!" Truet spit out viciously.

"I need you alive, Truet. We're going back to Boise City tonight. I will not allow you to engage in a gunfight with two or three men in a saloon, while they have two or three other friends out there somewhere. I won't put myself in that kind of situation. And I won't allow you to, either."

"I'm not your prisoner, remember? I can do as I please," Truet said with finality.

Matt's eyes opened wider, his temper was beginning to rise. "No, you're not my prisoner, but you are my friend. Now, I'm asking you as a friend to keep your head and trust me. I understand what you're feeling, but it isn't the time,

Truet. We could both end up dead tonight if you insist on blindly going down there. Let me assure you that a stranger will put a bullet in your back and mine too as soon as they hear about the reward money." Matt shook his head and added, "What you want to do is absolutely foolish. This is no time to react on your emotions. You need to sit down, relax, and think this over a bit. You'll get your chance with Mick, I promise you that. But let's pack up and leave while we can. Part of the reason I'm still alive is because I learned a long time ago not to let my emotions control my actions. Especially, when I don't know where the enemy is, or even who they are!" he finished strongly.

Truet stared at Matt with contempt while he battled to control the surge of rage that built within him. He had every desire to kill Mick Rodman, and he was going to do it whether Matt helped him or not. It was his fight and he would kill Mick or die trying. Truet didn't care what happened afterwards. He had nothing to live for anymore now that Jenny Mae was gone.

Barry McCracken said solemnly as the two friends glared at one another angrily, "You can't leave. They're staying in the livery stable. That's where they plan to ambush you in the morning."

Matt's eyes went from Truet over to Barry and then back to Truet again. "Sounds like you're going to get your chance in the morning, Truet. Why don't you two tell me about these individuals that came here to kill me."

Truet sighed heavily and sat down on the foot of the bed. "You know them, Barry. Tell him what he wants to know."

Through a series of questions asked by Matt, Barry told the character traits of each man, what little history he knew of them, and which ones had killed a man before. With great interest and probing questions, Matt got a better understanding of the caliber of men that he was going to be facing in the morning, whether he like it or not. A five-thousand-dollar bounty was a temptation for any man who played those kinds of cards for a living. There were many bounty hunters that came into the territory to collect on Truet for five hundred dollars. What difference would a federal badge mean compared to five thousand dollars? Matt took the threat seriously and told Barry as he was leaving in the late hours, "I appreciate you coming to warn us, but I don't have any reason to trust you. If I see you tomorrow morning I will be forced to shoot you. Leave town tonight or stay indoors, but don't let me see you in the morning. I will be looking."

Barry seemed insulted by Matt's implication. "Marshal Bannister, I no longer hold any loyalties to Bob Thacker. Tomorrow there's going to be five men trying to kill you. I can't let that happen in good conscious and if you let me, I'll fight beside you against them," he offered sincerely.

Matt shook his head. "No, Mister McCracken, I appreciate what you've done, but you'll do yourself a favor if you just stay away from me until the shootings done. That's your warning," he finished strongly.

After Barry had left, Truet asked Matt, "You don't trust him?"

"Nope," Matt said as he lowered the lamplight and peeked out the window to look up and down the dark street. He continued, "For five thousand dollars a man might put our attention on his pals and shoot me in the back of the head and you in the leg, while he fights beside us." He looked at Truet. "I'd dead, you'd hang, and he'd be five thousand dollars richer. No, I don't trust him, do you?"

Truet laughed slightly, "Not anymore."

49

Barry McCracken had mentioned the burned-out shanty that stood directly across the street from the livery stable. Joe Warren's plan was to send two men across the street at sunup to the ruins of a once solid log cabin. When Matt and Truet neared the livery stable, they'd be caught in the middle of a cross fire with nowhere to go for cover. They'd be surrounded by men with rifles. Matt could easily be picked off and Truet would have to surrender. It was a good plan and would've worked well, except for Barry's telling them about it.

During the night Matt and Truet left the hotel down the back alley and quietly entered the remains of a solidly built cabin that had caught fire. Its log walls were burnt, but still strong and stable. The roof was gone and what wasn't burnt had collapsed into its center, leaving it full of debris. It had two windows facing the livery stable and a doorway missing its door. The charred wood left blackened marks on the clothing and skin of both men while they waited for early signs of life. A new morning gradually showed itself in a glorious sunrise over the eastern mountains.

Mick began to lower his hands slowly to undo his gun belt.

Truet taunted him, "Grab your gun, Mick! Die like a man. You're going to die today for what you did to my wife."

"No... Please, Truet," Mick begged, as he unbuckled his belt and let it fall. "I'm sorry," he pleaded with desperation and began to cry while he begged for his life.

"I've been waiting for this day," Truet said grimly. He was about to continue when a gunshot exploded the window jamb beside him splintering the wood. It was followed by two other shots and then a volley of shots were fired from the livery stable.

Truet stepped back away from the window and glanced at Matt, who was firing back towards the livery stable already. Across the street, Joe Warren and Ezra Loften were shooting from the top two windows and Dave Redl was shooting at them from the bottom left side window.

Mick Rodman had dropped to the ground quickly; scrambled up and began to sprint away from the gunfight as fast as he could.

Truet stepped into the window fully exposing his body to the men in the livery stable; careless of the danger, he aimed carefully at the running figure of Mick Rodman and fired. He watched Mick fall to the ground immediately. Truet had placed the rifle shot perfectly into the back of Mick's left knee. Mick screamed out as he held onto his leg writhing in pain on the dusty Louden street.

Truet's attention came immediately back to the livery stable as a bullet whizzed past his head and another narrowly missed his shoulder, as it splintered the wood. He turned and fired quickly at Dave Redl before stepping out of view again.

Matt took cover behind the wall. It seemed most of the

firing from the livery stable was directed at him. He was on the right side of the window in the corner and turned to shoot out of the window at Joe Warren, who was on the upper left side of the livery stable. He had Joe in his sights when a bullet from Ezra Loften shattered what was remaining of the window and Matt was hit by flying glass. Matt spun back around into the protective corner; he could feel the blood running out of a large cut on his scalp and another on his cheek. With a touch of his hand, he pulled a small shard of glass out of his right cheek. He was sure there was more, but he didn't immediately feel any with his hand.

"Truet!" he called loudly, "The upper right window. I can't get him."

Truet nodded. He looked concerned at the blood that ran down Matt's face. He changed his position in the window to get a better angle at Ezra. He waited until he was sure he had a killing shot. When Ezra turned his body just a bit in the right direction, Truet pulled the trigger with the bead on Ezra's upper chest, just below the throat. He watched Ezra Loften drop backwards out of sight with the force of the bullet. He glanced quickly back at Matt, who was bleeding heavily from his head and cheek. "He's down!" he called and returned fire towards Dave Redl directly across the street.

The shooting quieted momentarily, leaving an eerie silence. Matt peeked at the livery stable. No one was visible in either the upper windows or in the lower windows. He scanned the stable carefully looking for the slightest movement or sound.

"Are you all right?" he heard Truet ask.

Matt nodded while he wiped the blood off of his face. "Yeah," he answered without taking his eyes off of the stable windows. Blood ran down the right side of his face from his scalp wound.

Suddenly, Dave Redl appeared in the bottom window with a shot at Matt. It hit the outside wall of the window. Because of the angle, Truet didn't have a shot. Matt, however, quickly returned fire and ejecting the spent cartridge, reloading his lever action Winchester.45, he fired again hitting Dave Redl near his heart. Dave Redl fell.

At the same time, Joe Warren fired down from the window upstairs at Matt. It hit the bottom windowsill near him. Matt spun out of the window and out of sight behind the protection of the wall.

Truet returned fire at Joe, though again, he didn't have a good enough angle to hit him. Truet fired again and moved across the window to the open doorway to get a more accessible angle.

Joe fired again, but not having a target in sight; it quieted to an eerie silence. It was made more uncomfortable by the cries of Mick Rodman as he continued to cry out for his friends to help him. Joe waited for Matt or Truet to appear in a window to take another shot. "Dave, hey Dave," Joe called downstairs to his friend. There was no answer.

Matt made eye contact with Truet and said, "On the count of three- one, two, three!" Immediately both men sprung quickly into action, aimed their rifles at the upper left window and fired. One shot hit the outside of the wall and the other buzzed past Joe. Joe aimed and fired again at Matt. It hit the wood of the window jamb just an inch from Matt's face.

"That's it!" Matt stated under his breath and adjusted his body fully in the window to get a better shot at Joe. He aimed and fired, hitting the window frame Joe was hiding beside. He reloaded and waited for Joe to reveal himself. Again, it fell silent, except for the cries of Mick.

"Cover me, I'm going in there," Matt said while laying his rifle down. He quickly ran out the door towards the livery stable. Joe Warren appeared in the window and fired down at Matt. He missed and Matt kept running.

Truet fired quickly and watched Joe double over with a shot to his abdomen and regain his composure to some degree to lift his weapon towards Truet. Truet fired again and watched as Joe fell out of sight. "He's down!" Truet called out as Matt reached the livery stable doors.

Matt drew his revolver and said, "Stay out of sight!" He slipped into the stable.

Truet stepped out of the doorway of the burned out home and onto the street. Townspeople were beginning to fill up the street now that the shooting was over. It was dead quiet, except for the pain-filled cries of Mick Rodman. He was in the middle of the street trying to crawl somewhere safe, but he had nowhere to go.

Truet walked toward him carrying his rifle up over his shoulder. "Roll over," he ordered dangerously. Mick was pulling himself along the ground on his belly. His shattered and bloody knee left his escape attempt nearly impossible. Mick's body stiffened when he heard Truet's voice and saw Truet's shadow standing over him. Mick began to cry.

"Roll over!" Truet commanded strongly, "I want you to see who's killing you. After what you did to Jenny Mae it's the least you can do!" He stepped to Mick's side, kicked him in the ribs, and forced Mick over to his back with his boot. Mick screamed in pain as his knee twisted.

"Truet, please!" Mick begged helplessly, "Please don't kill me. It wasn't my fault; I'm not the one to blame. It wasn't my idea. You gotta believe me!" he cried out desperately to

Truet who slowly walked back around to Mick's feet. "It was AJ's idea; I didn't want to, I had to! AJ would've killed me!" Mick yelled out desperately.

Truet grit his teeth. "No, he wouldn't of," he said much too calmly. "AJ's dead, so are the others. You're the only one still living. This is the moment I've been living for since Jenny Mae was killed." Truet's countenance slowly changed, as he grew more aggressive with every word. The ferocity he'd been concealing for so long now showed in his eyes. "My wife died in my arms, Mick! Our stillborn son was wrapped in a blanket across the room. A son we could've raised together if it wasn't for AJ and you! You had no right to go into my house and touch my wife!" Truet yelled. He stomped viciously down onto Mick's shattered knee, causing Mick to scream in terrible pain. The shock of the pain caused Mick to automatically sit up to reach for his knee. Truet kicked him back down to the ground with a hard kick to his face. "Shut up!" Truet snarled and took his rifle in both hands and slammed the wooden butt straight down onto the shattered knee.

Mick yelled out with a blood-curdling scream that was unparalleled to any other that Truet had ever heard. Mick rolled from side to side quickly as the pain was too much to bear. He begged through his desperate tears, "Please stop. You don't have to kill me," he cried out bitterly. "I'll do anything. Please stop, Truet."

Truet lifted his rifle to his shoulder and aimed it at Mick. "I don't care how sorry you are. I'm sure you didn't stop when Jenny Mae begged you to stop, did you? Did you!" he yelled, demanding an answer.

Mick shook his head bitterly as he began to sob. "I'm sorry," he choked out, "I never meant to hurt her."

Truet glared down at Mick with an ice-cold expression

on his face. His voice held no compassion, "I'm giving you the same mercy you gave Jenny Mae. Goodbye, Mick!"

"Wait!" Mick yelled desperately, putting up an arm as if to block the forthcoming bullet. "Please, I don't want to die! Truet, please. Please don't!"

"Truet," Matt's voice sounded urgent, "Don't do that!"

"Stay out of this! This is none of your concern, Matt!" Truet stated with a glance towards Matt. "You know that," he finished without lowering his rifle.

"I understand what you're feeling, Truet. But…" Matt waved off the sheriff of Louden, who had come to Matt's side. He knew how passionate Truet was to get revenge on the man who harmed his wife, but he also knew how volatile it could be to interfere into another man's fight. Especially one that was so personal.

Truet cut Matt off as he snarled angrily, "You can't possibly understand what I'm feeling!"

"Yes, I do," Matt replied. He explained, "When I was a kid, the Dobson Gang attacked some friends and me at our swimming hole. They hung my best friend, and they forced me to watch him strangle to death as he hung from a tree. I went back the next morning to kill every one of those so-called men. You probably know the story," he paused for a moment to make sure Truet was listening. "I killed all five of those men all right, but I stood over Clay Dobson just like you're standing over Mick, Clay was begging for his life, too. I blew his brains out anyway just like you want to do. Trust me, Truet," he said softly, "you don't want to. You don't want to live with what I do. That memory will haunt you forever. Let me arrest him and the court of law will hang him for what he's done."

"She was my wife," Truet said painfully through his gritted teeth, tears slipped from his eyes.

"I know," Matt said softly. "But she's not coming back even if you kill him. Let's do this right and let the court sentence him to death legally. Isn't that how Jenny Mae would've wanted it? The right way?"

"You never even met her! So how would you know what she'd want, Matt?" he questioned bitterly. He continued to hold his rifle on Mick.

"I know Lee and Regina, Reverend Grace and Felisha, and I've gotten to know you, Truet. Jenny Mae was loved dearly by her friends and had a good man for a husband. The caliber of people she chose to have as friends tells me enough to know she was a godly lady with a great deal of integrity and a heart of gold. I have a feeling Jenny Mae was the kind of person who believed in doing what's right, no matter what. I know that because she married a man who believes in doing what's right. Even when it hurts." He watched Truet's body begin to tremble slightly. Matt continued, "I promise you, we'll seek the death penalty for his crimes. You will have your justice and be able to sleep at night too, without seeing his face exploding in your dreams." Truet looked at Matt, but still didn't lower his weapon. "It's over," Matt said, "Let's go home."

Truet lowered his rifle slowly. The emotions he felt raging within him got the better of him and his bottom lip began to quiver. He growled with rage and kicked Mick's ribs as hard as he could before he walked away to be alone. To be alone, Truet entered the livery stable and found an empty stall where he dropped to his knees in emotional exhaustion and wept.

50

Sunday morning, Matt and his deputy, Nate Robertson, led the way to the Thacker Ranch followed by twenty-some U.S. Cavalrymen led by Lieutenant Gerald Tompkins. The lieutenant agreed to follow the federal marshal to the ranch to thwart the threat of an ambush or an all-out gun battle. They rode up to the front of the house and Bob Thacker walked out onto the front porch dressed in his usual dark suit and a white shirt. He was angered by the intrusion. "Get off my property! You have no business here. None of you do. Now get!" he ordered roughly.

Matt sat on his horse with a contented smile. "Beautiful morning, isn't it, Bob?" he asked pleasantly.

"I told you to leave! I have nothing to say to you, except that Truet will be found guilty in Boise City, too. You haven't changed anything; I'll see to that. What?" he asked with a shrug of sarcasm as he waved his hand towards the soldiers on horseback. "Are you afraid to come out here and face me alone after betraying me? Marshal, you are a yellow, lying coward. That's what you are!"

"Where's Saul?" Matt asked, ignoring the insult. He

looked over towards the bunkhouse and the cookhouse where a few men stood outside watching curiously.

"He's working! This is a ranch and we're busy. Now get off my property and let us work. Good day!" Bob spit spitefully at Matt and turned to go back inside.

Matt said, "Lieutenant, will you send two of your soldiers to escort one of those cowboys over there to retrieve Saul Wolf from wherever he's working and bring him back here to me, please?"

"Absolutely," Lieutenant Tompkins agreed and gave his orders to two of his men.

"What are you doing?" Bob asked heatedly. His face grew red with growing fury and he began to shake. "Saul's working! I didn't give my permission for anyone to do that!"

Matt stepped down out of the saddle and walked towards Bob with a hardened countenance. "Bob, it is my great honor to inform you that you are under arrest for soliciting the murder of a U.S. Marshal. Give me your hands, sir." He revealed a pair of wrist shackles to put on Bob.

"What," Bob cursed. "Are you accusing me of something, Matt? I ain't going nowhere with you! How dare you, you little lying coward!"

"Your hands!" Matt ordered harshly.

"No! Do you know who I am? You can't arrest me, I'm Bob Thacker; I'm the one that wired for you, you son of a..." he yelled and then turned his back to Matt to go into the house.

Matt ran up behind him quickly and shoved him forcefully face-first into the wall beside the doorjamb. He pressed his shoulder into Bob's spine to hold him there while he grabbed Bob's right arm and aggressively pulled it behind his back. He shackled the wrist tightly, while Bob yelled out from the pangs of pain, but even more from the distress of his own building fury. Matt spun Bob around and forcefully thrust Bob's back against the wall, while he shackled his other wrist. Bob's nose bled, and he began to spit out obscenities. Matt ignored the foul words directed at him and physically walked Bob forward and forced him to sit on the top step. "Rest assured, Mister Thacker, you are under arrest and your influence stops with me," Matt said carelessly. He noticed Bob's nose bleeding for the first time.

Bob saw the blood drip down onto his white shirt. He wiped his face with the back of his shackled hand and yelled out with great anger, "You're going to pay for this! I don't care who you are; I'm going to see you bleed! Do you think you can arrest me, Matt? I'll see you buried if you don't let me go. Now take these off of me. Now!" he ordered loudly, shaking his shackled wrists in the air.

"You're under arrest. You conspired to have your men kill me. Unfortunately for you it didn't work. They are all dead. Now it's my turn; you're going to jail and then to prison, Bob. Because, at your trial, I am going to testify to the jury myself to make sure that you do."

Bob smiled wryly. "You can't prove any such thing. You killed my men and now you're framing me. You're a crooked and evil man, Bannister! You won't get away with this, I've got witnesses to back my story, and you haven't got anything. You're wasting your time!" Bob scoffed with a confident smile that barely parted his lips. He glared up at Matt and said, "Save yourself a heap of trouble and get off of my property."

Matt smiled. "Oh, I forgot to mention that a couple of your men did survive. Barry McCracken told us about your men's ambush plans in Louden just after he quit working for you. And Mick Rodman is willing to testify as well. Both of those men are waiting in Boise City for your trial. You're still under arrest, Bob."

Bob began to yell bitter threats and accusations tossed out with intermittent cursing.

Matt turned to Nate and said, "Find me something to gag him with. I'm tired of listening to him."

"Gladly," Nate said with a growing smile. He gave Bob a hard nudge with his knee as he passed by going into the house.

MATT RODE his horse beside the wagon that was being driven by Saul, as they made their way towards the home of Brit Thacker. Ten U.S. Cavalrymen rode along as well, led by Lieutenant Gerald Tompkins. As they approached the isolated home, Brit stepped outside of the front door with a shotgun in his hands. Brit said coarsely, "You have no business here!"

Lieutenant Tompkins ordered his men to encircle the front of the house and to raise their weapons to give a show of force. Brit was taken back by the unexpected midmorning visit and his breathing quickened. His eyes hardened on Matt when he noticed Saul waiting on his wagon behind him.

"Lay the gun down!" Matt ordered forcefully. His hand was on his revolver and he was ready to spring it out quickly if necessary.

Brit shook his head, refusing. "This is my property, you're trespassing!"

Matt dismounted cautiously, not taking his eyes off of Brit as he did and walked towards Brit by the door.

"What do you want?" Brit shouted, growing nervous. He began to turn his shotgun towards Matt, but the stern warning of Lieutenant Tompkins, who held his rifle on Brit, stopped him. The marshal had quickly turned to his side and pulled his revolver already, though it was still pointed up in the air. The marshal's eyes were deadly. Brit froze. His breathing grew quicker and his hands began to shake more noticeably the closer Matt came to him.

"What's going on?" Brit asked nervously.

"Give me the shotgun," Matt ordered, leaving no other option.

"Not until you..."

"Give me the shotgun! It's my last warning!" Matt yelled dangerously with his hand resting on his freshly holstered .45 Colt. His eyes were hard and mean. He no longer seemed the unthreatening man he appeared to be in town the first time they had met. Now he fit his lethal reputation.

Brit slowly handed the shotgun over to Matt. Brit's voice was softer in tone and quivered as he asked, "Why are you here? What do you want?"

"Stand over there and be quiet," Matt ordered him away from the door and then said to the lieutenant. "Keep him over there, please." He handed Brit's shotgun to one of the soldiers and with a glance at Brit, he went inside the small home.

Abby was standing fearfully back against the back door. She wore only a thin and filthy cotton dress with straps holding it on over her bare shoulders. Her bare feet were dirt-covered and her red hair hung straight down, lifeless and greasy. Her lip was scabbed over, a black eye was healing, and various bruises as large as a hand were on her upper arms and near her throat. She was frightened and her deep blue eyes seemed hopeless and desperate. She held her hands nervously in front of her.

"Abby, my name's Matthew Bannister. I'm the U.S.

Marshal from Branson. Your parents asked me to come here and bring you home. Do you want to go home?" he asked gently.

Her eyes brimmed over with thick tears. "My parents?" she asked.

Matt nodded. "Yes. I'm here to take you home."

She seemed overwhelmed and then looked at Matt with panic suddenly filling her eyes. Brit's voice threatened from outside. "Abby, you aren't going anywhere! You're staying here with me. You know you are. You know better than trying to leave me!" His voice sounded harsh and dangerous. He was out of her sight, but she was afraid at the very sound of his voice. She eyed Matt with an expression of terror in her blue eyes.

Matt said with a friendly expression on his face, "Don't listen to him anymore, Abby. From this moment on he won't touch you again, I promise you that. You have nothing to be afraid of anymore, especially him." Matt added softly, "Pack up what you want and let's get you home."

Abby's tear-filled blue eyes released their warm tears that fell quickly down her face. "I can go home to my mother and father?"

Matt's own bottom lip quivered lightly, as a wave of compassion passed through him. "Yes," he said reassuringly. He stared into her eyes compassionately. "You're going home, where nobody's ever going to hurt you again."

Abby's hands covered her face as she began to tremble and cry.

Matt was about to step over and hold her, to offer some comfort to her when Brit's brutal voice suddenly erupted uncontrollably and the sound of a scuffle broke loose from outside as Brit fought to get past the guards. The soldiers forcefully restrained him despite the wrath of his words and the venom in his voice to stop Saul from entering the house. Abby screamed in fright thinking it might've been Brit, but it was Saul who stepped in through the door. His attention was on Abby even though Brit's enraged threats were vehemently directed at Saul to stay away from his wife. The commotion of the soldiers ordering Brit to stay back continued as he was determined to break through the soldier's guard.

"Abby," Saul said lovingly. He stepped past Matt, and she stepped forward weakly to meet him in a loving embrace. They held each other tightly. She sobbed into his chest and momentarily tried to regain her composure.

"It's over. We're leaving, Abby, we're really leaving," he whispered to her. He kissed her quickly and said, "I love you."

She smiled in his embrace and sobbed into his chest, which muffled her words, "I'm going home." Saul held her tight.

Matt nodded to Saul approvingly and then stepped out of the house to leave them alone. Matt stood outside the door and eyed Brit with disgust and anticipation all at the same time. Brit stopped yelling to focus his attention on Matt, who said coldly, "I'm taking Abby back to her parents."

"You're not taking her anywhere. She's my wife! Abby, you better stay put or I'll come find you! Don't make me hurt you!"

Matt leaned against the doorframe and waited; while he watched Brit grow more and more agitated the longer Saul was inside. Just in case Brit somehow got past the soldiers keeping him contained, Matt kept his hand near his revolver. "Saul," Matt finally called out, "put Abby on your wagon and take her to Felisha's. It's time to go."

Brit's eyes grew wide. "Saul, I'll kill you! You're a dead man if you do! Abby," he cursed, "I'm warning you!"

Matt peeked inside and saw that Abby was afraid to come outside where Brit was. "He can't hurt you anymore. Come on out," he said with his reassuring voice.

Saul stepped out first and glanced at Brit nervously. He held Abby's arm as he led her out.

"Saul, stop!" Brit nearly begged Saul to stop. "Abby, please don't go. Look at me, please." He stepped forward before the soldiers, acting as a barrier, stopped him. Brit continued, "Please, don't leave me. I love you, Abby. You're my wife. I'm sorry. You can't leave me," Brit begged and dropped to his knees with tears filling his eyes desperately. "I need you, Abby. Please don't leave me. Abby, please. I love you. I swear I'll make you happy. I'll give you anything you want, just please don't go." He closed his eyes tightly in an emotional display of tears. He looked up at Abby who was slowly walking over towards him. "Please, don't leave me," he begged from his knees, folding his hands together resembling a prayer.

Abby stepped closer to the soldiers separating them and then suddenly spit in Brit's face. "I have nothing to say to you!" she said coldly and quickly turned her back and walked alone past Saul towards his wagon.

Saul was surprised by her sudden bold actions and was even more taken off-guard when Matt stepped over to him, nodded down at Brit, and asked, "Want to go a round with him? I'm giving you the opportunity."

Saul glanced at Matt and then looked down at Brit, who was bitterly lamenting for Abby to come back. Saul looked over at Abby who was waiting for him beside his wagon. He looked back at Matt and said through a growing joy-filled smile, "No thanks, I've just got everything I wanted. Thank you, Matt." He shook Matt's hand and walked away.

Suddenly Brit stood up and tried to run through the wall of soldiers trying to reach for Saul. "I'll rip your head off, you..." he flung out a paragraph of obscenities. "She's my wife! Don't you touch her or I'll kill you," Brit screamed, looking like a wild man. "Get back here, Abby, or I'll cut you up and feed you to the pigs! I'll find you! Abby don't you leave me or I'll cut his throat and your parents! I know where they are! I'll find you! Don't you take her!" he warned Saul, as he once again tried to break through the line of soldiers, but to no avail.

Saul looked at him and wordlessly walked away. He helped Abby onto the wagon, climbed up himself, and drove his wagon away from Brit's home. Brit watched Saul leaving with Abby sitting close beside him, holding his arm. She never once looked back towards him, no matter how furiously he yelled. When they were out of sight, Brit fell to his knees in exhaustion.

Matt unbuckled his gun belt and handed it to a nearby soldier.

"Marshal, what are you doing?" The lieutenant asked Matt.

"I've got some personal business to take care of," he said to the lieutenant and walked past the soldiers who guarded Brit. Matt used his boot to nudge Brit. "Get up."

Brit looked up from the ground at the unarmed marshal who was glaring down at him mercilessly. "You got what you came for. Please leave," Brit sounded defeated.

Matt continued, "You're a pretty tough guy. You could sure beat the snot out of that young lady, huh?" he nodded in the direction of the departed wagon. "Beat her black and blue. It takes a real man to beat up a woman, and to humiliate a child too, remember that? Well, I'm not a woman and I'm not a child, so let's see how tough you really are!"

Brit wiped his tears off his face as he stood up straight. "I'm no fool. You're trying to trick me into fighting, so you can arrest me and keep me from going to get my wife back." He smiled bitterly. "I ain't falling for it. When you leave I'm bringing her back. She married me for better or worse."

Matt smiled slightly. "You're under arrest for the murder of five Chinese men. I believe they are buried on your property somewhere along Hopewell Creek. I've got three witnesses that can correct me if I'm wrong. You're not going anywhere, except to the gallows or prison if you're lucky." Matt watched Brit closely; Brit's eyes widened and his face drained of color. Matt continued, his eyes growing colder with every word, "No, this is personal. This is for Abby's father!" he said with his fist already speeding towards Brit's face.

51

The Reverend Richard Grace was sitting with some of his congregational members in the churchyard for a potluck when he slowly stood up from the table and smiled excitedly. He walked to the side of the dirt street where Matt Bannister rode beside a cavalry officer, followed by a wagon that was being driven by two soldiers. Three more soldiers rode in the back, guarding Bob Thacker and his son, Brit. Behind the wagon were more mounted soldiers, five of whom were leading the horses of the men who rode on the wagon.

Bob sat with his hands shackled in front of him and a gag tied tightly around his mouth. His nose showed traces of dried blood and his shirt was heavily spotted. His eyes were water-filled and his face was redder than anyone had ever seen it before. Bob was deeply humiliated to be driven through town this way. Brit Thacker sat beside his father with his hands shackled as well. However, Brit kept his eyes downcast. The front of his shirt was covered with bloodstains that had fallen from his obviously broken nose, which had bled profusely. His face was covered in dried blood and both of his eyes were swollen and blackened already. His top lip was also split open. He appeared to have been severely beaten.

The sight of the two men took Richard by surprise; he looked up at Matt and smiled. Matt's light-colored shirt had a couple of spots of blood on it, so did the knuckles on both of his hands, as well as his knee and boot. "Matt," Richard said through his smile. "It is good to see you again. Well, you did it. You tracked Truet down and brought him home safely! We've been praying for you all this time. Are you hungry? We've got some food left." He motioned to the congregational potluck behind him on the grass. Almost the entire congregation neared the street to look at Bob and Brit. Some laughed, others stood in disbelief and others in simple relief.

Matt shook his head with an appreciative smile. "No thanks, I thought I'd bring these two by so you all could say goodbye. Bob and Brit are going to be gone for a while," he said glancing back at the two men. He added as an explanation, "We all got tired of listening to Bob, so we gagged him."

"Thou preparest a table before me in the presence of mine enemies," Richard quoted from the twenty-third psalm. With a growing smile Richard said, "The Lord is awesome, isn't he? A month ago I was beat up in my own home by his men, and I certainly wasn't the only one. Bob threatened to burn our church down and run our congregation out of town. Now look at him," he sounded nearly compassionate. "Thank you, Matt, for coming to Sweethome."

"It's been my pleasure," Matt replied and shook the reverend's hand.

"Mister Bannister!" Dillon yelled, as he ran around the side of the church with three other little boys. "Hi, Mister Bannister!" he exclaimed with excitement. He stopped next to Reverend Grace and stared up at Matt with his big brown eyes that looked so much like his mother's.

"Hi, Dillon," Matt replied and added, "Do you want a ride home?"

"Yeah," he exclaimed. He stepped forward and reached his hands up to be lifted. Matt reached down and pulled him up behind him easily.

"Reverend, I'll see you soon," Matt said and gave Betty a soft kick, as he led the procession of cavalrymen.

"Dillon, do you know how to ride a horse?" Matt asked as they rode away from the church.

"I rode on Truet's," he answered after a short pause.

"Does that mean you know how to ride one?"

"Uh huh."

"So, if I let you borrow mine, do you think you could ride to China for me and buy us some tea?"

"Yeah," he said confidently and then added thoughtfully, "Well, if my mother will let me. It's not far, huh? Maybe you could tell her it's okay."

Matt laughed lightly. "I don't know if she'd listen to me."

MATT STOPPED in front of Felisha's home, let Dillon down, and stepped out of the saddle himself to tie Betty to a hitching post. He stood for a moment to talk to Lieutenant Tompkins, then the soldiers moved on towards Boise City. Bob and Brit both glared at Matt murderously as they passed by in the wagon. Brit's eyes widened and his head lifted up when he saw Saul walking out of Felisha's house towards Matt. Brit tried to stand and called out for Abby, but he was pushed down and quieted by the soldiers riding with him.

Saul watched them pass by and then asked Matt, "Did you do that to Brit?"

"For her father," Matt explained with a nod. He watched the soldiers man-handling Brit to keep him sitting down and silent for the trip to the Boise City jail.

"It looks like you worked him over pretty well. Was he being held? It doesn't look like you were touched," Saul commented, looking Matt over.

"He wasn't being held!" Matt scoffed with a shake of his head. "I was raised by my uncle, Charlie Ziegler. He was a bounty hunter for a while. Before he taught me how to shoot a gun, he taught me how to use my hands to protect myself. I have three older brothers, a younger brother and sister and we all learned how to fight." He nodded towards the wagon and continued, "Men like Brit are generally the biggest cowards when it comes right down to it. They like to talk tough and intimidate whoever they can, beat the hell out of women, and maybe even shoot an unarmed man. But, stand up to him and he'll back down once his tough-man routine doesn't work. Force him to fight like I did, and you'll find he doesn't know how. Now, my friend," he continued with a friendly slap to Saul's belly. "If you'll excuse me, I'm going inside." He turned around to walk toward the large front porch.

Dillon, who was walking beside him said, "Maybe you could teach me how to use my hands, Mister Bannister. A boy named Johnny always says he's going to hit me. Maybe you could teach me how to hit him, like you did that mean man. Did you hit him?" Dillon didn't wait for an answer, he quickly added, "My mother always says not to hit anyone because it doesn't prove anything and real men use their brain not their brawn."

Matt put his hand around Dillon's shoulder and stopped

when they reached the bottom step of the porch. "She's got a point. Anyone can fight, but a smart guy uses his noggin to make a good life for himself and his family. Tough hands and tough guys don't mean anything." Matt bent over slightly; as he spoke to Dillon he tapped his own head with his finger. "This means everything," he finished just as Felisha stepped out of the door and onto the porch.

Matt gazed up at her as he straightened up with a smile. She looked lovely in her blue Sunday dress and her brown hair was neatly rolled in a tight bun. Her brown eyes gazed upon him affectionately as she stood at the top to the stairs. "Miss Felisha, you look exceedingly wonderful today," he said sincerely. It was the first time he'd seen her since he'd left.

"Thank you, Mister Bannister. I'm sorry to have missed you this morning when you came by for Mister Robertson. I went to Rebecca's after breakfast to bake for today's potluck," she explained needlessly. Matt already knew that from his disappointment of not seeing her that morning. She added sincerely, "It's good to see that you made it back."

"Thank you," he replied with a smile, his hand still on Dillon's shoulder.

Dillon asked quickly, "Mother, may I ride Mister Bannister's horse to China to buy some tea? He said I could, probably."

Felisha frowned and her brow narrowed questionably while she watched Dillon's hopeful expression and Matt's guilty smile. "Dillon, why don't you go inside and look on the world globe and try to find China on it? C-H-I-N-A," she spelled it out. "When you find it, then we'll talk about it."

"Okay," Dillon replied and then ran up the steps to go inside.

"Matt, are you trying to get rid of my son?" she asked Matt sounding annoyed.

"No, not at all," Matt replied, surprised. "I meant nothing by it. We were talking about being able to ride a horse. He said he could, so I asked if he could ride to China," Matt explained with a smile and a shrug. "I meant nothing by it," he said staring into her eyes.

She nodded. "That's good because he's a part of me, and he goes everywhere I go. I love my son, Matt. Nothing will ever change that," she finished with a strange lingering stare at Matt.

"I know," Matt said simply. He suddenly felt awkward.

"Okay," she said with finality in her voice and then added, "It's a beautiful afternoon and I'd like to take that buggy ride you promised. If you feel like it," she added questionably.

Matt smiled. "I'd like that. I'll go rent one and be right back."

"Matthew," she said, "I'm walking Dillon over to Rebecca's so she can watch him. I'll pack a lunch too."

"Dillon's not coming?" he asked curiously. "I don't mind if he comes along, Felisha. I was just playing around with him about the whole China thing. I honestly meant nothing by it."

Felisha laughed with a pleasant smile. "We'll take him next time. I think I'd like to talk to you by myself for a while. If you don't mind, that is."

Matt gazed at Felisha with a smile. She looked beautiful. "I'll be right back."

52

Matt drove the buggy under Felisha's directions about four miles north of town to a birch tree-lined creek that ran through its rock-lined bed. The sound of the water gently passing by left a soothing sound that filled the silence like a song. Within the grove of birch trees, they laid a quilt over the grass and sat down in the coolness of the grove's shade. They continued the long conversation they'd carried on for the four-mile journey to Hopewell Creek where they decided to stop. They talked about Matt's journey to find Truet and the gunfight they had in Louden. He told her about the arrest of Mick Rodman and their journey to Boise City where Truet was now waiting under guard for his own safety until his name could be cleared. And he told her about his morning spent arresting Bob and Brit Thacker. She listened intently and at times asked reasonable questions. She told him about Bob Thacker coming to her house twice, and how she appreciated his sending Nate Robertson to watch over her and her household. They talked about Abby and Saul, Dillon, The Graces, Truet and Jeannie Bartholomew.

It wasn't until after they had eaten the late lunch Felisha had packed that the conversation focused more on them. Felisha lay on her side with her hand supporting her head. She watched Matt sitting in front of her eating a piece of rhubarb cobbler. She said in a timid, soft voice, "I got your letters."

Matt smiled slightly, almost embarrassedly as he swallowed the last of the cobbler. He looked at her as he laid his small plate down. "Did you like them?" he asked for a lack of anything better to say to her statement.

Felisha closed her eyes with a short quiet laugh and answered sarcastically, "No, I burned them all and never wanted to see you again." She hesitated and added with a grin, "Of course, I liked them, silly. I wouldn't be here if I didn't."

"Good."

"Good?" she asked. "Is that all you have to say?" Her brown eyes flickered with concern and misted just a touch. Her smile remained. Her anxiety was becoming evident. "I mean; did you mean what you said in them or...?" she left it open for his response.

Matt looked deeply into her eyes and answered awkwardly. "I have never meant anything more in my life." He glanced out into the grove of birches and continued, "I came here to settle down a town and maybe help out one of Lee's friends. Checking in on Abby was on my secondary agenda." He looked down at her and added sincerely, "I never expected to meet someone like you. I never expected to feel the way I do. I am drawn to you in a way that I've never ever felt or imagined I could feel drawn to someone. I'm not a letter writer, Felisha, but I couldn't stop writing to you. Did I mean what I wrote? I meant every word that I wrote."

"And now?" she asked softly.

Matt looked into her eyes and smiled. "Even more so. You're a very beautiful woman, Felisha."

"Thank you," she said softly, as she stared back at him.

"Hmm-mm," he nodded simply and glanced away towards the creek awkwardly.

"Hmm-mm? That's all you have so say?" she asked quietly.

He turned back to her. "No," he hesitated. His words wouldn't come easily. He hesitated to speak, but when he did, he spoke with a great anxiety in his voice, "I don't want to leave you, Felisha. I have to take Abby back to Branson, but I don't want to. I want to stay here with you."

"Will you lie down so I don't have to look up at you? It's beginning to hurt my neck," Felisha said patting the quilt beside her.

"Oh, yeah," Matt said and lay on his side about a foot from Felisha. He rested his head on his hand as well.

"Thank you," she said, and continued, "You could send her back with Nate. She'd be safe with him."

Matt wrinkled his nose. "No. I want to be there when her parents see her for the first time."

"You could come back."

He eyed her curiously. "You'd want me to?"

"Yes," she replied in a whisper, "I do." She reached over and touched the beard on his cheek. "You're a very handsome man, Matthew Bannister."

"Thanks," he answered with an awkward smile.

"What are you thinking?" she asked softly. Her hand still softly rubbed his cheek.

"I'm thinking," he hesitated, "I was just wondering."

"Wondering what?" she asked as her hand moved from his beard to his hair, which was tied back in a ponytail.

"Well," he spoke awkwardly, "I poured out my feelings in my letters and have done most of the talking today," he sounded nervous, "I was just wondering how do you feel about me. I mean, do you have the same kind of feelings that I do, or just kind of a friendship? Because you've never said," he explained quickly.

Felisha laughed and then grabbed his hair and shook his head playfully. "Yes. I do!" she exclaimed dramatically and smiled as she stared at him.

Matt smiled slowly. "You're kind of interested in me?"

"Um, kind of," she responded sarcastically.

"Really?" his face grew serious.

Felisha's smile softly faded. She explained in a soft and fragile voice, "I feel like I'm falling and I can't stop it. So if you're not serious, Matthew Bannister, then please don't come back after you leave. I don't want to fall for a man I can't have." she finished with a touch of a tear glossing her eyes.

Matt smiled ever so slowly. Almost dream-like, he moved forward and touched his lips to hers. Their mouths opened and their eyes closed. He took her in his arms and held her close. The kiss was long, gentle, and passionate as he laid her down on her back. They separated their lips slowly, and he lifted his head just enough to look down and see her face.

She looked at him lovingly. "It's about time," she said softly.

53

Maude Lesko stood over a table measuring out material to sew a child's dress. The Lesko Clothing and Shoe Repair store had done well in Branson. They stayed busy; Maude had a solid clothing market and tailoring business. Robert had a strong demand for his shoe and boot repair, even though he sold a good number of new shoes and boots. Business was good. They were more financially stable then they'd ever been before.

A bell rang as the door opened and Maude quickly glanced over to it and saw a giant of a man walk in. On the other side of the man she saw just a head of red hair looking away from her. The giant sized man was looking at Maude sheepishly with a strange expression on his rough face.

"I'll be with you in just a moment," Maude said busily, as she went back to finish her measuring.

"Mama?" she heard and immediately recognized the voice. Maude inhaled a deep breath and her body stiffened at the sound of the voice. She looked up and saw Abby.

Abby's blue eye's no longer sparkled with life, but they were staring at Maude, brimming with heavy tears. "Mama,"

Abby's voice broke, and she began to shake uncontrollably as she waited for her mother to come hold her.

"Abby!" Maude gasped in disbelief and then ran around the counter quickly and went to her daughter. She took hold of Abby tightly and began to sob. She felt her daughter's arms, holding her tighter than she ever had before. "Robert!" Maude yelled through her tears. "Robert!" she yelled louder.

Robert Lesko appeared from the door to his private workroom and his mouth dropped open when he saw Abby and his wife holding each other tightly, sobbing. "Abby!" he yelled and ran to hold his daughter. He sobbed along with Maude as they swarmed over Abby. In the midst of her homecoming, they did not hear the bell ring again as Matt stepped into the store. He stood beside Saul, who was wiping his own eyes as he happily watched Abby.

Matt nudged Saul's arm and spoke quietly, "Well, she's home. It's been a long time coming, huh?"

Saul nodded. "Yes," he smiled touched by emotion.

"Before I leave, come see me tomorrow and I'll get you a job lined up at my uncle's granite quarry. Unless, you want to keep fighting?" Matt questioned.

"No. I'm never fighting again, Matt. I'll come see you tomorrow."

"Mama," Abby said, regaining her composure and stepping back enough to look at both of her parents. "This is Saul. I brought him with me, I hope that's okay."

"Of course it is, dear," Maude said through her tears. She looked up at Saul and saw Matt standing beside him. She wiped her eyes and held her daughter closely. "Thank you for giving my daughter back to me. God bless you, Marshal. Thank you," she said as her face contorted into grateful tears. She glanced up at the ceiling. "Thank You, Jesus. Oh Lord, thank You!"

Matt watched Abby being held by her parents and nodded to Saul with a smile. He pulled an envelope out of the inside pocket of his jacket. "Excuse me, Mister and Misses Lesko, but I have a little present for Abby to sign." He stepped over to the counter and laid the official-looking document out on the counter.

Robert Lesko spoke quickly as he walked towards Matt, "Marshal, I will gladly pay any fees for bringing her home."

"There are no fees, Mister Lesko," Matt replied.

"Then may I ask what you want her to sign? She's just come home, Marshal."

"What is this?" Abby asked as she looked at it curiously.

Matt smiled warmly. "It seems Brit wants a divorce. All you have to do is sign it. You see, the judge and Brit have both already signed it." Matt looked into Abby's eyes and said, "Once you sign your name, you are a free woman. I will take care of everything else."

Abby gasped, as did her mother. Tears filled her eyes. "How? How did you get him to..." she was speechless.

Matt smiled. "It is amazing what a man will do to spare his own hide. The judge, lawyers, and I worked out a couple of deals. For divorcing you, the prosecution won't seek the death penalty in Brit's case. He's facing a minimum of twelve to sixteen years in prison. To save his life he was very willing to agree to a divorce."

A tear slipped down Abby's face. "You mean I won't be married to him?"

"As soon as you sign your name he will no longer be your husband."

"I'm going to grab a pen!" Maude Lesko stated and quickly walked around the counter.

Saul asked quietly, "What about Bob? Do you know what will happen to him?"

Matt frowned. "They might sentence him to seven or eight years, but most likely he'll be out in three to five."

"You knew all of this, all the way from Sweethome and you didn't tell me?" Saul asked sounding hurt. "What about Truet? I know we're going back tomorrow to testify on his behalf. But do you really think he'll be acquitted?"

"Shh," Maude said and handed the pen to Abby to sign. "The last time you signed your name on a piece of paper like this, you left us, Abby. I don't know what that man did to you, but when you sign your name he will be out of your life forever, and you'll be forever in ours. Sign your name!"

Abby took the pen and signed her name with a trembling lip.

"Welcome home, my child," her mother said and hugged her. Abby cried.

Saul watched Abby with a smile and turned back to Matt. "What about Mick? Does he get a deal for testifying against Bob?"

Matt shook his head. "No, the prosecution will seek death in his case. Mick will face a jury of citizens, but with all the evidence stacked against him, I'm sure he'll hang. And you can count on Truet being there to watch it."

"You know, Matt, I'm a little afraid of seeing Tru. I lied about AJ. What if he never wants to see me again? I may have lost my best friend."

"Well, you're going to see him in a few days. You can certainly make amends by telling the truth at his hearing. What more could he ask for from a friend?" Matt said with a shrug.

"Marshal," Maude asked, "I have overheard parts of your conversation with him," she pointed at Saul. "I don't know what all has happened to get my daughter home, but I sure thank you. For three years we pleaded with that sheriff, Martin DePietro, to do something for us, but he is useless!"

Matt frowned and replied, "Well, you're right about that. He is no longer the sheriff of Sweethome by the way. He's been removed from office and Henry Kyle is the new sheriff."

"You are just full of secrets today!" Saul exclaimed. They had ridden from Sweethome to Branson together over the past four days and Matt had kept silent about all of the information he was now sharing. "Why didn't you tell me any of this?"

Matt reached over and picked up the divorce document off of the counter carefully to not smear the ink. "Because, I wanted to tell you and Abby in front her parents. Abby, I hope I never have to say this to anyone again, but congratulations on your divorce. Remember, no man has a right to hit a woman, and by no means should a woman stay married to a man that does. Take care my friend," he said and held out his hand to shake her's. She hugged him quickly and held him tight for what seemed a long moment. Maude hugged him when Abby released him and afterward Matt shook Robert Lesko's hand and walked to the door. "Saul, I'll see in the morning. Have a good day," Matt said and stepped out of the Lesko's store.

Outside, he folded the document and replaced it into his pocket. He would give it to the judge when he returned to Boise City for Truet's trial. It was a beautiful day and he couldn't help but to smile at a passing lady who appeared burdened by her troubles. A genuine smile is refreshing, especially in a constant world of troubles. Excitement glowed from Matt's grin. He was leaving to go back to Sweethome and the thought of seeing Felisha made him smile.

EPILOGUE

Saul Wolf and Abigail Lesko stood in front of the altar of the Baptist church and shared wedding vows. Abby had transformed from the frightened, dirty and bruised, hopeless girl trapped in a cottage on the Thacker Ranch to the beautiful, radiant and life-filled bride that she now had become. She smiled brilliantly as she gazed up into Saul's eyes. Saul wore a tailor-made black suit, which fit him perfectly. With a proud smile on his face, he softly held Abby's fragile hands in his giant palms. He looked tenderly upon his beloved bride with the greatest of affection.

The Reverend Eli Painter directed the couple towards the large church filled with wedding guests and said, "Ladies and gentlemen, may I introduce to you, Mister and Misses Saul Wolf." He turned to Saul and smiled, "You sir, may now kiss your beautiful bride."

Saul smiled widely and bent down to kiss Abby. Their lips met in a love-filled passionate moment as he took her in his arms.

The guests applauded as the newlyweds made their way

through the church aisle towards the front of the church where a buggy was waiting to take them to the dance hall where the reception was to be held. They were lost in their wedded bliss as they left, hand in hand.

THE BRANSON COMMUNITY Hall was decorated appropriately for a celebration of some importance. There were three tables filled with various foods and desserts. There were many tables surrounded by chairs for the guests to sit on and eat. The Leskos' had paid for a band to play for the evening so the newlyweds and the guests could dance.

Matt Bannister walked into the dance hall wearing a gray suit with his long hair tied back in a neat ponytail. Holding his hands were Felisha Conway and Dillon, both equally in finer dress. Matt smiled as they neared the newlyweds. Saul and Abby were talking to the Reverend Richard and Rebecca Grace, Lee and Regina Bannister, and Truet Davis.

"Congratulations, you two," Matt said as he shook Saul's hand and gave Abby a quick hug. Felisha hugged them both.

"Thank you," Saul said, "I can't believe this day is really here. If it wasn't for you, Matt, we wouldn't be here today."

Matt shook his head, "I had very little to do with it."

Saul scoffed with a smile on his face. "Take some credit. If it weren't for you, we wouldn't all be here together. You've given Abby and me a new life together and we can never thank you enough."

"The Lord's been in charge of this all along, Saul." Matt shrugged. "I just made the arrest. Thank Jesus, because this started long before I got there."

Saul crinkled his brow as he asked, "When?"

Matt looked at Truet, who lowered his glass of champagne and answered for Matt. "When Jenny Mae died," he paused to get Saul's attention. "If she hadn't died, Matt never would've come to Sweethome. Jenny Mae never would've let me go after those men and we would've sold out and come to Branson with our tail between our legs like we were going to anyway. That's when it started, Saul." He finished sadly. He then added in a more cheerful tone, "She would've been extremely excited for you two, though. It's actually kind of comforting to think her death wasn't in vain. She'd be pleased to know that."

Richard Grace said, "Being a preacher, I have to just add that the Lord can and does use the most painful experiences to further His eternal kingdom. The Bible says God can bring the good out of every situation. Sometimes we see it, sometimes we don't. We have very finite sight; we see right now what's before us and hope for a tomorrow. God sees eternity and works in our lives to prepare us for it. My quick example is Apostle Paul. He wanted to go spread the Gospel, but he sat in prison. He didn't want to be there, but God wanted him there. Why? Because Paul belonged to the Lord and the letters he wrote during his time spent in that prison are invaluable to the eternal scheme of God's plan today. We wouldn't have the Bible without them.

"My friends, we have an amazing, living God who loves us despite our weaknesses and knows what's in our best interest. And if we let Him, He'll lead us down the path He has planned especially for us. There will be storms along the way of course, but let us never lose hope in our Lord Jesus Christ. He has us in the palm of His hand, even when it feels desperate and dark. The truth is as Christians, we always have hope even in the darkest times, because we have the Lord. Sometimes it may not seem like it, but the Lord is faithful and He will honor hope that's built on Him. In short, how important is the Lord to you? Do you believe in Him? If so, can you place your hopes in Him? Because when it hurts and you don't understand, you still must trust Him. It's then that He's got a plan for you," Richard finished purposefully, as he looked around at his friends.

"Amazing, isn't it?" Matt asked no one in particular. "There's a living God who loves us all so much that He sent his Son to die for us, just so that we can know Him. And, there are people who will spit on the Bible and reject the creator and judge of their own souls. Well," he added with a shrug, "the Lord has proven himself to me. I know I will spend eternity in heaven with my Lord and Savior, Jesus Christ."

Regina Bannister stepped into the circle of friends and reached out for Felisha's hand. "Come with me, you too, Rebecca, there's someone I want to introduce you to," she said and led the two ladies away to meet another guest somewhere.

Truet sighed, "When Matt and I were coming back from the logging camp, I remember him saying the Lord could bring some good out of all that had happened. I got angry and yelled, 'like what, Matt?'" He looked pointedly at Saul and Abby, "Now I know. Congratulations to you both," he said with a small smile and quietly walked away towards the table set up with a punch bowl and cups.

He stood near the table sipping the cup of punch he held and watched the many guests finding seats, getting food, and generally having a good time. The band was getting set up to play and by the appearance of the guests, there would be many who wanted to dance. He glanced to his right just in time to see Regina, Felisha, and Rebecca leading a dark-haired beautiful woman in a green dress towards him. He turned towards them waiting, his eyes nervously meeting the angelic face of the beautiful stranger with them.

Regina spoke as they approached, "Truet, I'd like you to meet my sister-in-law, Annie. She's Lee and Matthew's baby sister. Annie, this is Truet Davis."

Annie held out her hand politely. She stared at Truet with deep brown eyes as she said, "Oh, Matthew's new deputy marshal. It's nice to meet you. I've heard a lot about you."

Truet nodded. "Likewise," he said shaking her hand gently. He looked over at Felisha, who raised her eyebrows twice quickly and smiled pleasantly before stepping away. He turned back to Annie. "You're much prettier than your brothers," he said uncomfortably.

Annie frowned dramatically and said naturally, "I've got swine better looking than my brothers."

Truet laughed heartily. It was the first time since Jenny Mae was taken away that he had laughed, though the thought did not occur to him. He answered, "Well, I didn't mean to insult you."

Annie laughed lightly. "It's best you don't get into that habit. You might be a deputy marshal, but I have guns too. And my brother's the marshal, so I'll get away with shooting you if you insult me like that again," she finished in mock sincerity.

Truet stared at her momentarily and then laughed loudly. He put his hand out to shake again. "Let's try this again. It's nice to meet you, Annie. You are a very beautiful lady."

"Better," she said questionably, "But, I don't ride side-saddle and I wasn't kidding about the guns, so the 'lady' part is out," she said with a shrug.

Truet laughed as he rolled his eyes. "Why am I not surprised? I would ask you for the first dance when the music starts, but I'm afraid of insulting you again."

Annie smiled a pretty smile. "I'd be insulted if you didn't ask me," she said sincerely.

He stared into her brown eyes. "Then Annie, before any other man asks, may I have the first dance with you tonight?" he asked very sincerely.

Annie scoffed, as she flung her hand toward the crowd of guests. "Uh! I've got bovine better-looking than any of them!"

Truet laughed.

THE BAND HAD BEEN PLAYING for over two hours to the delight of the wedding party. The first dance was for the newlyweds only. The many friends and guests watched Saul and Abby dance together for the first time as a married couple.

When that dance was over the band opened up the dance floor to anyone and played a series of songs that led many onto the dance floor where they smiled, laughed, and enjoyed the celebration. There were many tables filled with groups of friends visiting together and a few loners standing idle searching for a single lady to ask to dance or a group they could converse with. The wedding reception was a splendid success, and every guest had a great time.

The Reverend Richard Grace stood closely beside his beloved Rebecca at the edge of the dance floor watching

Saul and Abby lovingly dancing together. He held Abby probably closer than a man should in public, but considering it was their wedding night, it seemed perfectly appropriate for the couple who had been through so much.

"Look," Rebecca said pointing her hand towards Matt and Felisha. They were dancing close together and as they met each other's eyes, they slowed to a stop and kissed softly. They spoke a few words, kissed again and with a smile they began to dance slowly once more. Felisha glowed in Matt's arms.

Truet Davis and Annie Lenning, Matt's widowed sister, had been dancing together throughout the evening and sitting at the table talking when not dancing. They seemed to be enjoying one another's company a great deal as neither one had stopped smiling all evening. They were having more fun than any other couple on the dance floor. Quite often their laughter had been heard above the band.

For Rebecca Grace, it had been a joy to watch the two of them act like children at times. As the last dance of the night was announced, she watched them begin to dance together. The evening was coming to an end.

"Oh, the awkward last dance," Richard said with a pleased smile. "He likes her, Rebecca. I can see it from a mile away, and she likes him," he said of Truet and Annie.

Rebecca smiled and turned to speak into Richard's ear. "Maybe we should consider moving over here, too. It looks like we might have a couple more weddings to attend pretty soon," she said nodding towards the dance floor.

Richard turned his head to watch as Felisha affectionately held onto Matt on the dance floor. He had never seen her look so peaceful and beautiful. He glanced over at Truet as he spoke something into Annie's ear, and her response brought a hearty laugh from Truet. The first laugh Richard had heard from Truet since July. He found Saul holding his bride tenderly, still dancing on this their wedding day.

Richard laughed to himself as he said joyfully, "Oh, God is good!" He led his beloved Rebecca out onto the dance floor to dance with his own special lady, while the music still played.

A LOOK AT: BELLA'S DANCE HALL (MATT BANNISTER WESTERN 3)

Welcome to Bella's Dance Hall, where Christine Knapp found a career dancing and singing after her husband and child died along the Oregon trail. Three years after this devastating loss, Christine is ready to find love again and is drawn to Matt Bannister at first sight.

After being heartbroken by Travis, Christine meets Kyle Lenning, Matt Bannister's brother-in-law. During a group date, tragedy struck and Kyle is killed. In the fall out of the tragedy, Christine's reputation is stained, and the immoral town sheriff and his friend take the opportunity to accuse Christine of murder to blackmail her into doing their wicked will.

With no hope, no escape and no way out of it, Christine is about to sell her very soul to three of the most powerful men in Branson when Matt Bannister comes to her door. Will he demand justice for the death of his sister's husband or rescue her from a horrible fate?

AVAILABLE NOW

ABOUT THE AUTHOR

Ken Pratt and his wife, Cathy, have been married for 22 years and are blessed with five children and six grandchildren. They live on the Oregon Coast where they are raising the youngest of their children. Ken Pratt grew up in the small farming community of Dayton, Oregon.

Ken worked to make a living, but his passion has always been writing. Having a busy family, the only "free" time he had to write was late at night getting no more than five hours of sleep a night. He has penned several novels that are being published along with several children stories as well.

Made in the USA
Las Vegas, NV
15 November 2020

10956441R00231